HELEN
OF SPARTA

AMALIA CAROSELLA

LAKE UNION
PUBLISHING

15 April 2
B+
1495 (91:

Published by Lake Union Publishing, Seattle

www.apub.com

Amazon, the Amazon logo, and Lake Union Publishing are trademarks of Amazon.com, Inc., or its affiliates.

ISBN-13: 9781477821381

ISBN-10: 1477821384

Cover design by Anna Curtis

Library of Congress Control Number: 2014950871

Printed in the United States of America

For Mom, Dad, Zan, D., Biz, Laur,
and, of course, Adam

Zeus, the lord of all, who displays his might in everything else, considers it right to approach beauty in a spirit of humility. For in . . . the form of a swan, [he] won Leda for his bride, ever pursuing his quest of this gift of nature by stratagem and not by force.

—*Isocrates,* Helen

TABLE OF CONTENTS

FOREWORD

The world of Helen and Theseus is difficult to place precisely into the historical and archaeological record, but we do have some clues. Evidence suggests the Trojan War and the events leading up to it took place during a transitional time in history, at the tail end of the Bronze Age, and just a blink away from the collapse into a period referred to as the Greek Dark Ages. Homer is the first writer to emerge from these dark ages, some four hundred years later, and to ancient Greeks, his epics were more than just entertainment; they were the preservation of cultural history and memory. In ancient Greece, it was fairly well accepted that these events really happened, and the heroes involved really lived.

The archaeological record of Bronze Age Greece points to a highly organized and centralized government revolving around large palace complexes, which took insignificant inventories of goods from the surrounding communities, and then redistributed those same goods to their people and the larger region through wide-reaching trade. Craftsmanship was highly specialized, and of incredible quality, which itself suggests a foundation much more stable than subsistence living. It's even possible that there was a healthy middle class at work! And these weren't isolated communities, but, judging by the distribution of trade goods, complex networks in regular communication with their centers, as well as their neighbors, near and far.

This is the world into which Helen and Theseus would most likely have been born, although at least one generation apart. Theseus, a son of both the god Poseidon and the mortal King Aegeus of Athens, was a contemporary of Heracles and Tyndareus, Helen's adopted father. Helen, a daughter of Zeus (in the form of a swan) and Leda, was part of the generation that followed, including such heroes as Odysseus, Menelaus, Agamemnon, Diomedes, Achilles, and Paris and Hector of Troy. But as with all the most important and famous characters of myth and legend, Helen and Theseus's generation gap doesn't stop them from crossing paths.

By Helen's time, Theseus was well into his reign as king of Athens, his heroic exploits far behind him. Theseus was known as a just and wise king once he settled to the task, and is even credited with the introduction of democracy to Athens. That isn't to say he didn't still engage in the occasional adventure. His best friend and fellow king, Pirithous of the Lapiths—another child of Zeus—wasn't the best influence. It was in Pirithous's company that Theseus made two very grave errors. The first was the abduction of Helen from Sparta, whom he then turned over to the custody of his mother for safekeeping before engaging in the second error, the failed abduction of Persephone, which resulted in the imprisonment of both Theseus and Pirithous in Hades. Pirithous, the instigator of both events, was never permitted to escape, but Theseus was rescued by Heracles. He returned home to Athens to find Helen stolen from him, and his people no longer interested in keeping him on as king. Ultimately, abducting Helen cost Theseus everything.

What Helen had to say about any of her experiences with Theseus, we don't really know. Ovid addresses the abduction in passing from both Helen's perspective and Paris's in the *Heroides*, but beyond Helen's insistence that Theseus treated her honorably—far more honorably than Paris intended to—and Paris's implication that Theseus was a fool for not taking every advantage of her while he had Helen in his hands, very little is said.

And in the myths that follow, Helen isn't a very sympathetic character—maybe because her motivations are so unclear. No one can quite agree whether Helen went with Paris willingly, or even if she got as far as Troy in his company. Homer tells us she regrets intensely the Trojan War, even while it's occurring, but she's unwilling to act in the interests of either Troy or the Greeks (whom Homer refers to as Achaeans) to stop it. Though she helps Odysseus sneak in and out of Troy and speaks longingly of home, inexplicably she never gives herself up. She finds Paris to be cowardly and despicable, but she still makes love to him and stays by his side throughout the fighting. Even in the stories where Helen never arrives in Troy, it isn't because she takes action on her own behalf but rather because Hera whisks her away to Egypt to wait for Menelaus, or because the pharaoh, offended by Paris's violation of *xenia*—the most sacred law of hospitality—takes her from him before they can leave again. Helen appears to have very little power beyond the singular ability to incite lust, and even less agency. She is a plaything, a pawn of the gods, used to bring about the destruction of civilization, and an end to the Age of Heroes.

But she doesn't have to be. So much of Helen's early life is a mystery, and even her abduction by Theseus is a footnote of *his* story, more than it is hers. In *Helen of Sparta*, I wanted to give Helen the opportunity for something better—a chance to take her life into her own hands.

After more than twenty-five hundred years of texts in which she's been pushed around by men and gods, I think she's earned it.

CHAPTER ONE

I gasped for breath, but my head was already beneath the water again, hard fingers digging into the back of my neck and holding me down. I tried to force my body to relax and willed myself not to struggle while my lungs burned for new air. My scalp stung. It must have been bleeding.

"How could you, Helen?" Leda said, pulling my head back up.

The ocher and walnut dye from my hair stained the water a muddy brown. I stared at it, gripping the edge of the raised tub to support myself while I caught my breath in great gasping heaves. My mother had always resented me, but I'd never expected to be half-drowned by her hands. As queen, she had always left this sort of mothering to the maids.

"Do you not realize how this affects us all? Your beauty will secure you the finest marriage, and secure Sparta the finest king!" Leda attacked my scalp and hair with more sand and soap.

The servants would be scouring brown dye off the stone tiles for days. If they scratched the finish, Leda would never forgive me.

"And just when Tyndareus is returning home with Menelaus!"

She shoved my head back down into the water. I managed not to inhale any of it, but only just. I could still hear her cursing over the sloshing.

Menelaus. After long years in exile, he and his brother, with the support of my father, had spent the last year at war to reclaim Mycenae from his uncle Thyestes. Would the man who returned be the friend who had left me? I feared a year on campaign, a year at his brother's side, would have hardened him, stealing the kindness he had always shown me. Or worse, what if he returned, and all he saw was my beauty? There was no denying this last year had changed me, and I could not bear the thought that he might look upon me with nothing but hunger and lust. So I had dyed my hair, and hoped it would be enough to keep him from wanting me at all.

But of course Leda could not understand my reluctance. To her, to Tyndareus, to all of Sparta, Menelaus would make the best match, the best king. Had he not been raised by Tyndareus as a son all these years? He was familiar already with Sparta's strengths, Sparta's people, Sparta's needs. Even better, once his brother, Agamemnon, had retaken the throne at Mycenae, it would secure an alliance between our peoples. And he had always been my friend, showing kindness to me even when my brothers had grown tired of including me in their games, encouraging Tyndareus to soften my punishments, and taking the blame for some of my wilder escapades.

But friends or not, I couldn't marry him. Not after everything I had seen of what would follow. And the dreams were only getting worse, not better. Once, Menelaus might have looked upon me as a sister, but it would not be long before that changed. And I wouldn't marry him. No matter what he desired. No matter what any of them wanted. I knew my duty to Sparta, to my people. Marrying Menelaus would only make the dreams, the nightmares, come true, and I could not allow that to happen.

My lungs ached and my thoughts spun. Leda pulled my head back up at last, and I coughed and spluttered. She thrust a towel into my hands, but when I did not dry my face and hair briskly enough for her tastes, she took it back from me, rubbing hard. Water from the floor soaked through my shift. I already knew from testing the color that the dye would leave brown stains and the valuable linen would be spoiled. Leda would not forgive *that*, either.

"I don't want to be beautiful," I said once I'd caught my breath. "I don't want any of this."

She tugged painfully on my hair with the towel. "You are a princess of Sparta, Helen, and you will behave as one, with all the grace and beauty you're capable of. Hera help us—you certainly won't entice any man with your tongue."

"You always told me that my beauty was my greatest curse, and I would never be free because of it," I said, snatching the cloth back to dry my own hair more gently. "You said it would only cause trouble for everyone, that men would be driven mad just from looking at me."

Leda made a noise of exasperation, deep in her throat. "I did not mean you should ruin yourself, Helen."

I caught one of the wet strands, relieved to see the dye had not washed away entirely. My hair was an even muddier brown than the water—dull and unattractive where it had once been shining gold, bright as the sun.

"It will grow out, Mama."

"Not before the banquet tonight." She stepped back, studying me through narrowed eyes. "Perhaps a scarf of some sort will hide the worst of it. If only you had done a proper job of it. Walnuts and ocher. What will Menelaus think of you now? He will hardly want you as a bride with spotted brown and black hair."

"I thought there would be other men, greater men than Menelaus. Isn't that what you said when he left?"

"King Theseus did not let even his Amazon bride cause trouble like you do! If you insist on behaving like a drunken centaur, we will be lucky if any man at all will have you."

"Good." I stood, twisting the cloth of my shift to wring the worst of the water from it before letting the embroidered hem fall back to my ankles. Even the braided ends of the belt at my waist had been stained. "I don't care. I don't want to marry any of them."

"Impossible child!" She grabbed me by the arm, her nails digging into my skin. "Would you leave your people without a king? Let them be conquered and made slaves? Put to their deaths? If only Sparta were inherited by its sons. Better the kingdom fall to Pollux than to such a spoiled, foolish girl."

"Let Clytemnestra be queen of Sparta instead. She is Tyndareus's true daughter. By all rights, it is her husband who should rule."

"You are the daughter of Zeus, Helen. It must be you! The gods demand it, and I will not let this kingdom suffer because of your selfishness. When you are queen, the gods will smile on Sparta, and then perhaps Zeus will grant us his forgiveness at last."

The gods. Always the gods. Useless statues and temples—what power the gods might have had was spent on punishing us for their own divine sins. Leda feared Zeus especially. Everyone knew the story of her rape by the swan, though why Zeus would take such a form escaped me utterly. However violent the circumstances of my conception, I could not believe Leda would ever let a bird assault her in such a way, no matter how beautiful. But here I was, named a daughter of Zeus, and Clytemnestra, merely the daughter of a mortal king, though we had been born twins. Conceived the same day, according to Leda. First Zeus had come, and then she had sought the comfort of Tyndareus's embrace.

It wasn't the first time Zeus had claimed her, for my twin brothers, Pollux and Castor, were said to be the result of a similar affair, but it was certainly the first time Zeus had shamed her so utterly by the act, inspiring her with unnatural lust. And then to see me, the daughter Zeus had forced upon her, named heir to Sparta—it was insult to her injury.

"You rely too much on the favor of fickle gods, Mother."

Leda struck me so hard, my head snapped back.

I stumbled, steadying myself on the tub before I fell. My lip had split. I sucked at the wound, and flashes of nightmares danced behind my eyes. Blood and a golden city, burning bright in the darkness. Menelaus, the man who had always treated me as a sister, regarding me with a loathing that made my stomach turn even more violently than the stench of burning flesh rising from the smoldering ashes. The bronze taste of my own blood only solidified the images in my mind.

I didn't dare speak of it. One dream might be overlooked, but as often as I woke screaming in the night, I was sure to be taken by the priests if they knew the truth, if they knew I remembered the nightmares as clearly as my days. And it was not likely they would ever give me back. As a daughter of Zeus, I was too great a prize. Tyndareus might be king of Sparta, but not even he could protect me if the priests claimed me for the gods. For themselves.

I would not be their slave, and I was not so great a fool as to believe an oracle's life was anything else but that. Slavery and servitude, and poppy milk until I could not tell the world around me from my dreams. No. If I must serve—and as a Spartan I knew my duty, no matter what Leda believed—I would serve my people. Not the gods who punished us so cruelly, and not the priests who grew fat on our offerings, either.

Leda dragged me from the small single tub, past the wide spring-fed pool, which served as the communal bath for the women's quarters, and into the hall.

"You will not insult the gods while you live under my roof, princess or not." Her voice was as hard as her hand had been, and her nails dug deeper into my arm. "I have suffered enough for you already! That you live at all is only for Zeus's favor."

She flung open the door to my room and threw me inside. I tripped into the bed, my wrist twisting uncomfortably beneath my weight. I cried out, but she did not soften.

"You will stay in your room until your father arrives to decide your punishment. Do you understand me, Helen?"

I nodded, mute. In her anger, Leda had lost all her grace and beauty. Her face was cold, and I flinched beneath her glare. She looked upon me as if I were the broken shards of an urn, useless to her in every way. And then she swept out of the room, shutting and barring the door behind her.

This was another reason why I had kept the secret of my dreams from everyone but my brother Pollux—Leda would be all too happy to see me sent away to Delphi with the blessings of the gods, and gone from her sight. She would never risk the anger of the gods by fighting the future they had ordained; Zeus had taught her too well to fear him. But me? Zeus had no use for me at all but for this death and destruction, and in that, I would never serve him willingly, no matter what my mother feared would result.

My mother barked at a servant to guard my room, her tone sharp. I would miss my lessons today, but my tutor, Alcyoneus, was not foolish enough to bother Leda when she was in a rage, especially when he was guilty of telling me how to make the dye.

It would be a bad day for the palace slaves, and Leda would make sure they all blamed me.

~❦~

I lay on the bed, staring at the star-painted ceiling as the morning sun rose to its zenith. From my room I could hear Leda shouting at servants in the kitchens, the noise of preparation floating up from the courtyard below my window.

Clytemnestra and I had been given an inner room to ensure our safety if the city ever came under siege, for Tyndareus had never forgotten how it had been taken from him once before. My sister complained frequently that she wished we had a room on the opposite side of the women's quarters, so she might watch the men sparring in the practice field beneath the palace wall. From the second story, the view would be ideal, and we might even have glimpsed the edge of the city over the wall, with its red-tiled roofs and square, whitewashed homes.

I tried to stay awake, but my eyelids began to droop. As I drifted toward sleep, the shouts took on the quality of warriors and crying children instead of servants preparing a feast. I could hear Menelaus sometimes, calling my name, his voice hoarse with fury, and Agamemnon bellowing at the soldiers. Or worse, I heard him laughing while women screamed.

In this dream, I am naked. Ajax the Lesser pulls me from the temple, dragging me through the streets of the city. Bodies and blood spill in the dust, and the Achaean soldiers are ransacking the houses of the dead. Women huddle against the brick walls, sobbing as they try to cover themselves with the tattered shreds of their robes. It is now beyond the point of fighting. All those who might have struggled are dead or subdued. When I don't move quickly enough, my captor jerks me forward, shoving me before him. My legs are slick and sticky, my body sore, but I keep walking, through the courtyard and into the palace, and then into the megaron. The central hearth fire has been smothered with corpses of soldiers, stripped naked, and piles of bloody swords and armor sit waiting to be loaded into carts and hauled to the shore. The room stinks so much of human waste, I would be grateful to choke on smoke.

Agamemnon sits on a golden throne, richly detailed with rearing stallions among emeralds and rubies. He leans forward when he sees us and smiles slowly, his eyes traveling over my body, full of lust and greed. A chill slips down my spine.

"Helen, my dear sister-in-law. It is so good to see you delivered safe at last."

Two bodies lie at his feet, a gray-haired man, a king by the circlet he wears, and a woman with black hair shot with silver. Seeing their lifeless faces brings tears to my eyes, as if I know them well, but no names come to mind. I raise my chin and stare over Agamemnon's head. Splashes of red and brown coat the brightly colored fresco behind him. So much blood, so much death, so much waste, and for what? My hands ball into fists.

"My brother has been waiting for this day for years. Menelaus says he plans to kill you for what you've done, for making a fool of him all this time." Agamemnon stands, stepping down from the throne and treading upon the dead woman's fingers.

He holds a golden cup in his hand, a king's goblet filled with wine. As he passes the dead man, he tilts the cup as if offering a libation to the gods. The wine splashes over the body, and he lets the cup drop from his hand. It clatters on the tile floor, rolling into the pool of blood seeping from the dead man's skull. Agamemnon grabs me by the arm, pulling me close. His breath is hot against my ear, in my hair, and sour with wine. "It seems such a waste, don't you think? I could save you still. Speak to my brother on your behalf. Ask him to show you mercy."

"No." I push him away, twisting my arm to free it.

He laughs and lets me go. "You'd rather die at your husband's hands?"

"Menelaus has paid for me in blood. If he wants my life, he'll have it."

"So be it."

His words make me shiver, and I stumble back into the prince of Locris. Ajax's hands close over my shoulders with the weight of mountains, though he is hardly much taller than I am. He makes up for his lesser size with meanness, taking strange pleasure in the pain he inflicts upon others. If only it had been Ajax the Great who found me, I would not be standing before Agamemnon now.

"Tie her up," Agamemnon says. "Bind her to the throne, and leave us. If she's going to die, I may as well have my share of the spoils before Menelaus snaps her pretty neck."

⚜

The sharp clop of hooves on stone and the cry of a messenger shouting for Leda jarred me from the dream. My bedding was damp, but my throat did not feel raw from shouting, and I was grateful for that much. I rubbed my face and sat up. My wrist still ached, but it took my weight.

A horse whinnied, drawing me to the window. The messenger stood with his animal, greaves, cloak, and leather chest-plate covered in dust from the road. My brothers greeted him, looking as though they had come straight from the practice field. They certainly didn't look like twins, but of course the priests had attributed that to parentage, and said the same again when Clytemnestra and I were born, three years later, different as moon and sun in appearance and temperament. Leda swore Zeus had been in her husband's guise the first time he came to her. She only realized the deceit later that night, when Tyndareus himself had returned and took her to bed a second time. The priests believed, then, that fair, green-eyed Pollux had been born of Zeus, and dark-haired and olive-skinned Castor came from Tyndareus's mortal seed. When my brothers' looks were repeated in Clytemnestra and me, their declarations were only made more convincing.

If only my sister Nestra shared Castor's temperament as well as his looks; Pollux's twin could always be counted on for kindness whereas my twin seemed filled with nothing but spite. She still hadn't forgiven me for spilling the walnut dye on her gown, though it had been an accident, and she was certain everything I did was to make her look all the worse beside me. Leda didn't help; filling the entire palace with her moaning over my beauty and how it would cause all men and even gods to be overtaken by lust, she made Nestra even more jealous.

Pollux laughed at something I didn't hear and glanced up at my window, then looked again, his mouth forming a thin line. Castor followed his gaze, his eyebrows rising. I pulled my head back into the shadows so they would not see my hair.

Leda glided out from the megaron and into the courtyard, waving for a boy to take the horse to the stables. The messenger bowed, and I recognized him as the son of one of the nobles.

Tyndareus had sent most of Sparta's men home after Mycenae fell almost half a year ago, but some two dozen warriors had remained with him as guards and aides. From Mycenae, it was two long summer days by foot to Sparta, three if one stopped to rest and eat along the way. I had never been there, but by all accounts the palace at Mycenae was immense and the city at least twice the size of Sparta. Only Athens was richer than Mycenae.

But Tyndareus had not laid siege upon Mycenae for any share of its wealth. Just as Heracles had helped him to reclaim his own kingship, Tyndareus had marched to support Agamemnon and Menelaus, to help them win back the throne of their father, Atreus, now that Agamemnon was old enough to keep it. I was simply glad to see Agamemnon gone, after all these years in our household, for he had never been anything other than sour, and as for Menelaus . . .

I had missed him this last year, but the time apart was for the best. Let Menelaus go live as prince of Mycenae and find what pleasure he might among his own people. Perhaps Corinth would desire him for a son-in-law, and he might become king elsewhere. Anywhere but here, as my husband.

"King Tyndareus comes, my lady. He begs you to have refreshments waiting for his men and his guests. Menelaus and Ajax the Great accompany him."

"All is prepared for my husband's arrival," my mother said. "Go make use of the baths. Wash the dust from your skin before finding your wife."

The messenger bowed again and left; Pollux and Castor disappeared with him. No doubt they sought to avoid any last duties Leda might find for them.

As children, we had all scrubbed the painted-tile floors and frescoed walls of the megaron until our knees grew calloused, and then had been forbidden from the feasting we had worked toward. In recent years, Tyndareus had allowed us to take part in the celebrations, but not even my brothers were old enough to escape the work demanded beforehand. At least being confined to my room kept me from that particular unpleasantness.

I sighed and withdrew before Leda could see me and be reminded of my disobedience. I had meant to sneak out of the palace to watch the soldiers parade home. From the height of the city wall, the valley spread out below in rich greens and fertile fields, our crops and our city sheltered by the mountains, but I was not often permitted the view. I had stood at the wall when Tyndareus marched away with his men, shining bronze armor and glossy horses turning to dust, and I had hoped to see the dust turn into men again. But that would be difficult to accomplish while my door was locked and guarded.

Leda had returned to the megaron, and I leaned out the window. The drop to the ground was not so far even from the second story. If I hung from the ledge, I might be able to climb down the stone face, and if I fell, I would not be seriously hurt.

I dug through my chest for a scarf to hide my hair and face so if I were seen, I might avoid being recognized at once. I would go to the wall to see my father and then make Pollux help me climb back into my room the same way I'd left it. He would understand, I was sure, even if he thought me a fool for dyeing my hair.

With the scarf wrapped tightly around my head, I climbed backward out the window, glancing down only once to be sure I would not tumble onto any of the drying amphorae where they waited to be refilled with wine. The clatter of breaking pottery would bring half the palace slaves.

I hung from the ledge, my sandaled toes searching for some kind of purchase below, but finding nothing. I would have been better off barefoot, but it was too late now. I took a deep breath and prepared to drop.

"Helen!"

I slipped, choking off a scream that would certainly bring Leda. The wall fell away, and my arms flailed until I remembered not to panic at the whistle of air in my ears. I closed my eyes tightly and went limp just before a pair of strong arms caught me.

"Helen, what on earth are you doing?" Pollux demanded.

I breathed more easily when I heard my brother's voice. I had been sure Menelaus called my name. But when I opened my eyes, it was not Pollux who held me; he stood nearby, arms crossed. I shoved at the dusty chest I had fallen into, trying to free myself.

Menelaus laughed and set me down on my feet. "You haven't changed a bit, have you?"

My face burning, I wrapped my scarf more securely around my hair and gathered what dignity I had left, raising my chin. I refused to even look at Pollux, and glared at Menelaus instead. "What are you doing under my window?"

"I rode ahead of the others." Menelaus caught a strand of my hair, pulling it free from the scarf, his eyebrows rising. "By the gods, Helen! What did you do to yourself?"

I knocked his hand away, dropping my gaze to the bronze greaves he still wore, dusty and scarred by battle. I didn't want to see his dismay, even if I had hoped for just such a response, and his amusement would be worse. He had changed so little. It would have been easier if he were different.

I crossed the courtyard, intent on leaving the palace before Leda found me. I wanted to see my father before he learned what had happened, to have just one moment of happy reunion before his anger found me, too. If I could only get beyond the palace walls without being seen . . .

"She dyed her hair." Pollux's tone was grim, and I heard the ping of leather against bronze, the song of a soldier's jog, as they caught up with me on the broad porch of the palace entrance. "I told you she's been in trouble. Leda's furious with her."

I shook my head, quickening my pace. "You gossip like a kitchen slave."

"It isn't as though you could hide it for long." Pollux walked on my right side; Menelaus on my left. They had no trouble matching my stride, and Menelaus seemed not to be weighed down by his armor in the slightest. "Or that you meant to."

"Oh, Helen." Menelaus sighed. "I suppose I should have expected it, with all the things Leda says. As if Zeus would rape his own daughter—"

"No," Pollux said. "It has nothing to do with Leda's carrying on about Zeus. If only it did."

"Pollux!" I regretted, then, having told him anything about my nightmares, but at the time I had been desperate to share the burden, and at least Pollux could be trusted to act in my interests.

"What's this?" Menelaus caught me by the arm, turning me to face him.

We stood on the near side of the palace wall, by the gate. Leda would greet Tyndareus at the porch, and I expected her to step from the palace at any moment to be sure the stone had been swept clean.

"She's still having nightmares," my brother said. He wasn't looking at Menelaus, but at me. I hadn't told him what I meant to do with my hair. His jaw tightened, and he looked away.

"You promised." I couldn't meet Menelaus's eyes and glared at Pollux instead. "You promised you wouldn't tell."

"You would've told him anyway." We both knew this wasn't true. From the start, Pollux had felt Menelaus should know what role he might play, if the dreams were visions. I had refused. The less anyone knew, the safer we all were.

"You remember them?" Menelaus asked, and I could feel him studying me. "But why would nightmares make you dye your hair? I don't understand."

"It's nothing." I pulled my arm free. "It doesn't matter. Please, if Leda sees me here, I'll be in even more trouble."

"For dyeing your hair?" I could hear the laughter in Menelaus's voice again, but he let me go, walking with me.

"Not exactly," I said.

"Then what?" Menelaus asked.

I pressed my lips together and sped up, leaving them both behind. I was so angry that I could not even look at Pollux. He had no right to say anything at all, and now Menelaus would never let it rest, asking questions until I told him everything. Before the nightmares had come to me, I would never have kept such a secret from him.

I slipped through the gate, relieved to have the wall between me and my mother.

"Helen." Menelaus caught my hand this time, his skin warm and dry against mine. My fingers closed around his without my permission, and I let myself be drawn to a stop. "You can tell me anything. When have I ever betrayed your trust?"

I bit my lip, looking up at him. His forehead was creased with concern, unruly red hair falling over his ears. His skin had bronzed this last year, and his shoulders had broadened. He looked like a man, now. And I was no longer a girl. The way he looked at me, it was as if he had starved on campaign, and only now realized his hunger.

"You've been gone for over a year, Menelaus." It hurt me to say it, and it would hurt him, too, if I went on. But I had to. I would not give him any encouragement. "Things have changed. You're different now, and I am, too."

His brown eyes sharpened, his gaze moving down my body before flicking back to my face. He stepped closer, and I realized how truly I had spoken. This was not the boy who had been kind to me because I was a child, or treated me with the fondness of a little sister. This was not the boy I had counted as my closest friend.

"Are you?" He kept his voice soft, but there was a determination beneath the words that I had never heard before. "How different, Helen?"

My face burned again, and I had to look away. I should never have said it. With Clytemnestra shouting her change from the highest windows of the palace, I would not be able to keep my own a secret for much longer. My sister was mad for a husband, but the sooner I married, the sooner the visions would come for me. The sooner the stranger would come to take me away and mountains would be built of the dead.

Menelaus took my chin in his hand, lifting my face to his. "Even if you have changed, Helen, I haven't. Not in any way that matters to you. I am still your friend."

"I'm sorry," I said, grasping for any excuse to leave him behind. Not even Menelaus would risk Leda's ire so soon after his return. "Mother says I am too old to have friends who are men. Not even you."

Menelaus dropped his hand as if I had burned him, and I turned away before I could see the pain in his expression. I left him beneath the wall of the palace and did not dare to look back.

CHAPTER TWO

I stood before Tyndareus's throne in the megaron, the raised central hearth too hot at my back. A skylight above me lit the room with bright sunlight, making me even warmer. During the feast, the gallery overlooking the hearth would be filled with children and young women not permitted to attend. Long tables had been set and benches and stools brought out to seat our guests, but the food had not been laid out yet, nor would it be before these household matters were addressed. The megaron was not just our banquet hall, nor even just a center for ritual. As Tyndareus's throne room, it was where Spartans could come with petitions and the nobles gathered when he called a council, but family affairs always came first.

Gray flecked Tyndareus's black hair at the temples where there had been none before, and the lines in his face cut deeper around his eyes and mouth. The war for Mycenae had aged him, and I felt ashamed for behaving as I had. His homecoming should never have been ruined by my disobedience.

"What do you have to say for yourself, Helen?" he asked, his voice soft. Tyndareus did not seem upset, but he rarely did, dismissing most of our misbehavior as childhood mischief. Mine most of all.

Leda stood beside him on the dais, her skirt tiered in shades of red. Now that Clytemnestra and I had seen thirteen summers, my mother did not believe we should be treated as children anymore. She raised her chin, her eyes as cold and flat as the great bronze-colored eagle that stared down on us from the wall behind the throne, flanked on either side by mustard-yellow griffons.

When I had managed to climb back in through the window, tripping over a stool and nearly falling over a table, my mother had been waiting for me. A servant had seen me talking with Menelaus and Pollux, and said as much to Leda.

"I am sorry for leaving my room. I only wanted to see your return to the city." I bowed my head, trying to ignore my father's guest. Ajax the Great stared at me beneath hooded eyes, and I wished I did not have an audience for my disgrace.

"But you do not apologize for speaking ill of the gods."

I glanced at my father's face, trying to judge his mood. His expression was empty of emotion, a perfect mask for a king. Pollux sat on one of the low benches skirting the interior of the megaron. I was not sure why, or what he had said to Tyndareus, but after this afternoon, I did not trust that he would keep my secret for much longer.

"I only said that they were fickle." I raised my chin to match my mother's. This much, I did not deserve punishment for.

Ajax's roar of laughter startled me into stepping back. He leaned against a pillar painted with lightning bolts, one of four central columns set around the hearth, each with the symbols of a different god. He was so immense a man that I wondered the stone did not move from the weight of him.

"You would have her punished," he gasped between laughs, "for speaking so plain a truth? One every child should grasp at the earliest age?"

Tyndareus rubbed his forehead. He studied me for a long moment, waiting for Ajax to regain himself. His eyes were tight and dark, his expression weary. He dropped his hand back to the arm of his chair and sighed.

"Knowing this and proclaiming it are two different things, I fear. Can you not see, Helen, how this might offend them? We should not criticize the gods in any small way. Your mother and I know this better than most." He took Leda's hand, and I looked away from the intimacy of the gesture.

"I cannot put my fate in their hands, Father. I cannot trust them."

"I do not blame you for your fears, Helen, and Ajax is right that I cannot punish you for speaking honestly. But nor will I turn a blind eye to insult beneath my roof. You will make an offering to Zeus directly after the morning meal, begging his forgiveness."

"But my lessons—"

"Alcyoneus has taught you quite enough." And I knew then that he had guessed where I had learned how to make the dye. "One day missed will hurt nothing."

I bowed my head again. "Yes, Father."

"Let me see your hair, Helen."

I swallowed hard, glancing quickly at Ajax, who had straightened and fallen silent at my father's words. At least he was not the other Ajax, from my dreams. Even the thought of standing in the same room with Ajax of Locris made my stomach twist into knots.

I unwound the scarf from around my face and hair, staring hard at my father's sandaled feet as I did so. Tyndareus rose, coming toward me. He took my chin in his hand and raised my face to his, giving me no choice but to look at him. His mouth formed a thin line, and his brown eyes narrowed. The way he looked at me, inspecting the damage

I had done to my beauty, reminded me of Agamemnon's touch in my dreams. But Tyndareus, my true father or not, would never hurt me.

"I do not think I need to ask why you have done this, Daughter, but it grieves me all the same." He met my eyes, and I could not look away. "I am sorry that you have been driven to this, but I did not think there was purpose in sheltering you from the truth of your birth and the danger of your beauty. I would not see a daughter of mine kept in ignorance and shadow. You deserved the light of knowledge."

"I just wanted to be free," I said. Tears burned behind my eyes.

I had not expected his understanding, his grief. Disappointment in me I could have lived with, but I could see he blamed himself for the second rape my mother had suffered by Zeus, from which I had been born, and for the future my beauty threatened. Tyndareus did not just fear the men who might abuse me, but the gods as well.

"I'm sorry, Papa."

He squeezed my shoulder and let me go. "For disobeying your mother, you will be forbidden from the feast. A servant will bring you dinner in your room, and this time, you will not leave it. Do you understand me?"

I nodded. It was a much kinder punishment than I deserved, and I saw Leda glaring at me over his shoulder. She did not think it severe enough, either, but would not contradict Tyndareus in front of his guest. Perhaps that was his purpose in keeping Ajax near. If so, I was grateful.

"In the morning, you will allow your mother to cut your hair. I will not tolerate any further trouble in this regard, Helen. You must accept who you are, and learn to live as the gods made you." He turned from me, toward the dais. "Pollux, escort your sister. She is to go directly to the women's quarters."

"Of course, Father." Pollux came forward, waving me ahead of him.

"Even with the ruin of her hair," I heard Ajax say before I left the megaron, "she is still beautiful, Tyndareus. She would make any man a fine wife."

"She would make any man a fine queen, my friend," Tyndareus said.

Then the door closed behind us, and Pollux and I were alone.

"Tyndareus was very kind to you," my brother said, "but you should have told him the truth."

"I will." I glanced up at his face. He walked stiffly beside me, eyes straight ahead. "But you can hardly expect me to confess my nightmares in front of Leda and Ajax the Great. It is a private matter, for his ears alone."

"And what of Menelaus?"

I frowned, trailing my fingers along the painted oak branches on the wall as an excuse not to look at him. We'd had this conversation dozens of times. "You heard Tyndareus. I'm to remain in my room."

"Helen, you can't really be serious. Rejecting Menelaus's friendship, hiding the truth. If the dreams reveal your fate, he is to be your husband!"

I whirled, grabbing him by the arm, but I pulled him to a stop only because he let me. He was so strong, now, so adult. The next time Tyndareus went to war, Pollux would go with him. And the time after that, he and Castor would lead the soldiers themselves. Would he lead men in the burning city for Menelaus as well? Would my brothers die there, with all the others?

"Promise me you will not tell him!"

Pollux searched my face, but he did not reply at once.

"Promise me, Pollux! Whatever happens, I must not marry Menelaus, and if he knows, it will only encourage him to love me."

He sighed. "Helen, with your marriage goes the kingdom of Sparta. Tyndareus will not choose a husband for you based on love. The best you can hope for is a friend. A man who will respect you.

Menelaus will be that man, and he will be a good king for our people. You cannot ask for more than that."

"I can ask for peace. I can ask for war to be averted. There are other men," I said. "Greater men than Menelaus."

Pollux shook his head. "You sound like Leda. To hear her talk, you would think the great hero Heracles or King Theseus had already asked for your hand. There is no shame in an alliance with Mycenae."

I flushed and began walking again. We were not far from the women's quarters, and Pollux would not be able to follow me there. Only the king could walk within that part of the palace; all other men were forbidden. When I saw the curtained entrance, I ran toward it.

"Helen, wait!"

I glanced back over my shoulder as I pulled open the curtain. "Enjoy the banquet, Brother." And then I let the fabric drop, cutting off his reply.

❦

The stranger holds me by the hand, drawing me past stalls of colored fabrics in brilliant purples and blues, even the rarest greens, and stands that overflow with finely wrought gold and silver in quantities that make even Agamemnon seem poor. The people around us smile, bowing as we pass, and the merchants call to us, waving their goods in the air. He looks back at me, grinning, his pale brown eyes alight with joy, and my breath catches. For the space of a heartbeat, I wonder if I came with him willingly.

The thought startles me, and I try to pull my hand free, but he does not let go. His smile fades and he tugs me closer, his fingers twining through mine. For all that he laughs and smiles, his grip is too tight, as though he fears I will free myself and run.

"Is my city not beautiful?" he asks.

We stand at a jeweler's stall. The man lays out a variety of gemstones before us. One is an emerald larger than my thumbnail. The jeweler grins, holding it up. "To match your eyes! Any setting that you desire, I can make."

I shake my head with a smile and step back.

"It is very beautiful," I agree.

"All of it can be yours, Helen." The stranger pulls me into his arms, and the heat of him burns through me. "If you will be my wife."

I look back at the merchant with his emerald, at all the bright colors, and all the people.

It turns to ash before me. The reds and golds and purples flame into smoke and shadow and darkness, stinging my eyes. I cough and push the stranger away, but he will not let go. He buries his face in my hair, his arm around my waist holding me firm. His lips move against my neck and throat, trailing fire with kisses, while the world is torn with screaming women and crying children, running through the streets.

"Helen," he murmurs, as though we are lovers. "Helen."

"No." I shove at his chest, but he does not move. "No! They're dying! Can't you see? Everyone will die!"

"Helen?" This time the voice is louder, no longer a whisper of passion. I feel a hand on my shoulder, and try to knock it away. I have to get free. I have to hide. Ajax will find me. And then Agamemnon—

"Helen, wake up."

My eyes flew open, and I screamed at the shape leaning over me. A hand clapped over my mouth, half suffocating me, with a hissed plea for quiet. The form bent closer, and I struggled to free myself, biting the hand and digging my nails into the arm behind it.

"Helen, stop!"

I stilled at once, blinking. My vision cleared as the tears slipped down my cheeks, and I could see Menelaus's face, the red of his hair shining copper in the moonlight. He sat on the edge of the bed.

"It was just a dream," he murmured.

He waited another moment after I quieted, then removed his hand from my mouth. I stared at him, my heart racing, and pulled the blanket up over my chest.

He brushed the moisture from my cheeks. "I didn't mean to frighten you."

"What—" My voice cracked, and I cleared my throat. I must have been screaming in my sleep. The noise of the banquet floated through my window, drunk men laughing and singing and stumbling through the courtyard. "What are you doing here?"

"I heard you crying from below. You sounded terrified."

"You shouldn't be here." I sat up with the realization. Clytemnestra? No, she was not back yet, or she would be shrieking now. But she could return at any time. And Leda. She might check on me, to be sure I was still in my room after what I had done today.

"Shh," he said, pressing me back. His breath smelled of wine. "Your mother is still at the banquet." He snorted. "And Nestra is so busy flirting with your father's guests, I think she'll forget to sleep tonight. I have never seen a woman her age so desperate for a husband."

"Please, you cannot be here. If Leda finds out, she will have me whipped."

"If Leda finds out, she will have you married. And how is it, Helen, that Nestra, in everything your junior, has become a woman when you have not?"

I froze at his words. Was that why he was here? To claim me? The wine had certainly given him courage, to bring him through my window in the middle of the night. But he was right. Better to have me married than dishonored. Leda would make me his bride if she found him here, even if he had not touched me. My hands closed into fists in the linens.

"I think you had too much to drink at the banquet, Menelaus."

He stroked my hair, winding his fingers through it. "I could not listen to you cry and do nothing. What do you dream of that upsets you so? Your brother refuses to speak of it at all now, and Nestra will only say that you weep."

I closed my eyes and turned my face away. "It doesn't matter."

"You never kept secrets from me before." His hand fell away from my face. "I wish I knew what I had done to lose your trust. To lose your friendship, after all this time. Have I not always treated you kindly? Have I not always kept my word to you in everything?"

The pain in his voice cut through my heart, and I caught his hand. Sword work and spear throwing had calloused his palms, and he wore a heavy ring now, on his thumb. My fingers brushed over it, imagining the lion carved into the gold, the mark of a true prince of Mycenae.

"Leda says I must remain distant from my suitors." It was the only excuse I could give him, and I clung to it. "I must trust my father to choose the best man for Sparta."

"And you think I am your suitor?"

"Aren't you?"

"Oh, Helen." He raised my hand to his face, pressing it to his lips, then his cheek, roughened with stubble. The moonlight washed the bronze from his skin and hid the breadth of his shoulders, and, for a moment, I saw the boy who had been a brother to me. "There is not a man who has seen you who does not wait for the day that Tyndareus calls us to compete for your hand. But I missed your friendship sorely. Did it mean so little to you?"

I pulled my hand free, glad that it was dark and he could not see my face flush. "It meant the world to me."

"Then why, Helen? Would it be so terrible to marry your friend?"

The pressure behind my eyes made his face swim into shadow. "I don't want you to hate me."

He was silent for a heartbeat; then he laughed, low and gentle. "Why would I?"

"You will!"

My voice rose, and he hushed me, touching a finger to my lips. I pushed it away, sitting up. My hand found his knee, and I gripped it so hard, he hissed.

"You want to know what I dream of? I dream of war, Menelaus. The world turned to ash and fire. A golden city that burns while I hide in a temple, begging the gods to protect me, and then Ajax of Locris—"

I stopped. I did not want to think of Ajax the Lesser. I did not want to speak of it, for fear I would have the dream again. My father worried about the gods, but it would not be the gods who abused me.

"Menelaus, in my dream, you hate me. There is no love between us, no kindness, no friendship. All of it is gone. And so many die, so many. I cannot risk it. You have to understand. Please."

He stared at me, and even in the dark I saw the whites of his eyes. He shook his head slowly, as if denying my words, and his hand covered mine on his leg, wrapping around it. His other hand was in my hair again, his fingers threading through the strands and cradling my head.

I smothered a sob, but he pulled me to him, pressing my face against his shoulder and holding me in his lap while I cried the tears I could no longer hold back. He stroked my hair and wrapped his arm around my waist, rocking me against his body, warm and solid, and as familiar as the scent of leather and wood smoke that clung to his tunic.

"It is only a dream, Helen."

But I did not think he believed it, either.

CHAPTER THREE

Leda came to me not long after dawn, touching my shoulder to wake me, and pressing a finger to her lips when I would have spoken. Clytemnestra had not come to bed until the birds had started their early songs, and she slept like the dead beside me, her breath foul.

I dressed and followed Leda from the room. Slaves already ducked in and out of the other sleeping rooms, linens draped over their arms. Morning light poured into the hall through high-cut windows where the roof of the corridor rose taller than the rooms on either side. It painted the plaster walls sky blue, giving life to the purple-and-gold-feathered peacocks, which chased one another along the bottom third.

My mother had forbidden any symbols of Zeus in the women's quarters, choosing to honor Hera instead. But Zeus's wife was not known for her sympathy when it came to those women her husband had taken interest in. Proof, I thought, that these gods were not worth our regard, if Hera could be so cruel.

Leda brought me to the baths, where she bade me sit on a high stool while she cut my hair. The sound of the shears filled my ears, and

I held still as the strands fell around me to the limestone floor, like so much flotsam in the painted waves. The terra-cotta tub where she had scrubbed the dye from my hair still bore darker brown splotches in the grooves of the fish swimming along its edges.

It had been for nothing. But I was not certain if I was more worried or pleased that Menelaus loved me for more than just my looks. We still could not marry. I still should not be his friend any longer. I had not realized how difficult a habit it would be to break.

"Undress, Helen."

Leda's voice was even and soft, but my nails dug into the wood of the stool.

"You may as well bathe, or you'll be scratching at yourself all day. I won't have a princess of Sparta fidgeting in her seat."

I had known from the beginning that it was only a matter of time, but I had hoped to hide my bleeding for another month or two. Until Menelaus left again, at the least. If I bathed now, in front of Leda, in front of Leda's servants, she would know the truth at once and my childhood would be over. Tyndareus could not afford to put off my marriage for too long once it was known I had become a woman. The sooner I had a husband, the sooner Tyndareus could begin to teach him about the kingdom he would inherit, and secure the succession.

Of course, if he meant me for Menelaus, he need not rush things quite so much. Menelaus was already well-known from the years he and Agamemnon had spent living in the palace, exiled from Mycenae, and now he had proven himself in war as well. Sparta would have no trouble accepting him as its future king.

I had to believe Tyndareus would consult my feelings before he chose my husband, or else I would go mad. What was the point of being so beautiful if that beauty could not at least ensure peace? Surely one of the men it might attract would serve Sparta better than Menelaus.

"Now, Helen." Leda tugged at the sleeves of my dress, urging me to lift my arms so she might pull it up over my head. I hesitated for only a moment. It would do nothing to help me if I fought her, and everything to increase her fury when she discovered what I had hidden.

I shrugged out from beneath her hands and stripped the fabric from my body, hiding the wool I had kept between my legs in the cloth as I did so.

Unlike the small tubs, the communal baths were fed from a hot spring and always warm, but I shivered all the same as I stepped down into the pool. It was large enough to swim in, and if I had not been so afraid the blood would show, I would have done so. Instead, I clamped my legs together and held as still as possible in the water.

One of the slaves picked up my shift, shaking it out. The wool rolled free onto the tile, leaving a trail of red.

Leda pressed her lips together.

"For how long?" she asked.

I said nothing, watching the warm water weave faint tendrils of blood through the carved dolphins on the bottom of the pool. Dolphins were sacred to Apollo, and I hoped I did not owe my dreams to him. Athena, the goddess of wisdom, was the only Olympian I could respect in the least. She was strong and beautiful, and no one would ever make her marry against her will.

"You will go straight to the shrine and make an offering of your morning meal to Zeus, your father." Leda scrubbed my back with a coarse sea sponge, making my skin sting. "And you will spend the morning on your knees, begging for his favor."

She shoved me deeper into the water to rinse the hard soap from my skin. Normally, the servants would have used sweet-smelling oils. But normally, a bath was not a punishment. My hair would stink all day from the tallow, like rancid fat. I grimaced. Perhaps it would keep Menelaus from coming too near.

"You will return by midday, and you will tell Tyndareus what you have done." She let me go, leaving me the soap to wash the rest of my body. "Let him decide your punishment, and determine your fate now that you're a woman. This is the last time you will betray *me*."

"Yes, Mama." The words sounded very small.

Leda did not spare me another look.

⸙

My morning meal waited for me at the table in the megaron, the remnants of last night's feasting still in evidence. Kraters, empty now of the watered wine mixed for the guests, still stood on their pedestals at each corner of the room for easy access by the servants. The long tables and benches, littered with wine cups and empty platters, had not been put away yet.

At the family table, Pollux and Menelaus sat on either side of my usual stool. Pollux looked as though he had barely slept, but he smiled and called for me to join them. I could feel Leda's glare, and only shook my head, collecting my bread, smeared with honey, and a pomegranate. It made a meager offering, and I wondered if Leda meant to shame me before the priests, too. More likely, she wished to keep me from eating any of it myself.

Pollux rose as if to follow, but Leda's sharp voice brought him back to his seat, and I left alone.

The path up the hill to the shrine had long turned into packed dirt, and in truth I preferred the sacred grove to the temples. It seemed more fitting to me that a god should be worshipped in a garden than trapped inside stone walls.

Of course the shrine had not always been a garden. It had begun as nothing more than a stone altar before the face of Zeus in the rock, but Leda and Tyndareus had made it into something finer. Flowering trees and bushes scented the air as thickly as incense before the shrine came into view, and a seashell path led to a raised limestone altar, exquisitely carved. They had also built the bower to shield the stone of Zeus from the elements and encouraged grapevines to grow over the frame.

It had been done after the swan came, before my birth, and Pollux claimed to remember playing in the dirt here while Tyndareus worked. It was a rare thing for a king like Tyndareus to build a place like this with his own hands. Perhaps they had hoped that with their sweat and labor, Zeus might forgive them for the insults they had given.

Now the shrine was tended by two priests, watering the plants and clearing away the offerings left for the god. It was peaceful and quiet, for most of Sparta's people prayed to Zeus at the temples. But not us. Tyndareus and Leda always insisted that we make our offerings here. Pollux and I had made almost daily trips to the shrine while Tyndareus fought for Mycenae, and we had offered kids, lambs, golden cups and bowls, and wine.

Steps had been cut into the hillside and an archway built at the top to remind those who passed through it that this was a sacred place. On either side of the arch, Tyndareus had planted oak trees, hiding the inside of the garden from sight. The bark of these trees would not be harvested for cork, unless the priests required it.

I did not notice the priestess until I had entered, removing the scarf from my head out of respect. When she looked at me, her mouth twisted, and then she laughed, a sound like silver chimes in the wind.

"Oh, Helen. What a sad sight you make now."

I flushed and walked to the altar, setting my offerings out and keeping my head down as I knelt before Zeus's image. Tyndareus swore he had once seen the face come to life, after I had been born, but I felt it more likely someone had put poppy milk in his wine. As a child, I had prayed and prayed for some sign from the god who was supposed to be my father, aching for Zeus's acceptance when my mother looked on me with such loathing, but I received nothing for my troubles. Pollux had never seen anything, either, and by my tenth summer I had given up.

Now, I pretended to pray so that I would not have to speak, but I felt the priestess watching me, and though she waited in silence, I did not think she was convinced.

After a time, she asked me, "What do you pray for, Helen?"

I sat back on my heels and covered my hair once more with the scarf. "My mother told me that I should beg Zeus for his favor, since I have lost hers."

The priestess laughed again. "Do you honestly believe you ever had hers to begin with? Pollux may have been born of love, for Zeus took Tyndareus's form when he came to her then, but you, Helen, you were born of rape and shame. She would have had you dashed on the rocks if not for fear of the gods."

My face burned, though I did not think my cheeks could become much redder than they were already. "No woman deserves to be treated in such a way."

"Leda was given a great honor, to bear Zeus's son. She cursed him for it, as did Tyndareus, who could not see beyond his own pride. If Zeus had not loved Leda so well, Sparta itself would have fallen. Leda's rape by a swan was less than your parents deserved in punishment. Zeus showed her mercy."

"And does Zeus punish me for the sins of my parents now?" I looked back at the priestess where she sat on a low stone bench.

Her auburn hair hung loose down her back, myrtle flowers floating in the soft curls like gulls on the sea. A scallop-shell pendant rested at the hollow of her throat, and sparrows and doves darted around her feet, picking at the crumbs of past offerings. Strange that I had never met her before, but I wished that she had not dedicated herself to the gods. Perhaps Menelaus might have fallen in love with her, instead.

"Do you feel so ill-used? The most beautiful woman alive, with a brother who loves you well—Pollux will never forsake you. And a man who would offer you the same, though you spurn him." She seemed to look right through me, pinning me to the earth. "Is there someone else you would prefer over Menelaus? You have only to name him and he will be delivered."

"No." I rose to my feet. I did not like the way she spoke of Menelaus, as if he were nothing more than a convenience. "I ask nothing of these gods. Let Menelaus love me for his own reasons, or better yet, not at all."

The priestess smiled, but there was little kindness in her expression. "To hear such a thing from your lips is absurd. Have you no idea of the power you hold over men? Menelaus will continue as he has begun. I could not stop it if I wished. Nor could Zeus."

Her words sent a prickle of unease down my spine, though I did not know why. I had never heard a priestess speak as she did. By all rights, the gods should have taken great exception to her arrogance, priestess or not.

I did not want to worship gods as cruel as this—gods cruel enough to rape my mother after she objected to being deceived, or willing to waste the lives of hundreds, perhaps thousands of men in a useless war. I did not want to believe we could not be free.

"Menelaus has the right to make his own choices," I said at last.

"And yet . . . ," she said.

My stomach twisted at the weight of those two words, and at the thoughts that followed in my own mind. *And yet*, I kept from him his fate. I kept from him the truth of what I saw coming. But this priestess could not have known what I had done.

I shook my head, trying to clear it. The dreams had come to me as a warning, I was certain, for I had dreamed of smaller moments in the past and seen them brought to life through my inaction, and avoided when I interfered. Once I dreamed that Pollux would be thrown from his horse and break his arm while riding with Castor, and I begged him not to go. He had come back with a sprained wrist and claimed if it had not been for my warning, he would have suffered worse.

The dreams did not tie me to the future, but they gave me the opportunity to alter it. I saw it even in the small details that changed from nightmare to nightmare. One night, Ajax the Lesser would find me in the temple; the next, I cowered in a bedroom, listening to a warrior break down my door. It was as if the future itself were still in motion, unset until the moments claimed us.

The priests would not see it that way; nor would Menelaus, I was certain. He would see my dreams as proof that we were meant to marry, and he would use it to win me.

But if I did not marry Menelaus, no stranger could steal me away. Everything rested upon that choice.

"Good day, Princess," the priestess said.

When I looked up, she was gone.

⊰⊱

I did not spend the morning on my knees as Leda had ordered me, but I sat where the priestess had been, trusting that as angry as my mother was, she would not come to check. The only other person who came to the shrine that morning was Pollux, and I made room for him on the bench.

"I'm sorry, little sister," he said. "I heard Nestra speaking of it last night and meant to warn you. She promised me she wouldn't tell Mother until morning, but then I saw them speaking together at the feast, and it was too late."

At the feast. I traced the carving of a bull in the stone, worn smooth from wind and rain and the touch of other fingers. "She told Menelaus, didn't she?"

Pollux's jaw tightened. "She had no business speaking of such a thing to anyone but our parents. No right to spread the news of your bleeding like gossip. Tyndareus will not be pleased to realize he is the last to know."

"I'm to speak to him at midday." I sighed and rested my head against his shoulder. At least it explained why Menelaus had come to my room the previous night. He had wanted the truth of more than just my dreams.

"When you tell him why, he'll understand."

"I hope so."

Pollux squeezed my hand. "If he doesn't, I will speak for you. I'll tell him I told you to keep it a secret. That I made you conceal the truth. He can be angry with me, instead, if he must."

"Don't be ridiculous." I laughed, sitting up to look at him. "You didn't even know yourself."

When I saw his face and the grief in his eyes, my stomach twisted. I had never seen him look so wretched before. Pollux was at worst serious, but never miserable.

"What's the matter?"

His gaze slid to the grapevines. "He spoke as if he knew it all, as if you had told him everything, or I swear to you I never would have said a word."

My heart turned to stone in my chest, making it difficult to breathe. "What?"

"It was after the morning meal. We were on our way to the practice field. He said you had told him. That you had cried in his arms, confessing that he would hate you if you let him love you now. He wanted my counsel as to how he could reassure you."

I released my brother's hand. The back of my throat burned with bile. "You told him he will be my husband."

"Helen, I thought he knew. You have to believe me. The way he spoke of it, it seemed impossible that he did not."

I stood and paced to the altar, staring at the empty stone eyes of Zeus. What was Menelaus thinking? Everything else rested on that.

Maybe I was wrong. Maybe he would not see it as proof. Last night he had told me they were only dreams.

"I'm sorry, Helen." I heard Pollux stand up behind me, but I did not turn. "I know that I said he deserved to hear it, but I never would have told him without your permission."

"What did he say? When you told him."

"He did not say anything, but the color drained from his face, and when he sparred against Castor, I thought he would batter our brother into the dirt. He left the field soon after, and I came here to warn you. I would not have you caught unaware by Menelaus as well as Leda in the same day."

"Leda is finished with me. She says now I am a woman, I am to be Tyndareus's trouble, not hers."

The face of the statue unnerved me. There was no kindness or sympathy in the rock. But there was no kindness or sympathy in the gods, either. Not the Olympians, nor had I ever heard Alcyoneus speak of his Egyptian gods as compassionate, though I had begged my tutor for stories of his people, fascinated by the differences as much as the similarities.

I rubbed my face and turned to my brother. "I should go, or I'll be late to see Tyndareus. Will you come with me?"

Pollux's mouth relaxed from the thin line it had become. "I intended to, whether you asked it of me or not. Leda will have poisoned him with her anger already, though I expect he will be more upset with Nestra than you."

"I hope you're right."

We left the shrine together, and walked back in silence through the cork oaks that had taken root all over the hill. I could see in Pollux's face that he meant to make it right.

If Tyndareus did not punish Nestra, I had a feeling my brother would.

Tyndareus pushed away his meal of bread and goat cheese, the lines on his face more pronounced than ever. The megaron had been cleared of all but me, Pollux, and Leda, though Pollux's attendance was more oversight than anything else. He had slipped in while the others left, and he stood now in the shadow of one of the large pillars, out of Leda's sight.

"This has gone on long enough. Helen betrays even her kingdom with this deceit. You must take your daughter in hand!"

Tyndareus leaned back in his chair, giving Leda a long look. "And why is it only when she has misbehaved somehow that she is my daughter and not yours?"

Leda drew herself up, regal and furious. "If you had allowed me to punish her as she ought to have been punished, instead of letting her behave so willfully, none of this would have happened. What she has become is your doing, Tyndareus, not mine!"

"And what precisely has she done?" Tyndareus asked, his gaze resting on me. The plaster floor beneath my feet was painted with two charging bulls, one the gray of a thunderstorm and the other sea-foam white. I would have gladly faced a herd of them, horns sharp and nostrils flaring, rather than Tyndareus now. "What is it that has offended you so utterly?"

"Ask her yourself." Leda did not look at me.

"Helen?"

I bowed my head. "I hid from my mother that I had become a woman, out of fear of marriage."

"According to her sister, Helen has been bleeding for the last six months at least!" Leda said. "I will not tolerate it, Tyndareus. This lie is too great to be overlooked, even for you."

"And yesterday you would have had her punished for speaking the truth." Tyndareus's voice was cool. "What would you have her do,

Leda? No matter how she behaves, it will not please you. You punish her for nothing more than her birth."

"And you have spoiled her for it!"

"Enough!" Tyndareus rose from his seat. "You have brought her to me for punishment, and I will see to it. You may go."

Leda opened her mouth, then shut it. Tyndareus had spoken as her king, not her husband; the dismissal was clear. Leda might rule absolutely as queen and high priestess when leading rituals of thanksgiving and mystery, but in this, she had little power. She glared at him and left, the heavy door slamming behind her.

Tyndareus sighed and retook his seat. The rest of the tables had been cleared away by now, the floors swept and washed. No wonder Pollux had come to see me. While I had been at the shrine, the rest of the palace had been cleaning. Someone had even thrown herbs in the fire, and the scent of lavender hung in the air.

"Princes should not slink about in the shadows, Pollux," Tyndareus called. "Nor should a son of Zeus lower himself to such behavior. If you are intent on remaining, you will stand before me openly."

Pollux straightened, stepping out from behind the column. Tyndareus waved him to my side.

"Am I correct in assuming you are here to defend your sister?"

"I am."

"I wonder that you think she cannot defend herself, after everything she seems to have accomplished in my absence." Tyndareus studied me as he spoke, but the anger he had betrayed in Leda's presence was gone. "If Pollux will stand beside you, there must be some good reason for your behavior. Unless your brother has lost the wits he had when I left?"

I smiled. "No, Papa. Pollux is still Pollux."

"And yet, he could not seem to keep you out of trouble altogether." Tyndareus picked grapes from a dish of fruit. "I should have realized that yesterday was not the end of this, but it never occurred to me that you might take things this far, Helen, and to find Pollux has a hand in it makes it all the more alarming." He held my gaze, and there was no humor in his expression. His brown eyes were hard and sharp. "My patience wears thin. I will have the truth of it now before this goes on any longer."

I swallowed against the tightness in my throat and stared at the bulls. The gray animal stood for Zeus, lord of the sky, and the white for Poseidon, god of the sea and the earth. Before the swan, Sparta had worshipped Poseidon the Earth-Shaker above all others, but the priests had felt Zeus's appearances warranted a change. Alcyoneus said it did not make any difference. No matter whom we worshipped first, the other gods would take exception. That was the way of things among the Olympians. His own gods, he had assured me, were much more reasonable, but I doubted it.

"Pollux had no part in my actions, Papa. He did not know I planned to dye my hair, nor did he help me to conceal that I was no longer a girl."

"But he knows why you did it."

"Yes," Pollux said. "And had she asked me for my help, she would have had it."

"What of Castor and Clytemnestra?"

"They had nothing to do with any of it," I said.

I took a deep breath to steady myself, and felt Pollux step closer. I was shaking just thinking about what I must say, feeling my freedom slip away with every breath, but I made myself look at Tyndareus.

"It is the nightmares, Papa. I thought they would stop when you left with Menelaus and Agamemnon, but they have not."

"You remember them." Tyndareus watched me closely. "Or have you always? No, never mind that. I know well enough why you might hide that truth. Tell me, now."

"After I am married and made queen, a man will come from another land. A prince, I think, but a stranger to us. He will feast at my husband's table, live with us as a guest, and accept our gifts. But he will betray us and steal me away with him." I could feel the pressure behind my eyes again, and the dream lapped at the edges of my vision.

So often, I saw the stranger, on the deck of the ship, holding his hand out to me, golden-brown eyes flashing with power I could not understand. Did I go with him willingly? It seemed impossible that I could be so faithless, to Sparta or my husband. I saw the golden city, walls rising into the heavens, as beautiful as any Olympus. Then the fires, all of it turning to blood and cinder. Ajax of Locris in the temple, grunting as he raped the woman above me before finding me beneath the altar, his surprise turning to lust. And Agamemnon, too, rutting like a boar. Menelaus, calling my name as if he would battle me to the death. And perhaps he would. Agamemnon had said he intended to kill me.

"There will be a great war, Papa, and it will be fought over me."

⁂

In the end, I told him everything I could. Tyndareus sat in silence, listening as I spoke.

"You said you are married in the dream," Tyndareus prompted.

I pressed my lips together and looked away.

"It's Menelaus," Pollux said softly. "And he knows. I did not mean to tell him, but I did."

Tyndareus sighed, staring out the window. "Then there is no reason to exclude him now. Have him brought to me, Pollux. We can use his counsel, and if need be, we will call upon Agamemnon as well."

"Not Agamemnon," I said. But I knew that at some point we must, since he would lead the looting of the golden city. Agamemnon would never allow such an insult to Menelaus to go without reprisal, seeing any slight against his brother as one to himself. "I cannot look at him without seeing the dream."

"You have nothing to fear, Helen. We are warned. Forearmed. The gods are giving us the knowledge we need to prevent this." Tyndareus smiled at me. "You will be safe, I promise you."

I wanted to believe him, and so I nodded. But before Pollux left, I caught my brother by the arm. "I did not tell Menelaus about his brother. I would not pain him further without need."

"He will not hear it from me," Pollux promised, and I knew he meant it.

When we were alone, I crossed the room to my father, taking his hand and dropping to my knees before him. "Please, do not let me marry him. If I am not married to Menelaus, I cannot be stolen from him!"

"Helen." He stroked what was left of my hair and raised me to my feet, holding my hands in his. "We need not fear a man we know will come. When he arrives, you have only to point him out to Menelaus, and this stranger can be killed. His threat to you will be extinguished with his life. If Menelaus knows what may come, it will make him all the more determined to protect you. You could not be in safer hands than his."

"But what if it is exactly this that poisons his love for me? It is too much to ask of him, too great a burden to ask any man to bear."

"Menelaus will choose his own fate. I will not deny him that right. But he will still be a valuable ally. We may need the resources of Mycenae." Tyndareus squeezed my hands and let me go. "Trust in the gods, Helen. They smile upon you."

I wanted to scream, but Pollux had returned. My father promised Menelaus the right to make his own future, but at what cost to mine? I already knew what Menelaus would choose. My nails dug into the skin of my palms.

Tyndareus went at once to Menelaus, clasping his arm and drawing him to his side. He greeted him as a son.

Pollux smiled reassurance, but I could not return it. I would keep trying. Tyndareus could not marry me off without hearing the suit of the other men who might want me, or else invite war. And Leda had been right. There would be greater men than Menelaus coming to win my hand.

Perhaps I could persuade my father that one of them would be the better match, or if he did not listen to me, I would give these other men the encouragement to convince him for themselves.

Anyone but Menelaus.

CHAPTER FOUR

Theseus was largely untouched by the jostling of men while he waited. Feasting with a hero-king, a son of Poseidon, and offering due honors was one thing; rubbing elbows with him in a crowd was another. He wondered if Helen noticed the same in her own life. Perhaps she and her brother were still too young to realize what it meant to be a demigod. Or perhaps Helen's beauty was too tempting to those who might otherwise have kept a greater distance.

Judging by the number of men who had made this journey just for the chance to see her face, Theseus was beginning to think the latter more likely. He almost felt sorry for her.

"Isn't this supposed to be a celebration of Helen's birth? She looks miserable," Pirithous said. "If this keeps on, the only competition you'll have for her hand is me."

Theseus smiled, not looking away from the dais where Helen sat on a litter with her sister. They had strung Helen with so much gold, even Apollo might have mistaken her for the sun, and then they had set her out for everyone to see before the gates of the palace walls. The polished oak of the gate, bare wood stained crimson and carved with olive trees and vultures, made an imposing backdrop.

"If she truly is a daughter of Zeus, then she's your half sister, Pirithous. Don't you think you're better off breeding a little bit farther from your own blood?"

Pirithous snorted. "If we refused to marry our own family, we'd be left only with mortals to choose from."

"A fate worse than death, I'm sure," Theseus said.

Helen closed her eyes, the polite smile fading from her expression as she turned her face toward the sun. He had not really doubted, but there was Zeus, in her cheekbones, and the shape of her eyebrows. Her father's looks were softened and much more delicate, but there was no mistaking her parentage. She was as beautiful as any goddess.

A year ago, word had spread all across Achaea that Helen had ruined her beauty, but he saw no evidence of any lasting stain in her golden hair, and since then he had heard only of her loveliness, so widely acclaimed, he would not have believed it to be true if he had not looked upon her with his own eyes. There was not a single well-born man in all of Achaea who would miss this opportunity to see her, even if Tyndareus refused to hear any offers of marriage.

Any man, if so moved, could climb the dais, under the watchful eyes of no less than a dozen guards in addition to her brothers, and offer Helen his good wishes for her birthday along with a gift. A sizable pile of gold trinkets and guest-gifts behind Pollux told Theseus at least four dozen men had felt so compelled, and the line had only grown since his arrival, snaking most of the way down the main road to the city wall. Palace bakers had begun offering stuffed breads to those unwilling to risk losing their place.

Tyndareus couldn't possibly think Helen could speak to all of these men before the evening feast. Even if he had limited the number to only those with the fortune and bloodline to make a suitable husband, there would have been too many. What could Tyndareus be hoping to accomplish?

"Pollux looks just like his father," Pirithous said.

"All Zeus's children seem to share a certain resemblance," Theseus agreed. "Though I've never seen any child of his with hair the color of wheat and honey."

"Can you not tear your eyes away from the woman for one moment?" Pirithous laughed and clapped him on the shoulder. "I'm not sure why you bother. If she does like you, it can only end poorly."

He brushed Pirithous's hand away, not quite able to stop himself from glaring. "You go too far."

"Perhaps so." Pirithous's smile faded, all the humor leaving his expression. Theseus tried to ignore the concern that replaced it. Pirithous had been the one to persuade him that he ought to come to begin with. Athens had been without a queen for too long. "So be it, then. If you're so determined to win her, I will not interfere with my own attentions."

"You're not the kind of man she'd be interested in." Theseus forced himself to smile. "Nor do I think Tyndareus would trust his kingdom to a king who resorts to thieving cattle from his neighbors for sport."

"After hearing so much about your heroic self, you were bound to be tested by your neighbors sooner or later. I simply chose to be first."

"You're a scoundrel and a pirate, Pirithous, and every king south of Macedon knows it. Tyndareus is unlikely to be an exception."

Pirithous chuckled. "But he would trust Sparta to you, when your hands are already full with Athens? If Mycenae threatened this city, you'd have no way to defend it. Sparta has no practical port, Theseus, and all Agamemnon need do is hold the Isthmus road to keep you from marching to its rescue. Neither one of us would make an ideal match for Helen, regardless of our bloodline."

She was laughing with Pollux now, her face alight. His heart caught at the sight, and he swore. Helen was better off with another husband, one the gods favored, but perhaps as a favored daughter of Zeus herself, she wouldn't be brought to ruin because of his ill luck. Evidently, the loss of two wives had taught his heart nothing about the dangers of marriage, or else Aphrodite and Artemis were taking fresh interest in punishing him for the sins of his past. He shook his head. He'd paid and paid again. Not everything had to be fated for agony.

He waved one of his servants over. "Two skins of the watered wine we brought, and a basket of Attic cheeses with some fruit. See if you can get fresh bread from the palace, too."

The servant bowed. "Yes, my lord."

The line had advanced, but it would still be some time before he climbed the dais himself—time enough to get what he needed.

Helen adjusted one of the golden cuffs on her arm and then motioned for the next man to be allowed on the dais. Clytemnestra looked on with clear disdain, leaning back to speak to her brother, Castor. Her sister might have been beautiful in any other company, but beside Helen, her dark hair and olive skin looked plain. Helen glowed next to her, with her fair skin and honeyed hair. And when she smiled, truly smiled, the mood of the entire crowd lifted.

"Do you really think the gods are going to give you Helen?" Pirithous asked.

Theseus shook his head. "I've never claimed to know the will of the gods, but I hope Aphrodite will smile upon me, if only this one time."

"The next man, please," Helen called from the open litter, her voice lilting and lovely.

Theseus took the steps two at a time, leaving his servant with the wine and the basket of food below. Red linen had been draped over the top of the litter to shield the young women from the sun, and they sat among a dozen cushions of red, yellow, and blue cloth, which set off the gold cuffs on Helen's arms and the headdress of electrum framing her face. Helen was dressed in a long gown of pure white, the loose cut of the fabric covering her from neck to ankle, and girdled close at the waist, holding a thickly fringed, flounced overskirt in place. Every movement Helen made caused the small gold and silver trinkets among the pale yellow fringes to jingle and flash in the sun. Theseus could only imagine what the crowd would have become if she had worn something more traditional and left her breasts bared. She would never need to expose herself to capture the attention and adoration of men.

He bowed low and did not allow himself to look anywhere but at her face.

"It is a great honor to meet the daughter of Zeus at last." He kissed her hand before straightening. "I am Theseus, king of Athens, Hero of Attica, and son of Poseidon."

Her eyes widened, and her gaze faltered for a moment, sweeping over him. Even to her young eyes, he would not look old. The gods gave many gifts with their ichor; retaining one's youth for longer than purely mortal men and women was the least of it.

"Noble King Theseus, we are honored by your presence."

He smiled, then half turned, waving for one of his servants to join him. A guard tried to stop him, but Helen leaned over to look, raising her eyebrows. A good sign, he thought.

"Let him come," she said.

"An early gift for the princesses." Theseus inclined his head politely to Helen, and then to her sister. Clytemnestra sat forward, her expression filled with naked surprise. No other man to climb the dais had addressed her so.

He took a wineskin from the servant's shoulder and let Pollux see that it was sealed before he opened it and raised it to his lips. He took a long drink before offering it to Helen. Pollux scowled but did not stop him.

Helen accepted the wine, her green eyes lighting with the fire of emeralds, though he could not tell if it was with amusement or pleasure.

"I thought you might like some refreshment after baking in the sun all day. Wine from Athens." He repeated the performance with the second wineskin and passed it to Clytemnestra. She accepted it without any hesitation. Dismissing the servant, he set the basket between the two women on the litter. "You'll find Attic cheeses and fruit inside, enough to share with your brothers, and bread as well."

Helen smiled. "You are very kind, King Theseus. We thank you for your attentions."

"Lovely young women like you should not starve on the dais while the common men stuff themselves and look their fill." He bowed to Clytemnestra, another gesture no other man had made. It would be hard for her, he thought, living always in Helen's shadow and being ignored today, when it was her birthday, too. "An honor to meet you as well, Princess. May the gods grant you joy in the coming year."

"Thank you." Clytemnestra smiled, but without Helen's warmth. "We look forward to seeing you at the feast."

"I would not miss it." He turned back to Helen. Her eyes were such a unique color, the depth of green like nothing he had ever seen before. "It is my wish to see more of you, if you would do me the honor."

Helen inclined her head, the electrum blazing as it caught the sunlight. It was not quite an acceptance, but nor was it a refusal. He doubted that she would have much control over whom she was able to spend time with over the course of the celebration. It was clear by this display that Tyndareus and Leda meant to attract as many suitors as possible, all hoping to claim a seat beside her for a meal. Theseus had already counted at least a dozen other kings and the same number of princes, from Macedon—even farther north than Pirithous's people lived—to the southern island of Crete. But what preference she might show, he hoped to have won in this moment.

"Until tonight, then." He bowed again.

When he left the dais, he felt Helen's gaze follow him.

❧

Theseus went to the temples while the men still stood in line to give Helen their good wishes for her birthday. He could not watch them fawn over her any longer once he had seen her fed and offered her wine. Each imposition, each ogling eye, made him more and more irritable on her behalf. And he had other respects to pay.

The temple to Poseidon was modestly sized compared to what he had built in Athens, but the stone buildings had been designed in the same style as the palace. Tall columns stood in the entrance, painted with cresting waves and leaping fish from their bases to the roof and leaving the temple open to the sun on one side. Inside, the walls were covered floor to ceiling with horses of every color, stamping, rearing, and charging. Nostrils flared as they tossed their heads, their manes flying in the wind.

Offerings of hard bread, goat cheese and milk, figs, pomegranates, and wine covered the altar. Theseus knelt before his father, setting a golden trident the length of his arm before the rough clay form of the god, and bowing his head.

"Father, hear me. Accept this offering in thanks for our safe passage."

He rubbed his palms against his thighs, ignoring the seashells digging into his knees. It had been more than a decade since Poseidon had granted him audience or aid, and perhaps he was foolish to look for it now. But what else could he do? He hadn't meant for any of this to be about marriage, no matter what Pirithous had said. Helen had been more curiosity than anything else, as she was to so many of the other men who had come at Tyndareus's invitation.

"If she is not meant to be mine, Father, harden my heart. Make me like the ocean, callous and unfeeling. But if I might have her, if this is not too great a prize to ask for, give me your blessing, your protection. Give us both peace, and let it last."

He stayed on his knees for a long moment, waiting, listening with all his being. Theseus lifted his gaze to his father's painted face, but there was no life in the worn features there. No kindly smile or wrathful glower, just the silence he had come to expect. He rose, pausing to kiss the altar, and left the small temple.

"I should have known you'd be here, bending knee to your father." Pirithous leaned against one of the pillars, shaded from the sun. "He does you few favors, Theseus. You'd have done better to offer sacrifice to Athena or Aphrodite."

"Neither Athena nor Aphrodite is my father." Theseus nodded to the palace below, set behind its walls. Guards walked the tops, wearing leather breastplates, no doubt ready to respond with bow and arrow if the mass of men below became a mob. "Did my servants make room for you?"

"Oh yes. As always, they were most accommodating." Pirithous pushed off from the pillar and fell in beside him as he walked back toward the city. As usual, Pirithous had chosen to join his party at the last possible moment. "Helen seemed most impressed by your gift. Though I hear rumors that Agamemnon negotiates with Tyndareus for the hands of both his daughters."

"And if that were true, and Tyndareus decided, what possible purpose could this celebration serve? Why invite so many eligible men to Sparta and wave Helen in front of their faces, only to tell them they may not have her?" Theseus shook his head, staring at the crowd still gathered outside the wall.

The temples were not far from the palace, but built upon higher ground to honor the gods. From this height, they could see the gold of Helen's jewelry flash, almost blinding in its intensity. Goats and sheep grazed on the near side of the settlement, taking advantage of the uneven ground inside the greater city walls as it rose to the temples. A few shepherds, young boys for the most part, sat among them, their crooks resting over their shoulders as they watched the festivities below more than their flocks. Where the animals had not yet cropped the grass, poppies bloomed bright red, and violets in vibrant blues. No doubt the flowers would be trampled before the moon had filled, with so many men trudging back and forth from the temples to secure safe travel back home.

"No," Theseus said. "Tyndareus would not risk a mob, and that's surely what he would have if he meant her for Agamemnon, after all of this."

"Not Agamemnon," Pirithous said. Theseus had long since stopped wondering how Pirithous obtained such information so quickly; he could talk any man or maid into giving up his or her secrets in the time it took most men to survey a room. "It is Menelaus who seeks Helen's hand. The servants in the palace say they are much in the company of one another. Menelaus follows her as though she were a bitch in heat and he driven mad to mount her."

"Servant gossip. Menelaus and Agamemnon are like sons to Tyndareus. Their frequent visits could have nothing more to do with Helen than the interest of a brother."

Pirithous snorted. "Do you honestly believe that even Pollux and Castor can look at Helen without their own loins stirring? She's nearly as alluring as Aphrodite herself."

"Careful, Pirithous." Wars had been started over less, and he would not see Helen punished because Pirithous did not guard his tongue. "Aphrodite is not forgiving of such comparisons, and I have no desire to suffer her rage again."

"Nearly, I said." Pirithous flicked his fingers in dismissal. "And regardless, it's only the truth. Zeus gifted his daughter great influence and power when he gave her that form, and recognizing the work of the gods as impressive can never be a sin."

"Can't it?" Theseus glowered at the mass of men.

Agamemnon climbed the steps to the dais, his swagger and the flash of bronze armor impossible to miss. The king of Mycenae bowed to Helen, but Theseus could see even from this distance the coldness in his manner, and Pollux's expression darkened further with every word exchanged. Helen recoiled from Agamemnon's touch, pulling her hand free as quickly as possible.

Tyndareus was sure to consult Pollux and Castor about her potential suitors, to ensure the man chosen would be respected and that his daughter would not be mistreated. No, if Agamemnon sought Helen's hand, even for Menelaus, he was not yet successful, and antagonizing her brother was hardly the way to seal a marriage.

Theseus rubbed at his face and looked for the angle of the sun. It wouldn't be long now. Perhaps he could impose on Tyndareus's hospitality just a little further, and secure himself a seat beside Helen at the feast. No king would dare refuse such a modest request from a hero.

Father, help me. Uncle, grant me your favor.

If things went well tonight, he would go to Zeus's shrine in the morning and thank the gods properly.

❦

Seats were scarce in the megaron, but Theseus had received a place at the family table in exchange for a gift to Leda of the rarest green linen from Troy. The most noble of Tyndareus's guests had been given places at the tables below, or at worst on the benches that lined the walls, but it did not account for half the men Helen had seen. The gallery above the hearth was filled again with more men, the women and children who might normally watch from above ousted in favor of those who had presented Helen with gifts.

She leaned forward, refilling his cup with wine, and their shoulders brushed. Theseus's head filled with the scent of the white windflowers woven into the braided crown of her hair. She looked even more striking without all the gold and jewels from her earlier display.

"Is my company so unappealing that you wish to see me drunk?" he teased.

She smiled over the rim of her own cup. "I am pleasantly surprised by the good fortune of your company, my lord. I feared my mother would think it necessary to seat me beside King Nestor this first night, to do him honor, and I'm afraid I have no taste for stories of war."

"You've spoken just in time to prevent me from launching into my own," he said, forcing himself not to smile. "What of the tales of raiders, outwitting their foes?"

"It seems to me those, too, often end in bloodshed," she said, the light of humor dimming from her eyes. She looked away, picking at the bread on her plate. "What makes men hunger so for such contests? Is there no suitable glory to be found in other pursuits?"

"Plenty, if a man has the temperament and the patience to find it." There was more to her words than idle conversation, and he wished he knew where her distress had come from, but now was not the time to ask. "Does your brother Castor not find glory in his horses? He is known already as the finest horseman in the Peloponnese without even the benefit of being Poseidon's son."

Her eyes were the color of mint leaves in the lamplight, meeting his with all the warmth of gratitude. "Yes. Castor takes great pleasure in his horsemanship. I'm sure that if you asked it of him, he would share with you what he knows."

He smiled. "I think your brother's skill is not something that can be taught, but I will speak to him, if only to say that if he ever wishes to leave Sparta, he and his talents will be welcome in Athens."

"You're very kind, King Theseus."

"It is only in the best interests of my city and my people, I assure you."

"And would you put your people and your city above all else? If you saw some greater threat to them, some future that might be avoided at the cost of some smaller risk in the present, would you act, or refuse, to save them from the nearer pain?"

He laughed and picked figs from a dish at the center of the table. "That isn't a question I can answer without knowing the nature of both events. Nor would I make such a choice without consulting Athena, for Athens is her city more than mine." He offered her the figs, and she accepted one. "Why do you ask?"

She bit her bottom lip, toying with the stem of the fruit. "A good queen would collect wisdom from those who have led before her."

"Very wise, indeed."

Helen's eyes widened slightly in surprise; then she smiled with such brilliance, he could not help but grin in response.

Nor would he risk losing such a gift by pointing out that a decision as she had described would fall to the king. His marriage to Antiope, the Amazon queen, had taught him the difference between a queen who took interest in the fate of her people and one who concerned herself only with the affairs of running the palace, as Phaedra had. There was no question in his mind which he preferred to have at his side, beautiful or not, but not all men would agree that a partnership between equals, ruling in all things together, made for a stronger kingdom. His gaze slid down the table to the king of Mycenae, Agamemnon, and his brother, Menelaus. Neither one had the strength of character to stand as an equal beside an Amazon.

"The younger Atrides takes great interest in you, Princess." In truth, Menelaus had been watching them all night with an intensity that made his shoulder blades itch against the pressure of a phantom knife.

Helen glanced at Menelaus, where he sat with her sister and Agamemnon. Clytemnestra seemed to be enjoying herself, even if the two men were not as pleased with their seating. She smiled and laughed and flirted with Agamemnon as if they were alone in the room. For the banquet, Helen's sister had changed into a gown that bared her breasts, her dress dyed pomegranate red and her black hair oiled to shining. Theseus did not let himself give her more than a fleeting look.

"Menelaus has been a brother to me for most of my life," Helen said, returning her attention to the figs on her plate. "He comes often from Mycenae as my father's guest."

"I can imagine. Agamemnon would be foolish not to take advantage of his brother's easy manners as an ambassador."

"I do not think he does it for his brother." The smile that he had only recently won back faded again, and a crease formed between her eyebrows. She picked an orange from the nearest fruit bowl, turning it over in her hands for a moment. It was a gift from one of the eastern princes, no doubt, for such fruits did not even grow so near as Troy.

He took the orange from her fingers and scored the rind with his knife in one long motion, keeping the actions as casual as he could. Had she really never considered that Menelaus might serve as a spy on Tyndareus?

"Agamemnon does not seem a very sociable man."

From the corner of his eye, he saw her brothers watching them, though they lacked the intensity of Mycenae's prince. If Helen meant to know the men whom she might marry, Theseus would oblige her with more than the truth of his own character. He worked the peel free as he spoke, being careful to keep it all in one piece.

"Menelaus, on the other hand, smiles more than he frowns, though tonight he seems too distracted for diversion. Agamemnon needs a man like him to forge alliances and build friendships if he plans to extend the influence of Mycenae."

"And how do you know so much, when you have only just encountered them tonight?"

He smiled, passing her the fruit, free of its rind. The peel, he coiled back into its original form and set as if it were still whole onto the table before her.

"Agamemnon is much too young to have lines carved so deep in his face if he is not a taciturn sort of man, and there has never been a king in Mycenae who did not grasp for more. Menelaus is loyal, or Agamemnon would not wear the crown at all. He will serve his brother. Though I think it likely Menelaus will not suffer his brother's demands longer than he must." He grinned when she stared at the orange peel, her eyes widening again just slightly before meeting his. "If you know what to look for in a man's face, there is much to be told of his habits, and I have had many, many years to master the art."

"How old are you, to possess such wisdom?" Her good humor had returned, her mouth softening. She ate a piece of the orange.

"Do you really want to know?" He liked to tease her. When she played along, her eyes sparkled. But if she valued wisdom in a man, her choices were limited to those many years her senior. "I'm afraid if I tell you, it will frighten you away, and that will hardly help me to win your hand later."

She laughed. "You can't be much more than thirty, even if you are a friend of Heracles."

He said nothing, taking a drink of his wine. Perhaps it was not fair to keep it from her, but he'd prefer to let her make up her mind before she realized how much older he was. He set down his cup and leaned forward.

"Tell me, did anyone else think to bring you something to eat after I left? I thought to stay and watch, but I did not wish to offend your father by not paying respect to him before the banquet."

Helen broke off another section of the orange and offered it to him. "If I answer your question, will you tell me your age?"

He accepted the fruit and pretended to consider while he ate it. "Perhaps if it is a very good answer, I might be persuaded to give up my own."

"What would make it a good answer?" she asked, smiling.

"If I had intended to make it easy, Princess, I would have told you already."

She reached out, uncoiling the orange peel, her lips pressed together. When she looked up at him again, she was not smiling, but there was a surprising new warmth in her expression. It was more than just gratitude, this time, as if he had passed some sort of test.

"Of all the men who climbed the dais, none showed the courtesy and kindness that you did, to me or to my sister." She wound the peel back together again before meeting his eyes once more with a look that made his heart soar. "I will not forget it."

He swallowed the words he could not say and struggled to keep his tone light. "That is a very fine answer, but I wonder if you will be as pleased to know mine."

"Surely the great Hero of Attica does not fear a young woman's opinion?"

"You are not just any young woman, Princess. If I were afraid, it might be justified." He lowered his voice and leaned toward her, brushing her hair behind her ear. "I confess to having seen forty-eight summers."

"Impossible!" She clapped her hand over her mouth the moment the word escaped, her eyes wide, though he was not certain if it was because she shouted, or because of his age.

He laughed. "The truth, I swear it by my father, Poseidon. Does it disturb you?"

Her eyes narrowed, and she leaned forward, studying him more closely; then she shook her head. "I can hardly believe it's possible. The gods must love you."

Theseus forced himself to smile. Beyond Helen, Clytemnestra had turned her attention to Menelaus, who looked as if he had tasted something bitter. The younger son of Atreus looked away, smiling at Helen's sister the moment he realized Theseus's attention. Just a heartbeat too late.

"Somehow I do not think your sister would have responded to my confession with quite so much grace."

Helen glanced down the table at Clytemnestra just as Menelaus stole a look in her direction. Helen's face flushed. Theseus ducked his head, trying to catch her eyes, but she would not look up.

"It was meant to be a compliment, Princess."

Her smile was forced and distracted. "Forgive me, King Theseus. I think the wine has given me a headache."

"Of course." He called for a servant. "You've had a long day." A boy came forward with a jug, and he poured most of the wine from her cup into his own, refilling hers with water.

"Thank you." She took the cup but glanced down the table again.

"Perhaps it would be best if you retired for the evening? A good night's sleep might help."

Helen went white around the eyes and shook her head. "No. Thank you. Perhaps just some fresh air." She set the cup down and rose.

Theseus stood with her. "I'll join you."

She smiled at him. "You are very attentive, King Theseus, but I won't be gone long. Stay."

He didn't like it. Much as he would have enjoyed her company, his greater concern was the crowd of men deep in their cups with too few women to sate their appetites. Helen's presence was temptation enough, but if she were alone in the dark—opportunity had been encouragement enough for worse than rape. Still, this was her home, her father's palace. Imposing himself upon her would not do him any favors.

She squeezed his hand, and when she left, he did not follow. But he caught Pirithous's eye, where he sat at a lower table, and lifted his chin. Pirithous followed his gaze to Helen as she skirted the tables toward the main doors, thrown open to admit the cool night air and keep the smell of wine and sweat from overcoming the lavender tossed periodically into the hearth fire.

Theseus retook his seat, his gaze traveling over the other men in the megaron. A few had watched Helen as she passed, but now that she was gone, they had returned to their wine.

All but Menelaus. The son of Atreus had followed Helen.

CHAPTER FIVE

Menelaus had stared at me throughout the banquet, his expression growing darker with every word I exchanged with the king of Athens. But Tyndareus had not promised me to Menelaus yet, even if he had not discouraged his hopes, either. I was not Menelaus's to own, Menelaus's to guard. I could not stand to sit beneath his glare any longer.

The cool night air made it easier to breathe. I had not realized how stifling it was inside the megaron, with so many men at the banquet. So many men, and yet the one we hoped for had not come. The stranger, the prince who would steal me, had not shown himself. But if he was not Achaean, if he was some foreigner, why should he? He might not yet even know that I lived. It was folly to think that just because I was known in Achaea, the rest of the world knew of me, too. Or worse, perhaps it was the rumors spread by this very celebration that would bring him here later. Tyndareus and Pollux had refused to even consider it.

The torches in the courtyard had guttered for the most part, and the servants had been too busy pouring wine and refilling platters to replace them. The columns of the entry loomed over me, drained of color by the moonlight and casting deep shadows over the walkway. I followed the wall far enough that I would not be tripped over by drunk men stumbling about and took shelter in the darkness, sliding down the wall and wrapping my arms around my knees. The chill of the stone beneath me raised gooseflesh on my skin, but I didn't care. I needed to breathe and think and settle for myself what I must do now that Tyndareus's plan had failed.

It had been a year in the making, spreading rumor of my beauty to the far corners of Achaea before inviting the men of every city to this celebration, and the stranger had not come. For me, his absence brought relief more than anything. I did not want to even allow this strange prince to see me. I did not want him ever to come this far. I did not want to follow the path the dreams had laid at my feet any more closely than I must.

But Theseus, king of Athens, Hero of Attica, had not appeared in them at all . . .

"Helen?"

I sighed. Of course Menelaus had followed me. I should have expected as much.

Pottery clattered against stone, and Menelaus's low curse followed, then my name again, with less patience.

"Here," I called.

It would be better than having him trip over me in the dark. I saw a flash of moonlight on gold and caught his arm before he stepped on me. He sank down, his back against the wall, and held my hand in his.

I stared at the shape of our hands together in the dark. "You should go back to the banquet."

His thumb caressed the back of my knuckles. In the last year, since learning of my dreams, Tyndareus had allowed him too many liberties. Perhaps I had as well. I pulled my hand free from his, and tucked it away where he could not take it.

"And leave you to be stolen away?" he asked.

"I won't be stolen. Not tonight." Our shoulders touched, the heat of his body seeping into mine. If we had been younger, I would have nestled myself against him and wrapped myself in his warmth. But we weren't young anymore, and it would have been cruel to encourage him. "Tyndareus doesn't want us to be seen together."

He put his arm around me, and when he spoke, I felt his breath against my ear. "We won't be seen."

I shivered and pushed him away. "Stop, Menelaus. If anyone saw us, it would ruin everything."

He laughed, pulling me closer. "You're going to be my wife, Helen. It hardly matters."

"You don't know that." I slid out from beneath his arm, my body cold where it no longer touched his. "Tyndareus might still promise me to someone else. And better for everyone if he does."

"You cannot mean that." All the humor had left his voice, and I was glad I could not see his face clearly. "You can't really want to be married to some fool who only sees your beauty and your kingdom, who cannot appreciate you for the sharpness of your mind, or the kindness of your heart. You think that Athenian will treat you as anything more than his whore?"

"Better that than see your friendship turned into hate. Better that than to let the world burn!"

I stood, intending to return to the feast, but he rose and caught my arm.

"I love you, Helen."

I tried to pull myself free, but he tightened his grip, jerking me back. The force of it startled me, and I stumbled into his chest before regaining my balance.

"I would kill a thousand men, burn a hundred cities to have you!"

"Do you think that's what I want? Wars and death, bodies and ash?" I shoved him, forcing him back a step. "Maybe a son of Atreus can live with all that blood on his hands, cursed as you are, but I can't! You understood that once. Before you went to war with Agamemnon."

"The curse." He flinched, turning his face away, his jaw working. "What could you possibly know of that? Of any of it! This has nothing to do with my family. Nothing to do with my brother, at all. I've made sure of that much."

"It has everything to do with him." I was shouting, but I didn't care. "Do you know what your brother will do to me, if this future comes to pass?" I didn't wait for him to answer, but he had stepped back again, releasing me. "Agamemnon will rape me on corpses in the palace while the city burns!"

Menelaus grabbed me by the shoulders, almost throwing me into the wall. His face was so close to mine, I smelled the wine on his breath, felt the sour heat of it against my cheek.

"Do you spread these lies to your father, too? Do you think it will stop him from making you my wife? After everything I have done to help you, to protect you? The promises I made!" He shook me, and my heart pounded in my chest. His body pressed against mine. "Do you think this was what I wanted? Bad enough that I must bend my knee to my brother, but now you would give him reason to mock me with your refusals, and for what? A child's fear of a passing nightmare?"

I swallowed against the tightness in my throat.

"You don't believe me," I rasped. "After everything. You don't even believe me!"

"My brother will never touch you," he snarled, his fingers digging into my arms and bruising my skin. "He swore you would be mine when I went to war with him, and he will not break that vow."

"When you went to war?" I could barely hear anything over the roar of blood in my ears, and I clawed at his fingers on my arm. "What has that to do with me?"

His hands gentled at once, as if he had only then realized what he had done. He raised his hand to my face and stroked my cheek.

"Helen." It was more a sigh than anything, and he dropped his forehead to mine, our noses brushing. "Don't you see? I have done everything for you. To protect you. To keep you."

His mouth hovered over mine, sharing my breath, and I felt his body growing harder against me. He pressed closer and my heart raced, even as my body stilled and my stomach lurched. He could claim me, now, and I would not be able to stop him. If I screamed for help, there would be no hiding my shame. And Tyndareus would have no choice but to marry us.

His lips brushed against mine, hesitant, and then fierce, forcing my mouth to open. I heard myself sob.

There was a crash of clay, and Menelaus jerked back. I turned my face away, biting my lip and holding my breath to keep from crying out with relief. A man laughed and began to sing. Menelaus let me go, slipping into the shadows.

I ran back to the entrance, eager to step into the light that spilled through the open doors. In the light, he could not kiss me or press me back against the building. In the light, he could not bruise me and shake me in rage.

I wiped my face and raised my chin, forcing a smile to my lips. I walked back into the megaron, the tang of men and rich aroma of the food almost overwhelming me after the crisp air outside. But when Theseus rose to meet me, I knew at once that I was safe.

❧

I waited, hoping Menelaus would return to the banquet, so I might go back to my room without fear of meeting him on the way. Many of the men in the balcony had left, or been herded out by Tyndareus's guards, but the megaron was still more full than empty. Most of the nobles would find beds on the tile and plaster floor, outside on the porch, or within the courtyard, though the most honored had been given rooms of their own.

Castor and Pollux had been forced to give up their beds for guests, according to their grumbles, and would be sleeping in the stables with the horses. It was one of the few benefits of being a woman in the palace; Tyndareus would never put warriors in the women's quarters, and our rooms would always be our own no matter how many men descended upon Sparta. At least until marriage.

"You're falling asleep, Princess," Theseus murmured.

He shifted slightly, and I realized I had been leaning against his shoulder. The table had been cleared of everything but figs and honeyed nuts. Oil lamps glowed softly beside the platters, lighting the hall without the smoke of torches. As long as the kraters were still full of wine, a good portion of Tyndareus's guests would stay up to drink it.

"No," I lied, sitting up. "I'm fine."

"My lady, I would not be offended if you went to your bed." His lips twitched, forming something between a smile and a frown. "Let me call your brother to escort you."

I hid a yawn behind my hand and glanced down the table, but Menelaus hadn't returned. The last thing I wanted was to meet him in the corridors on the way to my room.

"Too much wine, perhaps."

"Wine does not account for the circles beneath your eyes." He tilted my face up with a gentle finger beneath my chin. "You hide it well, you know. But I wonder what could keep a princess from sleeping at night."

I flushed. "I appreciate your concern, my lord. You're very kind."

"But not kind enough to have earned your confidence."

"Kind enough to have earned my respect," I said. Never before had I spent an evening in the company of a man who only looked on me with consideration and not lust. "More than any other has done in one day."

He laughed, waving for Pollux. "You are more generous than I deserve, Helen."

It was the first time he had used my name so informally, and I searched his face. His eyes were like the sea, sunlight glinting off water. Fitting in the face of a man who called himself Poseidon's son.

"Little sister." Pollux joined us. "It seemed almost as though you had forgotten the rest of us existed."

"I apologize for keeping her to myself." Theseus turned his smile on my brother. "But I wonder if you would do me the favor of helping your sister to her room. There are too many men who have had too much to drink for her to wander the palace alone."

Pollux arched an eyebrow, a smile tugging at the corner of his mouth so slightly that I doubted Theseus would notice. He bowed. "I appreciate your caution, King Theseus, and your attentions to my sister."

I took Pollux's hand when he offered it, and rose from the table. "Thank you, my lord."

Theseus stood and bowed. "Please, Princess. We are equals. Call me Theseus."

"Thank you, Theseus." I met his eyes again when he straightened, and for just a moment, I heard the sound of waves crashing against the shore. Too much wine, almost certainly, and exhaustion, playing tricks on my senses.

Pollux pulled me gently away, and I stilled the desire to look back.

"You must have impressed him," Pollux murmured as we passed through the side door and into the hallway.

In the semidarkness, the painted oak trees seemed to grow faces to stare at us. The owls in the branches came alive, golden eyes glinting.

"If you're not careful, you'll have another admirer. Menelaus won't like competing with the king of Athens."

I pulled my hand free from his and glared. "And what about what I like, Pollux? Or do you think I should not try to prevent my future as well?"

"You know that isn't what I meant." He frowned, slowing his pace and pulling me with him. "What's the matter with you, Helen?"

"I don't need to be reminded of Menelaus's feelings." I pressed my fingers to my lips. There had been so much hunger in Menelaus's kiss.

"He did follow you, then. I thought he had, but when he didn't come back, I just assumed he'd taken one of the servants to bed."

I stopped dead in the hallway and stared at my brother. "What?"

Pollux laughed. "Please, Helen, even you can't be so naive. How else do you think he can stand it, spending so much time in your company?"

The fact that it shouldn't have surprised me did not make me feel any better. My face burned, and my stomach twisted into knots. I should have known. Pollux had not kept his own trysts any kind of secret, and that Menelaus would find relief elsewhere made just as much sense.

"You really didn't know?" Pollux's voice had softened. The concern in his expression made me feel even more foolish. "You shouldn't let it upset you, little sister. The women he beds complain that he calls your name in his release."

"Am I so great a burden, Pollux? Is loving me so difficult a thing?"

He laughed again. "Don't be ridiculous. Any man who marries you will count himself the most fortunate in all the world. It would be worth any difficulty, I'm sure."

We went the rest of the way to the women's quarters in silence, for I could not bring myself to speak further. I should have been relieved Menelaus had found other lovers. I should have felt secure and safe knowing he would not come looking for release in my bed. But the idea that he could not stand to be near me, that my very presence drove him to use other women as whores, made me feel sicker than before.

"Theseus would make a good match for you," Pollux said before pulling the curtain back. He smiled when I looked up at him, surprised by his words. "If you married him, there would be no dishonor in it."

He kissed my forehead. "Good night, little sister."

I watched him go from the other side of the curtain before I climbed the stairs to return to my room. Sometimes I forgot how well Pollux knew me.

❈

My maid, Clymene, rose with me at dawn and helped me dress. She slept on a pallet in the corner, behind a curtain, where she might be woken by my cries and wake me from my nightmares if need be. I no longer shared a room with my sister. It had been one of the first changes Tyndareus had made when he had learned the truth of my dreams, and Nestra had gotten her wish; her bedroom looked out over the practice field. Of course, now she complained it did her little good since Agamemnon rarely came to Sparta, and when he did, he did not bother to spar with the other men.

Clymene laid out my gown on the chest at the foot of my bed, and arrayed rings, cuffs, and jeweled combs for my hair on the table. I took the low stool beside it and, as was my usual habit, began studying the weaving on my loom in the early-morning sun.

So often, I worked only by lamplight, too restless to sleep, or too disturbed by my nightmares, but my loom leaned against the wall with the best light from the window. In daylight, I could see where I had chosen the wrong color, or if the weft threads were not tight enough in the warp.

This morning my eyes seemed to cross, and I sighed.

"Would you like mint leaves, my lady?" Clymene asked when she finished combing my hair. "You hardly slept."

"Yes." I rose and went to the window, sitting down on the bench beneath it and hoping the streaming sunlight would counter my exhaustion. "I don't want to yawn my way through the sacrifice this morning."

Few were awake aside from the servants, who were moving in and out of the kitchens, where they were baking bread and preparing the morning meal. Though I had expected to see the courtyard filled with sleeping bodies, there were none to be found. Two immense amphorae dried in the grass, emptied of their wine and tipped upside down. I would not have been surprised to see far more than that. Leda must have ordered it cut thin with water for the lower tables, unwilling to waste good wine on men of little consequence. Perhaps she had also made them pitch tents in the practice field rather than allowing them to sleep in the courtyard after the porch and megaron had been filled. Or perhaps Tyndareus had not wanted them to hear my screams in the night.

Tyndareus left the megaron, scratching his jaw. He stared at the lightening sky as if it surprised him, and I wondered if he had even left the banquet at all. He went straight to the storerooms, no doubt to be sure of our foodstuffs and guest-gifts, though that was Leda's duty. There would not be time for him to sleep before the morning's sacrifice.

Clymene brought ornaments for my hair and worked them into the braids as I sat. There was no point in wasting the effects of the mint before I needed it, and by now she knew to fetch it last. My eyelids drooped, lulled by the gentle tugs on my hair.

"You should be honored that so many men have come to see you, my lady," Clymene said. "The gifts from King Theseus of Athens alone are enough to keep you in gowns and jewels for the rest of your life."

"Oh?" I hadn't been aware of any further gifts from Theseus, beyond the food and wine he had brought me on the dais.

There had been gifts of gold from others, tripods and platters, cups and bowls, even jewelry, but nothing terribly valuable as anything outside of guest-gifts. No one actually used golden tripods or cauldrons, after all, except to regift them later, as proof that one could afford to keep such things as luxuries. For everyday use, gold was far too soft to be practical beyond a cup here or there, and as far as metals went, iron, copper, and tin—for bronze—were by far the most valuable and would be made into weapons and armor. Tyndareus lamented constantly that he could not find a man who knew how to work iron for Sparta, for the knowledge was rarer than the metal, and he feared that without it, we would be disadvantaged in any war.

"A chest each of gold, silver, and copper," Clymene said. "And at least a dozen bolts of fine linens and wool, plus the animals for the sacrifice this morning."

"So much."

Theseus had practically gifted me a dowry. And he thought I was too generous? A man did not give gifts of such wealth to a whore, no matter what Menelaus said. Perhaps a bracelet here, or a necklace there, but nothing so grand as bolts upon bolts of cloth and chests of metals.

"What else have you heard of the king of Athens?" I asked.

"His servants think he is a very fine master, and a better king. Athens has known great prosperity beneath his rule. Perhaps that is why he brought you such gifts."

"To prove his worth as a king to my father."

If he married me, he would bring the same peace and prosperity to Sparta. But I did not see how he could rule Sparta and Athens. The distance was too great between them. Still, it would serve me better to be away from here. If I were in Athens, the prince would not find me when he arrived in Sparta. And even if he did, Theseus was a hero and much wiser than Menelaus.

"King Pirithous of the Lapiths joined his party. The servants say he spends much of his time in the kitchens, gossiping. I've never heard of a king behaving in such a way, even if he is a son of Zeus."

"King Pirithous must be a good friend of Theseus, to be his travel companion." I did not remember meeting Pirithous, but there had been another tall man at the feast, head and shoulders above everyone but Ajax the Great, son of Telamon. Men did not claim to be children of gods unless they had the height to prove their words.

A man ducked out a side door from the servants' quarters. His red hair would have marked him, even if the line of his shoulders hadn't. I had spent more time than I cared to consider watching those shoulders on the practice field before and after Mycenae had been won. It had been time foolishly spent, and no doubt half the reason he felt so confident in his pursuit of my hand.

Menelaus went into the kitchen before reappearing again with bread in his hands. He glanced up at my window, and I was a moment too late in jerking back. I had not meant for him to see me. I didn't want to see him after what Pollux had told me last night.

"The mint leaves, please, Clymene?"

She nodded and left. I kept a window box of the herb in one of the empty rooms for mornings like these. They happened far too often.

"Helen?"

I swore under my breath and leaned out the window, searching the courtyard for anyone who might see or hear, but it had emptied even of the slaves. Menelaus stood beneath me, only an arm's length from the wall, eyeing it as if he might climb up. He stepped back when he saw me. I did not smile or offer him any greeting.

"Good morning, Princess." He bowed with a formality that seemed absurd. "Did you sleep well?"

"No," I said. He could hardly have expected otherwise.

I couldn't help but glance toward the slaves' quarters from which he had come. My window faced them directly, a long wing across from the family's own. The megaron, with the majority of our store-rooms, linked the two sides of the palace on one end of the courtyard opposite the wide-porched entrance, which completed the enclosure. A dark-haired girl had just emerged, her cheeks flushed and her face glowing. I may have been a maiden, but I knew the signs of a woman who had been well loved. Would he have done as much to me, if we had not been interrupted? The memory of his imposition made my own cheeks burn.

"Helen." The formality was gone, and he stepped closer to the wall again, lowering his voice so that I could barely hear. "Forgive me."

I shook my head. I couldn't. I wouldn't. It had been unforgivable. "You fly into a rage when another man treats me with kindness during a banquet, but I'm expected to overlook other women in your bed?"

His face turned red. "And who told you that?"

"Does it matter?" I asked. "It's the truth, isn't it? Because you cannot bear to be near me otherwise. Give me up, if I am so troublesome. It's all I've ever asked of you."

"You are mine, Helen." His jaw locked, and his eyes flashed with fury. "You are meant to be mine."

My own temper rose, and it took all my strength to keep from shouting. "I am a princess of Sparta and a daughter of Zeus. I belong to Sparta, not to you! And if you do not care for Sparta's future, I will never allow you to rule as its king. I will *never* be yours."

I jerked my head back from the window and threw myself on my bed. Menelaus called my name, but I buried my head beneath the cushions and blankets so I could not hear him. I would not answer. I would not come to his call like a dog trained to heel.

And I would never, ever, be his bride.

CHAPTER SIX

W ell." Pirithous leaned back on the cushions that made up his seat beside the low table in Theseus's rooms. Somehow he'd diverted an entire haunch of mutton from the feast the previous night, as well as bread, grapes, and a soft goat cheese. "If Tyndareus has not settled on Menelaus as a husband for Helen, he had better put a guard on her or he will be left with little choice in the matter before long."

Theseus forced his jaw to relax and laid his hand flat against his thigh so that he would not be tempted to throw his cup across the room. The space he had been given was generous, two bedrooms and a receiving room, the walls painted with galloping horses on green fields and fish-tailed hippocamps, leaping over ocean waves on one side, and soaring eagles and griffons in a storm-dark sky on the other. By the grumbles of Helen's brothers, these were Pollux and Castor's own rooms, and Theseus thought it would be poor repayment to return them damaged because he had been too irritated to remember his strength.

"It's a relief to know I wasn't imagining the man glaring daggers into my back. He followed Helen, then?"

He did not bother to ask where Pirithous had taken himself the night before, after Helen had returned to the feast. Nor did he ask when his friend had finally found his own bed, if at all. Morning had come too early, but the sacrifice today was not one Theseus could miss; the victims were his own bulls.

"He was not pleased about your attentions to her. The man is half-mad with jealousy." Pirithous shook his head, reaching for a loaf of bread. When he broke it, the inside steamed. Theseus prayed that whichever poor kitchen slave Pirithous was cultivating, he would have the good sense not to plant her with his seed. "I only hope that he was drunk, for I cannot excuse his behavior in any other way."

"What exactly did he do?"

"They argued. Something about nightmares she's been having and Agamemnon threatening her. Menelaus insists he'll marry her, regardless of any cost, but it seems that Helen is reluctant to accept his terms."

Pirithous picked at a stem of grapes and spit the seeds into his palm as he ate them. He seemed much too focused on the food, and Theseus was certain there was something more he did not say.

"I suppose it will depend on how much weight Tyndareus gives to her feelings on the matter, but if it were up to her, she would not wed him at all. That much was quite clear."

A weight lifted from his chest, and Theseus grinned. "She does not want him."

Pirithous's smile disappeared and he leaned forward, brushing the grape seeds onto his plate. "My friend, I would not do this. To yourself or to her. Ariadne, Antiope, Phaedra. You loved them all, and the gods turned them to poison. You've already lost one son because of love. What if the gods take your kingdom this time? Helen spoke of seeing a war coming. You risk Athens, in this."

"It's too late, Pirithous." He felt as though he had freed Atlas and shouldered the world himself with the words. It was not even her beauty that captivated him, either, so much as her concern for her people, and the way she fished for wisdom rather than compliments. "If there is any hope she might love me, I cannot turn from her now."

"It has only been one day, Theseus. You barely know her."

"Proof, then, that it is the will of the gods. Aphrodite and Eros, involving themselves." He did not like to admit he did not have control, but he did not see how he could explain his feelings in any other way. "Tell me if there is hope. You can see more clearly in this than I."

Pirithous sighed, leaning back again. His reluctance to speak was an answer itself, but Theseus needed to hear the truth.

It had been Pirithous who had believed coming to Sparta would be the answer to his troubles; Zeus would surely protect his daughter from the meddling of the other gods and goddesses. And Theseus had risked war before, when he took Antiope as his bride. War had not been the problem for Athens, then. The Rock would never fall. It had been the gods—the goddess of maidens and Amazons, Artemis, to whom Antiope had broken her vow—who had doomed them. No, it was not war he feared. Not at all. But Helen was a daughter of Zeus, the only daughter Zeus had ever sired with a mortal woman. Surely that must mean something.

"It is hard to say after only one day, Theseus," Pirithous said at last. "Whether or not she could love you, only the gods can know so soon."

"Then I will pray for a sign."

Pirithous laughed, but it was sharp and humorless. "Of course you will. For all the good it will do." He pushed the rest of his food away and rose. "I suppose that I should dress and make an appearance at this dedication to show our allegiance."

Theseus smiled, breaking off a large piece of the bread. "It has only been one sleepless night, Pirithous. Surely you cannot be tiring so soon."

❦

Every potential suitor seemed to have arrived to see the sacrifice made to Zeus. No doubt they hoped the god would send some sign in blood of who might be favored as Helen's future husband.

Or else they had hoped she would dress in the Cretan style, with her breasts bared for the ritual. Theseus had been relieved to see she had chosen otherwise, but the red gown she wore was still stunning. The bodice was a brilliant poppy shade, with the tiered skirt fading into deep purple at her feet. A practical choice when dealing with animal sacrifice or any amount of blood.

Theseus frowned. Perhaps he should have spoken to Tyndareus the previous evening and made his intentions known. Theseus still wasn't sure he should be intent upon anything, but he could not seem to stop himself. Helen was charming and brilliant, and she did not look at him as though he were anything more than a man. She did not fear him, or simper, or offer him any undue honors simply because his father was Poseidon. The last woman who had treated him in such a way had been Antiope.

But Helen was no Amazon. Unlike Antiope, Helen would be capable of returning his love fully as an equal, without the disdain of years spent among a people who would rather spear a man than marry him. If she wanted him. If she loved him at all.

Aphrodite, I beg you. Smile on me, now. Let her return my love.

From where he stood, Theseus could see Helen's hand shake as she held the knife to the bull's throat. Tyndareus noticed, too, and his hand covered hers, steadying the blade. Helen's brothers stood beside her, ready to offer two more victims to Zeus. The priests droned on as they scattered the barley, taking advantage of such an audience to remind those gathered of their duties to the gods.

Theseus did not listen to the words of the priests, but he said his own prayer to Zeus, his uncle. *Give me your blessing, Zeus. Let Helen*

*be mine, if you will it. You will find no man more capable of guarding
your daughter, no man more fitting to be her husband.*

Helen, with Tyndareus, made the cut across the animal's throat,
and blood poured out, steaming in the morning air. The priests pressed
golden bowls to the skin to collect it.

Someone touched his elbow, and he glanced down to see a
woman near Helen's age. He had seen her in the palace. She was one
of Tyndareus's servants, almost certainly. She gestured him closer,
and he ducked his head that she might speak without disturbing the
others around them.

"My lady Helen wishes to speak with you, my lord."

He grew still as stone, and his gaze leapt to Helen at the altar. She
watched him closely as her maid went on.

"In private, if it might be arranged without drawing attention.
She trusts you will not betray her confidence in this matter."

The woman released his arm and he straightened. Helen met his
eyes and inclined her head as if confirming her maid's words. The
motion was so slight and smooth, the gold and silver ornaments in
her hair did not even chime.

Is this your sign, Zeus? Or is it only Helen's?

It didn't matter. He could not deny her either as hero or man.

Theseus nodded.

Helen's posture relaxed almost at once, and she turned her gaze
back to the priests as they spoke the final words of the ritual, carving
the thighbones and fat from the carcass to burn for the gods.

Theseus glanced down at the maid, but she had disappeared.
Pirithous arched an eyebrow, following the girl's movement as she
slipped back through the crowd. Of course Pirithous would have
made it his business to overhear.

Tyndareus led Helen away from the altar. A few men stepped
forward to make their own offerings, but most followed after the
princess, and Theseus joined them.

She dropped back as the procession became more of a mob, hemmed in only by the thickening oak saplings on either side of the path. Adult oaks bared chestnut trunks where the cork bark had been harvested, but not yet regrown, and sword lilies bloomed in the pinks and oranges of a sunset around the shrine, more poppies scattered among them like drops of blood.

Helen walked with Pollux, and Theseus smiled to see the men around them kept a respectful distance, though it meant they bumped elbows with one another. When Theseus managed to reach them, that distance increased even further. Pollux excused himself almost immediately, grinning at Theseus, and Helen frowned as she watched her brother go.

"I hope it isn't my presence that causes your displeasure, Princess."

"No, not at all." She smiled. "I did want to thank you for your generosity. My maid tells me that the gold and silver in my hair come from your gifts, in addition to the bulls."

"A daughter of Zeus deserves more than I have to give. You look lovely."

Her face flushed, and she ducked her head, causing the decorations to ring against one another. "I'm afraid it won't last, my lord. The ornaments are beautiful to look at, but heavy to wear."

"Yes, I would imagine so." He lifted one of the delicately wrought discs from her hair and shook his head. "I admit that when I gifted them to you, I had not intended for you to wear them all at once."

"In your honor, King Theseus." She bowed her head, and the silver and gold chimed again. She grimaced at the noise. "And I hope you appreciate my sacrifice," she teased. "I'll have a headache before I reach my room."

"I may have something to cure that ill since it seems I am responsible for giving it to you. Should I have my physician sent to you?"

She glanced up at him sidelong, and he smiled. If Menelaus had not been glaring at them, he might have been tempted to ask her what she wished to speak with him about. But if she wanted privacy, better that he play along with her ruse.

"I don't think my father would permit him in the women's quarters."

"Then perhaps you could come to him," Theseus suggested, pretending innocence. The excuse should hide a short meeting without trouble. "Surely your father cannot object to that."

Helen raised her eyebrows with all appearance of curiosity, and he had to struggle not to laugh. "Has your physician made great strides for the treatment of headaches in Attica?"

"Quite so." He hoped no one was studying him too closely, or they would see the amusement in his eyes, even if he kept it from his lips. "In fact, he has invented a powder of his own that, when mixed with water or wine, can cure any ache. A very closely kept secret. I'm afraid he would not be willing to share even a sample of the medicine with your father's physician, for fear of the mixture being deduced. If you are to be well enough to take part in today's festivities, you must allow him to treat you."

"You are too generous, King Theseus. I will have my maid bring me to his rooms as soon as I have removed the ornaments from my hair."

"I imagine it will take you some time to free yourself, or does your maid make quick work of such a chore?"

Helen started to shake her head, then stopped when the metals sounded. She pressed her lips together as if to keep herself from a curse before forcing a sheepish smile.

"I'll see him before the meal is set on the table," she said. "Would you ask him to wait for me?"

"Of course." He did smile then, hoping to reassure her. But Menelaus watched them both like an eagle about to strike; she would have a difficult time getting away from the man. "I'll see that everything is arranged. If for some reason you cannot come, send your maid."

"Thank you, my lord." She squeezed his arm, looking up into his face. Her eyes were the green of spring grasses and myrtle leaves. Last night, he would have sworn they matched the turquoise of the sea.

"Theseus!"

He jerked at the call, tearing his eyes from hers and excusing himself. *Athena, help me. I must keep my wits.* He thanked the gods it was only Pirithous who had noticed. Theseus joined him.

"Do you want Menelaus to have you killed in your sleep, Theseus?" he hissed.

"He wouldn't dare."

Pirithous gave him a dark look that suggested otherwise. "All the same, you would do well to keep your admiration to yourself until you speak to her father. I don't understand how you ever got on without me. Even with Antiope you did not behave so foolishly."

"Antiope would have sneered if I had." He shook his head, hoping to clear it, but it did not help. All he could think of was Helen, and he searched for her again in the crowd.

Menelaus had gone to Helen's side, leaning down to whisper against her ear. Helen stiffened and pulled away. She raised her chin, her voice sharp even at a distance, though Theseus could not make out the words. Helen walked quickly away, joining Castor and Pollux instead.

"Menelaus takes too many liberties," Pirithous murmured.

"Let him. He only succeeds in driving her away." But his hands had balled into fists at his sides. Whatever argument they'd had the previous evening, Helen had clearly not forgiven the son of Atreus.

"Whatever it is she wants of you, Theseus, it will have something to do with him."

Menelaus's expression was dark as he watched Helen, but he recovered himself and offered his company to Clytemnestra. Helen's sister welcomed him without reservation.

Whatever she wanted, Theseus hoped it was within his power to give.

⁘

Theseus paced his physician's small room, really no more than a short hall and a sleeping chamber, though the walls were painted richly with leaping fish and dolphins. Bread and watered wine sat ready on a small table, but he could not bring himself to eat while he waited.

The sun had risen, and the morning's entertainments had begun in the megaron. Pirithous was there, no doubt enjoying himself with whichever servant made herself available, and none the worse for his lack of sleep the night before. He claimed his stamina was a gift from Zeus; considering his other appetites, Theseus did not doubt him.

"My lord, would you prefer to sit? Is there something I can have brought for you?" Ariston asked.

"No, thank you." Theseus forced himself to stop, standing before the window. He clasped his hands behind his back. Ariston was a good physician as well as an old friend, but Theseus was still his king, and a king should not show anxiety or worry. Certainly not over a young woman.

A knock on the door cut through him, and he turned. It could not be anyone other than Helen, but the woman who slipped into the room kept her hair and face covered by a scarf. The green eyes that met his were unmistakable, and splashes of her red gown peeked out from beneath a pale blue robe.

Ariston shut the door behind her.

"My lady." Theseus crossed the room to meet her and brought her hand to his lips.

Helen squeezed his hand. "My lord. Thank you for seeing me."

"It would be rude of me to refuse you." He nodded to Ariston, and the man disappeared into the bedchamber without a word. "May I offer you food or drink?"

She shook her head, reaching up to unwrap the scarf from her face. "Thank you, but no."

Her golden hair fell free of the scarf, no longer encumbered by the ornaments. A single diamond rested against her throat. It was something he had found in Egypt before he had settled into the kingship of Athens, and one of his gifts to her.

Theseus lifted the stone, rolling it between his fingers. "I thought this would suit you, when I heard of your beauty. I'm pleased I could finally offer it."

A blush began at the fair skin of her chest and rose all the way to her cheeks. "It is very beautiful."

"So beautiful, it would shame any other woman who wore it but you." He dropped his hand and again met her eyes, which were the green of olives now. He had never seen a woman with eyes so arresting, and when she looked at him, he felt it like fire on his skin. Zeus had outdone himself. "I'm honored that you seek my counsel, Princess."

"I seek your help, my lord, not just your counsel." She swallowed, all the color leaving her face. The scarf twisted into knots between her fingers.

"To you, Princess, I am Theseus." He took the scarf from her hands and guided her to a low bench along the wall. "Sit, please, and tell me what makes you so anxious."

She sat and stared at her lap, her fingers pleating the fabric of her skirt before smoothing it again. He poured her wine and pressed the cup into her hands, but she only frowned into the liquid.

"I hope that you are as generous when you hear what I have come to say."

Theseus pulled a stool around to face her and seated himself close to her side. From the way her fingers barely closed around the cup, he feared she might drop it.

"Barring a declaration of war against my city, or a curse upon my sons, I believe there is little you could say that would offend me."

He leaned forward, brushing a strand of her golden hair behind her shoulder. It was smooth as silk, and he knew he should not touch her, but somehow he could not quite stop himself.

She stilled when his fingers brushed the column of her neck, and her gaze rose from the wine to his face. "Menelaus says that if you married me, you would treat me as nothing more than a whore."

He drew back. A hundred responses came to mind, many of which he would have spoken in his younger days, but it was not the insult that mattered now. "What do you believe?"

Her face flushed. "I believe you are a good man and a fair king. You look on me with kind eyes and listen to me as though my words carry weight. If that is how you treat your whores, I would be lucky to be counted among them."

"I would treat you as a queen of Athens," he said. "And if we were married, my city would love you. But I would give up Athens for you, if you wished it."

"No." She grabbed his knee, her fingers lighting a fire that traveled up his leg. "I would join you in Athens, if you would let me. When this celebration has ended and you leave Sparta, take me with you. That is all I ask."

Her nails bit into his thigh, but he did not free himself from her grip, and the warmth spread to his stomach. Her eyes were wide, pleading, and her other hand held the wine cup so tightly, her knuckles turned white.

"As my wife?"

"If you wished it."

"Helen." His voice sounded rough even to his own ears. "I do not know of any man who would not wish it."

He could not stop himself from stroking her cheek, his fingers trailing along the soft skin of her jaw. He brushed his thumb over her lower lip, and her eyelids fluttered shut, her hold softening on his leg.

He sighed and dropped his hand, though he could still feel the texture of her skin on his fingers. "And if I were younger, if I were not responsible for the people of Athens, I would leave with you now without hesitation."

She turned her face away, her hand slipping from his knee. "If you do not take me, you risk an even greater war. So many Achaeans will die that even when they win it will leave our lands in ruins for generations. The kings who survive will be twisted in spirit, but most will not return from battle. Is that not worse for Athens?"

The prophecy felt like stone in his stomach, worse now that he heard it from her lips than as a rumor shared by Pirithous.

"How do you know?"

"The gods have granted me visions of the future, horrible dreams of what will come." She swallowed again and stared at the wine cup in her lap. Her face was so pale that he could see the veins beneath the skin. "If I remain here, if I marry Menelaus, it will mean blood and death and fire."

He rose, turning away to keep from drawing her into his arms and giving her comfort he shouldn't. She offered him not only herself, but a reason why he should take her. The gods were cruel to present him with this, if they did not mean for him to have her. *Athena, help me to think clearly now.*

He stared at the window, shuttered to keep their privacy, and rubbed his face. "And how do you know that if I take you from here, it will be avoided? How do you know it will not incite the war you fear?"

"Because in the dream I am Menelaus's wife."

He heard her stand, and the wine cup clinked softly as she set it upon the table. Her hand touched his elbow, and the warmth of her fingers spread up his arm.

"Theseus, if I am not here, I cannot be stolen from him by this stranger who will come, and if I am not his wife, he and Agamemnon cannot start a war to reclaim me. If there was another way, another man whom I thought I could trust, I would not impose myself on you—"

He laughed, looking down at her. "You offer yourself to me as my wife, and you think it is an imposition?"

She pressed her lips together. "I know what I am, Theseus. And you are wise enough to know it, too. The man who is my husband will not have an easy life. Every man in my father's hall seeks to have me as his alone, no matter what the cost, or how much blood it spills."

Yes, he knew. But life as the wife of a hero would not be easy, either. Was it possible she did not know what his love had brought down upon his wives? By Zeus's thunder, he hoped she didn't. If they were to have a future, let it not be shadowed by death.

"I'm flattered you think me any different," he said.

"Haven't you proven it? Just now, you refused me when I offered you myself. But I will beg you, my lord, if I must. I cannot stand by and do nothing to stop so much destruction. This is my future, and if the day comes because I did not act now, the guilt will fall on me along with the blood."

Her eyes held the fire of emeralds, and he knew why she had chosen him. It wasn't because he could refuse her. She did not care if he wanted her for her beauty, or for her kingdom. She only cared that he would act to save the lives of others. She would trade herself for the lives of strange men she had never met, prostitute herself for peace. At least if she were his, he could see that she went unpunished for her generosity. In Athens, she would be honored above all others. He could make her his equal.

"I am not your lord, Helen."

He fingered a strand of her hair, then tucked it behind her ear. There was nothing left to do but accept the burden the gods had placed upon his shoulders. Just as he had accepted it as a youth and gone to Crete for the freedom of Athens. Perhaps now he served to free Helen, too. There were worse things to fight for.

Father, help me now as you did then.

"I am your servant," Theseus said. "I will speak to your father and bargain for your hand, but even if I cannot bring you to Athens openly as my wife, I will see you made safe. You have my word."

CHAPTER SEVEN

Clytemnestra spent the evening at Theseus's side, shooting glares at me from across the length of the table, and I forced myself not to consider the things she might be telling him. Theseus would not listen to her lies. I had to believe he was too wise for that.

Beside me, Agamemnon put down his cup, wiping the wine from his mouth and beard with the back of his hand. He watched Clytemnestra with small, dark eyes, his mood souring more with every smile my sister gave to Theseus.

"He's too old for her," I said. "She would never have him."

He glowered at me. "But not too old for you?"

I broke a piece of bread from the loaf between us and tried not to show the chill that went down my spine when his eyes traced my body beneath my gown. "My marriage will be to the man who will best serve Sparta. Age brings wisdom, and I would be a fool to turn down any man who offers my people such a gift."

"Just because you are beautiful, you think it gives you the right to choose a king?" I tried not to flinch when his fist hit the table.

"Tyndareus will see you married to the man who offers him the greatest gifts. The wealth of Mycenae will ensure that man is my brother."

"Is Mycenae richer than Athens?" I kept my voice light though my heart raced. "I'm surprised it has recovered so quickly from the war. You must be a very fine king, my lord."

"It's a shame you do not have your sister's manners." He bared his teeth at me and refilled his wine cup. "What good is beauty without grace?"

My face flushed, and I stared at the bread on my plate, biting my tongue on an even ruder reply. Nestra's laugh rose above the sounds of conversation, but I did not let myself look up to see if Theseus smiled in return. The king of Mycenae must have been truly blinded by love for my sister if he believed her manners were an improvement over mine. If I hadn't been so irritated by her incessant flirting, I might even have told her so. Not that she would listen.

Agamemnon left to go carve himself more meat. Unlike Theseus, he did not offer me any of the food from his plate, and I did not ask for any. Sitting beside him was punishment enough without allowing him further excuse to insult me with his refusal. At that point in the night, I would even have been grateful for one of King Nestor's war stories. At least he had always treated me with courtesy. I would never understand what Nestra saw in Agamemnon. It could not just be his muscle, or she would fawn over Menelaus just as much if not more so.

I picked a pomegranate from the fruit bowl and stared at the bloodred skin. I dug my nails into the rind and breathed in the fresh scent of its fruit, hoping it might dispel my exhaustion.

"My lady?" Clymene touched my arm. "Menelaus asks you to meet him in the courtyard."

I frowned. I had already refused to meet with him earlier this afternoon, and I had no desire to see him now, either. Not after the things he had said to me this morning, standing beneath my window.

"Tell Menelaus I cannot leave my father's guests."

She nodded and left. I dropped the fruit on my plate and noticed Theseus watching me. He raised his cup and I smiled. Then Nestra tugged at his arm, draping her body against him, and I had to look away.

Neither Agamemnon nor Menelaus returned to the table. If I had been sitting with Theseus, or even my brothers, I might have found a sympathetic shoulder to lean against, but alone, there was no point in forcing myself to stay awake after I had spent the last night sleepless.

I rose, picking my way through my father's guests. There were fewer now, many of the poorer admirers having left that morning, and the balcony above was open to women and children again. Most of those left were princes and kings, men who believed they could win my hand by gold or athleticism. I recognized a few as good friends to Tyndareus—Ajax the Great, of course, and his half brother, Teucer, known for his skill with a bow; and Ajax the Lesser of Locris, whom I wished I did not know at all. Adrastus and Diomedes, his grandson, had come from Argos, but Diomedes was not even my own age, and Adrastus could not truly hope we might marry, no matter how exceptional he believed his heir to be. Sparta did not need a boy-king.

Too busy looking for the men I knew at the tables, I did not notice the one who stepped in my way until he had caught my arm.

"Surely you do not wander alone with so many guests present in the palace, my lady."

I pulled my arm free, looking up into a face that reminded me of Pollux. "It is early enough yet that I need not fear. No man with his wits about him would violate me in my father's hall."

"Your pardon, Princess." He bowed, offering me a charming smile. "Theseus would not forgive me if I did not see you safely to the women's quarters."

"King Theseus is very attentive."

The man laughed. "Only to beautiful women, I assure you."

"And who are you to know the limitations of Theseus's kindness?" I asked, stepping back.

"Pirithous, king of the Lapiths, son of Zeus." He grinned again, his gaze flicking over me, and I felt even in so swift a glance, he had taken in everything about me. "I apologize for not introducing myself sooner, but I did not wish to steal your attention from Theseus. He's quite taken with you, but that can hardly be surprising. What man isn't?"

Pirithous certainly had the height of a demigod. I refused to take another step back even if it meant I had to crane my neck to meet his eyes. And this was Theseus's closest friend? His manners left something to be desired.

"King Agamemnon does not seem to have any use for me, even as a dinner partner."

"King Agamemnon is a fool," he said. "Be grateful you have not caught his eye. The way the servants speak of him, he's nothing more than a brute."

I smiled. "I do not have any interest in procuring King Agamemnon's favors."

"No, of course." His eyes narrowed. "But there are many rumors about your relationship with his brother."

I raised my chin. "You shouldn't believe everything you hear from servants, King Pirithous."

"I've seen enough to know it is not all talk," he said softly. "He is determined, Helen. If he was a brother to you once, he isn't any longer."

My throat tightened. Was it so obvious? "I don't know what you mean."

He smiled grimly. "I'm afraid if you won't permit me to accompany you, I'll have to follow."

I swallowed hard and surveyed the room. Menelaus's seat still sat empty at the table, and the idea of an escort did not seem so unwelcome anymore. He would not be happy that I had refused him and gone to bed instead.

"If you insist. I cannot stop you."

He inclined his head. "I won't be far behind."

Strange, I thought, to find such comfort in the words of a stranger. When I heard his footfalls echo mine in the corridors, I did not turn, and as I slipped through the guarded and curtained doorway to the women's quarters, I caught no sight of him at all. But he had been there, and on Theseus's behalf, he kept me safe.

~❀~

I did not need to light the oil lamp to find the way to my dressing table, and perhaps if I kept the room dark, Menelaus would not notice I had returned to my bedchamber. I would not be able to weave tonight, if I could not sleep. Not if he watched for me. I shook my head. He'd probably found another slave to take to his bed in my place. Was it terrible that I hoped so, just this once?

The soft sounds of movement told me Clymene had arrived before me, and I lifted my hair up off my neck. "Can you undo the clasp of my necklace?"

The delicate wire slipped free, and I caught the diamond pendant in my hand, letting my hair drop. The stone flashed in the moonlight, and I smiled. Even darkness couldn't dull its beauty. Clymene's fingers moved through my hair, plucking out the silver and ivory pins and dropping them to the floor. She wasn't usually so careless.

"You'll never find them again in the dark," I said, glancing over my shoulder.

I froze.

A figure loomed behind me, too tall to be my maid. My hand closed around the diamond.

"Clymene will find them in the morning, I'm sure." Menelaus's fingers slid down my neck and along my spine, prickling my skin. "I sent her to the feast. Agamemnon should keep her occupied until dawn."

"You shouldn't be here." I slipped out from under his hands but did not turn to face him. My heart pounded in my ears.

Clymene was with Agamemnon. Leda would not check on me; she barely even looked at me. And Nestra no longer shared my room. Clymene had been my only protection, but she would obey Agamemnon and Menelaus as she would my father or brothers. All the servants did.

"I could not stand to think you would go to your bed still angry. If you had only come to me earlier, I would not have been forced to climb in through your window like a common thief, but I had to speak with you." He touched my hair again, and I willed myself not to flinch. "I don't know what I said to upset you this morning, but whatever it is, I apologize a hundred times. A thousand. Surely you understand it is only that I love you too much—"

"It doesn't matter," I said, interrupting him. I could not stand to hear more of his love. Not when he showed no regard for my own feelings. "No matter what you say, or how many times you apologize, tomorrow you will still look at me as though you own me. You still consider me to be your prize."

"When all this madness is over, we'll be married. Tyndareus only waits for his guests to leave to announce it." His hand fell to my shoulder, his thumb sliding over the sleeve of my gown and slipping it down my arm. "Clytemnestra will be given to Agamemnon and be made queen of Mycenae. Even she can't complain about such an arrangement. And you and I, we will be free to love each other openly."

"No." I fought back the tears pressing behind my eyes. Tyndareus could not have done this to me. Not without my agreement. Not without at least consulting Pollux and Castor. Surely my brothers would not have kept this from me. "Menelaus, it is not so simple. You know it isn't."

"I told you Agamemnon would keep his word," he said, kissing my shoulder. "Tyndareus has always hoped we would marry. Did you never wonder why I sought you out, even when you were still so young? Once I knew you, it hardly mattered how it had begun. You were so sweet to me as a child, so delighted with my attentions. How could I resist?"

"But you can't. He wouldn't." I turned to face him.

The line of his mouth in the moonlight showed no kindness, and his eyes glinted with a hardness I had never seen before. It reminded me too much of Agamemnon and the way he stared at serving girls. The way he had stared at me during the banquet.

"You can't want this," I said. "The future it will bring. The war. You can't want to have me this way. To put me in the path of harm, and your brother—"

"You should be grateful," he said before I could speak further, as if he had plugged his ears against my words. "If I had not bargained with my brother, leveraged my support in his desire for Mycenae, Agamemnon would have taken you for himself, instead. Can you imagine? You say I only look upon you as another prize to be won, but at least I can give you my affections, my love. My brother never understood. He never realized how much more you are than just your beauty and your kingdom. But I do. I know you, Helen."

I shook my head, sidling away. The things he was saying—no wonder Agamemnon was so sour, and if Nestra had known . . .

But it did not matter. No matter what argument he made, it did not change what would come to pass. Better if I had been promised to Agamemnon than Menelaus. Perhaps there would not have been any affection shared between us, but that would be nothing if it meant all that death, all that horror avoided.

"Think, Menelaus," I said softly, urging him to see reason. "Think what you're saying. Think what you would be allowing to happen!"

"I would be allowing you to become my wife. You cannot truly be so surprised by it all when I have made my feelings so clear." He stepped closer, crowding me against the table. Jewels fell to the floor, ringing against the tile. There was not enough wine on his breath for the excuse of drunkenness. "Have I not always cared for you? Always protected you? Who better than I?"

Theseus, I thought, the diamond biting into my palm. I stepped back, tripping over the low stool. Menelaus frowned, reaching for me, but I batted his hand away.

Theseus, who does not look at me as though I am a chest of gold, or speak to me as though I do not know my own mind.

I lurched around him toward the bed, hoping to put space between us, but I banged into the chest that held my gowns, bruising my shin. Menelaus followed, his eyes dark.

Theseus, who listens to more than just his lust. Like you used to. A king who cares for his people.

Menelaus caught me by the wrist and pulled me back against his body. "If you had only come to speak with me this afternoon, or even during the feast, I would have told you all of this. Explained everything."

"You don't understand," I said. "You don't understand what will happen if we marry and the stranger comes."

"It's you who doesn't understand, Helen." His fingers tightened around my wrist, his other hand a fist in my hair. He didn't pull, but nor could I move away. "Do you think you're the only one who dreams? The only one who suffers? Do you have any idea what you've done to me? I can't sleep at night without seeing you, without growing so hard, I feel as though I will burst from the pain of not having you beneath me."

"Not like this."

His hand held me bound. If I screamed, would anyone come? The slaves were used to hearing me cry in the night. They would only think it a nightmare. And anyone outside would mistake it for noise from the feasting, just another kitchen girl shrieking when she's caught by the man she teased all night.

"Please, not like this," I begged. "If we're going to be married, can you not just wait a few months longer?"

He laughed again, rough and low. "A few months of agony. And days of watching you expose yourself to these dogs. Days of suffering your refusals. It would be crueler of me to leave you in doubt of our future, to let you work your wiles on other men." He kissed me beneath my ear, his fingers leaving my wrist to trace my collarbone. "You will not tell me I cannot have you, after tonight, and I would not see those men you tease suffer as I have. It is unkind of you, Helen. Unkind to them, and even unkinder to me. Or is that the truth of it? The reason for your nightmares? All this time you say you are unwilling, that you are taken by force, but watching you with that hero—"

His hand wrapped around my throat, and his eyes, narrowed and dark, glittered in the moonlight. I went still, my lungs seizing. The beat of my heart filled my ears louder than ever while his fingers pressed into my skin, closing, squeezing until my breath caught. I grasped his wrist, but the way he stared at me, the way his lip had curled and his grip tightened, I did not dare to struggle.

"No," he murmured, the pressure upon my throat easing at last. I took a gasping breath, my chest aching, though whether it was my broken heart or the air I had been denied, I could not tell. "No, I cannot believe you are so cruel as that. But you are mine, Helen, and I will have you remember it when you sit beside that Athenian tomorrow."

Theseus.

I closed my eyes and clutched the diamond in my palm. If I fought Menelaus, there would be no forgiveness. Even if I scratched and clawed, he would not free me. He would only look on me with the same hate I saw in my dreams.

He kissed my neck, and I shivered. Menelaus, whom I had loved as a brother. As a child, I had dreamed of our marriage. I had dreamed of how he would take me in his arms, gentle and fierce. Dreamed of his kiss on my lips and how kind a husband he would be. The best I could have hoped for.

A sob caught in my throat, and I turned my face away.

"I am owed this, Helen," he murmured against my ear. "I am owed you."

There was nothing gentle about him, then, when his lips claimed mine, and I knew I would give him this. Not because it was owed. Not because he had earned it. Not because I was his. I would give him my body, because he could not have my heart. Because I would not marry him, no matter what Tyndareus had promised. Because once, long ago, he had been my friend, and regardless of what happened between us, I could not bear for him to hate me yet.

I unclasped the pins that held my dress and let the fabric fall to the floor.

Because before the week was ended, I would be free.

CHAPTER EIGHT

Menelaus half growled, his hungry gaze sweeping over my nakedness. For a moment, a brief moment, he only stared, but then he was pushing me back against the bed. One hand was at my waist, biting into the soft flesh as I fell into the bedding. He crawled atop me, pulling me toward him by my hips when I flinched away.

"I've dreamed of this for so long," he murmured. "So long."

I shut my eyes and lay limp, my fingers closing all the tighter around the diamond still in my palm. But I did not want to think of Theseus. I did not want to think at all.

His lips traced the line of my jaw, the column of my neck, the slope of my collarbone, and the shape of my breast. "Beautiful," he said between hard kisses as he worked his way to the peak. "So beautiful."

But I did not feel beautiful, then. I did not feel anything but sick. Before the nightmares had come, I had imagined these moments between us, imagined his kiss, his caress. I had imagined a considerate lover, a friend as concerned for me and my pleasure as his own. Before the nightmares, each brush of his hand against mine had lit a fire inside me, but now I lay bare before him, and felt only the twist of snakes in my belly and the chill of gooseflesh.

He moved away only long enough to pull his tunic over his head, and I turned my face away before I saw his nakedness. I did not want to remember him this way, to remember any of this at all. This man, whoever he had become, was not the man I had admired, even loved. He was no friend, nor any kind of protector. I did not know him, or understand the desperate, panting hunger of his breaths.

Pirithous had been right to warn me, and in that moment, I only wished he had spoken sooner. That I might have kept Clymene by my side at all times, or stayed in the hall until I could be certain Menelaus had found his own bed.

But I had thought—what had I thought? That Menelaus would never betray me. That Menelaus above all would protect me from harm. Had he not been my closest friend since childhood? Had he not always loved me, cared for me, stood as my champion in all things?

Menelaus pressed me into the bedding, heavy and rough, until all I felt was the ropes beneath the furs, and bruises across my back. His hand wrapped in my hair, forcing my head back and baring my throat to his mouth.

I cried out when he drove inside me the first time, tears pricking my eyes. He groaned my name, and I hushed him. The servants might not come if they heard me, but they would certainly be startled by a male voice.

"Let them come," he growled. Before I could prepare myself, he moved again. His red head bent over my body, his teeth closing over the tender skin of my breasts.

He did not seem to notice when I began to cry, hot tears burning as they slipped down my cheeks and pooled in my ears. I wrapped my legs around his waist to try to slow him, fisted hands pushing at his chest and shoulders to give myself space, to give myself time to breathe, but he only drove himself deeper inside me.

"Mine, Helen," he murmured. "You will always be mine."

I closed my eyes and focused on the feel of the diamond in my palm, the sharp cut of its edges against my skin. I tried to shift my body beneath his to avoid the worst discomfort, sickened by my own whimpering, by the roar of laughter rising from the courtyard outside. Gods above, but it burned, as if I were torn apart with every thrust. And the ropes beneath me—I could feel each knot, each overlay, digging into my spine. He groaned again, like a rutting boar, and stiffened.

My breath caught, and I prayed that he was through. That I would never again know his weight upon me, or the staleness of his hard pants, or the sourness of his sweat, mixed with a too-sweet musk.

A moment later, he rolled away, his fingers slipped from my hair, freeing me at last. I curled up on my side and covered myself with the blanket.

He laughed and drew me against his chest, fondling my breasts. "Just knowing you're still beside me makes me harden again."

I swallowed the sob in my throat and pretended I did not feel him pressed against my backside; I pretended not to hear him at all.

"Helen?" he murmured, kissing the back of my neck.

I did not answer, and with a sigh, he rolled to his back. I lay still and silent, listening for his breathing to slow, waiting for it to steady. The snakes in my stomach writhed, cold sweat breaking from my skin.

I could not lie beside him any longer, with his seed spilling from between my legs, surrounded by the scent of his body, all musk and leather, until I gagged. But I forced myself to wait, counted my racing heartbeats until I had no more numbers, and Menelaus snored softly at my back.

Only then, biting my tongue against even the slightest hiss of discomfort, did I dare to move, slipping from beneath the blanket and contorting myself in order to escape. I half fell from the bedding and froze, searching his face for any sign that he had heard.

Menelaus didn't stir, his expression relaxed in sleep, all the lines I had grown so used to seeing smoothed away. For a moment, I stared at the boy I had known, the one who took me fishing when Castor and Pollux had refused me, and who swore to Leda it was his fault I had come back muddied from toes to chest, another gown ruined.

And then I saw the rest of him, scarred and hard muscled. The body he had used to claim mine, careless of my feelings, of my distress and discomfort. The boy I had known once was gone.

I caught up my sleeping shift, laid out still upon my chest at the foot of the bed, and left the room.

The water in the small bath had long turned cold in the moonlight, but I did not stir. Even the idea of moving from the tub made me wince. I should have used the pool instead, but I had not been certain I could keep my head above the water, and after everything that had happened, I refused to let myself drown. He had not been gentle, but he had been thorough. More than one area would blossom purple, black, and blue before morning, and so be it. This was all he would ever have of me. I would no longer feel any guilt for leaving him behind.

I opened my hand and stared at the diamond. The rough edges of the stone had cut into my palm, but I had not been able to release it. The sharp bite of the facets had been a welcome distraction from the pain of our joining.

When I had eased my sore body into the warm water, I did not think I would ever rise again. But now, I sat in cold water and my teeth chattered, gooseflesh rising on my skin. I could not stay here until morning. If the servants learned what had happened, my father would be shamed in front of all his guests and I would be as good as married. Any hope I had of escape and freedom would be destroyed with the gossip and the announcement of betrothal that would follow.

I washed the blood from the diamond in my hand, and forced myself to rise from the water, wishing for Clymene. Bending over to reach the towels on the benches along the wall made me gasp, and I moved with less grace than an old grandmother as I dressed.

I crept back down the corridor, trying to ignore the way the peacocks' eyes followed my progress in the dark. Menelaus snored still, the sound traveling through my door.

Theseus. I needed to speak to Theseus. Menelaus would not be able to wander the halls of the women's quarters in search of me if he woke. As long as I did not return to my bed, I would be safe from him until tomorrow.

The sounds of the feast outside had faded though the moon had not yet set. If Theseus was not in his rooms, surely his physician could find him for me. A much softer snore greeted me from the other side of the curtain at the main entrance, and I had never been more thankful for a sleeping guard. I slipped past him, my bare feet making little noise on the painted tiles.

The halls were mostly deserted, splashed with moonlight and shadow. The owls watched me tiptoe past the open door to the megaron and through the storerooms beyond it. Ariston's room was on the opposite side of the palace, inside the servants' wing, since he had only common blood. When I heard footsteps, I hid behind pillars and waited for the rare servant to pass. I did not forget Pirithous's warning, and prayed I did not meet any of my father's guests, drunk from too much wine.

I knocked on the door. *Please, let him be awake.*

I knocked louder.

"Princess," a voice hissed.

My heart pounded in my ears. I had no place to hide but the door frame, and it was not deep enough to keep me out of sight.

The man came forward, still half in shadow. I could just make out the glint of his eyes, tracing the shape of my body through the thin shift I wore. A flush rose from my chest to my cheeks as the silence between us roared.

He stepped into the moonlight, and I recognized his face.

"King Pirithous." I slumped against the stone, my hand pressed over my heart.

"I had hoped that when I saw you to your room, you would stay there." He reached around me to open the door and pushed me through it into darkness. He glanced back out into the hall and then pulled it shut behind him.

I groped for the wall, and Pirithous grabbed me by the wrist when my hand brushed his tunic, guiding me deeper into the room.

"Ariston!"

The physician appeared, carrying an oil lamp. The flicker of the small flame cast shadows over his rumpled hair and accentuated the blanket-lines impressed on his face, turning them into gruesome scars.

"My lord Pirithous?" Then his gaze fell on me, and his forehead furrowed. "My lady?"

"If you've any wine, she'll need it. Nothing cut, mind you." Pirithous sat me down on a stool. "Might I assume you came looking for Theseus?"

I nodded, mute. My heart still raced, and I winced in discomfort. Had Pirithous been following me the entire time? If I had screamed when Menelaus had arrived, might he have heard and come?

No. Even if he had heard, how could he have reached me? And Menelaus would only have been enraged.

Ariston set the lamp on the table, a wineskin over his shoulder. He poured me a cup and pressed it into my hands. I drank, hoping for the numbness it might bring. At least the uneven lamplight kept him from seeing the marks on my body.

"I'm sure he's in his room by now," Pirithous said. "Ariston, keep her here. Apparently she hasn't the sense not to wander, even when she's been warned."

I glared at him, but said nothing, and when he was gone, I stood. I was too sore for the stool, and my damp hair dripped cold water down my back.

"My lady, please," Ariston said. "My lord will be here shortly, and he will not be happy to find you gone."

"I don't intend to leave after I went to so much trouble to arrive." I could not bring myself to smile, but the tension in his shoulders eased. "Tell me, does King Pirithous often lurk in the hallways at night?"

Ariston's lips twitched. "My lord Pirithous does not sleep much, but when he lurks, it is usually for a purpose."

I rubbed at my arms to warm them. "Like following me?"

Ariston took the lamp with him to the hearth, using the small flame to light a larger fire. When he didn't answer, I moved to the window and pulled the shutters closed before the light could spill outside. I hadn't wanted to risk waking Menelaus when I left my room, but I wished I had reached for something warmer than the light shift I slept in. Even the gown I had discarded would have been an improvement.

The door opened, and I turned to see Theseus, still dressed in his long tunic from the banquet, the gold filaments of the embroidery glittering in the hearth light. He took in my appearance with clear eyes, his mouth a grim line.

He shut the door and barred it. "Ariston, one of your cloaks. She's freezing."

The physician rose from the hearth and disappeared into his sleeping room.

"My lord—" But I could not manage more than those two words before my throat closed and my eyes filled with tears.

Theseus crossed to me at once, and I nearly fell into his arms.

I shuddered and hid my face against his chest, gulping back a sob. And then I could not hold my grief back any longer, and I cried in earnest.

"Shh." He smoothed my hair. Warm wool settled over my shoulders, and he tucked the fabric around my body. "I do not know what has brought you to me in the middle of the night, Helen, but if it is within my power, you need only whisper it and I will see it done."

I shook my head, unable to speak around the lump in my throat. Theseus sighed, lifting me up and carrying me to a bench nearer the fire. He sat me in his lap and let me cry against his shoulder. I struggled to control my breathing and stop the hiccupping sobs. I could feel Menelaus still, his touch, his body against mine, in mine, and I clung to Theseus, the solidness of him, the warmth, the gentleness of his touch, to put it from my mind.

"You're safe," he murmured into my hair when I had calmed. "Whatever's happened, you're safe now."

I felt him pull back to brush my hair from my shoulder, but he froze in the middle of the motion, his whole body stiffening beneath me.

He lifted my chin gently and turned my face. His expression blanked into a king's mask, the warm blue eyes becoming the flat gray of a hurricane on the sea.

"Whoever did this to you will answer to me, and he will be lucky if I do not kill him in his bed."

I covered the mark on my neck with my hand, my cheeks burning.

Theseus's eyes narrowed. "Was this Agamemnon's work? The way he looked at you at the feast, I would not be surprised if he did you harm."

"Not Agamemnon." I stared at his chest and felt the pressure of tears behind my eyes again. Would he still protect me now that I had been used? I didn't know. But I could not ask him to help me and not tell him the truth. "Menelaus was waiting for me in my room. He said my father had already given his word that I would be his wife. That Agamemnon had arranged it all."

Theseus's expression hardened to stone, and his voice was cold. "Menelaus oversteps himself."

My hands trembled, and I pressed them against my thighs so he would not see. "Forgive me, my lord. I did not know what else to do. If I had not given myself to him—"

I couldn't continue. I did not even want to think the words, but I had felt the violence behind every gesture he'd made, every word he'd whispered. I had felt his fingers close around my throat. There would have been no hiding what happened, if I had refused. No hope of freedom. I'd have been married the moment Tyndareus and Leda caught sight of me.

Theseus set me down on the bench and rose, pacing to the window. His hands balled into fists at his sides. "Where is he now?"

"Asleep in my bed."

Without Theseus's warmth, the chill returned to my skin and settled into my bones. The flames danced, the shadows making the painted river on the opposite wall look as though it flowed. I pulled my knees to my chest, though it made me wince. At least it kept me from shivering.

"Perhaps I should not have come," I whispered.

Theseus swore a low oath. "The only person who did not act as he ought was Menelaus, and if he were within my reach, I would end his life with my own hands."

"He asked me to meet with him before the feast and I refused. If I had just gone to speak to him, he would not have been tempted to climb through my window—"

"No." He crossed back to me and sank down on one knee, forcing me to look into his eyes. "This is not your fault. He had no right to climb through your window, no right to touch you at all. Do you not see he lied to you?"

I shook my head. It made no sense. No matter what else had happened, Menelaus had always been my friend. I had trusted him with everything since the age of six. Even if we had fought—I had never tolerated Menelaus's temper, but to betray me like this?

"I spoke to your father just this evening, and he swears he will not promise you to any man until the proper ceremonies have been observed. Tyndareus will make no exceptions. Not even for Menelaus."

My heart tripped heavily against my ribs, and I closed my eyes for a moment, rocking on the base of my spine. The ache in my body was nothing compared to this new pain.

"But he said that Agamemnon—"

"Agamemnon has been bartering for a bride, but not for Menelaus. Your sister, Clytemnestra, will be his queen. Pollux gave me the news of it himself."

I shook my head again. How could he have lied? I wanted to weep.

"I'm sorry, Helen." Theseus's thumb brushed over my cheek, wiping away my tears. "I'm sorry that any of this had to happen. I wish I had been able to stop him, but if you had not given yourself to him, things would have been worse. A man that desperate would not have taken no for an answer."

"I thought—" My voice broke, and I tried again. "I thought he loved me. As a sister, if nothing else."

"Crazed by his love, perhaps," Theseus murmured. "But to abuse you this way is unforgivable."

I swallowed, staring at the worn fabric of the cloak. My fingers knotted in the cloth. "If you no longer wish to have me as your wife, I beg you still to help me leave the city. I cannot stay. I will not be his wife, and I will not give him Sparta."

He stroked my face. "When I leave, I will find a way to take you with me. If you still wish to offer yourself as my wife after you are made safe, that will be a different matter."

The pain in my chest eased, and I pressed his hand against my cheek, comforted by the dry warmth of his palm, the kindness in his eyes. As long as I had his protection, I could believe that all would be well. Poseidon's son or not, my father would think twice before he moved against the king of Athens. Even Agamemnon would have to hesitate.

I forced myself to rise, though my muscles protested. Theseus helped me to my feet, steadying me with an arm around my waist.

"If Menelaus wakes and finds me gone, he'll be furious. Better he think I am resigned to our marriage and the fate it will bring." I pressed my lips together. "He cannot know we have spoken."

Theseus's eyes flashed, his face turning to stone again. I could have sworn in that moment I heard the crash of waves against the cliff. "You need not return to him at all. And better if you do not expose yourself to more of the same."

"And how will I explain myself if I don't return to my room? He will be furious, Theseus. Already he thinks me ungrateful—disloyal."

"Tell him, if he questions it, that you were hurt, and went to your father's physician for relief. If he is any kind of man at all, he will not press you further, if only for the sake of his own pride. And from the way you move, I have no doubt you've suffered. He will see that, too. Find another bed to sleep in this night, I beg of you."

I looked away, hoping he would not see the truth in my expression. For all that I had been willing, it had not felt like loving.

Theseus turned my face back to his, lifting my chin. "I will never hurt you, Helen. I promise. Not like that."

I forced a smile. "I thought the same of Menelaus, once."

Theseus rapped on the door to the hall, unbolting it, and Pirithous opened it from the outside.

"Stay close to me," Pirithous said, "and pray to the gods we meet no one along the way."

I glanced back at Theseus as the door closed. He stood with his back to me, his shoulders bowed and his head bent. For everything I had asked of him, perhaps I could at least give him some happiness in return.

I owed him that. I owed him everything.

CHAPTER NINE

Theseus paced his rooms and concentrated on keeping his hands from balling into fists. What little peace he had gathered shattered with the memory of the marks on Helen's neck and the visions of Menelaus forcing himself on her that rose in his mind.

The door opened and he spun, reaching for the nearest weapon at hand. It was nothing more than a table knife, but the ocean roared in his ears, and he knew it would be enough to cut down whatever came. *Let it be Menelaus!*

"Peace, Theseus," Pirithous said, his voice low. He didn't move from the doorway, his eyes trained on the knife. "She made it back to the women's quarters without being seen, and you have no enemies here yet. I should think Menelaus will feel quite secure after tonight."

He forced himself to release the knife, but he couldn't stop the growl. "If he weren't hiding in her room, I would see him dead by my own hands this night, guest of Tyndareus or not."

"Not without bringing war upon Athens." Pirithous entered and shut the door behind him. "Peace, my friend. For her sake, if not your own. You do her no good if Mycenae rises against you as you leave, to say nothing of what it will mean for your people. Athens is strong, but breaking the sacred laws would mean incurring the wrath of the gods as well as men."

Theseus ground his teeth. "And if it were the woman you loved who had just been raped?"

"Then I would depend on you to speak reason until my judgment was restored. Is that not the greatest purpose of friends and allies?" Pirithous's eyes blazed with Zeus's fury, but he poured wine for both of them and kept his voice level. "Come, Theseus. Drink and be seated. If you intend to steal her, we will need a plan. Your love for her is obvious to even the blindest of men, and Menelaus will accuse you first, even if Tyndareus would not."

"If you had seen her face when she spoke of it, Pirithous, you would not be so easy now."

"I saw enough." Pirithous's jaw tightened. "And heard more. You have my help in this, Theseus, and not just for the sake of our friendship. Helen is a daughter of Zeus, and she deserves better than what Menelaus will give her. He's proven that tonight."

Pirithous's face was lined with the strain of too little sleep and too much wine. For the first time since they had met, Theseus glimpsed his age. They had both lived too long with all the appearance of youth, and all the weight of wisdom earned by hard years as kings, but until that moment, Theseus had always thought his friend wore it lightly.

Theseus took a long drink of the wine and dropped to a seat at last. He had not been sleeping as he should, spending too many late nights drinking with Tyndareus, and all for nothing now. He needed rest, but he did not know how he would manage it, knowing what Helen had suffered. And dawn was already coming.

"I have spoken to Tyndareus, offering him gold and iron and beasts in numbers that would tempt more powerful kings than Sparta. I cannot be certain it is me he objects to, or simply that he does not wish to barter her without full honors. But he must realize even Mycenae cannot match the offer I've made."

"Then she will have to be stolen," Pirithous said quietly. "And if it is to be done, we should do it quickly."

Theseus rubbed his face. "And so I take her from the prison of her nightmares of Menelaus and death, to a gilded cage."

"Shall I see if there are any black sheep in the city to be bought?" Pirithous asked.

Theseus nodded. "A sacrifice would not go amiss. At the very least, I must beg my father for calm seas and fair winds on the voyage back to Attica."

"Will he hear you?"

He pressed his lips together and met Pirithous's eyes. "I can only pray."

❦

Ariston arrived not long after dawn with news that Helen's maid had come and gone, white faced. Helen would not be at the morning meal, so Theseus excused himself from it also, leaving Pirithous to see to her safety while he went to pray.

He had already made offerings to Zeus tenfold, but he could not forget his father when he traveled by sea, nor Hera and Aphrodite, if he wanted his relationship with Helen to grow, and they would need Athena's protection now more than ever if Mycenae rose in arms.

He saved her offering for last.

Olives would have made a better gift than the wine he brought, but he did not trust himself not to slit Menelaus's throat on sight if he ran into the man in the palace on his way to collect them. Just thinking about it made the ocean roar in his ears. No, he could not see Menelaus yet, and Pirithous was right; it would affront more than

Tyndareus to violate the laws of hospitality. War he could win, but he could not fight the gods if he meant to keep Helen safe.

Athena's temple stood a little ways from the others, in a thick grove of sacred olive trees, though Theseus could not tell if the trees or the shrine had come first. Snakes wrapped around the columns, winding and weaving into braided patterns, and owls were painted across the lintels between them. The temple itself was little more than its roof and one back wall where a statue of Athena, carved from olive wood, fit into an alcove above a stone altar. Olive trees formed the other two sides, fit between the columns, their branches reaching beneath the roof for their mistress.

Theseus laid the wine upon the altar and dropped to his knees before the image of the goddess. They had given the temple a stone floor, and he felt no grit or dirt beneath him, though he had seen no sign of any priestesses.

"My lady, you know what I beg of you. Athens is yours, and will rise as far as you wish, giving glory to your name in everything we do. But if we must fall, if it is your will that such a fate waits for your people, let it not be for this."

A dark-haired priestess stepped up to the altar, opening the wine-skin and pouring a measure into a golden cup etched with owls. Theseus sat back on his heels, staring as she lifted the cup to her lips.

"My lady—" He rose to his feet in shock, one arm outstretched to stop her.

But she had already drunk.

Priests and priestesses were kept on the offerings given to the temples, but he had never seen one profane an offering at the god's own altar.

"Attic wine," she said. "A fitting gift from the man who holds Attica to the goddess who has made it so."

"I would not give the goddess anything less," he managed to say.

"No." She set down the cup and fingered an offering of wool that rested beside it. "No, you have always done your duty to us."

She looked up at him, then, with bright silver eyes, and smiled.

The beauty of her face rivaled Helen's, but even suggesting the comparison in the silence of his own mind made him tremble, and he fell to his knees at once before Athena, bowing his head.

"Forgive me, my lady," he said. "I did not know you."

"And how could you know me, if I did not reveal myself?"

He thought she might be laughing, but did not dare to raise his eyes. Her hand, cool and gentle, touched his face, lifting his chin so that he looked at her. Her flawless skin seemed to glow, and her eyes danced.

"You need not grovel before me, Theseus. We are family, after all."

He shook his head. "I am nothing, my lady. Only your servant."

"You are my champion, Theseus. My hero. Is that not what you have been named? Hero of Attica. Do you think you would be called so if it were not by my favor? Rise, for you have done nothing to displease me, and I would speak with you as my cousin, not as my servant."

She held out her hand to him, and he had no choice but to accept it. As her fingers closed around his, a shock traveled through his bones like lightning. Her lips twitched. When he stood, he barely matched her height.

"I am honored, my lady."

Athena pressed her lips together, her eyes flashing. "I did not come to listen to you give homage. Had I wanted that, I could have heard it from the comfort of Olympus."

He had to stop himself from stepping back, and for a dizzying moment he wondered if this was how men felt when they met him for the first time. "Forgive me, my lady, but what is it you've come for?"

"To help you, Theseus. As far as I'm able. Neither one of us, I think, wishes to see Athens in ruins over a woman, but you seem to be committed, and if I do not help you, no one will. Certainly not Aphrodite, jealous as she is. And Hera has never had any love for Zeus's misbegotten children."

"Helen has done nothing to deserve their enmity." He looked away and swallowed the rest of his words. It was not his place to judge the gods. "I would give them any offerings they desire. If they will not help Helen, would they not at least offer me their blessing? Help me, instead?"

Athena sighed, turning his face back to hers with a cool hand on his cheek. "It would be easier if it were only a question of incense and the blood of bulls, Cousin, but it will never be so. Not with Helen."

He stared at the goddess, turning her words over in his mind. She was so beautiful, it hurt to look at her, but to look away would have been an insult. "Then what?"

She shook her head, her silver eyes filled with sympathy. "Nothing, Theseus. There is nothing you can do, and certainly nothing that Helen will, poisoned against us as she has been. If Leda had only kept her spite to herself—but no. It is too much to expect of any mortal woman, or immortal for that matter."

Her lips thinned again as she searched his face, though he did not know what she looked for. She held his head still, and her fingers curled around his ear, her nails biting into his flesh.

"Swear to me that you will not forget where your loyalties lie, no matter what Helen might say. Swear you will not turn from us, and I will give you my aid, even if they will not."

"I swear it." But he frowned at the crease in her pale brow, as if she listened for the lie in his words. "My lady, how could I turn from you? No matter what else comes, I am my father's son. I cannot turn from my family, even if they do not love me as well as I might wish."

She barked a sharp laugh, and her hold on him eased. He freed himself carefully, watching her face for any sign that she might take offense.

"Not half as well as you deserved."

Athena stepped back and turned away, seeming to stare at the altar before them. Her dark hair fell past her waist in a thick braid, woven with strands of gold and silver. The gown she wore moved like silk, and he imagined it would be nearly translucent in sunlight.

"I am sorry for that," Athena said after a moment. "It was cruel of my sisters to make you suffer so, in love. Especially what happened with Phaedra and Hippolytus."

He flinched at the sound of his son's name, his jaw clenching. Hippolytus. Poor Hippolytus. Hippolytus, who had paid in blood for sins he had not committed. He almost wished Phaedra had been successful in her seduction of his son and that Hippolytus had happily gone to his stepmother's bed. If he had, perhaps his son would still live.

"I beg you not to speak of it, my lady."

Athena bowed her head. "Yet you risk it all again for Helen."

His stomach turned to ice. "Do I?"

"Theseus." Her pale face seemed even whiter than before, the warm glow of her skin dampened with grief. "It breaks my heart to pain you further when all you ask of us, all you have begged for these last years, has been peace. Love her, if you must. It is too late for us to stop you, for no god can undo what another power has done. Marry her, if you will. I will see you safely to Athens. But there will be a price that must be paid, and I can do nothing to stop it."

He shook his head, stumbling back a step. The ocean roared in his ears, the surf pounding against a cliff. He had paid with his own blood, with the blood of his son, with the lives of his wives twice over. He had given up Ariadne, whom he loved, to Dionysus when it was asked of him. He had paid with his own sweat, serving them in everything he had done. And now they would ask for more? They asked him to pay, when he acted at Helen's request to save the world.

"Is it this war from her dreams?"

She looked at him with pity, silver eyes liquid with regret. "The price is not mine to name, but Zeus's."

He shook his head again and nearly fell against the altar. The cup of wine spilled, washing him in red. He stared at it in horror.

"It's the only way," she said softly.

"Zeus would punish her for this? For coming to me for help, for wishing to save the lives of her people and stop a war?" The wine dripped from his fingers, and he closed his hands into fists, trying not to feel it as blood. How much blood would Zeus ask for in exchange? And for what? The chance of happiness for his daughter? A future where she need not fear war or abuse? "You would let him!"

"I will give you my help, as I have promised, but I cannot change Zeus's mind." She shook her head. "If you cannot resign yourself to the cost, perhaps you should not marry her."

Athena disappeared in the space of a breath, and he stood alone in the temple, her words ringing in his ears more loudly than the ocean of his fury.

Wine-stained and trembling, he fell to his knees.

All he could do was pray.

CHAPTER TEN

At the banquet the next day, Pirithous rose from his place when he saw me and under the guise of courtesy, helped me to my seat beside him. I had spent the rest of my night in one of the spare rooms, waiting until Clymene came in search of me before returning to my own bed. I did not know when Menelaus had left it, but I was glad he had gone.

I bit my lip to keep a hiss of pain from escaping as I moved. I could feel my mother's eyes following me and swallowed against a swell of panic. If Leda realized what had happened . . .

I refused to consider the possibility. Clymene had promised me she would burn the linens, and I had made her swear not to speak a word of it. Leda would never know. I would not let her force me into a marriage to Menelaus simply because he had barged in through my window.

"Easy, now," Pirithous murmured. "Smile, or you will not fool anyone."

I forced a laugh, adjusting the scarf at my neck to be certain it covered the marks Menelaus had left on me. "Are you so skilled in the art of deceit, then, King Pirithous?"

Pirithous filled my cup with wine. The first bitter taste told me he had added more than water. His eyes met mine over the rim of my cup, and he smiled as if nothing had passed between us before now.

"Ariston sends his regards," he said.

"You'll give him my thanks?"

"Of course." He waited until I had set down the cup, and filled it again to the brim. I tried to protest but he only laughed. "By order of your physician. Drink up and enjoy it. I promise the potion is not better without the wine."

Whatever he had put in my drink worked quickly on my empty stomach. I must not have hid my relief any better than my discomfort, because Pirithous passed me bread and meat from his own plate a moment later. He did not have to tell me to eat. My stomach sloshed with too much drink.

By this part of the day, even those who had drunk until dawn were awake, and there were few empty places at the tables. Servants wove through the guests with jugs of water and mixed wine, filling cups until they had none left of either, then returning to the kraters for more. Platters of bread emptied faster than they could be replaced, and when I saw Leda rise, leaving in the direction of the kitchen, I did not envy the slaves working there when she arrived.

Pirithous seemed to prefer discussion of sword work and spear throws with Pollux to conversation with me. Even so, he was far more attentive than Agamemnon, and I did not have the energy for the farce of conversation we would have shared, regardless. More than anything, I wished for my bed or at least the reassurance of Theseus beside me. The seat meant for him remained empty, and as much as I tried not to notice, I could not help but glance up every so often.

When the roasted boar had been cleared away, I touched Pirithous's arm.

"I do not see King Theseus," I said, my voice low.

Pirithous covered my hand with his, squeezing it lightly, but his gaze traveled over the others in the hall.

"He is anything but faithless, Princess, if that is what worries you. Theseus cannot seem to go two days at a time without bending a knee to his father." He released my hand and poured me more wine. "Not that it has ever done him much good in matters like these."

"Like these?" I asked.

He searched my face, the humor drained from his expression. Then he turned toward my brother, clapping Pollux on the shoulder with all the appearance of a man who has had just one too many drinks.

"Tell me, Brother," Pirithous said, "what do the Spartans say of Theseus, our great Attican hero?"

Pollux laughed. "Much the same as the Atticans, I'm sure. Is it true that he went willingly to Crete as tribute, in the place of another youth?"

"Against good King Aegeus's wishes, he did indeed, to free Athens of the blood debt. They say that Minos made him dance with the bulls, but Theseus charmed them so they would never gore him. And why not, when he is Poseidon's son? Minos was so furious, he threw him into the Labyrinth against the Minotaur. Do you know what Theseus used to kill the beast?"

"Aegeus's sword, of course," Pollux said. "We all know that."

Pirithous grinned and shook his head, as a man does who wants only the excuse to tell a secret.

"Then how?" Pollux asked.

"A length of string." Pirithous slid a finger across his neck. "So strong and thin, it slit the beast's throat when Theseus tried to strangle it. He keeps it still, dyed crimson from the Minotaur's blood. It's the only token he has of Ariadne, since he was forced to abandon her at Naxos to the gods."

"Did he love her?" I asked.

Pirithous met my gaze, and though he smiled, lines of sadness fanned around his eyes. "It was years before the grief of her loss left his heart. Of course, she was a goddess to the Cretans, Minos's daughter or not, and heroes like Theseus are born to serve the gods, not to wed them. She used him to secure her freedom from the power of the Labyrinth. Once that was done, she had no more use for his love. She chose Dionysus instead."

I picked at some bread, but my stomach felt sour. "You make her sound a terrible creature to abuse him so."

Pirithous shrugged. "That's the hero's fate. Used and abused by the gods for whatever they see fit."

"Do you not count yourself as a hero, King Pirithous?"

He laughed. "Princess, I am no Heracles, even if I am a son of Zeus. After witnessing what misfortune it has brought Theseus to serve the gods, only a fool would not choose otherwise."

"But Ariadne helped him."

"Yes, she helped him." Pirithous took a drink of wine. "And then she and Dionysus broke his heart, and took King Aegeus's life in payment. Better for him if he had not gone to Crete at all."

"And what of his people?"

"The people of Athens would have kept their king awhile longer. The cost of freedom was very high for Theseus, but of course he did not realize the price when he left, and he was young enough then that he did not know better." Pirithous poured himself more wine. "You and Theseus are not so different from each other, you know. He serves his people first, himself second, and the gods above all."

"You give me more credit than I deserve," I mumbled.

I stared at my wine before taking a long drink. The bitterness of the potion had left it, but Pirithous did not seem as though he would ever let my cup fall empty. I did not know how much Theseus had told him, or how much he had guessed, but the numbness that came with too much drink did not come quickly enough.

The conversation between my brothers and Pirithous stopped abruptly, and I looked up. Theseus stood at the far end of the hall, his expression set into a king's mask. He seemed to search the room until his eyes found mine. I looked away at once, hoping Menelaus hadn't noticed.

Pirithous rose to his feet. "Excuse me, Princess."

I murmured something appropriate and watched him walk away, unsurprised when his path led him to Theseus. For someone who had been praying, Theseus looked as if he had been through a war.

Pollux slid over to my side, taking Pirithous's seat. He stole the pomegranate from my plate. "String, of all things. I never would have believed it."

I glanced at my brother and frowned. "Perhaps you still shouldn't. Clymene says King Pirithous gossips like an old slave in the kitchens."

Pollux peeled the fruit, dropping thick pieces of rind on my plate as he worked to free the jeweled seeds inside. "King Theseus asked Tyndareus for your hand, you know."

The wine turned to stone in my stomach. "And what did Tyndareus say?"

"Theseus would make a good match, but Menelaus understands more fully the risks involved. Father thinks he will protect you more fiercely."

"None of you understands," I said. "We should not be risking any of this! Menelaus does not care if this war comes, nor for the men who might die fighting it, as long as he wins me."

Pollux sighed. "They are only dreams, Helen. You worry overmuch."

"You and Father and Menelaus do not worry enough."

He rolled his eyes and slid back to his seat, taking my pomegranate with him. Pirithous sat down beside me again, his gaze following Theseus as he took a seat of honor beside Leda. I had not seen her return, but there was no longer any lack of bread on the tables.

"Theseus must speak with you," Pirithous murmured in my ear, so low I barely heard it.

"I am watched."

Pirithous twitched a shoulder. "Tonight, then. At the evening banquet."

"Are you sure it's wise with so many who might hear?"

"I am sure it is necessary."

"But Menelaus—"

"He will not find your window unguarded." Pirithous pushed my cup closer. "Drink. You'll be made safe tonight, no matter what comes."

I planned to accompany Tyndareus to Zeus's shrine before the evening meal, for an excuse to stretch my legs. I was so thick with wine that I nearly fell when I got to my feet, but Pirithous steadied me, and it seemed natural that Pollux should invite him to come with us as Zeus's son.

"Won't suspicion fall on you, if you stay so near?" I asked him while we walked together up the hill.

Tyndareus and Pollux had outpaced us some time ago, though they were not out of sight. Even with the wine, I still moved stiffly, but the sun poured over us, warming my muscles, and I enjoyed the exercise if not the scenery. The stampede of men, after yesterday's sacrifice, had trampled the grass and poppies into dust on either side of the path. Not even the goats would find sustenance from what was left.

"I count upon it," Pirithous said. "And better me than Theseus, as I will be innocent of the crime, in spite of my reputation."

"Theseus will be innocent, too," I reminded him. "I've asked to go."

"Do you really think Menelaus will see it that way?"

I stumbled on the path, for a moment feeling Menelaus's body pressed against mine, crushing me beneath him. Pirithous steadied me, his hands gentle.

"Menelaus is a fool if he doesn't realize it," I snapped, jerking away from his touch, but it only made me trip again. Pirithous's eyes lit, his lips curving, until he saw my face.

"Then he would only behave true to his form. He has already proven himself a fool to pursue you this way. I wonder if you would be so determined to be free of him if he had not."

"I'm determined only to free Achaea's sons from the war that will come." I glared up at him. "Whether Menelaus had pursued me or not, a marriage to him is still part of that future."

"What of love?" Pirithous asked. "Have you not given it any consideration?"

My face flushed. "As heir of Sparta, I do not have the luxury of marrying for love. My husband will be king."

"And is that all you think of Theseus? That he will make a good king for your people?"

I bit my lip, and Pirithous half smiled.

"Is it his power, then, that attracts you?"

I shook my head. "It will help to keep me safe, but if it were only power that mattered, I'd have looked no farther than Mycenae."

"Then what, Helen?"

"He treats me with kindness, as more than just a trophy." I frowned. My mind was still sluggish from wine and the potion, and I struggled for the words. "And I think—I hope—he respects me. Enough to offer me the right and freedom to choose my own fate. For that alone, I could love him."

Pirithous laughed. "I thought you did not have the luxury of marrying for love."

"Theseus is a good king, well loved by his people and his friends. He will do everything within his power to save his people from the devastation of war. To save Achaea itself. With or without love, he is the right choice."

"And what of Menelaus? Did he never have your love?"

"It doesn't matter now, whether he did or not," I said. "He would see Sparta burn as long as he had what he wanted from it. I would not willingly make such a man into a king of my people."

Pirithous nodded but said nothing. We had reached the shrine, and he offered me his arm at the steps. With his help, I did not stumble. Tyndareus and Pollux had already slaughtered the victims, and I had only to lay my offerings of gold and silver on the altar before Zeus's stone face. Had it not been for the wine Pirithous had encouraged me to drink, I likely could not have bowed at all. What I managed was barely respectable.

"Too much sitting at banquet?" Pollux teased me, when he saw how stiffly I moved. "Perhaps we should go hunting tomorrow morning, before the festivities begin."

Even the idea of sitting a horse made me wince. "I don't think Leda will approve."

"Since when does Leda approve of anything you do?"

"Best not to test your mother's patience, Pollux, when we have a palace full of guests," Tyndareus said. "And it would not do for Helen to be thought wild by the men who might marry her."

"I was given to understand that Helen was all but promised to the younger Atrides," Pirithous said. "Or so your people say."

Tyndareus shook his head. "Helen is promised to no man until the games are played and a winner is found. Before Zeus himself, I have sworn this. Helen's husband will be chosen as much by the gods' favor as by mine."

"Then I will tell Theseus to make sacrifice," Pirithous said. "And pray that the gods favor him, when the time comes."

"I did not think the king of Athens would take another wife," my father said.

"Nor did he," Pirithous agreed. "Until he looked upon Helen. But surely you could not find fault in such a match. The blood of Poseidon joined with the blood of Zeus could only strengthen the line. Their children would be as gods."

"But at what cost?" Tyndareus asked. "I would not see Helen suffer the fate of Phaedra."

Pirithous glanced at me, and I pretended not to listen. Even so, he guided my father back down the path toward the palace, and I did not hear what else he might have said.

"Do you know what happened to Phaedra?" I asked Pollux.

My brother shrugged, and I took his arm as we followed. Even if I had wished to eavesdrop, Pirithous had lengthened his stride to leave me behind.

"Only that she was cursed by the gods," Pollux said. "They say Aphrodite made her fall in love with Theseus's son, Hippolytus, and they both died for it."

"Hippolytus is an Amazon name."

"Yes." Pollux matched his pace to mine. "Hippolytus was Theseus's son with Antiope, the Amazon queen. But the story I heard of how it came to be does not seem much like him."

"What happened?" I asked.

Pollux hesitated, glancing down at me. "They say he stole her while he traveled with Heracles. Then he took her maidenhead, that she would have no other choice but to leave her people, dishonored. When the goddess Artemis learned of it, she cursed them both, and the Amazons attacked Athens to take revenge for the insult to their queen. In the battle, Antiope fought for Athens in order to protect her son, and the Amazons killed her for breaking her vows."

I did not know what to say. For the first time, I wondered if I had made a mistake in placing myself in Theseus's hands, but the man in the story did not sound at all like the man I had come to know. Was this what the people of Sparta thought of him? If Tyndareus believed it, he would never let me marry him, no matter how great a hero he might be.

"I suppose Tyndareus thinks he is protecting me," I said.

"Isn't that what all of this has been for?" Pollux asked. "So the man from your nightmares has not come as we hoped he would. When he does, we will be ready. Zeus will protect you and all of Sparta."

I pressed my lips together and said nothing. Zeus seemed much more willing to take than to give, and I had no intention of leaving my fate or Sparta's in the hands of any god.

But I could not turn my mind from the story of Antiope . . .

CHAPTER ELEVEN

When I returned to the megaron, we spoke of nothing beyond the level of wine in my cup and the amount of food on my plate. Theseus seemed even more intent than Pirithous to keep my cup filled, and though he smiled and laughed as he had the first night of the feasting, his eyes remained the flat blue-gray of the sea before a storm. When our gazes met, his jaw would tighten before he looked away.

I had seen Tyndareus behave the same way when something troubled him, but I did not know what could have happened between last night and this evening. I did not dare ask where I might be overheard, just as I could not ask about Antiope.

"If you're worrying over Menelaus," Theseus said finally, after a bard had taken a seat by the hearth and the carcass of the bull that had been our supper was cleared away. "Two of my men carouse beneath your window even now, ready to feign drunkenness until Pirithous relieves them himself in the morning. As long as I am in Sparta, you will be safe."

"And when you leave?"

His mouth formed a grim line. "I've given you my word, Helen. You can depend upon that much, if nothing else."

"But my father has refused your offer."

"It isn't your father's refusal that worries me." He poured me more wine. One of his men had brought us a jug of Attic wine, and though it felt disloyal to admit it, I liked the sweetness of it better than our own. "As long as this is what you wish for, removing you will be the least of my concerns."

I swallowed around the thickness in my throat and forced myself to look at him. "I have heard you have experience with abducting women."

He froze in the act of setting the jug back down on the table, and for a moment, the song of the bard and the conversation in the megaron faded completely. All I heard was the roar of the sea pounding against stone as Theseus's eyes met mine.

"What exactly," he said, speaking so softly that I had to strain to hear him, "were you told?"

I swallowed again, but I could find the breath for only one word. "Antiope."

The pottery handle shattered in his palm.

How he caught the wine jug before it dropped, I did not know, for he had not looked away from me for even so much as a heartbeat. But he steadied it, and then he brushed the dust of the pottery from his hands with every appearance of complete control. He shook his head just slightly, and the voices of my father's guests and the music of the lyre crashed back around me.

"Ah," he said. "Of course."

I glanced down the table, but no one seemed to notice the accident, or if anyone had, they did not care.

"Of course?"

Theseus took a long drink of his wine and said nothing.

"Theseus, please."

He set down his cup but did not look at me, his gaze trained on the bard. "Do you believe it?"

"Should I?"

"Oh, Helen." He laughed, but it was bitter. "What am I to say? I could tell you what happened, but why should you believe me? Why should anyone?"

"They said—" I bit my lip, but I had come this far, and if it was true, better that I learn it now than after he had taken me to Athens. "They said that you raped her."

"Yes," he said. "I can see why that would upset you after what Menelaus did."

I flushed. "That's different."

He shook his head, his expression full of sorrow. "They say," he said softly, "that I raped her to make her marry me. So that she would have no other choice but to be mine."

"Oh," I breathed, feeling it like a kick in my gut. I closed my eyes against the tears that pricked behind them and tried not to think of the things Menelaus had said, or the feel of his body over mine. I focused on my breathing and felt some of the tightness in my chest ease.

"Would you like to hear the truth?" he asked. Concern made crow's-feet around his eyes, and I knew he was only offering to distract me. He did not wait for me to nod.

"Antiope was a wise queen, and a better warrior," he said. "Her people loved her to the point of worship. When she chose to leave them, to break her vows and become my wife, they could not believe she would do so willingly. They did not *want* to believe it. So they told themselves a different story, the one that you had the misfortune to hear."

I felt the cold metal of my wine cup in my hands and drank from it while he spoke. He smiled, but his expression was filled with remembered pain, and my heart ached for him.

"It was not long before they came to Athens with Artemis's blessing, thinking to rescue her and take revenge on me, but by that time we had our son, Hippolytus, and I do not think any force on earth could have persuaded her to leave him, even if she had not cared for me. She fought for Athens, and Artemis made sure she fell in the battle. Later, the goddesses took our son as well."

"I'm sorry," I said.

He refilled both our cups with more wine than water. "So am I."

The bard began singing of Heracles and how Hera had driven him so mad, he killed his wife and children.

Theseus grimaced, and rose. "I'm afraid I have no stomach for song tonight. Will you walk with me?"

I took his hand and let him help me up, ignoring Leda's glare. She could hardly complain that I was not doing my duty for Sparta, and even if Theseus had not been a suitor, he would have deserved any honors we could heap upon him as a hero, my companionship among them.

Clymene trailed behind us as Theseus led me from the megaron. I wished I could send her away, but under Leda's eye, I did not dare. In the courtyard, she dropped back several paces. It was enough space, if we kept our voices low, that we might speak with some privacy. Theseus pulled my arm through his as we walked beneath the shadows between the pillars and the walls.

"I wish I could promise you an easy life," Theseus said when we had outpaced her. "Or even that I could tell you what avoiding your war will cost. I will not even be able to give you freedom, at first."

"It is a great freedom to choose my own husband, my own fate. That is all I have ever asked for."

"So you say." He stared ahead into the darkness. The moon was bright, but after the lamps and fire of the megaron, I could barely see. "But a month from now, a year spent locked away, what then?"

I stopped, pulling him with me. "I have been ogled by men since my tenth summer, Theseus. Every year, it is worse than the last. If leaving here means I need not be seen by anyone but you, I cannot imagine it will make me unhappy. At least I will be spending my days without fear of my nights."

He caressed my cheek, his touch featherlight. "Nothing to fear but the gods."

I caught his hand, holding it to my face. "I will not fear them, either."

"Careful," he said, "or they might hear it as a challenge."

"The gods do not listen to me. Sometimes I doubt they hear any of us."

He laughed, dropping his hand from my face and walking on. "Knowing they hear you does not change things for the better, I promise you."

I sighed, taking his arm again. The two men beneath my window stood when they saw us, their grins flashing in the moonlight. Theseus flicked his fingers, and they went back to their game, but I waited until they would not hear before I spoke again.

"You said before that you have some greater worry than stealing me away."

Theseus was silent long enough that I looked up. His lips were pressed together, and his hand over mine tightened.

"The gods have never loved me, Helen," he began, seeming to choose his words carefully. "They have taken every woman I have ever loved, my father, even my son. You think I am different from these other men who wish to win you, but in truth, it is only that I fear what will happen to you if you become my wife. Now more so than ever, for though Athena will help us, Zeus demands we pay a price."

Zeus. Always Zeus! Why should he care now, what I did? After all the years he had spent ignoring me. I glared at the sky. "Zeus has never had any use for me before now. I do not see why that would change."

"I think it is this war you dream of. By taking you from Sparta, we deny the gods. Men are never more attentive to sacrifice and honors than during battle, and Zeus will ask for something in exchange. I fear—I fear it will mean blood. A life."

"No," I said, but I wanted to scream. "I cannot believe it. The gods sent me these dreams as a warning. Why should Zeus feel cheated when he never meant for it to happen? The gods seek to avoid this fate, not court it."

"Athena has never lied to me, Helen. Not in all the years I have been her champion and king."

"Then perhaps Zeus has deceived her, or means for us to be deceived. That is his way. That is always how he accomplishes his goals, through trickery and lies." My nails dug into his skin, but I did not care. "We make our own fate, Theseus. I have seen it in my dreams. And whether or not he is my father, I will not let Zeus take that from me."

Theseus pried my fingers from his arm and raised my hand to his lips. The warmth of his kiss spread up my arm, making me flush.

"You have the courage of a hero, Princess. As a queen you will have no match."

"But you do not believe me."

"I know the gods. They have never taken less than what they asked for." He nodded toward the entrance to the megaron, guiding us back. "But if there is any woman who could succeed in thwarting Zeus, I can believe his daughter has the fairest chance."

When we stepped back inside, the sour smell of men and wine brought with it Menelaus's breath in my ear, his weight crushing the air from my lungs.

"You need only make it through this evening and tomorrow," Theseus murmured. "I only wish I could free you from the heartache so easily."

I forced myself to smile, for many of the men in the hall had turned to look at me as I walked back to my seat. Menelaus stopped his conversation with my mother, and when he looked at Theseus, his lip curled.

"He'll suspect you first and convince my father it was so," I said.

"Perhaps." Theseus squeezed my hand and leaned down to speak in my ear with the excuse of helping me seat myself. "But it will change nothing. The Rock has never fallen, and Athena will not see her city brought to ruin for the glory of Mycenae. Once we reach Athens, you'll be safe from Menelaus."

But his face when he sat down was lined, making him look for the first time as old as Tyndareus.

In Athens I would be safe from men, his expression said as he urged me to drink my wine. But not from the gods.

CHAPTER TWELVE

O ne more cup of wine, Helen, and then I'll call Pollux to
see you to your bed."

She mumbled something in her sleep that sounded
like a denial, and he smiled. Theseus helped her to sit up, and her
eyelids fluttered open, her eyes like emeralds in the lamplight.

"Here." He pressed the cup into her hands. "To help you sleep.
You will need as much rest as you can get, I'm afraid, for tomorrow
night will bring little."

She widened her eyes with an effort and hid a yawn behind her
hand. "Forgive me."

"I would not have bothered to wake you at all, Princess, but I fear
we push Menelaus's temper too far."

"He hates you," she mumbled.

Theseus nodded and helped her lift the cup to her lips. "Drink."

She took a sip, and her nose wrinkled, the taste seeming to wake
her more thoroughly than his words had. Her eyes narrowed in a
glare over the rim of the cup as she swallowed down the rest in one
long draft.

He turned a laugh into a cough, fearing she might spit the wine in his face if he showed his amusement. She did not seem to be fooled.

"It did not taste like that when Pirithous dosed me," she muttered, setting the cup down on the table.

He poured more wine to wash the bitterness from her mouth. "Pirithous likely did not make you drink it all at once."

"Hmph."

She drank the second cup without complaint, though, and the tension around her eyes eased. He took the cup from her hands before she had finished. As it was, he'd be surprised if she could walk.

He leaned down so he would not be overheard. "Tomorrow, after you retire for the evening, can you find your way out of the women's quarters without being seen?"

She considered it for a moment, blinking slowly. "Perhaps through one of the windows in the bathing room. They look out on the back side of the palace and the practice field, rather than the courtyard, though I would not want to risk jumping."

"I would not let you fall." He stroked her hair from her face. "I will not let any harm come to you again, Helen. I swear it."

"But we will still need to get beyond the palace gate and the city walls. Both are well guarded. And if anyone notices your absence—"

"I will be conspicuously present, with witnesses to vouch for me. Your brothers, if I can manage it. Menelaus can hardly accuse them of complicity. You need only excuse yourself from the feasting when full dark has fallen and slip out of the palace without being seen. Not even by your maid. Can you do it?"

She bit her lip, her gaze sliding down the table to Menelaus.

"Helen." He caught her chin and turned her face to his. "Can you do it?"

She blinked the moisture from her eyes as quickly as it had come. "Yes."

"Good." His fingers trailed along her jaw as he dropped his hand, her skin so soft beneath them. "Then you need not worry about the rest. Pirithous is the most successful raider I have ever known. In the dark, he moves like fog and shadow. You will not be seen as long as you are in his company."

"But if he is absent for too long, he will be accused. Will that not point suspicion back at you as well?"

Theseus grimaced. "Pirithous slipping away for a few moments during a feast will be expected by now. I only hope he does not leave too many children behind."

"Is that why he's always gossiping in the kitchens?"

"He is even more accomplished at talking women into his bed than he is at raiding."

Helen fell silent and looked away, her brow creased. Theseus wished he had never mentioned it, but perhaps it was better for her to know the kind of man Pirithous was, if she had not realized it already.

"They are always willing, Helen." He brushed her hair from her face, so he could see her expression. "There are many women who think it an honor to bear the child of a demigod, legitimate or not, and Pirithous at least ensures they enjoy themselves as much as he does."

She shook her head just slightly, her hair falling in a golden curtain between them. "It isn't that."

"Then what?"

"Nothing," she said. "It's nothing."

She tried to stand but lost her balance, falling back to the stool. Theseus steadied her. He should not have let her drink so much wine, perhaps, but she had needed it. A good part of it was probably the potion; he had not meant to keep her up so long after giving it to her.

"Are you well?" he asked.

"Just tired. I think I'd better go to bed." Helen pressed her hand to her forehead, her face almost green. She swallowed so hard, he heard it, and he hoped she wouldn't be sick.

"Pollux!" Theseus called.

Her brother glanced up, then excused himself from the company of Ajax the Great. The warrior's eyes lingered on Helen until he noticed Theseus's glare. Could none of these men hide their lust for even the length of a feast?

"King Theseus." Pollux bowed.

"Would you see your sister to her room? I'm afraid she's asleep on her feet."

Pollux laughed. "Little sister, how much wine did you have to drink?"

"Too much," she mumbled, reaching for his arm. "But you needn't gloat. I've learned my lesson."

Theseus helped her to her feet, and Pollux swept her up into his arms, tutting softly. She rested her head against her brother's shoulder and groaned.

"What on earth possessed you to drink yourself sick?"

"Does it matter?" she moaned.

"Thank you for your attention to my sister, King Theseus." Pollux smiled, looking very much like Pirithous. "I'm sure that in the morning she'll have the grace to thank you herself, if not to apologize for her excess."

Theseus shook his head. "No apology necessary. I am sure the fault is mine, I should have cut more water into her wine."

He squeezed Helen's hand once, then let them go. From the corner of his eye, he saw Menelaus rise as Pollux and Helen disappeared through the door. Pirithous slipped out a moment later, and Theseus retook his seat. He did not dare follow Menelaus to see what happened when he found the Athenians in his way.

"Are you sure you will not let me send a slave to warm your bed, King Theseus?" Leda asked, touching his shoulder. He had not noticed her cross the room.

"My thanks for your hospitality, my lady, but I think King Pirithous has already had my share."

She smiled. "Sparta is not so poor that we do not have enough women to serve both the son of Poseidon and the son of Zeus. After spending the evening beside my daughter, you would surely benefit from the relief of a woman."

"You cannot think your daughter's beauty is an imposition."

Leda twitched one shoulder, neither confirmation nor denial. "It is simply my observation that she is a trial to the self-control of other warriors."

"Lesser men, I'm sure." His knuckles were white with the effort of keeping his tone civil. "Unworthy men."

"You waste your time on Helen, my lord."

He stiffened, rising to his feet to face the queen of Sparta. "Do I?"

Leda did not even step back, though he loomed over her. She raised her chin, and he could see where Helen had come by her courage, though he was fast beginning to think courage was the only virtue Leda possessed.

"She will not make you a biddable wife, even if her father will allow it. And Tyndareus has his heart set on making Menelaus his son, no matter what he says otherwise. Whatever games are played to test her suitors, you can be certain they will favor the younger Atrides."

"I'm sure you do not mean to insult me, Queen Leda, for you must recognize that the son of Poseidon is a match for any man. Or do you mean to suggest that Menelaus and Tyndareus conspire to cheat?"

Leda only smiled politely. "Helen has already given Menelaus her maidenhead to secure his claim. Of her own free will. She teases you, King Theseus, and I would not see you abused in such a way while you stay as our guest."

His hands closed into fists at his side, and it took all his strength not to reach for the woman's throat. "You know this as fact?"

"I arranged it at my daughter's request." Leda touched his arm, all sympathy. "I am sorry to give you such news, but better that you learned it now than later."

He ground his teeth and looked away. The girl who had come to him in the night in tears had not arranged for anything, and had he been in doubt, her pain when he had told her the story of Antiope would have been proof enough. That Leda knew what had happened only made her Menelaus's accomplice, and for that she deserved punishment much greater than he could dispense.

Hera, make her suffer for this betrayal. Spite her for everything she has done.

"Send the slave," he said softly, so she would think he believed her. "And let Menelaus have Helen, if she is so determined to be his wife."

He took the wine jug with him when he left, and thanked Athena for giving him the chance to sow the seeds of doubt. Let Leda believe he thought Helen ruined.

CHAPTER THIRTEEN

Theseus did not so much as look at me the next morning. He did not smile at me across the table, or ask if my sleep had been disturbed. I could not even tell him that his men had done their job and kept Menelaus from my room.

"Did I do anything foolish last night at the banquet?" I asked Pollux. Surely Theseus could not be angry that I asked about Antiope. It was the only thing I could think of that might have caused him to dismiss me, though the later part of the evening was fogged with too much drink and exhaustion, and I could not remember it all clearly.

"Other than pass out, I didn't notice a thing," he assured me. "Why do you ask?"

I glanced at Theseus, seated beside Leda. "He does not even acknowledge me."

Pollux laughed. "Perhaps he is simply too distracted with arranging his departure to give you all of his attention."

"His departure?" I frowned.

"Theseus and Pirithous leave tomorrow after the morning meal. I heard him tell Father and Mother this morning. I'm surprised he didn't mention it to you last night."

I shook my head. "Not a word." It made little sense for him to leave so soon after my own abduction. Tyndareus would suspect him immediately, no matter how many people had seen him at the banquet.

"I was surprised myself, but Mother didn't seem to be. Tyndareus did not dare take offense, of course. He wouldn't risk upsetting two demigods. But I think he is relieved to see them go, all the same. Pirithous has been free with the servants, and Theseus has kept you much to himself."

Menelaus joined us then, and I did not dare ask Pollux anything further.

"Did you sleep well, Helen?" he asked me. Beneath the table, his hand found my knee.

My face flushed, and I tensed beneath his touch. "Well enough."

I stopped myself from mentioning the disturbance of his cursing the men beneath my window. The sound of his voice had brought me out of a deep sleep, and I had lain still as stone in my bed, waiting until he had gone and dreading he would find a way around them into my room.

"I meant to come to you yesterday, but the Athenian did not seem as though he would let you out of his sight."

I glanced at Theseus again, but even with Menelaus beside me, he gave no sign he noticed. Pollux and Castor laughed together, oblivious as always. I hoped they would stay that way. If Pollux thought I had arranged my own disappearance for any reason, I had no doubt he would find me.

"Just as well." My voice wavered, and I had to clear my throat before I could go on. "Tyndareus would not have been happy if I had slipped away to see you."

"Tyndareus would not have cared. Leda herself has given us permission, and she would not have done so without your father's acceptance."

His hand slid up my thigh, and I pressed my legs together to stop him, my heart racing. If I looked at him, I would cry.

"Come for a walk with me, outside," he said.

My hands shook, and I crossed my arms, pressing them against my ribs to keep him from seeing. "I'm sorry, Menelaus, but Tyndareus told me yesterday I was to stay with our guests."

His fingers dug into the flesh of my leg, then released me. "Later, then."

I repressed a shudder at the thought and forced myself to smile. "Perhaps."

"Menelaus!" Pollux slapped him on the back. "We need you on the practice field. Castor is bragging he will have you beat in the sword and sorely needs a reminder of his inexperience."

For the first time since the celebration had begun, Menelaus grinned, and for a moment I saw the man who had been my friend. "It would be my pleasure, if you can talk your sister into coming to watch. Perhaps she will offer the winner a prize from her gifts."

"Little sister, you would not deny us the pleasure of Menelaus's sword arm, would you? Castor has been insufferable all week."

"A golden cup to the winner, then," I said, glad for the excuse to put distance between us. "And I will come to watch."

Maybe if I was lucky, Menelaus would lose.

Pirithous found me by the yard during the first round of fighting and dropped to the ground beside me. More than just Castor and Menelaus would challenge one another today, and somehow the prize had become not only a golden cup but a kiss from me as well. Menelaus's idea, so sure he was that he would win. I hoped he tripped.

The practice field was kept cropped by the palace goats where it was not soft sand for wrestling. During larger games in honor of Ares or Athena, logs were used to mark out arenas. Pollux had made me help pour libations to both the war gods, and Zeus as well, though this would be an informal occasion. The ritual bound everyone to the rules of the fight—the object today was only to disarm—but it did not always keep people from being seriously wounded. Agamemnon in particular never scratched where he could stab.

Of course, Clytemnestra had come, with our cousin Penelope, to watch. Nestra giggled and cooed from the other side of the field, making cow eyes at Agamemnon. Tyndareus must have told her of the betrothal, or else she simply had no shame at all. The latter, I decided, when she admired the other men just as openly. She whispered something to Penelope, and they both looked at me before breaking into a titter. Penelope and I had been friends once, but she spent so much time with Nestra now, it seemed unlikely we ever would be again.

"You look much improved this morning." Pirithous raised my hand to his lips, and I smiled, happy for the distraction he offered. "Not the worse at all for the wine. A true child of Zeus."

"I would think it would be a truer test for a child of Dionysus."

"Ah, but is not Dionysus a child of Zeus as well?" Pirithous grinned. "Won't you fight with the others?"

Pirithous stretched out in the grass, folding his hands beneath his head and crossing his legs at the ankles. "I'm not sure it would be fair, really. I could perhaps give Pollux a lesson or two, but they wouldn't have any hope of winning against me in a fight."

Watching Menelaus and Ajax the Lesser circle each other, I couldn't decide whom I hoped to see pummeled more. "Very considerate of you."

He laughed. "You don't sound pleased, Helen. Would you like to see someone in particular driven into the dirt?"

Ajax snarled and lunged, but Menelaus deflected the blow, dancing back with a laugh.

I picked at the grass, shredding the pieces between my fingers. "If the war comes, Ajax of Locris will be the first to rape me. I've seen it happen a dozen ways, but most often he is the first."

Pirithous said nothing, though his body grew taut as a bowstring.

"And when he finishes, he brings me to Agamemnon, who does more of the same." I nodded to where the king of Mycenae stood, cheering on his brother. "Of course, this is only when Menelaus himself does not find me and press a knife to my throat. In those dreams, things go much worse for me."

"You told him this? Menelaus?"

"Yes."

Menelaus slid his sword under Ajax's guard, nicking his bicep. Ajax charged him, and they tumbled to the ground. Agamemnon roared with laughter, but Pirithous watched with narrowed eyes.

"And what of your mother?" he asked finally. "Does she know what your future with Menelaus holds?"

"When I was a child, my mother warned me countless times that all I could expect from men was violence because of my beauty, but she all but disowned me a year ago. What Leda knows of me now, she learns from Tyndareus, and Clytemnestra's gossip. She and Nestra are like sisters, now that she is old enough to marry, always whispering and laughing together." Just as Nestra did this day with Penelope, as though determined to turn every woman in the palace against me.

Pollux forced the two men apart, barely avoiding a bloodied nose in the process. Ajax and Menelaus squared off again, grinning at each other like wolves.

Pirithous sat up, and I turned to see what had caught his attention. Theseus stood on the side of the field beside Pollux, sword in hand. Even from a distance, his knuckles were white.

"What on earth is he doing?" I asked.

"Being a hero." Pirithous rose to his feet and stripped off his short tunic, revealing a kilt beneath. He grabbed one of the practice swords, flipping it end over end to test the balance, then chose another, casting a glance over his shoulder at Theseus.

"I thought it wouldn't be fair if you fought?"

"Theseus has other ideas, it seems." He brandished the swords, one in each hand, and nodded to himself. "Whatever happens, Helen, stay off the field. The farther from the fighting, the better."

Theseus stepped forward, and Ajax and Menelaus broke apart. Pirithous strode out onto the field, planting the second sword in the ground on the way, hilt up. Theseus said something I didn't hear, and Pirithous grinned, taking up a place at his back. When the others drifted from the edge of the field toward them, I began to understand.

Pirithous and Theseus meant to fight them all at once. Nearly two dozen men, all in their prime. Menelaus circled around Pirithous toward Theseus, and Agamemnon came to his side. Pollux and Castor stepped back out of the group, tossing their swords to the ground and taking the position of judges.

"To first blood," Pollux called, raising his arm. "Any farther, and you forfeit your prize. Don't forget that the ladies watch."

❧

When the melee began, I could not bring myself to look away.

Theseus's sword arm moved so quickly, I could barely see it, but each stroke caught a man's arm, or shoulder, or leg, sometimes even a cheek. Pirithous was much the same, and in the first few moments, the crowd of men who attacked them had been thinned to half its number. Neither one of the demigods had even broken a sweat.

"Is that the best you can do?" Pirithous taunted. "What kind of suitors will you make for Helen if you cannot even last a heartbeat in battle without shedding blood?"

Pirithous grinned at me. I shook my head, afraid to speak for fear of distracting either one of them. Menelaus did not look as though he would limit himself to scratching his opponent, and Agamemnon rarely played any game fairly.

The bloodied men fell back, lining up at the edge of the field with my brothers. Of the second round, Pollux called only Ajax of Locris from the field, and I thought it pleased him that the man did not last longer. Truth be told, it pleased me, too, and from the look of him, Pirithous had not been gentle with his sword. Ajax limped away from the fight to join the others, his kilt stained red with blood.

In contrast to Pirithous, Theseus said nothing, not even grunting. Though he deflected the blows of others, his gaze never left Menelaus. There were only six men left now. Ajax the Great, son of Telamon, of course, and the brothers Atrides among them, cheered on by Clytemnestra and Penelope. Patroclus, a young man but a fierce and quick fighter, also held his own, unbloodied by Pirithous's sword.

The last two I knew only by reputation, for they claimed they were the twin sons of Ares, but I did not know their names. They pressed Pirithous hard, fighting together as I had seen Pollux and Castor do, as if they knew each other's minds. But Pirithous caught one of them on the forearm, and without his brother, the other did not fight half as well. Pirithous flicked his wrist and disarmed the man, catching the sword in his free hand in time to block a blow from Ajax the Great.

"Theseus, stop playing with your opponents, and send them off the field."

At his side, Theseus snorted. Agamemnon and Menelaus fought him together, but in a move I did not see clearly, Theseus put Agamemnon flat on his back.

"Foul!" Clytemnestra called. "King Theseus does not fight fairly!"

A thin line of blood appeared on Agamemnon's cheek, and he slammed his fist into the dirt, murder in his eyes. Pollux silenced Nestra with a sharp glance and called Agamemnon from the field.

"It is not as though you need compete for favor," Castor said. "And Clytemnestra would never forgive you if you accepted a kiss from Helen."

Agamemnon grunted and dabbed at the cut on his cheek as he climbed to his feet. "True enough."

Nestra was already on her feet, rushing to make overmuch of his wound, and Agamemnon let her pull him away from the other men. But the look he cast over his shoulder at Theseus made me shiver. Athena help him if he ever called on Mycenae for hospitality. After today, Agamemnon would be pleased to see Theseus dead.

Patroclus darted beneath Pirithous's guard, while the son of Zeus blocked a blow from Ajax, focusing on wounding the giant. It was well timed, and Pirithous had no hope of deflecting the cut, which caught him along the ribs just as he laid open Ajax's thigh.

Pirithous laughed and saluted Patroclus, stepping away from Theseus's back. "Menelaus and Patroclus are yours, my friend. I am cut."

Theseus's sword flashed, and Patroclus leapt back, his arm bloodied.

"Let that be a lesson to you, Pirithous," Theseus said through gritted teeth as he circled with Menelaus. I had no doubt that he had meant for it to come to this, the two of them alone on the field. They moved like panthers, with swords flicking in place of tails. "Never trifle with a Myrmidon."

Patroclus gave me a wistful look as he left the field, but I did not think he was even old enough to grow a beard. Ajax turned and saluted me, and Pirithous laughed, having returned to my side. He cleaned his sword on the grass, but his gaze did not leave Theseus.

"Next time perhaps, Ajax," Pirithous called.

"Perhaps," Greater Ajax agreed. "But I will settle for seeing Menelaus soundly thrashed."

Pirithous's eyes narrowed as he watched the two men still on the field, circling, testing, dancing, together. He shook his head just once, keeping his thoughts to himself.

My lungs burned, and I realized that I held my breath. I forced myself to exhale slowly.

"Theseus will win, won't he?"

Pirithous grunted, and spoke so only I could hear. "He should have won already."

"Why hasn't he?"

"Can't you guess?" Pirithous's expression was grim. "He means to shame him, if it can be done in a fight like this. But it is a dangerous game to play with a man who wants blood."

"Menelaus will never forgive it."

Pirithous shrugged. "Then they will both bear their grudges, for Theseus will not forgive what Menelaus has done to you, either."

"Is that why he fights?"

Pirithous grinned. "You didn't really think he'd let Menelaus have the prize, did you?"

I pressed my lips together.

Theseus's sword glinted. He flicked his wrist, the blade finding Menelaus's throat. A clean red line bloomed against pale flesh. A mortal wound, if it had not been a game. If Theseus had not meant for it to be otherwise.

Menelaus touched the spot, then stared at the blood on his fingers.

Theseus tossed his sword to the ground and left the field without a word. Though I watched him until he disappeared inside the palace, he did not even glance at me.

Pirithous left my side to collect the sword, handling it with a reverence that he reserved for little as far as I had seen. He wiped the blade on the linen of his kilt, careless of the blood, and then wrapped it carefully inside his discarded tunic.

The other men spoke quietly among themselves, glancing after Theseus and then to me. They paid little attention to Menelaus, though Agamemnon had joined him on the field again. The two brothers glared at the palace, while Clytemnestra spoke loudly of how splendid they had looked.

"Did I do something to offend him?" I asked Pirithous, unsure if I should be relieved or insulted that Theseus had not claimed his prize. It would have served Menelaus right to stand witness, if he had, but I had no desire to suffer the consequence of his anger, later, either.

"Not you, no." His bright eyes traced every part of me so closely, I nearly stepped back. He smiled slowly. "But perhaps you should give his prize to me, all the same."

I tried to laugh, but Pirithous stepped forward, looming over me in a way that caused my heart to trip with fear. The sound stuck in my throat, and I swallowed against it.

"Please," I said. "Don't do this."

"But it's for Theseus," he said, so near that the words tickled my cheek.

Tears pressed against my eyes, and I shook my head. When I tried to pull away, he drew me back, tight against his body, his bare chest hot beneath my hands. I had forgotten, for a time, that I was too beautiful, and Pirithous was a man like any other. Like Menelaus. I couldn't breathe through the memory. His rough hands, the violence of his touch . . .

He bent and kissed me. I beat against his chest for freedom, clawed his skin, but his lips parted mine, his mouth tasting of mint and sweet summer grass as he crushed me to him. Another heartbeat of struggle, while he pillaged my mouth, and I bit him, hard. Pirithous let me go, chuckling low in his throat, and my own fury broke through against the fear, the helplessness I had relived, so briefly.

I slapped him so hard across the face that his head snapped to the side.

And then, I turned and ran.

CHAPTER FOURTEEN

Y ou should know better than to walk alone," Pirithous said as I slipped into the corridor after the evening meal. If only the trees on the wall were not just painted, and I could hide among them instead of facing him.

I neither slowed nor glanced in his direction. "Menelaus is at the banquet. Unless you plan to molest me again, I am safe enough. It is early yet."

"Have I angered you?" Laughter rippled beneath his words. "What's a stolen kiss between friends and allies?"

I raised my chin and walked on.

He kept pace with me. "It was for the best, Helen. To misdirect those who might have been watching. After Theseus's display on the field, something had to be done."

"Theseus has not spoken or looked at me all day," I snapped. "No one will think of him."

"You're a fool if you think Menelaus will forget him. One day of disinterest will undo nothing. Especially after Theseus humiliated him."

"And one kiss will do what?"

"Divert half the guests with gossip, at least, and you cannot tell me you did not enjoy striking me, if nothing else."

I shook my head and walked faster, refusing to even consider his words. I could see the curtained partition of the women's quarters, and could not wait to leave him behind. He stopped at the entrance, and the guard held the curtain back for me.

"Good evening, King Pirithous. May the gods speed you on your travels tomorrow."

His lips twitched with some hidden amusement, and he swept me a bow. "It will be my greatest sadness to leave you."

I ducked into the corridor, and the guard let the curtain fall, blocking him from my sight. Pirithous chuckled quietly as he walked away, and the sound made me grimace.

I went to my room and collected the bundle I had made earlier. It included a change of clothes, borrowed from Clymene, so that I might pass for a slave rather than a princess, and some of the finer jewels Theseus had given me. No one would notice their absence, they were so new. I wore the diamond at my throat already, but I did not dare to take too many of my things. If I had been abducted, I would not have had time or the inclination to pack, and I did not know how Theseus intended for me to travel.

I changed out of my linen gown, the fabric so thin it would do nothing to keep me warm, and mussed the blankets in the bed to make it look as though I had slept. For the journey, I dressed in the rough-spun and undyed wool of the slaves. By the time Clymene came to the room, I would already be long gone. Menelaus had seen to that, sending her away again in hope that he might find a way into my room, but I could hear Theseus's men outside.

The corridors were empty, all the servants gone to help with the banquet, and I had no trouble making my way to the bathing room without being seen. I leaned out the window, searching the shadows.

A man stepped out of the darkness beneath me, and I breathed more easily.

"Theseus."

"We must move quickly," he said, his voice low.

I dropped my bundle to the ground and climbed over the sill, feeling for the ledge with my toes. Theseus caught me by the waist halfway down the wall and set me to my feet. I turned in his arms to face him, and he stroked my cheek. Even in the moonlight, I saw the warmth in his eyes that I had missed in his manner all day.

He smiled, his fingertip tracing the shape of my lips. My heart raced, and my face flushed with heat. "If you only knew how much it pained me to turn from you, even for a day."

"You should not be here. You must be seen in the megaron."

"Pirithous told me you worried, and I did not want you to leave thinking I was angry." His hand fell away from my face. "Once you are out of the city, Ariston will take you to the shore where my ship waits at Gytheio. Do as Pirithous asks until you are outside the city wall and you will be safe."

I hid my face against his chest to keep myself from speaking out of turn. If Theseus did not know what Pirithous had done, I would not give him reason to worry. Theseus trusted him. I had little choice but to do the same.

He kissed my hair. "I hope to join you three days from now, but I fear you will not be comfortable while you wait. Ariston will do what he can to help, but you must remain hidden."

"Of course." I pulled away, bending to collect my things. "I will do whatever is required to protect your people from reprisal."

"Theseus," Pirithous hissed from the shadows, and I wondered how long he had been there. "You must get back before you're missed, or all of this will be for nothing."

Theseus tipped my face up to his and held my gaze. "You have my love, Helen. No matter what comes, know that."

Then he released me, and Pirithous stepped forward as Theseus melted back into the night. My heart ached to see him go.

Pirithous took in my appearance and grunted. "Have you a shawl to cover your head?"

I dug through my small bundle and pulled one out. It was rough-spun wool to match my shift. He nodded when I wrapped it over my hair.

"That will do." He held out his hand to me. "The sooner you leave the city and get to Ariston, the better for your comfort. You do not want to have to travel hidden inside a basket for too long."

I hesitated, my hand balling into a fist at the thought of touching him.

"Come, Helen. We have not the time for this. You must trust me."

"Can I?"

He grabbed my hand and hauled me after him. "If you couldn't, you would not have to wonder."

I did not know by what trick Pirithous got us beyond the walls unseen by any of my father's guards, but not one of the men stood at his post while we slipped among the shadows, though I knew them all to be reliable. We did not walk very far beyond the sight of the city gate before Pirithous stopped me. He whistled a phrase from a hymn I recognized as Athenian, and Ariston rose out of the dark, leading a mule with a small cart.

Ariston bowed. "My lady, we have a long journey ahead of us."

"A good day's walk, yes." I smiled at him. "I thank you for your help in this, Ariston."

Pirithous stroked the mule's nose and checked his feet while we spoke. "If you pass anyone on the road—"

"Yes, my lord," Ariston said. "The princess must be hidden in the basket. My king has made it clear to me she must not be seen."

"Good man, Ariston." Pirithous clapped him on the shoulder and glanced at me. "Do not let her argue. And be sure she is not seen on the ship, either. We cannot afford for loose lips to carry word of a woman smuggled away by Theseus."

"How can you hide a woman on a ship?" I asked.

Pirithous met my eyes. "Uncomfortably. Until Theseus arrives, you'll be in the hold inside that basket." He nodded toward the basket sitting in the cart.

"Theseus lined it with cloth, my lady, and straw beneath to cushion you. And I will bring you food and drink," Ariston said.

I pressed my lips together. The basket would grant me little freedom of movement. If I was on my knees, my head would clear the top.

"I'm sorry, Helen," Pirithous said. "There is no better way."

"If it will get me safely from Sparta, that is all that matters," I said.

"We must go, my lord, if we wish to travel by dark," Ariston reminded him, before I could ask anything further.

"Yes, of course." Pirithous caught my hand, kissing it. "Good luck, fair Helen. And a safe journey."

Ariston urged the mule from the copse, and I followed.

When I glanced back again for one last glimpse of my home, Pirithous had vanished and so had Sparta's walls.

⁓⁂⁓

Ariston helped me into the basket before dawn, and I sat with my knees drawn to my chest. He gave me bread and cheese and grapes, but I had no appetite. I leaned against the inside of the basket and closed my eyes, letting the cadence of the mule's hooves on the dirt road lull me to sleep.

⁓⁂⁓

Orange light spilled through the weave when the cart finally stopped. My bones ached with the constant jarring of pebbles beneath the wheels.

"My lady?" Ariston spoke in an undertone. "We're coming to Gytheio now."

My stomach still roiled from the stress of the night, and I picked at the bread, hoping food would help settle it. If nothing else, eating would keep me awake, and I did not dare doze now that we neared the port in case I made some noise in my sleep.

I heard a shout, and Ariston answered; then I heard a bustle with the jingle of metal clasps and the thump of leather that only came with soldiers. Their accents were Attican, and Ariston spoke to them in friendship. Theseus's men.

"When do we sail?" one asked.

"King Theseus intends to join us by nightfall, unless there is some delay. He bids us to make ready to sail the moment he arrives."

"Is the princess as beautiful as they say?" a different voice asked, muffled by the basket.

Ariston strangled a laugh. "Even more so."

"What does the king say?"

"Our king made an offer for her hand, but King Tyndareus refuses to accept any until the appointed time, a year hence." Ariston sounded convincing for a man with said princess hidden in a cart behind him.

"A new queen for Athens!"

"Surely King Theseus will win her."

"Nothing is certain, my friend," Ariston said, quieting the others. "Mycenae wants her, too, along with half the other men in Achaea. Better for Theseus to find a woman elsewhere, who is not so coveted. Help me unload the cart, and I'll tell you all the news from Sparta."

Two of the men hefted the basket, grunting at the weight. I stayed as still as possible and held my breath while they carried me. The crunch of dirt and pebbles under sandals was replaced by the sound of the wood deck of the ship and the stale scent of salt. Ariston warned them not to toss the basket below, making some excuse of trade goods, but they still thumped it hard against the ladder rails. I bit my tongue on a curse.

Finally, they set me down on a solid surface, tilted though it was, and I heard them clamber back up the ladder. The sunlight that had filtered through disappeared with a heavy thud of wood against wood, leaving me in darkness.

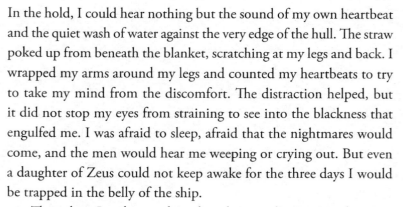

In the hold, I could hear nothing but the sound of my own heartbeat and the quiet wash of water against the very edge of the hull. The straw poked up from beneath the blanket, scratching at my legs and back. I wrapped my arms around my legs and counted my heartbeats to try to take my mind from the discomfort. The distraction helped, but it did not stop my eyes from straining to see into the blackness that engulfed me. I was afraid to sleep, afraid that the nightmares would come, and the men would hear me weeping or crying out. But even a daughter of Zeus could not keep awake for the three days I would be trapped in the belly of the ship.

Three days. I took a steadying breath, struggling against the panic that threatened to explode from my chest. Three days in this darkness, in this silence so heavy, so enormous, I could barely stand the sound of my own breathing. I pressed my forehead to my knees and told myself it did not matter. I was safe here, and soon, Theseus would join me. We would sail for Athens, and I would be his queen. The stranger would come to Sparta and find another woman at the king's side, one not so beautiful as to be worth stealing. He would leave again, empty-handed, and there would be no cause for war. The walled city of my dreams would never burn, standing gilt and shining for generations to come, and Theseus and I would laugh at our escape. We would tell the story of my abduction to our children, and one day, when it all lay behind us, perhaps we might return. Pollux would forgive me, and Castor, too. Pollux had always forgiven me, no matter what I had done.

But I had never left him before. Never abandoned him altogether. We had been a pair, he and I, grown so close these last two years, since before Tyndareus went to war, taking Menelaus with him. Menelaus— Menelaus would never forgive this.

I shivered. In the darkness, I could almost hear the panting of his breath, feel the weight of him crushing me, smothering me, his fingers wrapping around my throat. The creak of the ropes beneath the bedding. No. Not creaking. Scrabbling. Squeaking.

Rats.

I was trapped in a hold, in a woven basket, with rats. And they were drawing closer, by the sounds. Something even brushed against the outside of the basket. Nibbled against it. I kicked at the sound, shook the basket as much as I dared to startle them away.

The food. The bread and cheese and water that Ariston had left me. They could smell it, I was certain. They could smell it, and how long would they be stopped by the small noises and movements I could make?

My legs cramped and my whole body ached, but at least the rats kept me awake. I had tested the lid of the basket, hoping I might throw the cheese, at least, from it, and distract them, but it had been tied securely shut on three sides. Knowing I was trapped so completely only amplified my discomfort, and my legs screamed for the chance to move, to stretch out long and straight. Worse, I had nothing in which to relieve myself, and from the pressure building in my belly, I could not last much longer.

It was the only measure of time I had, that growing urge, and the heaviness of my eyelids, and the pain of sitting in such a small, confining space for so long. I counted again. Each prick of the straw through the blanket, each scratch and scrabble of the rats, each heartbeat filling my ears so loudly, I thought I would scream. And then they were inside. Crawling over me, biting my arms and legs and back and scratching at my skin with their sharp-clawed naked paws.

I swatted them away, crying, sucking back sobs and screams for fear the men might hear, and they couldn't, or Menelaus would come, and steal me back, and fire would swallow me whole. The rats would burn, all char and ash and smoke and the stink of singed flesh and fur, choking me, gagging me until the bile rose, sickly sweet and bitter on the back of my tongue. I swallowed back my own vomit, afraid to give them more to eat, and curled into the smallest ball possible, covering my face and head, and weeping into the blankets and straw until I had no tears left.

Was escaping Menelaus worth this? I imagined Theseus discovering me three days from now, flea-bitten and half-eaten by rats, covered in my own waste. I would be dead. I would be dead and dead and dead, and the war would not come, because I would not live to be stolen again.

The thud of wood against wood brought me out of a doze, and I stiffened, listening hard for any sound, any sign of who it might be. If it was one of Theseus's men, I did not dare even to breathe too loudly. If it was Ariston—oh please let it be Ariston. I bit my finger to stop a whimper of need. Ariston, Ariston, Ariston, and the freedom to stretch my legs at last, at last, at last. And relief. My thoughts veered away from the temptation, for if I thought about it any further, I would lose control.

"Princess?" Ariston called softly, and I cried out. He hushed me almost as quickly, fumbling with the ropes that secured me inside. "I could not risk coming sooner. Forgive me for making you wait so long—the men are asleep. I brought you food and water."

I groaned, even the word making me desperate. "Hurry. Please."

The lid came off, and hands caught me up. A strangled cry broke from my throat, my muscles so sore, burning now that I might move. I tripped over the edge of the basket, and my legs gave out the moment Ariston released me. But I did not care, even when my knees stung, scraped on the rough boards.

"A pot, I beg of you."

"Here." He helped me up, guided me toward the overbright lamplight. I had been in the dark for so long, it was blinding. "Careful, my lady. Watch your head."

He steadied me as I took my relief, then supported me as I stood, both of us half-stooped. "Three days."

"Just two, now," Ariston said softly. "Perhaps if I gave you a potion for the discomfort."

"I can't," I said. "I thought I could, but I can't. Don't make me go back, please. Don't shut me inside again, in the dark, with the rats. They gnaw at the sides, chew through me."

"Rats?" Ariston frowned. "There are no rats on this ship, my lady."

I shook my head. "I can hear them, feel them biting and clawing, crawling all over—"

"A potion for your discomfort, and to help you sleep as well," Ariston said. "It will help the time to pass more swiftly."

"The nightmares—"

"Better to risk them than risk your mind altogether." He sat me upon a chest, then turned back to the lamp and the supplies he had brought, taking a pinch of some powder and mixing it with another in a cup. "Not too much water, or you will not last until I can return again."

I closed my eyes, leaning back against a bundle of some other good. It was too dark to see outside the circle of Ariston's light, and I was tired. So tired.

"Drink this, my lady," Ariston said sometime later, holding a cup to my lips.

I did not have the strength to argue.

CHAPTER FIFTEEN

I t would have been faster if Theseus had ridden a single horse, rather than hitched the team and gone by chariot to the coast, but he did not dare appear too much in haste. Pirithous had taken the worst of the suspicion after so many had witnessed the kiss on the practice field. The temptation to break Pirithous's jaw for that imposition had nearly won out, but Theseus resisted. No wonder Helen had hesitated to travel with Pirithous when he had led her from the city.

"It was kind of you to give us your aid, King Theseus," Leda said.

Her face was still pinched and gray over her daughter's disappearance, but Theseus wondered if part of it was not fear for what the sons of Atreus might do to her for losing their prize.

The news of Helen's abduction had flown through the palace almost before Clymene had whispered it in Tyndareus's ear. Menelaus had glared blackly at anyone and everyone who came too near or drew too much attention, and more than once it had nearly come to bloodshed in Tyndareus's hall. Somehow, Agamemnon had kept his head and prevented his brother from such a breach of conduct, but only by luck and the grace of the gods. Ajax the Lesser had been so insulted by Menelaus's baseless accusations that the man had left for home, which had served Theseus well enough. Pirithous had told him Helen's words at the practice field, and he could not even look on Ajax of Locris without envisioning the future that Helen saw.

"It was only right to offer you what help I could, as your guest," Theseus said, checking the horses' hooves and bridles. "But I am afraid I cannot put off my departure any longer. Athena has given me the sign, and I must obey."

"Of course," Tyndareus said. "May the gods give you a safe and swift journey home to Athens, by land and sea."

"I will keep my eyes and ears open for any sign of your daughter, sir. If word comes to me in any form, you shall hear of it at once."

"You will have my eternal gratitude if you see her safely found and returned home, King Theseus," Tyndareus said. "And, ah, if you hear from King Pirithous?"

He had not been pleased with Pirithous's plan to flee almost before they had begun searching. Theseus thought it went too far, but as Pirithous could be accounted for by several of the servants, maids no longer, Agamemnon had been persuaded not to mount an offensive against the king of the Lapiths. Theseus could not deny the diversion had helped, but the conduct was unseemly.

He clasped hands with Tyndareus and tried not to let the man's trust disconcert him. He had done what was necessary to preserve Helen as her own father had not. Even Pirithous had agreed that leaving Helen would have been the more grievous offense.

Theseus did not have to force his scowl, with the thought of all that Tyndareus had not done for his daughter so fresh in his mind. "You can be sure that if Pirithous harbors Helen, I will see her delivered back into your hands."

The horses stamped as he took his place in the chariot, then lurched ahead with the order to move off. The men who had driven the cattle and livestock for sacrifice over land by the Isthmus road would return now by sea as would the guards who had come with him. None of his men would think it amiss if their king traveled ahead once they put the city behind them.

It had been three full days since Helen's abduction, and it would be four by the time he reached Gytheio. The only good to come from his delay would be the time it gave Ariston to arrange things above ship to accommodate her needs. He'd ordered a tent pitched, enclosed on all sides on deck—not so unusual for summer sailing. It would be small, fitted against the bow and barely large enough for himself, never mind the two of them, but it would allow her to stretch her legs and lie flat to sleep after days in the basket. At least it would be better than the pitch-black hold.

Theseus rode without stopping, pushing the horses hard. The others fell back, and he did not give them so much as a glance over his shoulder. Freed of the party and the press of people and animals at their sides, Theseus gave the stallions their heads.

All he could think of was Helen.

⁂

His men cheered from the ship when they caught sight of him at the shore, Ariston among them. The tent made an odd hump on the deck, almost the same brown as the wooden planks and larger than he had expected. The oars were still drawn into their banks, and the square sail had been laid flat on the rocks where two men mended small tears in the fabric.

Theseus dismounted with little ceremony, giving orders to the man who met his horses to see them sold. He leapt to the deck.

"My lord," Ariston greeted him. "All is arranged as you wished."

He clapped the physician on the shoulder. "Well done, Ariston. See the basket brought up to my tent as soon as it can be arranged."

"Of course, my lord."

Theseus let the man go, unwilling to ask about Helen's welfare with so many who might hear. He clasped hands with his men and grinned at their enthusiasm to be back upon the sea.

"Will we raid up the coast?" one man asked. The others seconded the suggestion.

Theseus shook his head. "Not this trip. Athena has given me her sign. We are needed at home, and I would not have delayed even this long if it had not been for the loss of the princess."

A mumble rose from the men that he understood as their acknowledgment. The news had been spread to every town within two days' ride of Sparta, and Gytheio, as the nearest port, would have been among the first to know.

"We wait only for the rest of the party, and then we sail with the tide," he told them. "Those of you with any business in town, see to it now and be back well before then. I will not wait."

A few chuckled, and a few more took his suggestion, vaulting overboard to settle their accounts or find the relief of a woman before they set sail. Others went about securing the sail back to the mast, climbing up and down with the ease of long practice. He was anxious to see Helen, but forced himself to wait and speak with the men until they had settled and he could slip away without drawing too much notice.

After a time, Ariston and another man hauled the basket up from the hold, and Theseus saw it carried into the tent. He waited for the men to leave before calling to Ariston for wine, food, and water for washing. A couple of the older oarsmen teased him for not just bathing in the sea, but he only grinned and waved them off. It made an adequate excuse to see to Helen's needs.

He ducked into the tent after Ariston had gone in search of his requirements and thanked the man's foresight for providing a shielded lamp. Dim light came through the canvas, but that was to be expected with the sun so low in the west. Helen had been in the dark for days.

The basket seemed smaller than he remembered, and he set his jaw as he untied the knots holding the lid in place and lifted it free.

Helen's pale face looked up at him, her hair tangled and dull. She blinked at even the little light inside the tent, and a long moment passed before her eyes focused upon him with any recognition. When they did, she sighed and her arms unwrapped, slow and stiff, from around her knees to reach for him.

"Helen," he murmured, pulling her up and out of the container.

Her body trembled, and she hissed as she stretched muscles that had gone unused for so long. Had she always been so thin?

Her gaze shifted from his, taking in the room, and she swallowed. Men laughed outside, and she flinched from the sound. Ariston ducked under the flap, with a jug of water for washing, food, and drink. The physician bowed his head respectfully and set the things he had brought atop another basket, upturned to serve as a table.

Ariston poured a measure of wine, and offered it to Helen. "I did take the liberty of adding a potion to the cup," he said quietly. "For I am certain you cannot be any more comfortable today than you have been the last three."

She reached for it, but her hand shook. Theseus helped her to bring it to her lips. She drank it down without complaint or pause.

"Thank you, Ariston," Theseus said.

"If you have further need of me, I will be just outside, my lord. Shall I tell the others you are not to be disturbed?"

"If they have need of me, but not before." Theseus set the cup back down, and sat upon a low stool, settling Helen across his lap. "See that it is only you who comes to speak with me, at all costs."

Ariston bowed and left.

Her body liquid against his, Helen rested her head against his shoulder, hiding her face in the curve of his neck. He stroked her hair and held her close.

"Soon enough, we will be home to Athens," he murmured in her ear. "But the worst is over now, I promise."

"You escaped without suspicion?" she asked, her voice cracked from disuse.

"With Pirithous's help and the grace of Athena. I owe them both a debt." But when she tried to speak again, he hushed her. "We have not left Gytheio yet, and we cannot risk any of the men hearing your voice. Speak only if you must."

She made a noise that sounded almost like a grunt and wrapped her arm around his neck. With one hand he refilled the cup with wine, and when he moved to drink it, she lifted her head, guiding the cup to her lips instead. He helped her drink, then finished what she could not.

"Don't put me back in the basket," she whispered. "Please."

"Shh." He kissed her forehead. "You're free of it now. You're free."

She shuddered once against him, then relaxed. From the way her arm fell limp back to her lap, he thought she slept.

The rest of his men arrived not much later, and he heard them come aboard, laughing and joking with the others. Ariston ducked into the tent and, seeing Helen asleep, spread blankets on the deck. Theseus set her down carefully, but she stirred, her eyes fluttering open with a groan when her limbs were moved. She gripped a handful of his tunic when he made to stand.

"Don't leave me."

He pried her fingers free from the linen and stroked her hair. "I'll be back as soon as I'm able."

She sighed and turned her face away.

"Stay with her," he ordered Ariston, and left the tent.

"My lord!" The master of the ship raised his fist to his forehead in salute. Theseus had brought the man back from Crete years ago, and now the entirety of his navy followed the Cretan custom in showing their respect. "We are ready to sail."

Theseus glanced over the bronzed backs of his men, seated at their oars. A bank of fifteen lined each side and no bench was empty. The handful of extra men, those who had driven the cattle, waited at the stern to push the ship back out into the sea before they might leap aboard. "Everyone's accounted for?"

"Yes, my lord."

"The sacrifices have been made twice over to my father, and Athena has promised us her protection on this voyage." He nodded to the water, the tide beginning to pull away from the shore.

In the moonlight the water was all black, but he felt it tugging at his bones. An affinity for the sea's mood came with being Poseidon's son, and it had served him well. He'd never lost a ship, never sailed into a storm. It was a calm night; Athena had honored her promise.

"Push off and take us home."

"Yes, my lord." The shipmaster saluted again and turned, calling out the order to the men. Wood scraped over sand, the ship carving a path into deeper water as smoothly as a swan, even while the men splashed around it, scrambling onto the deck again. A drummer at the prow beat the time, and the men took their first stroke. The ship creaked its own sigh of relief as it broke from the shore, echoed by the men who manned it and the flap of the great red sail in the wind.

Theseus walked the length of the deck, stopping to greet those he had missed earlier. He touched a hand to a shoulder here or an arm there, welcoming them back by name. They smiled, offering their own salutes when they were able and their nods when they were not.

"I'll be inside," he told the shipmaster when he had finished. "Send Ariston for me if I am needed."

The shipmaster bowed, and Theseus left them. They did not need him standing over them, urging them on.

He pushed open the tent flap and entered. Ariston had lit the shielded lamp, and Theseus was pleased to see the light did not carry through the canvas with shadows. Helen would be able to rise and walk if she desired.

She reached for him, and he took her hand. Cold fingers closed around his own.

"Sit with me?" She offered him a weak smile. "Or are you too great a king and hero to sit on the deck?"

He smiled, too, his heart easing at the return of her humor. "I am not too great to do anything that brings you comfort."

Theseus nodded to Ariston, and the man rose and left.

Helen struggled upright, and it took all his will to let her do so without help. She seemed so determined, he did not dare offer it. Her jaw clenched, and while she might have groaned, she made no other sound of discomfort.

She patted the blanket, and he lowered himself to the deck beside her. Leaning against him with a sigh, she said, "Can we speak more freely now that we've left port?"

"The drum and the creaking of the oars should keep our voices from their ears as long as we do not shout." He wrapped his arm around her, and when she shivered, he pulled the blanket up over her shoulders. "You're so cold."

She made a low noise in her throat, like a hum. "I feel much better now. And the cold will pass. It's the darkness I can't abide. And the silence. How long was I below?"

"Four days." He rubbed her arm to warm the skin. "I could not return sooner, though I wished to. Every night away from you I spent sleepless, thinking of what you must be enduring."

"I am well, Theseus, truly." She smiled when he frowned, searching her face in the dim lamplight. "I'll recover quickly now. You'll see. Just do not leave me alone in the dark."

He nodded and stroked her hair from her cheek. "Anything that you wish, Helen."

"And if I wish to be your wife?"

"Then I will make you a queen." He tipped her chin up to meet her eyes. "But not before you are ready. And not before it is safe. We have all the time in the world now."

Still he couldn't shake the goddess's words, worrying them in his mind. Perhaps spilling the wine meant nothing. Perhaps it did not mean their blood. It could not be something that would harm Athens. Athena would never permit Zeus to meddle in her affairs. But if it were wholly unrelated to them, the goddess would not have mentioned it. His mother's life? But surely as high priestess, Hera would not allow it. One of his sons? Theseus grimaced and tucked Helen's head beneath his chin. He could not bear to think of it. Not after Hippolytus. Surely the gods would not be so cruel as that. Athens could not afford to lose another heir. Athena would protect his sons. He had to believe it.

"You're very quiet," Helen said.

He grunted, forcing the thoughts from his mind. It would not do to worry her now, when she was so weak. "In the hope that you might sleep, that is all."

"I have slept for four days. Let me hear your voice."

He smiled. "If you wished for a practiced voice, you might have been wiser to seek the protection of King Nestor. He would have served you, and his sons are good men."

"Perhaps." She rested her head against his shoulder. He could feel the cold of her fingers against his ribs even through his tunic. "But I have never known a better man than you, Theseus. Even now, you would give me up if I asked it of you. If it were not what I wished."

"Only a fool seeks to hold a daughter of Zeus against her will."

"Then the world I have known is full of them, and you are the only wise man in it. How could I have chosen any other but you?"

"Heracles might have served you just as well."

She shook her head. "He might have kept me safe, but I could not have loved Heracles. You think you are fortunate that I have chosen you, but I believe I am the one who should give thanks that you came for me. I do not know what I would have done if you had denied me."

"What man could deny you anything?"

She fell silent, and he wished he had not spoken. They both knew the answer, and Menelaus's name hung unspoken between them. Trembling again, she hid her face against his chest. Menelaus, the fool. He should have done more than scratch his neck. He should have slit his throat and let the life bleed from him into the ground. He should have offered him in sacrifice to Zeus, in payment for Helen's freedom.

Perhaps he still would, if Mycenae marched against Athens. Zeus might require a lesser war, and if that were so, Theseus would count himself fortunate. But if Mycenae marched, Sparta would, too, and with their city, Castor and Pollux. For Helen's sake, he could not wish for it.

Theseus kissed her forehead. "Rest, Helen. No further harm will come to you now, and the morning is soon enough to speak of more serious matters."

"You'll stay?"

"As long as I am able."

"Thank you," she whispered.

He leaned back against the canvas wall, set against the forward rail, and tucked the blanket more firmly around her shoulders. The line of her mouth eased, her eyes closing. But it was not until the cadence of the drums signaled moonset that her breathing settled into sleep.

Turning Athena's words over in his mind, he did not rest at all.

CHAPTER SIXTEEN

I would never forget the days I spent trapped in the darkness below. I dreamed of my confinement, my limbs cramping and my chest tight as though I had too little air. But I woke to Theseus's presence, his even breathing, his heartbeat, and drifted back to sleep. Stiff, and sore, and weak, I found that first sleep cradled against his side did more to restore me than any draft of Ariston's, as if Theseus's own strength became mine.

But when I woke again later in the dark of the tent without the comfort of his warmth, or the steady rise and fall of his chest beneath my cheek, and the only sound in the blackness was the slap of water against the hull, my heart raced. I was in another tomb, like the basket. Even the thought made my legs cramp and my body stiffen with remembered discomfort. I couldn't breathe, too stifled by the blackness, and I dragged myself toward the sound of the water. Even drowning would be relief from another day trapped in the dark, with the rats chewing on my bones, and until I sank, I would be free, with the world around me.

My fingers touched thick cloth, oiled against rain and sea spray, and lifting it brought a splash of pale light. I sobbed at the sight, my throat thick, and crawled beneath the edge into fresh air and the false dawn before sunrise. How long I rested there, with only my head and chest free of the tent and gasping like a fish, I don't know. But gradually, I realized I lay upon the deck of the ship, and the slap of water against the hull was broken by the sound of creaking oars heaving and splashing in the sea.

Oars. Rowed by men. I took a steadying breath before the panic in my chest swallowed me whole. If they had seen me, they would have spoken. There would have been some call, some startled shout. As silently as I could, I tried to ease myself back, but the tent cloth rolled itself into the fabric of my shift, catching me, stopping me from slipping back the way I had come. I squeezed my eyes shut, pressing my lips together and holding my breath. Forward. I had to pull myself forward, and then, perhaps, I could dart back inside the tent through the main flap.

A quick glance at the deck reassured me that the men faced the other direction as they rowed, brown backs bent to their oars as one body. If I was silent and quick, it was possible I would go unnoticed yet. I slithered forward again, my shift unrolling from the oiled cloth as I did so, and then I forced myself to my feet, stumbling only for a moment before I steadied myself on the rail, and caught sight of the sea.

The sun had just begun to rise over the edge of the wine-dark sea, glinting and dazzling to my eyes. I could not stop myself from leaning out over the rail to see beyond the bow, where the kiss of sunlight turned the sky orange along the horizon. We traveled into it, east to Athens, and for a moment, I could see nothing else but the bright burning glow and the white sparks it threw on the water.

I had seen ships, of course. Tyndareus had taken me to Gytheio once in my fifth year, when he learned from Pollux and Castor I meant to run away for just a sight of the sea. We had only a river at Sparta, and at the height of summer, it ran so shallow, even the smallest fishing boats would grind against the bottom.

But the sea. The sea had stretched forever, as vast as the sky, the waves unending, sometimes no more than a ripple against the shore, and other times rising taller than a man. I could have stared at the sea all day and all night from solstice to solstice, and still I would not have looked my fill. Now, it entranced me, calling of freedom, of peace, of sun upon my face, and wide, open waters. My heart ached with it, my body rejoicing with the drum of its song, even as the sea spray stung my eyes.

"Aphrodite comes to us!" one of the men called out, startling me back. He pointed, and the dark heads of the men on the oars all turned together, just as they had rowed. The wind picked up, blowing my hair across my face, and Theseus called out for the sail to be raised even as he moved toward me.

"My lady, grant us your blessing!" another man shouted. "Grant us your favor and your protection!"

My heart tripped, and my throat closed. I turned my face away, hoping no one on the deck would recognize the princess of Sparta. Then Theseus stood before me, blocking me from the sight of the men, his mouth a grim line and his eyes flat gray and storming. His jaw went tight.

"May the goddess forgive me," he murmured, then dropped to one knee, clasping my hand in his and kissing it. The men roared behind him, stomping their feet against the deck until the vibration of the wood reached my heels.

He pressed my hand to his forehead, but I urged him up again, cold fear rippling down my spine. Thirty men stared at me—thirty men who would not forget what they had seen. I should never have left the tent, even to escape the nightmare of the rats, the darkness of the basket. They were not supposed to see me, their backs to the bow. But I could not have stayed inside without suffocating, then. It was the sea that had lured me, held me stunned by its endless beauty.

Theseus rose, and I saw what it cost him in the deep lines of his face, to treat me as a goddess when he knew I was only Helen. I turned from him, drawing the dignity of a princess around me like a shield against the terror in my heart, and I waited for him to raise the tent flap, as a goddess would wait upon a man to serve her. There was nothing left to do then but go back in, and hope the men would believe the goddess had gone again.

Inside, the strength I had found drained out of me, and I fell to my knees on the deck, burying my face in my hands. Theseus stepped in behind me and let the flap fall, throwing the tent back into darkness.

"Aphrodite forgive me, but for a moment even I saw the goddess, with the sun behind you." His voice was low and rough. "We will not give the men cause to doubt their hearts if they saw the same. I can only thank Athena for confusing their eyes and pray that Aphrodite takes no offense."

"I did not mean for them to see me," I said, "but I could not breathe, with the darkness pressing in and the closeness of the walls around me."

"Hush," he said, crouching beside me. He gently pulled my hands away, tipping my face up. "It is done now, and you are hidden safe still. Ariston will hear if one of them suspects something more, but there would be rumors regardless after how I treated you. Men will talk of how King Theseus could not keep his eyes from Helen of Sparta, but with luck and Athena's blessing, they will speak, too, of how King Pirithous stole my prize and fled after you were found missing. It will be enough, and if it is not, the Rock will not fall."

I nodded, though the suggestion of war made my stomach twist into knots. I should not have left the tent, no matter how suffocating or how desperate my need to see the open sky and the sun, but he was right. It was done, and I could not take it back. He was right, too, that rumors would spread, whether I had shown myself or not. I had been too partial toward him, too attentive, and too warm at the festivities. Menelaus had made that clear to me. I shivered at even the thought of his name, and the way his hot breath had haunted me inside the basket.

Theseus drew me into his arms, and I hid my face against his neck. The sea clung to him, salty and clean, and I breathed it in for comfort, banishing the memories of Menelaus.

"Shh," Theseus said, stroking my hair, for he must have felt the gooseflesh rise on my skin and the tension in my body. "These men are mine. Loyal to Athens and me. If they come to know you are not the goddess, they will only be proud of their king for taking honors he deserves. You are safe, Helen. I promise you."

It was enough to calm me in the dark, and in the golden light that bled through the tent during the day, with no word from Ariston that things were not as they should be, my fears diminished.

❦

We sailed directly for Athens, planning only one stop so that the men could sleep, though Theseus would not let them go ashore. It would be only two days of sailing around the coast of Achaea in good weather, and if I had not known better, I might have suspected Theseus had some power over the sea that we were sped so easily on our way. The men undoubtedly believed it was so, from the conversation that carried through the canvas to my ears, or at least that he had the favor of his father, Poseidon.

"Not Poseidon," he told me, half-asleep in the midafternoon heat.

The tent was hearth-hot when the sun beat down upon it, and, enclosed within the thick canvas walls, there was no breeze to lift the stale air. It was still better than the hold and the basket, even if it might have been cooler below.

"It is by Athena's grace we've escaped any trouble. My father has not favored me for a decade now, at least. Not since Hippolytus."

"What happened?"

Theseus sighed and rubbed his forehead. "It's a long story full of old sorrows better left alone. I had thought I would escape the pain of seeing my children die in such a way, though I should have known it could not be the case after I heard Heracles's tale. I suppose I am fortunate that my father's wife is not nearly so jealous as Hera, and I lost only the one son." His mouth snapped shut then, and he grimaced. "May the gods protect Demophon and Acamas from the same fate."

We had been lying together, flat on the cool deck, but I sat up at his words, staring at him. No wonder he had been so offended by the bard's song. "You killed him?"

He did not move, though I saw the ripple of tension in his jaw, and his shoulders bunched as though he prepared for battle. "Aphrodite felt herself spurned by Hippolytus's devotion to Artemis. She made Phaedra fall in love with him, and when Hippolytus refused the advances of his stepmother, my wife, Phaedra accused my son of rape to hide her shame. Hippolytus fled, but Aphrodite filled my heart with blind fury, and she used me as her tool to bring about his death. In that it was by my order he was pursued, I am responsible, but my mind was not my own."

A chill ran down my spine with his account. These were the gods we all served, so faithless! They demanded our sacrifices and attention, then made us their playthings and threw us away when we objected. They punished us with death to serve their pride.

"Did he?" I could believe Aphrodite would be so cruel as to use him in such a way. "Rape Phaedra, I mean."

"No." Theseus looked away, his jaw clenched and his hand balled into a fist so tight his knuckles turned white under the strain. "I learned the truth on my return home. Phaedra killed herself while I hunted my son, and Artemis told me what had happened. I don't know why the goddess confessed. Perhaps out of pity for Hippolytus. Perhaps to give me greater pain. Artemis could have protected him, but because he was the son of Antiope, she let him die. To punish me for marrying her sworn servant."

I wrapped my arms around my knees and stared at my toes. "You must have loved Phaedra very much."

"I thought I did," he said, "or I would not have married her. I had an heir in Hippolytus already, and he would have made a fine king for Athens when I was gone. But she was not Antiope. She did not know how to be queen."

"How do you mean?"

"She was interested only in how she might be served, not by how she might serve Athens. I should have known as much when I married her, for that was how things were done in Crete under her father, Minos. But I hoped she might change when she came to me. I thought in time she would become accustomed to Athens."

"Oh."

I was afraid to ask how he judged me, with all my talk of freedom. I was afraid of how he would compare me to these two women who had come before. Would he say to Pirithous that I was not Antiope? That I was not Phaedra? Worse still if his people thought it, too. But I could not be an Amazon, nor was I a princess of Crete. I was Spartan, and I served my people first.

"I did not think I would ever find love again, after Phaedra." Theseus sat up and brushed my hair over my shoulder. "Nor did I ever believe I might consider taking another wife, but you have the right to know what you might marry. I would not have you make this choice with blind eyes, Helen. You will have my protection, no matter what you decide."

I said nothing. I could not hold what the gods had done against him, but nor could I ignore what it might mean for my fate. If I tied myself to him, would his misfortune become mine? It was not a fair question to ask, and I had already answered it once, in the courtyard when he spoke of Zeus's price.

"Think on it, Helen. There is no hurry." He rose and slipped out of the tent, leaving me to my thoughts.

The master of the ship greeted him loudly enough that I heard the words through the canvas. Theseus spoke to him about nothing of consequence, and from the sound of his men and the calls that followed, he walked among his crew. Ariston had told me Theseus often took a turn on the oars when he sailed, and I wondered if that was what he had left me to do, while it was daylight still and I would not be troubled by the dark.

I sighed, aching to follow him, though I knew I could not risk being seen again. Yet the thought of Theseus working an oar, his back and shoulders bare to the sun, made my heart race.

My future would be what I made of it. My future, with Theseus.

CHAPTER SEVENTEEN

The storm blew up from a clear sky, and Theseus climbed the mast himself to roll the sail and secure it, trusting that Athena would not let him be thrown from the ship no matter how it pitched. The hair on the back of his neck rose when he heard the wind howl with a woman's voice. Laughter like silver chimes carried over the crash of the waves, and a dove lighted upon the snake's head of the prow.

"Aphrodite's blessing!" the shipmaster said. "She'll protect us through the storm."

Theseus stared at the bird, the truth of its presence sinking his stomach like rocks. Not her blessing, though he did not dare so much as whisper it to his crew, but her curse. His gaze fell to the tent snug against the bow, and Ariston, who stood outside it. Their eyes met, Ariston's expression as grim and dark as Theseus felt. The dove flapped its wings, soaring up into the clouds, and the rain broke in sheets.

Athena, protect us, and protect my men. An offering to Aphrodite would not go amiss, but he had only the cursed guest-gifts from

Tyndareus in his hold. Better if he had left them behind. *Hestia, goddess of the hearth, forgive me.*

No, he told himself. Helen had asked for his help, begged for his protection. As a member of Tyndareus's household, he was honor bound to do for her what he could as a guest-friend. He had not violated the sacred laws of the hearth or hospitality in this. If he had stolen her unwilling, that would be one thing, but this was in defense of Sparta as much as the rest of Achaea.

"If there is safe shore to ground the ship, do it," Theseus ordered. "We would be fools to do otherwise even with the protection of a goddess."

But there were only cliffs, and the men struggled on their oars to keep the ship from being smashed against them. The drum could barely be heard over the roar of the rain and the sea, wave after wave washing over them. Theseus took an oar himself closest to the bow, shouting the beat until his throat ached, but by then the men had the rhythm.

Father, give them your mercy, if not me. Let them see the shore again, and sleep in the arms of their wives.

Cold water, waves mixed with rain, covered their legs nearly to the knee, but the more water they took on, the more Theseus could feel the sea tugging at his bones, its currents as clear to him as the pulse of blood through his own body. He did not call the man back to his oar, for fear of losing him with the next wave over the rail, but he shouted his direction to the men.

"To the sea!" If they could find the current, it would carry them out of the storm. They could not hope to find a place to beach the ship; they could only pray for escape from the rain and the waves. "Into the storm!"

The men had sailed with him often enough not to argue, and the ship fought to turn. The wind rose as if in answer, and Theseus shouted for Ariston to take the oar. Perhaps Poseidon had taken pity on them after all, and sent the North Wind to guide them out. Theseus sloshed through the water to the mast, and climbed the slick wood again. The moment he pulled the ropes loose, the sail caught the wind. The ship lurched with the force of another wave, throwing him free.

Theseus struggled for the touch of wood, but the deck was no longer beneath him. Seawater filled his mouth, the water winter-cold on his limbs, seeming even to slow his heart. He kicked his legs, struggling up toward the muted cries of his men. Everything was gray, then black.

Father, please. Not this way. In Athens they said he could breathe water as easily as air, but the proof was here. His arms thickened, muscles screaming. The cold leached the strength from his body, dragging him down. He needed air. *Athena! Remember your pledge!*

To come this far and fail—and what would become of Helen, if he drowned? So black, so cold, and he could hear nothing now but the roar of the sea. It filled his ears, calling his name as a lover might. He struggled against the Siren song, swimming still, though he had lost his bearings. Did he only draw himself deeper? Air. He must have air. He must live, for Helen's sake, if nothing else. To keep his vow, to see her made safe.

He broke the surface with a gasp, his lungs burning, and a wave bore him up, pitching him toward the hard wood of the hull. A hand caught his, heaving him up over the rail.

"My lord!" It was Pallans, the man whose oar he had taken. "It looked as though Poseidon had raised you up out of the water by his own hand!"

"Not Poseidon." On hands and knees in the water that still flooded the deck, he coughed, his body shaking with relief. "Athena. Pray to Athena, or we will never survive this day."

The sail snapped against its ropes, secured by the other men after he had been thrown overboard. The clouds loomed green-gray, but the rain no longer beat upon his shoulders like stones. Blue sky blazed in a crescent ahead. As long as they kept the wind long enough to reach the current, they might make it out from beneath the storm. They must make it.

Another wave crashed over the deck, washing over the tent, and he dragged himself to his feet, fighting through the swells of water toward the bow. Helen. All of this was for nothing if Helen did not make it, too, and Ariston still worked upon the oars. Helen was alone.

"Pallans, keep the sail and steer us east as best you can. When you meet the current, do not fight against it. I must find an offering for the goddess." Theseus did not wait for his acknowledgment. Nothing would please Aphrodite more than sweeping Helen into the sea, but he would give her something else. Helen had some gold, from the gifts he'd given her. It would have to do, and he needed to see with his own eyes that she was safe.

He ducked through the dripping flap of the tent to find Helen a sodden heap, shuddering with the cold.

She let out a cry at the sight of him and crawled against the pitch of the deck. The bow was more sheltered than where the oarsmen sat, and the water flowed from the planks toward the benches, but the waves had soaked her still. He fell to his knees, gathering her close. She trembled in his arms, though she did not weep, and he felt pride for her courage. Had she left the tent in fear during the storm, he could not have blamed her.

"Brave Helen." He pressed a kiss to the top of her head. "The storm weakens even now. We will be through it before long."

"They said you were lost in the sea," she rasped. "I heard the men screaming your name."

"Athena saved me, as she promised. She would not let Aphrodite take my life or yours. It is the men I fear for now. The armband you wore the night I sent you off with Ariston—do you have it still?"

She struggled out from the wet fur around her shoulders and twisted the armband free, holding it out to him. "I took only what I thought would not be missed, but I have a bracelet, too, from what you gifted me."

"I will need something yet for Athena, when we reach shore." He took the armband and rose. "Stay against the bow if you can, and I will send Ariston back to you again as soon as I am able."

She grasped his arm before he turned away, her green eyes wide. "My life is not worth theirs, Theseus."

He squeezed her hand. "Athena has never abandoned her people. I do not believe she will begin now."

Then he went back out into the rain. He could not afford to linger with her, much as he might want to. The men would notice, and wonder, and if they believed Helen was the reason for this storm, he would not be able to stop them from launching her into the sea. Instead, he took the gold armband, dedicated it to the goddess, and threw it into the storm-dark clouds.

Aphrodite, accept this offering, be appeased, and spare the lives of these men, who only wished to honor you.

He was not the only man who watched for it to fall, squinting into the sea spray and the rain. The tightness in his chest eased when there was no sign of the gold dropping back to the sea. Where the armband had pierced them, the clouds broke, fingers of sunlight streaming down upon the ship. The men cheered, some singing hymns to the goddesses, others to Zeus and Poseidon.

Father, grant us your blessing. Send us home.

But it was sunset before they moved beyond the reach of the storm, and a long night, and a longer day before the storm cleared from the sky at their stern. By then, they were well caught in the current, whether by Athena's design or Aphrodite's, he did not know, and he could not risk turning back toward Athens as long as the clouds threatened more abuse. The ship would not take it and neither would his men, so Theseus ordered the oars pulled, and the men to turn their minds to prayer. The freshwater would last longer if they did not row, and Theseus did not mean to see them escape the storm only to die of thirst.

They sailed on in the hands of the gods, for everything around them turned to mist, and they would not have seen land until they smashed against it. He was able to slip away into the tent for a few hours' sleep with Helen, leaving Ariston to stand for him on deck.

"I have never been to sea before," she said, shivering in his arms. The clothes and blankets were damp still, and the mist did nothing to warm her, though the tent kept the worst of it from chilling her skin. "I would not ever sail again!"

He could not bring himself to tell her the trip might have been easy if the men had not taken her for Aphrodite. The goddess did not easily forgive insults of that kind.

"We will make land soon," he said. "I am sure of it."

"But where?" she asked. "There is no sun to guide you. How can you know which direction we sail?"

"It is in the hands of the gods, Helen. Athena will bring us home." He smoothed her hair beneath his chin, calming her mind with the touch. "If she did not mean to, we would have smashed against some cliff face long before now, or drowned in the storm."

"There are times I envy you your certainty," she mumbled against his chest. The chattering of her teeth had stopped, at least, and her words came soft on the edge of sleep. "But even if I have none in the gods, I will keep faith in you."

❧

It was the second sunrise after the storm when the fog finally lifted and they beached the ship on a sandy shore at the first sign of freshwater. Theseus sent the men up the river to hunt and bathe and stretch their legs after so long at sea. Better still if they found women, but he had seen no settlement.

Once all had gone but Ariston, he helped Helen down from the ship. With the physician, he made a second shelter for her from the sodden blankets between two oak saplings. They would spend the day checking the ship to be sure it had not suffered any breach in the storm, and the night resting weary bones on solid earth. If no repairs were needed, they could leave as soon as the following morning, when the tide allowed.

Helen's legs wobbled on land, but she only laughed when she fell, and Theseus thought her too grateful to have the sun above her and the sand beneath her feet to be troubled by anything.

"Where are we?" she asked, shading her eyes to see the sun.

"East of Achaea, perhaps in the Trojan lands. I cannot say for certain, though I am sure the men will meet someone to tell them. Pallans will not rest until he finds something worth raiding."

Helen's eyes darkened to the color of pine. "They will rape the women."

"Perhaps," he agreed, though he wished he had not mentioned it. "But if they do, they will likely keep them as slaves, or even as wives. Pallans is in want of a bride, and rich enough from raiding to be satisfied by one taken as a prize. None of the girls in Athens please him, though I had offered him any of the palace women he wished."

She pulled her knees to her chest, her hair falling in a shining curtain between them. "I had not realized the king of Athens lived the life of a pirate."

"In my youth I did many foolish things, but now it is only to keep my men sharp. If war comes to Attica, I will have blooded men to defend it." He brushed her hair over her shoulder that he might see her face, but he could not tell if she found it offensive. She already knew too much of war and blood for a woman who had never survived one, and he did not mean to make her think he would bring more of it. "In truth, it has been a long time since I set out to sea for any purpose. I only came to Sparta to quiet Pirithous."

Her nose wrinkled. "If you only came because of him, I suppose I owe him my thanks, though it galls me to offer it."

Theseus laughed. "He is a loyal friend, Helen. In time, I think you will come to see it. After what happened, he would have stolen you away himself if I had refused, though he would never own to it now."

"A son of Zeus through and through, then." But she smiled before she rose. "I think it is long past time I bathed. I feel crusted with salt and grime. Is it safe?"

He touched his fist to his forehead in respect, refusing to think of the pale skin of her breasts bared, or the softness of it beneath his fingers. He kept his eyes on her face. "I will guard your body as well as your honor, but keep your gown near to hand, in case the men return."

All he need do was think of Menelaus to smother his desire. He meant to give her every honor in Athens and make her his wife besides if she was willing, but until then, he would not touch her.

It was the least he could do to make up for what he had not been able to prevent.

CHAPTER EIGHTEEN

I bathed in silence, not wishing to talk to Theseus and test him further when he already sat stiff-backed along the bank, not even so much as turning his head in my direction. Perhaps it was cruel of me to ask it of him, but I had never felt so filthy in my life, between the time spent in the basket and the salt of the sea so thick in the fabric of my shift. The river water soothed my skin, and I turned my back to Theseus before dunking my head beneath the water to scrub the salt and sweat from my scalp. I couldn't decide if I was pleased or offended that he did not glance my way, but I would not tempt him, and I did not want to know if he looked.

When I raised my head and brushed the water from my eyes, I could have sworn I saw something stir in the trees on the other bank. The idea that the men might see me naked, and worse, with Theseus, had me reaching for my shift and covering my chest. I had hoped to scrub the fabric against the rocks before putting it on again, but the rinse I had given it would have to do. A branch snapped, and my head turned to the sound, searching for some sign of movement.

A boy's face appeared, peeking out from behind a tree, and I breathed a sigh of relief. We were so far from Achaea, it mattered little to me if rumors of a pretty girl spread. They would not reach Menelaus, and if they did, it would only lead him on a fool's chase. Perhaps it might even make me safer in Athens. It was Theseus's men I had to fear, for they would not mistake me for Aphrodite a second time.

The boy's face was mostly shadow, but he could not have been even my age. Certainly he did not have the height of Pollux, and his face was still soft more than masculine. When he realized I saw him, he waved to me, gesturing me to his side of the bank.

I glared at him and tied the belt of my shift before swimming back to the bank I had come from. I did not dare to call Theseus by name where someone might hear it. It was one thing for word to spread of a pretty girl seen bathing in the river, another if she was found in the company of the king of Athens so soon after my disappearance. He turned when I splashed into the shallows; then his gaze shifted over my shoulder, and he drew his sword so quickly, I barely saw the motion.

"Go back to Ariston," he said to me, his voice low and tense.

A crash in the brush told me the boy had run, and I could not blame him. The look on Theseus's face spoke clearly of his intention. "You cannot mean to chase him down."

"If he spies on you, he should be taught respect at the least, and I cannot risk his meeting the men now. Go to Ariston and wait."

"Theseus, he's only a boy."

But he was already running up the bank, moving with the easy grace of a wolf. I pressed my lips together. If I tried to follow, I had more chance of running into his men than catching him, and if Pallans was raiding for women, he was just as likely to take me as a prize, unwitting. Theseus leapt from one bank to the opposite side in one bound and disappeared into the trees.

I did not know what I would do if he came back with blood on his hands, but the thought made my stomach churn. I tied up my sandals and tucked the bottom of my shift into the rope belt, freeing my legs at the knee. Theseus was only a son of Poseidon, I told myself. A daughter of Zeus should be swift enough to match him.

I swam the river instead of jumping it, but Theseus had left a trail anyone could follow. I ran after him, realizing my foolishness too late. I had spent four days in a basket, and at least three more trapped idle in a tent barely as wide as Theseus was tall. My legs tired and my lungs burned; daughter of Zeus or not, I hadn't raced this way in years. I stumbled, and then I fell, but Theseus had married an Amazon, and I would not give him reason to say I was not Antiope. I picked myself up and pressed on until the trees thinned into a clearing.

Theseus had his knee pressed hard into the boy's back, pinning him to the ground. His head came up when I broke into the meadow, narrowed eyes going wide.

"You can't," I gasped, pressing my hand into the stitch in my side. "You can't hurt him. Just make him swear not to speak of it."

"Lady," the boy panted. "Lady, run! Up to Mount Ida, and the gods will protect you from these men! Lord Apollo will save you!"

"Fool boy!" Theseus rose, releasing him. "Is that what you thought? That you would rescue her from raiders with the men from the village?"

"Surely she must be a naiad, taken as your slave."

"Tell me your name, boy."

"Paris, son of Agelaus," he said proudly, climbing to his feet. "My father is a shepherd for King Priam, the greatest king Troy has ever known."

Theseus grabbed the boy by the tunic before he could escape, but he was looking at me. "He will tell the tale, no matter what he promises. You know what it will mean if word travels before we leave. Troy is not so far from Achaea that rumor will not spread."

I met the boy's eyes. They were honey brown, but bright with adoration when they fell on me. He did not even know my name, but Theseus's men would not hide his. Those they met would know they were Athenian, traveling with their king, and word that Theseus guarded a beautiful woman would send Mycenae to the Rock. But he was only a boy, so young, unarmed, an innocent shepherd, and I could not let him die for me. Not like this.

"I am not held against my will, Paris, but if anyone hears of me, that will be the least I suffer. This man is my hero, not my abductor. If you care for me at all, you will tell no one of this. Swear to me and to the gods you will keep this secret. Swear it to Lord Apollo."

He sagged against Theseus's grip, the brightness draining from his expression. He had wanted to save me, to make himself a hero, I guessed, but then he straightened and his boy's face turned grave. "I swear by Lord Apollo, and my love for you, my lady, I will never speak of this, if you will grant me one thing in return."

Theseus's eyes narrowed, and I swallowed, knowing already what he would ask. But he was only a boy, younger than me. I felt my heart trip with pain all the same, that even a boy could not look at me without wanting to possess me as well.

"What would you ask?" I said. I was already trembling, remembering Menelaus, his breath in my ear, the sour smell of his sweat, and the weight of his body on mine.

"A kiss, my lady, and I will keep your secret even from the gods themselves."

I turned my face away, blinking the tears back from my eyes. This was how it had begun. Love of my beauty, desire for my body. And it—I—had driven Menelaus into madness. But Paris was only a boy.

"You need not do this," Theseus said to me, his voice low. I heard my own pain echoed in his words. He would have spared me this, if I had gone to Ariston instead of following. "You need not give him anything. If you would not have him killed, I will cut out his tongue to finish it."

I shook my head. A kiss was a small thing to give, to spare his life and keep the fate I feared from coming. I had given much more to Menelaus, promised myself whole and consenting to Theseus, though he had honored me by refusing, and at least this boy had asked first, instead of taking.

"I will pay his price."

Theseus said nothing, but the boy stumbled free of his grasp. Paris grinned as if he could not believe his good fortune. I could not look at Theseus, for fear he would see how much it cost me, and perhaps out of fear I would see how much it cost him.

Paris stood a finger's width taller than me, and now that he had his prize, he did not seem to know how to claim it. I took a breath to steady myself and stepped forward to meet him. Rising to my toes, I pressed a kiss to his closed lips, the softness of them sending a trickle of dread through my heart.

I left them both without another word, walking back the way I had come, and wishing I had never followed Theseus to begin with.

⟞⟨❀⟩⟝

We arrived at Piraeus, Athens's port, four days later, before dusk. The return from Troy had been swift and uneventful, without storm or mist to slow us. The gods had exacted their punishment, it seemed. Theseus had lost one man in Troy, when the men had tried to steal livestock from one of the shepherds. A boy had fought them back, protecting the cattle long enough for more men to arrive, and dealing a lethal blow to one of our oarsmen. When Pallans told the story and named the boy as Paris in my hearing, my stomach heaved up what was left of my midday meal. Ariston had been forced to cover the sounds with a false coughing fit, and Theseus feigned exhaustion to sit with me inside the small shelter until I cried myself to sleep. It had been a hard journey for both of us.

From the tent, I heard the shouts of his people, cheering his return home. Theseus grinned at me like a boy before leaving the tent. The shouts and cheers became a roar. But what would they think if they knew Theseus had stolen himself a new bride? He was not a young man anymore, to be forgiven for his impulsive acts or ruled by lust, and Athens had not had a queen for a very long time.

Theseus left me behind with Ariston after seeing the rest of his men to shore. I paced in the tent as night fell, and Ariston poured me wine.

I sat down, staring at the cup in my hands. "How much longer?"

"Not long," he assured me. "On horse it is not even half a morning's ride to the palace and back."

"Do you suppose he went on horseback?"

Ariston smiled. "My lady, the king would never be left to travel on foot. If he requires a horse, it will be found for him. Is this not so in Sparta?"

I shook my head. "Tyndareus would never ride on horseback. It is beneath his dignity. He would wait for his chariot to be driven to the coast to meet him."

"King Theseus does not stand on ceremony in his own city, nor do the people expect it of him," Ariston said. "It helps that he has not aged. Sometimes we forget how old he really is, though most do not remember well a time before he ruled."

"It's so odd." Perhaps he'd keep his youth long enough that we might age together. But as a daughter of Zeus I might be gifted similarly. After all, Pirithous was a son of Zeus, and he looked no older than Theseus, though he could not have been younger.

Ariston shrugged. "He is a son of Poseidon. Why should he age like a mortal when he isn't one?"

Movement on the deck stopped my reply, and Ariston rose. He drew a small wicked knife from his belt and looked out, but the tension in his shoulders eased almost at once. Theseus ducked into the tent, a dark cloak over his arm and a small clay pot no larger than a fist in his other hand.

I let out a breath and he smiled. "Did you think I wouldn't return?"

"I knew that you would, but the waiting was an agony. If I never see the inside of a tent again, it will be too soon."

He helped me to my feet and wrapped the cloak around my shoulders, settling the heavy wool to cover me from head to toe. With his arms free, he produced a stick of kohl from the pot in his hands.

"To hide the beauty of your face in darkness," he said.

I grimaced, but when he placed a finger beneath my chin to raise my face, I did not argue. Smudged kohl was really the least of it. I would have colored myself blue if it would have protected Athens.

When he finished painting my face, he pulled the hood of the cloak up over my hair, tucking the stray strands behind my ear with black-stained fingers.

Theseus stepped back to inspect me. "How is that, Ariston?"

"She is unrecognizable, my lord."

Theseus nodded, glancing over my costume once more. "It will have to do, but I pray to Athena and Hermes we are not seen at all, or questions will be asked as to why a filth-covered servant rode before me on my horse."

"Just say I am a slave girl come from Egypt, and you meant for me to save my energy for your bed."

Theseus raised both eyebrows, his lips twitching. It seemed his good humor had returned with the sight of Athens on the shore. "And what do you know of Egypt?"

I smiled and dropped into the *henu* of the pharaoh's court, which Alcyoneus had taught me, my forehead nearly touching the deck in the deep genuflection.

"How may I serve you, my lord?" I asked in the Egyptian tongue.

Theseus stared at me, eyes wide. "Helen, how—?"

I rose from the bow. "I was always a good student, and Alcyoneus was a fine tutor."

"Perhaps she would do better as an ambassador to Egypt than your wife, my lord," Ariston offered, a laugh in his voice.

Theseus glowered at him. "And perhaps you would make a finer jester than a physician."

Ariston hid a smile with a bow. "As my king wishes, of course."

"Come," Theseus said to me, ignoring Ariston's false courtesy. I wondered if the physician had spent too much time with Pirithous, or if returning home had made him bold. "I'm sure you're tired. I'll have you to the palace before the moon begins to set, and my mother will have a bath already filled for you."

❈

Horses waited for us, and Theseus waved Ariston to a brown gelding.

"Go to your wife," Theseus told him after we had mounted. "But do not whisper a word of Helen to anyone."

"Yes, my lord. My thanks." Ariston saluted his king in the Cretan way, fist to forehead, and then rode away. Even in the moonlight, he disappeared quickly into the night.

Theseus glanced down at me in his lap and adjusted the hood of my cloak, tucking my hair beneath it again. "An Egyptian slave? And what shall I call you to keep the secret of your name?"

I ran my fingers through the horse's mane, thinking. "Miriam?"

"That isn't very Egyptian."

"No," I agreed. "It came from a Hebrew story Alcyoneus told me. He said there used to be thousands of them in Egypt, until their god told them to leave."

"Mmm." Theseus kicked the horse into a trot. Piraeus slept as if Ariston had slipped the entire port one of his potions, but Theseus wasted no time passing through it. "What of Selene, since it seems you travel so much by moonlight?"

I smiled. "I suppose that will do just as well. And it is only proper that a slave be renamed something in her master's tongue."

Theseus grimaced. "I do not wish to treat you as a slave, Helen."

"Selene," I corrected him. The road from Piraeus to Athens was well worn, and as quiet as the port had been. Few people traveled after the sun set, and at this time of night, even fewer would be awake at all. "And you need not pretend I am a slave unless someone sees us. Though I do not know how you will keep me hidden in the palace from your servants. There are not two women in Achaea with hair like mine. Better if we dye it."

He sighed. "I had hoped to find another way."

"Confine me to your rooms, then."

"And how will I explain to the palace that the king no longer wishes to be served in his chambers?" He shook his head. "No. That would arouse nearly as much suspicion. Better to dye your hair and call you a slave until rumors of your abduction fade."

I bit my lip to keep from asking how many slaves he had kept in his bed. Some things were better left unsaid. "And will you wait that long to marry me?"

"You're determined, then, in spite of everything I've told you?"

"I am." I held my breath, waiting for him to refuse me after all the trouble I had caused him. One of his men had died because of me, and Aphrodite had nearly swept the rest of them into the sea. I would not have blamed him if he had changed his mind. My heart pounded in my ears.

"If it is to be done, it will be done right, and that will take time. I must make offerings to the gods and see the priests and the augurs to determine the most auspicious day. I will do everything in my power to ensure our marriage is blessed by the gods, for I cannot bear to bring my misfortune to you. Can you wait at least that long?"

Even knowing his words promised delay, I felt relief beyond measure. If this was what he needed to be easy about our marriage, then I could accept it, and gladly.

"In the meantime, perhaps I had better dye my hair."

He laughed, brushing a golden strand back beneath my hood. "I suppose you're determined about that, too."

I rested my head against his shoulder, wishing it were not so dark and I could see more than just pale shadows of the land that would be my new home. Knowing Theseus would marry me gave me more peace than I had realized I wanted.

I smiled and said nothing, for Athens was before us, and in the moonlight it was too beautiful for words.

CHAPTER NINETEEN

The palace rose up above the city, set atop a sheer cliff, walled in stone. Moonlight framed it from behind, casting long shadows over the houses and the path leading to the Rock. The buildings and homes, one and two stories tall, grew closer together as they neared the palace, until they sat on top of one another against the palace wall. Even from here, I could see parts of it were made of boulders rather than rocks, too immense to have been hauled by men.

"It is a legend in Athens that the walls were built by the Cyclopes," Theseus said in my ear, reining in the horse so I could look my fill. "But you would have seen something similar in Mycenae, I'm sure."

"No," I said, not taking my eyes from the fortress on the Rock. A switchback road snaked up the hill, and what might have been torchlight winked from the gate above. "Menelaus promised me once he would bring me to Mycenae, but we never went. Is it much the same as this?"

I felt Theseus's shrug at my back, and the horse stamped with impatience beneath us. "The walls are made of the same tremendous stones. Tomorrow, I will show you all of Athens in the sunlight so you can see her beauty."

"It must rival the palaces in Egypt."

Theseus laughed. "How is it you have not even been to Mycenae but you know so much of the Egyptians?"

I flushed beneath the kohl. "It is only that I have heard the pharaoh's palace is very grand, and I can think of nothing grander than this."

Except perhaps for the burning city of my dreams, but I did not want to dwell on that, nor would I mention it to Theseus now and tarnish this moment.

"You have not even seen inside," he teased me. "But you are not wrong. It is a beautiful palace, and from the top you can see halfway to Troezen on a clear day."

He gave the horse its head, and we moved on. The outer wall grew larger, and the palace on its plateau loomed over us.

"Athens has never truly fallen to any siege," he told me while we rode, answering my questions before I could frame them. "The Rock will always stand, no matter what comes. Armies break beneath it like cresting waves, tripping over themselves as they fall. Ares may have strength and lust for battle, but Athena has the greatest mind for strategy and defense."

"Surely you do not depend on the goddess alone?"

"Athena has never betrayed me. And when we have spoken, she has never misled me. I am king of Athens by her will more than my own."

"You speak of her as if she walks the streets."

He laughed. "Not the streets, perhaps, but the temples." He fell silent for a moment. "She came to me in Sparta when I prayed for guidance."

He did not have to say what she had told him, and I knew we were both thinking of Zeus's price. I felt I had paid him already with tears and terror inside the basket. But I wondered if it had truly been

Athena who had spoken to Theseus or simply the priestess from the shrine. She was beautiful enough to be taken for a goddess, and I did not trust any message from Zeus not to be filled with lies.

We passed through the outer wall without difficulty, for it stood unguarded. Knowing Theseus, I doubted it would remain so for much longer. He might not arm it with warriors, but he would keep watch for Mycenae's march.

The small whitewashed homes inside the walls were all dark, with even the dogs asleep on the doorsteps as we passed. Doors and lintels were painted with what would be bright colors in daylight, and some design I could not make out. Pens for animals adjoined the outer walls of the buildings, and goats and sheep and cows slept in their sheds.

Theseus mumbled thanks to Athena under his breath when we reached the main gate of the palace; then he whistled softly. The massive wooden door groaned open, and it was too dark to see what had been painted upon it, but I would have guessed it was decorated with snakes and owls for their goddess.

"Good lad," Theseus said, and the horse trotted through into a dark courtyard.

"Lad?"

"My first son by Phaedra, Demophon, at the gate."

A boy no more than eleven appeared out of the shadows, taking the horse by the bridle and stroking its nose. Even so young, the child had broad shoulders and the look of height to come.

Theseus lowered me to the ground and dismounted with the ease of a man who had spent years on horseback. Like Castor. My heart twisted with the reminder of my brother, lost to me, now, by the choices I had made.

Theseus clapped the boy on the shoulder.

"See him stabled, fed, and watered, and then find your own bed, Acamas. Not a word of this to anyone."

Acamas glanced at me shyly. "Yes, Papa."

I stared again at the boy, grateful the kohl kept my expression hidden even if the moonlight did not. His second son, by Phaedra. Just a boy! Younger even than the one he might have killed in the wood. Theseus watched me, waiting for my response.

Acamas led the horse away. A cold breeze tickled the back of my neck. Somehow I had never considered his other sons, though he had mentioned them in passing.

"I did not realize how young your children would be."

"Demophon is a year older than you, but Acamas was too young to remember his mother at all."

"Will they hate me?"

He smiled. "Why should they?"

"I'll be their stepmother. That cannot be easy for them."

He took my hand, his thumb caressing my knuckles. "They know their duty, and I cannot imagine you will treat them unkindly. But come. My mother waits to meet you."

I let him pull me toward the palace, where torches flickered on the porch, welcoming him home. He took me up the broad stairs, lifting one of the torches from the wall as we passed, and led me down an unlit hall painted with owls and olive trees. The flames danced over the images, giving the owls flight.

He pushed open a heavy door engraved with a great bull and a group of dancers. I traced the shape of the largest figure, thinking of Pirithous's story. Was this meant to be Theseus when he charmed the bulls in Crete?

"This is my mother, Aethra," Theseus said, drawing my attention from the door.

She smiled, and though her pale skin held the lines of age, she wore them with the same grace and beauty as she did her fine gown, its layered skirt alternating blue and pomegranate red. With Theseus well into his forties, I did not dare to guess her age. Perhaps his own agelessness had come to him naturally after all, if his mother was so well preserved.

I dropped into a deep bow. "My lady, I thank you for your hospitality."

"Come now," Aethra said, urging me to my feet. "You need not bend your knee to me. Theseus tells me you are to be treated as a queen when we are in private, and I assure you no one is eavesdropping in the king's own chambers. He barely allows the slaves to clean it."

"The mother of the king deserves to be honored," I said. "And the mother of Theseus, doubly so."

"You must be eager to wash the kohl from your face, my dear, to say nothing of finding your bed."

I glanced back at Theseus when she drew me toward a door on the other side of the chamber.

He smiled, setting the torch into an empty bracket on the wall. "You are in better hands than mine," he assured me. "Have your bath and sleep well. I pray it will be dreamless."

Dreamless. I swallowed the swell of panic and forced myself to follow Aethra, though I wanted nothing more than to snatch my hand free and run. Fire crawled over my skin at just the thought of what might come when I closed my eyes without the sound of Theseus's heartbeat to distract my mind. The door shut behind us, and I fought for calm.

The room had two small baths, red ceramic surrounded by pale blue tile set in even redder plaster. Both had been filled, but two large cauldrons heated over a small hearth, waiting to refresh the cooled water later. This was the king's private bathing room, and unless I was mistaken, the door on the other side of the room led to the queen's room. I studied the paintings on the walls to steady my thoughts. Cresting waves and leaping blue dolphins danced across the room, while hippocamps swam beneath. Castor and Pollux had painted the fish-tailed horses on their walls, too. The images blurred, and I looked away.

"Theseus said you had a difficult voyage, though he did not explain how," Aethra said. "Nor did he tell me your name, but I can guess. Trust my son to fall in love with such a woman. Tell me at least that he did not steal you?"

I shook my head, then laughed from my nerves. "I suppose he did, for my father thinks I am abducted in my sleep, but I left with Theseus of my own free will."

She raised an eyebrow, helping to remove my cloak. Her gaze fell on my hair, and her lips thinned.

"Helen of Sparta." She sighed. "Well, what's done is done, and if it brings war to Athens, I suppose it will give the younger men something to do with themselves."

"I hope war will not come. At least not for some time. And it will be longer still if you will help me dye my hair."

"Dye it?" Aethra pursed her lips and pulled my shift over my head.

I sighed to be free of the rough wool, along with the days of sweat and dirt trapped in the fabric. In the basket, Ariston had at least given me a clay pot to relieve myself, so I had not sat in my own filth, but the one bath I had managed in Troy had not been enough. I felt as though the dust from the road had ground itself into my skin, sticking to the salt from the sea.

Aethra clucked her tongue at the state of my body. "I might have something, but it will wait until morning. I'm sure you're exhausted, and Theseus would not forgive me if I kept you up later than needed."

I stepped into the tub and sank into the steaming water, submerging completely. Closing my eyes in the tub made me feel as though I were trapped inside the hold again. I sat up, gasping for breath. The sloshing of water in my ears was too much, sounding like the sea against the hull, and I grasped the edge of the bath with both hands to keep myself from leaping from it.

Aethra frowned. "Are you quite well, my dear?"

"Yes," I managed to say, staring at the fire until all I could see were bright smears of white flame when I blinked. White was better than black. My breathing slowed, and I relaxed my grip on the tub enough to lean forward and let Aethra scrub my back and scrape the dirt from my skin.

Yes, I was tired, but I did not think sleep would come at all peacefully.

⚬

When the sun rose, painting the horizon with golds and oranges and reflecting rainbows off the whitewashed stone and red-roofed build-ings of the city below, I was awake still, but I would have been sorrier to have missed my first sight of Theseus's lands. I could only imagine what the palace might look like to those beneath the Rock.

Attica was even more beautiful in daylight, and I stood, straining for every glimpse of it I could take from the shadows of the queen's room, where Aethra had left me to sleep. Low shrubs and mountain pine covered the hills, so green that the orange of the morning sun turned them black. Where the light struck rock, it painted the lime-stone faces in sunsets.

All around the city, oaks, cypress, and olive trees reached dark limbs into the sky, some of the oak trunks stripped bare and red for the cork that would be used to seal jugs and amphorae. Lowing rose up as the cows woke, though I could not tell if it came from the palace or the city, and I thought I could see a trip of goats already climbing the hill beyond the city wall. More than anything, I wanted to step out upon the balcony and drink in the lands that were to be my new home.

The door from the baths swung open, and I shrank back behind the heavy curtains of the balcony until I realized it was only Aethra. She glanced from the bedding at my feet to the richly carved bed, one perfectly painted eyebrow rising, but she did not ask if I had slept. I had tried, but the furs and blankets and cushions of the bed had been so thickly layered, I had felt myself suffocating, trapped in their cocoon. It was far, far too richly appointed for me to find any comfort, even if I had not feared my nightmares.

I bowed my head. "My lady."

"My dear, it is no wonder my son has been swept away. Poseidon himself must find you tempting, even if you are his niece." She came forward to take my hands, pulling me into the light and looking me over with sharp eyes. "You are certainly as lovely as they claim. And then some."

I flushed. "Thank you, my lady, but I hope it is not just my appearance that has captured your son's heart."

She smiled and kissed my cheek. "If it were only that, he would not wish to make you his queen." Aethra let me go and turned her attention to my clothing. "Theseus asked if you'd like to share the morning meal with him in his rooms, but we must dress you first, in something more appropriate to your station than that frock you arrived in."

"But if I am to be a slave—"

"Nonsense," Aethra said. "If you are to be seen by the palace at large, we will find you something suitably humble, but I see no harm in dressing you properly while you eat with my son. It is the least he can offer you while you live in this gilded cage, and I assure you, if I sent you to him in slaves' clothing, he would never let me hear the end of it. Besides which, once his table is set, the servants know well enough not to disturb him until they're called again."

Before I could object, she had crossed the room to a large chest and thrown it open to frown at the contents. "We'll have to have new clothes made up, of course, but perhaps this will do for today."

She held up a skirt of finely woven linen, tiered in shades of green, from the palest hint of sea foam to a deep emerald at the hem. I had never seen anything like it, for green was impossibly rare. In truth, I had not realized such shades were possible.

"It will go well with your eyes, I think."

"It's beautiful," I said. "Too fine to wear just to eat a morning meal alone, by far."

"If you had arrived under any other circumstances, and the king invited you to share his meal, would you dress in rags?" She held the skirt up to my waist, then tossed it over her arm while she stripped me of my sleeping shift with brusque efficiency. "I doubt very much your mother would have allowed you to leave your room in anything less fine."

I could not argue with that, and Aethra took advantage of my silence to pull a soft ivory shift over my head and wrap the skirt around my waist before I could think of anything further to say. The fabric was so soft against my skin that I wondered how it could be linen at all. I opened my mouth, but Aethra gave me another of her sharp looks, belting a leather girdle at my waist.

"Not another word, my dear. It fits as if it were made for you, and we mustn't keep the king waiting. He can be very ill-tempered when he's hungry, and after the long journey you had, he's sure to be half-starved."

The idea of Theseus in an ill temper of any kind made my stomach twist, and I had no desire to be the cause of it.

I half dozed while Aethra combed out my hair and worked ivory pins into a crown of braids. Leda had never given me so much attention, leaving me in the hands of maids and nurses. Aethra's touch was softer than even Clymene's, and she hummed to herself as she worked.

When she finished, Aethra stepped back to look at me.

"The diamond is a very nice complement," she said, and I raised my hand to my throat, having forgotten it was there. The stone was warm to the touch. "I think Theseus will be well pleased, considering his last sight of you was covered in kohl and filth from your travels.

You've no real need for face paint at all with lips as red as yours, and a complexion so fair, unless you favor the fashion?"

I wrinkled my nose, thinking of the few times Nestra and I had been made up so formally. Having my face caked with white powder had been miserable. Leda had slapped our hands anytime we raised them above our chests, to keep us from smearing it. And the red sunbursts painted on my cheeks and forehead had itched. I did not know how anyone could stand it.

Aethra smiled. "No, I see that you don't. That's as well, I think. The less you remind Athens of Phaedra the better, and all that paint would only hide your beauty."

"Thank you, my lady," I murmured.

She opened the door to the baths, and I followed her through the empty room to the adjoining chambers without protest. I kept my eyes on my feet, determined not to trip on the full skirt, clumsy as I was after my sleepless night. The deep cut of the bodice made me self-conscious, though it did not expose me. I had seen Leda dressed in the Cretan style for rituals, her breasts bare and painted, but she had dressed me as conservatively as she was able from the moment my hips had begun to spread. I had never worn any gown even as revealing as this.

A complex knock by Aethra opened the door to us, and Theseus stood on the other side. I must have been pink from my chest to my forehead when I raised my eyes to meet his gaze.

"Helen," he said, his expression warmer than the sun.

He offered his hand, and when I took it, I felt all the tension of the night leave me at once.

"Thank you, Mother," he said to Aethra without so much as glancing away from me. "Tell Demophon to begin the day's affairs without me. I don't wish to be disturbed until the afternoon, and if he requires help with any of the more-stubborn issues, have him call on Menestheus."

"I am certain he will have no need," she said, and left without another word.

When we were alone, I nearly tripped into his arms, my exhaustion falling over me like a cloak with the relief of his presence.

He tipped my face up, searching my eyes, even as he pulled me against him. "You have not slept."

I flushed again, that he knew it so easily, and hid my face against his chest. "I was afraid if I did, I would dream. What if I cried out in my sleep?"

"No, I suppose it would not do if you were heard. Rumor spreads gossip through the palace faster than Iris can whisper the will of the gods. Tell me what I can do to ease your dreams. Shall I send for Ariston? There may be a draft he can mix . . ."

I shook my head. A potion would guarantee nothing. "I am well enough for a few days more."

"Even a daughter of Zeus must sleep." He pulled me with him into the room, past the low table set with fruits, bread, wine, and cold meats. "If you fear sleep in your room, you may have it in mine. I'll admit it was not how I intended to spend our first morning together in Athens, but I will not have you suffer more than you must."

I could not help but glance wistfully at the bed. "Won't the servants wonder if they hear weeping?"

"I'll wake you if you begin to cry, but they dare not question any sounds that come from this room too closely." He guided me to the bed, larger even than the one in the queen's room, but much more modestly appointed. The carved oak had been freshly oiled and polished, making the owls resting atop the posts gleam. No doubt Aethra had seen it done while he was away.

"It seems a shame to waste the gown," I said.

Theseus chuckled and swept me off my feet to lay me down. He removed my sandals and pulled a light blanket up over my body. The bed was soft, but not so plush that I drowned, and it lacked the excess of cushions and blankets that spilled over everything in the queen's room. My eyes closed the moment my head touched the bedding.

"It wasn't a waste." He kissed my forehead.

I wanted to argue, but it seemed too much effort, and the words failed before my lips would move. Just a few hours of sleep, in safety.

The sounds of Theseus in the room, pouring wine and breaking bread, sent me to sleep more effectively than any lullaby.

CHAPTER TWENTY

D ragging himself away from Helen after he had seen her rested was more difficult than Theseus would have believed possible. He'd left her a pomegranate, broken into pieces, but he could not spare the time for more. Aethra would see her fed, he reassured himself. And what good was he to Helen, if he did not act as king? Demophon waited, and so did the rest of the nobles.

"Father!" Demophon rose from the throne and came forward to greet him.

When had his son grown so tall? He easily matched Pollux in height now, and Helen's brother was several years older.

The nobles parted between them, and all conversation in the megaron ceased as they met before the central hearth.

"Demophon." Theseus clasped his arm at the elbow, greeting him formally as an equal. "I see you kept things in order."

His gaze flicked over the others, now bunching together and beginning to speak among themselves. His cousin Menestheus stood by the dais, and Theseus nodded thanks to him. It was not that he doubted his son's capabilities, but he was young yet, and it had eased

Theseus's mind to know he was watched over. Certainly Menestheus knew the politics of Athens and her people, even if he would never make a strong leader himself. He was too worthless with a spear for anyone to follow him, but he served loyally, as his family had served Aegeus before Theseus had become king.

"Any trouble?" Theseus asked.

Demophon shook his head, Phaedra's dark hair falling into his eyes. Theseus bit back the suggestion that he have it cut, smiling instead.

"Things have been quiet, of course, though when you did not arrive three days ago, the nobles began to fuss," Demophon said. "Aethra said Athena protected you and settled them. No one has any quarrel with Athens, and those who squabble within the city only do so out of boredom. We could use a war."

"Be careful what you wish for, Demophon. War will not do us any favors if we cannot win or the casualties are too high. Better the people be bored than starve under siege."

"And who could challenge Athens, truly?" Demophon smiled, and it transformed him. The boy he had left behind had become a man, ready to test himself for honor and glory. "We have Athena's protection, after all."

"Not all the gods are as reasonable as our lady." He clapped his son on the shoulder, trying not to think of Zeus. "Remember that when you are king."

"Of course, Father." Demophon bowed. "May the gods grant you many more years before then."

Theseus chuckled. "A taste of the kingship in my absence and you find it is not so sweet as you imagined?"

Demophon grimaced. "You make it look so easy."

"Decades of practice, I assure you. When it's your time, you'll be ready. And you'll have your brother to support you." Theseus let his gaze drift over the room again, but Acamas was nowhere to be seen. "Speaking of your brother . . . ?"

"Aethra let him sleep and moved his lessons to this afternoon. I can have him called if you wish it."

"No. Let him study. But we'll have a private supper this evening, and I expect you both to be washed and dressed to Aethra's standards."

Demophon raised his eyebrows, opening his mouth to speak, then shutting it again as he glanced at the nobles surrounding them. "As you wish, of course."

"I do." He had not been certain he should admit the truth to Demophon and Acamas, but it would have been cruel to deny Helen the small amount of freedom it would give her. At least with his sons and his mother, she could be herself.

"The nobles will be expecting a banquet to celebrate your return," Demophon said, "and the festival of Athena is coming quickly."

"The banquet will wait until tomorrow. Tonight I will spend with my family. As for the festival, that will be your responsibility this year. I trust it is not too much for you?"

Demophon paled. "But—"

Theseus grinned. "You can have Menestheus to help, of course."

"You want me to organize the entire festival?"

"If you're to be king one day, you'll have to shoulder the burden eventually. And time slips away from us, even now." He squeezed his shoulder. *Please, Zeus, let your price not be my son.* "As long as I live, you will have my help and my wisdom, but I will not be king of Athens forever, and the sooner the people trust you to lead them, the better for all of us. Aethra will help you with the women's rites, but do not forget that a king is both warrior and priest, just as the queen is priestess and mother."

Demophon's eyes shadowed at the mention of a queen. "And will we have a new queen in Athens?"

Theseus sighed. He wished making Helen queen could be as simple as placing a circlet on her head. "If the gods will it."

Demophon's expression filled with questions, but he only pressed his lips together, as if he would not risk their slipping free.

Theseus gave his son's shoulder another squeeze and released him. "Whatever comes, it will not be in time for the festival. Better that you begin to know Athena now than wait until I have been lost."

Demophon nodded, and Theseus hoped all of this was for nothing. What choice did he have but to prepare his son for the day as if it might be tomorrow? He did not know the price, and if he were given a choice between his own life and his sons', they must be ready to take their place on the throne. Not only for the people of Athens, but for Helen and all of Achaea. Whatever the price, Theseus would not let it be for nothing. To prevent the war, Helen must be protected, and if he were not living to do so, it would fall to Demophon.

"Rumor came to us that you went to Sparta to secure Helen, my lord," Menestheus said, speaking loudly enough for the assembly to hear his question. "And that Aphrodite herself wishes you to marry."

Theseus turned slowly, letting the entire room witness the flash of irritation for such an interruption, even if it came from his cousin. Menestheus had always been presumptuous, the more so because of his blood.

"King Tyndareus of Sparta invited us, as king of Athens, to celebrate his daughter's birth," Theseus said. "It's true that Helen is uncommonly beautiful, but even we cannot be in two places at once. We cannot hold Athens and Sparta both.

"Even if we had been tempted," Theseus continued over the mutters of some of the younger men, raising a hand to quiet them, "Queen Leda seems to have misplaced her daughter. Helen went missing four days before we left Sparta, stolen from her bed in the palace. When she is found, the girl will no doubt marry one of the sons of Atreus. King Pirithous will be disappointed to hear the news."

That remark earned him a rumble of laughter from the nobles, and Theseus forced himself to smile. Pirithous's proclivities were well-known, as he often came to Athens. Most of the nobles kept their daughters out of sight for the duration of his visits, and Theseus could not blame them. Had he a daughter of his own, he would have done the same.

"The brothers Atrides are cursed," one of the men called out. "Sparta insults us by choosing one of Mycenae's sons over the Hero of Attica and Athens herself!"

Theseus found the man in the crowd, one of the lesser nobles, and young, too. Not even of age with Menestheus and spoiling for a fight. It was long past time he led a raid to give the younger men experience in battle, but he would not leave Helen behind, now. Not until he knew whether Mycenae would march. If his nobles knew already of Aphrodite's supposed appearance on the ship, it would not be long before word spread to the Isthmus, then Corinth, then the Peloponnese, with Mycenae and Sparta listening eagerly for any news.

"If the House of Atreus is cursed, then we would not want them for so close a neighbor, never mind a tie by marriage through Helen's sister, promised to Agamemnon," Theseus said. "Let Mycenae have Sparta, if they can hold it. All of Attica follows Athens, and we are not so in want of a bride that we cannot find a suitable princess elsewhere." He nodded to Demophon. "You have your heir; Athens is secure. And in the meantime, we have guest-friendship with Tyndareus of Sparta."

"We heard that King Pirithous stole her," Menestheus said. "And if he has, will that not bring an army to our door as his ally? Surely they will march by the Isthmus road to Thessaly, and just as surely you will wish to stand in their way at Eleusis or Megara, and they will turn south toward Athens instead. Atreus always coveted these lands, and by all accounts Agamemnon is much his father's son."

"If they do, they will break upon the Rock," Theseus said, keeping his tone firm. Just as the Amazons had failed, so long ago, so would Mycenae, regardless of Agamemnon's greed. But he hated to even think of Antiope in the same breath as Helen for fear of giving the gods the reminder of the blood-price they had taken then. He forced it from his mind and met Menestheus's eyes. "And Corinth would not allow Agamemnon to overreach, besides. But Pirithous has sworn his innocence before the gods themselves. Helen of Sparta is not in his hands."

"If she were, you would still defend him," one of the younger men called out.

"Pirithous of the Lapiths is our closest ally and friend." Theseus searched the assembly as he answered, but he could not identify the speaker this time. It hardly mattered. He could not censure the man for speaking the truth. "We will not turn our backs on an honorable friendship. King Pirithous would come to the defense of Athens without hesitation, and we will do the same."

The older men nodded their agreement, for honor meant much to them, and he could see the younger men smiling at one another. Conversation broke out among the assembly. Theseus waited for another moment to be sure no one else had anything more to say, but it was only a susurrus of noise, now that their concerns had been addressed. Better for them to blame Pirithous than to realize Helen lay in his bed beneath their noses.

Menestheus grunted. "A shame the king of the Lapiths did not steal her, after all."

Theseus shook his head. "War will come in its own time without our helping it along, Menestheus. And if it does, we will all be grateful for the overabundance of young men looking to prove themselves in battle. There's no use in wasting their lives without need."

"But surely with Aphrodite's own blessing—"

"Aphrodite's blessings do not guarantee peace. Where she walks, Ares is quick to follow, and I will not risk the prosperity of Athens without need. Certainly not for the pleasure of a woman in my bed, no matter how beautiful."

"But it is not only her beauty, is it?" Menestheus pressed. "It is said once a man looks upon her, he will never be satisfied by any other lover."

Theseus snorted. "She is hardly some Medea, seducing men to her side only to see them suffer. She is just a girl, Menestheus. A young woman determined to serve her people as well as she is able. Nothing more."

"I will be sure to pass on your reassurances to the palace women." Menestheus bowed, excusing himself. "You are welcome home, my lord."

Theseus watched him go. He had not thought of the palace women until that moment, and the reminder from Menestheus's lips made his blood run cold. They would notice the change in his habits, even if no one else did. Not only would they notice, but they would also complain bitterly to one another, and worse, to any man whose attentions they sought. Menestheus may have been bold, but he was not foolish. If Theseus chose not to take any women to his bed, the man would wonder at the reason.

But Menestheus had already found a reasoning he liked—this curse of Helen's. Perhaps it would be enough. At least for now. He had to hope, for even if he had desired it, he could not in good conscience take the pleasures those women offered. Not as long as Helen was caged.

Theseus turned to his throne. He had never liked to climb the dais and take that seat, knowing it would mean entire days wasted while he listened to the imagined slights of men who had too little to keep them occupied. But now it was even worse with Helen waiting for him, locked away in his rooms.

If she could not be free, he had no wish to be, either.

CHAPTER
TWENTY-ONE

I sat on a stool before a great bronze disc so large it might have made a set of armor instead of serving as a polished mirror for the previous queen of Athens, Phaedra. All around its edge, it had been etched with bare-breasted women in tiered skirts, carrying bowls and platters, weaving at large looms, raising snakes into the sky. In Sparta, we had treasured the few mirrors we owned, only the size of an open hand at the largest, and kept them in fur-lined pouches so they would not be scratched. Had I known nothing else of Phaedra, this mirror would have told me everything that mattered. As it was, I now knew far, far too much.

Behind me, Aethra worked upon my hair. Most she had left to fall in thick chestnut waves down my back, but the top half she had pulled back into a knot at the crown of my head, holding it in place with ivory pins. The dye had stained her hands poppy red, and the bone comb, once a milk white, would never be less than orange again.

It would all be for nothing, if I still could not walk the corridors of the palace without attracting stares. It would not have been so bad if I'd had something to do, but Phaedra's room might as well have been empty for all the activity it offered. No loom, no fibers to spin into yarn or thread, and no spindles to wrap them around. It seemed all the queen had done in her room was lounge on cushions and drink wine, for the shelves certainly did not lack any cups.

"It isn't going to be enough," I said, staring at my reflection. "Is it?"

Her blue eyes met mine in the mirror. Pale and unchanging, they were nothing like Theseus's. "It's a beginning. If anyone catches sight of you leaving a room, they at least will not know you by your hair."

I sighed.

One day I had been in Athens, half of that spent in sleep, and already I felt if I could not leave the queen's rooms, I would go mad. Such was the price of freedom, I supposed, and I curled my fingers beneath the stool to keep from fidgeting. I would not leave until it was safe, not after the incident on the ship, but surely Theseus did not intend for me to sit idle all day long.

Aethra glanced behind her, checking the angle of the sun. The shadows had lengthened considerably since we had begun.

"My son would not have brought you here if he did not think he could give you some joy of it," she said, her hand dropping to my shoulder. She squeezed it once and then smiled. "Shall we see what Theseus thinks of your disguise?"

I rose and smoothed the green skirt over my hips, my fingers lingering on the fabric. In Sparta, I had worn fine linen, bordered with rich embroidery, but never something as smooth as this. It felt like the caress of water against my skin.

"Was this gown Phaedra's?"

"Mine, once, when I was not much older than you. King Aegeus sent me bolts of the finest fabrics after the news of Theseus's birth had spread. For months after, peddlers would come to Troezen, take one look at me, and declare that the gods had told them it belonged to me. I think if Aegeus could have acknowledged us, we would have been swimming in riches."

"But Theseus claims he is the son of Poseidon," I said, following her through the bathing room. "Did Aegeus not know it?"

"You must understand that Aegeus went to the oracle, desperate for an heir. The answer he received was a riddle, of course, for the gods never speak plainly. So he came to my father in Troezen, hoping his famed wisdom might discern the answer." Aethra's lips twitched as she pulled open the door to Theseus's bedroom, and the glance she gave me was almost sly. "My father realized at once the meaning of the oracle's words, and he saw an opportunity to advance the fortunes of his people, through me.

"When Poseidon saw that my father meant to trick Aegeus into my bed, he came to me first. Hair so black it was almost blue, and eyes that seemed to trap the ocean itself in their depths. I could hear the sea, when he looked at me, and seagulls calling to one another. He said he would not let me be defiled by a drunken man who did not know what he was about, for I was too beautiful not to be given my own pleasure in the taking. He did not leave my bed until Aegeus stumbled through the door to take his place. But it was clear from the moment Theseus was born, he had been sown from both men. He has Poseidon's eyes in Aegeus's face."

My cheeks flushed. "Poseidon must have loved you."

"Love or not, he honored me, and I have given him thanks for it every day since," Aethra said. "I would not have traded that night for all the silks and jewels in the world."

I turned from her, so she would not see the confusion in my eyes, pretending interest in the owl carvings on Theseus's bed. Aethra's story was nothing like Leda's. If Zeus had treated my mother so kindly, perhaps she would not have resented me so.

But what Leda thought of me did not matter anymore. And Poseidon had still abandoned his son. Why had the god not saved Antiope? Or Hippolytus? Or even Phaedra? Why had Poseidon not saved Theseus from so much grief and pain? It seemed the gods had only enough kindness for one mortal at a time, and Poseidon had given all of his to Aethra. But then, I did not think Zeus had any kindness for anyone at all. Aethra had been fortunate it was the Earth-Shaker who had come to her that night.

Aethra threw open the curtains of the balcony, and sunlight poured into the room. Now that I was better rested, I noticed how different it was from Phaedra's. In place of Phaedra's mirror, Theseus's bronze sword and shield hung on the wall by his bed, within arm's reach while he slept. The side table beneath them held nothing at all, though the dark wood was inlaid with ivory. I stared at the image for a long moment before I realized that one of the armies was all women. The war with the Amazons. I looked for Antiope on the side of the men, but could not find her.

Low stone benches wrapped around the room from the door to the hall to the entrance leading to the bathing room, around a round hearth where Aethra was building up the fire. There was room still for small tables to be set, if he wished to eat in private, and stools of the same height circled the other side of the hearth for more seating. They had cushions, of course, but not even the hint of a tassel, and all were fashioned from undyed fabrics and fleeces.

Even the walls were modestly painted, with borders of olive wreaths and branches in subdued tones along the ceiling and the doors. Phaedra's walls were overwhelmed by color, with so many bulls and horses and dolphins and fish that the eye could not follow any of it. I breathed a sigh of relief to be free of the oppression of such a crowded space and sat on the edge of Theseus's bed.

Perhaps these first days, if Theseus would allow it, I could remake the queen's room into something less suffocating.

The door swung open, and I rose.

Theseus wore a long tunic, belted around the waist. Embroidered fish leapt and flashed with gold and silver filament at the hem above his knees and the cuffs of his sleeves, matching the gold olive leaves of the circlet he wore as a crown. He glanced at me in passing as he entered, then stopped and looked again, his eyes narrowing and his expression falling blank.

I bowed my head. "My king."

He stood there for a long moment, the silence stretching between us.

"Where is your courtesy, Theseus?"

The sharpness of Aethra's tone tore his gaze from me, and he seemed to notice his mother for the first time. He pressed his lips together, but I could not tell if it was to keep from smiling or frowning.

"Can't you see she hoped to please you?"

"Of course," Theseus said, turning his attention back to me. He offered a formal bow, and when he lifted his head, sunlight glinted off the sea of his eyes. "Forgive me, Princess. It is only that I was caught by surprise."

"It had to be done, and better sooner than later," Aethra said. "All it would have taken was a glimpse of that hair, the color of sunlight, and word of it traveling back to the Peloponnese."

Theseus nodded, but his eyes did not leave mine. "I'm only sorry I could not give you the freedom to live undisguised."

"But you've given me the freedom to live," I said. "Without fear that I will be molested or harmed. That is enough to begin, Theseus, and we will build the rest upon it."

He smiled and crossed to me, fingering a strand of my hair. Aethra had refused to oil it, saying there was no reason when it already gleamed. "No matter what color your hair is, you are still the loveliest woman I have ever known. It is your spirit, Helen, that makes you so, and that much you will never have to hide as long as you live within my walls. I swear it."

"Then do not fret so," I said, though I knew I chided myself as much as him.

Theseus laughed, pressing his forehead to mine. "I will do my best."

His breath tickled my skin, sweet with honey, and I closed my eyes, lifting my face. Theseus had never claimed his prize that day on the practice field, and now he stood so near, I could think of nothing else. He caressed my cheek, and my face burned at his touch. Our noses brushed.

But he only sighed and instead of my lips, he kissed my forehead. I bit back my disappointment and hid my face against his chest. He smoothed my hair and rested his chin atop my head.

"Forgive me," he murmured.

I did not trust myself to respond.

The table overflowed with food, and it was fortunate the sun had not set, for there would be no room for oil lamps until after we had eaten. Demophon bowed to me formally, and Aethra prodded Acamas, too busy smiling, to do the same. Theseus's sons both had hair as black as jet, but I wondered if they had gotten it from Poseidon, their grandfather, or from their mother. From their manners, and the way Acamas looked to her for guidance, I had no doubt it was Aethra who had raised them.

"What will happen in Sparta?" Demophon asked after we had all eaten as much as we could. "With the heir missing, who will inherit?"

"My sister," I said. "Though if she is promised already to Agamemnon, my father might choose to give the throne to Pollux. I do not think the people would mind so much, if he passed over Nestra for a son of Zeus, but Sparta has always been inherited through its daughters, as long as one lived. He might wait to see if the people would welcome Agamemnon as their king before he decides."

"For the sake of your people, I hope the kingdom falls to Pollux," Theseus said. "He'll make a fine king when he's put to the task, and care more for them than Agamemnon will."

I brushed my thumb over the impressions of a chariot race on my wine cup. The hearth fire lit the room with a warm glow now that the sun had fallen lower, and the wheels almost looked as if they spun.

"I think Tyndareus will want to honor Zeus. That was what Leda always said. That it was not only that I had been born first, but that I was Zeus's daughter that made me heir."

"Is it true what they say of Castor?" Acamas asked. "Can he tame a horse with just a word? They say he knows the secret names the horses call one another, and when he whispers those names in their ears, they acknowledge him as their lord."

I buried the pang of grief that came with my brother's name, and forced myself to smile. "Castor is very good with horses, but as far as I know, he does not whisper secret names. The head of my father's stables swore my mare would never be broken, but Castor trained her to a bridle in a month, and she responded to every twitch on the reins as though she knew my thoughts."

Acamas sighed. "I suppose now he'll never come to Athens, or if he does, you will not be able to ask him to teach me."

The smile faded from my lips. "I suppose not."

"That's enough," Aethra said. "Demophon, see your brother to his bed."

Demophon grimaced, but he rose and dragged his brother with him by the arm before he could protest. "Good night, my lady."

Aethra guided them out the door, though I saw her paused long enough to kiss them both on the cheek before shutting it behind them.

"I'll have to call the servants in, or they'll wonder," Aethra said, moving my plate to the center of the table as if it were an empty serving dish and shifting the others so there were only four places set. "Theseus, they will not think anything amiss if you've disappeared to the baths. Take Helen and bolt the door behind you. I'll be sure they leave you the wine."

"And the fruit," he said, rising to his feet.

She waved us away.

Theseus opened the door to the baths, guiding me through with a hand at the small of my back, the heat of his touch seeping through the fabric of my gown. I still held my wine cup in my hand to hide the evidence of my presence at the meal.

He dropped his hand from my back to pull the door shut behind us, and everything went black.

I strangled a panicked scream into a whimper, my wine cup dropping to the floor. The basket. The hold. The black days with nothing but the sound of water against the hull and the rats, the rats scrabbling and gnawing upon my bones. Tears filled my eyes, and I choked on a sob.

"Helen?"

I tried to speak, but it only came out a moan. The floor rose beneath my feet, like the deck of the ship, and I stumbled back.

Theseus's arm wrapped around my waist, drawing me against his chest. His hand found my cheek, and I hated myself for the moisture he felt there.

"Shh," he said, brushing my tears away.

My hands closed into fists around the linen of his tunic, and I could not bring myself to release him. He swung me up into his arms, and I heard the clatter of my cup on the tiles as he kicked it away.

"I should have thought to bring a lamp," he murmured, pushing the door to the queen's room open. A noise of relief escaped me at the sight of moonlight and glowing embers in the hearth. "There, now."

He carried me to the bed, but my fingers still would not open, so he sat with me in his lap.

"Oh, Helen." He stroked my hair from my face. "Was this why you did not sleep last night?"

I tried to laugh, but the sound was pitiful. "I'm too old to be so frightened by the dark."

"Any man would be made uneasy after what you endured. Everything that has happened to you has come in the night, in the dark, in the shadows. There is no shame in wanting the light."

I hid my face in the curve of his shoulder. "Stay with me?"

His fingers wound into my hair, and his arm tightened around me. "Always."

CHAPTER TWENTY-TWO

I've brought oranges from the East for your lady—"

Pirithous stopped in the doorway to the king's room, staring at me in the same manner Theseus had months earlier when he had first seen my hair. He collected himself much more quickly, and a slow smile spread across his face.

"My lady." He bowed. "You are a vision. I would not have recognized you but for your eyes."

I dropped into the Egyptian bow that had so startled Theseus, and had the pleasure of seeing Pirithous's eyes widen with surprise as I rose.

"King Pirithous, it is an honor," I said in Egyptian.

Theseus laughed and clapped his friend on the back, propelling him into the room and shutting the door behind them. He came to me at once, taking my hand and kissing it before Pirithous could reach me to do the same honor.

"She is convincing, isn't she?"

"Even your brothers must doubt their own eyes, were they to see you now," Pirithous said, still staring at me as if I were a stranger. "Where did you learn Egyptian?"

"My tutor, Alcyoneus, was a scribe in Egypt," I said. "I learned so quickly that he taught me Egyptian just to keep me out of trouble. I can write it, too."

Pirithous shook his head. "Worthless then, if Tyndareus knows of it. Or Menelaus."

Theseus smiled. "But they don't. Why would Tyndareus have his daughter taught to write or speak so foreign a tongue? Helen says she learned it without their knowledge."

I nodded when Pirithous glanced at me, confirming Theseus's words. "Only my tutor knew. I did not even tell Pollux of it, for fear Leda would hear and forbid me from learning."

"An Egyptian, hmm?" Pirithous rubbed his jaw, eyeing me. "If she can manage to keep up the lie, it is probably the best solution. Far enough away that no one will know the difference and close enough to be familiar. But what happens when the Egyptians hear of it?"

"The pharaoh has at least a dozen concubines in addition to his wives," I said. I did not need Alcyoneus as a tutor to know that, for the number of the pharaoh's women was a point of awe to every king in Achaea. For some, this was because they did not know how he could control so many; for others, it was pure envy. I tried not to think of how many palace women Theseus kept. "Send him a gift and ask him not to deny the alliance if it is ever mentioned."

Pirithous's eyes narrowed. "Have you been to Egypt while our backs were turned?"

"Alcyoneus was highborn before he became a slave. His father's brother was a scribe for the pharaoh himself."

"You're a very strange woman, Helen." Pirithous's eyes bored through me, but I ignored his scrutiny, passing him his cup. "The more I know of you, the less I understand."

"Then it is fortunate I will be Theseus's wife and not yours." I smiled to take the sting from my words. In the months we had spent together since my arrival, I had not yet had cause to regret giving myself into Theseus's care, nor did I expect to find reason. There was nothing he would not do to bring me even the smallest pleasure, and I was careful not to abuse his generosity.

Theseus squeezed my hand and waved us both to our seats at the low table in the corner where I had shared my first meal with his family. "Fortunate indeed. Pirithous would not treat you half so well."

"I've never received any complaints," Pirithous said, all but leering.

Theseus's hand found my knee beneath the table, and I bit my tongue on what would have been an uncivil response, dropping my gaze to my cup. Picking a fight with Pirithous would not do us any favors now. Turning me into a foreign princess was the only way Theseus and I would ever be free to marry while Menelaus hunted for me still. If Theseus produced an Achaean bride of any beauty, he was sure to come, no matter what color her hair.

"Will you take the message to the pharaoh?" Theseus asked after Pirithous had filled his plate and taken a healthy bite of cold lamb. "On our behalf? I do not see why he should refuse, when it was not so long ago that one of his line went to Crete."

Pirithous stopped chewing, then picked up his cup and took a long drink. He set the cup back down slowly. "To Egypt?"

"You're the only one I can trust with it, save perhaps my sons. But Demophon is too young to go alone even if the nobles would not notice his absence."

"When you were his age, you were bull dancing in Crete."

"At Poseidon's command and against my mortal father's wishes—"

"And what difference does it make if the court knows Demophon has gone to Egypt to secure his father a bride? It sounds to me as though it would be more suspicious if you didn't send him. Going yourself would make the most sense."

My stomach lurched at the words. Acamas had told me the oars-men yet spoke of Aphrodite's appearance aboard ship, and while it was not proof enough on its own to raise an army against Athens, Agamemnon would use any excuse to nibble at Theseus's borders in his absence. So much the better if he found me here as well. Theseus only shook his head. "I won't leave Helen unprotected, and bringing her to Egypt unseen would be impossible even if she had not sworn off sailing after the storm. As different as she appears, she will still be noticed anywhere she goes."

Pirithous grunted, his eyes sweeping over me in a way that made me flush. "You should send Demophon, all the same. The boy is des-perate for glory, and a little raiding would go a long way."

"He is not even sixteen, Pirithous." Theseus's jaw was set, the muscles twitching with strain, and he ground his words between his teeth. "Athens cannot lose another heir, and I will not risk him. It would be one thing if he had sailed any distance before, but to send him on such a journey without experience would tempt the Fates."

"Only a fool coddles his son. Especially if he is to be king."

"Enough!"

Theseus's fist hit the table so hard, I flinched and the wine cups jumped. He swallowed and turned his face away, inhaling deeply through his nose.

"If you take such an interest in my son, by all means take him with you, but I will not send him alone."

Pirithous's lips twitched, and I wondered if he had been stopped by Demophon on his way through the palace. I'd never heard him gripe to his father, but from some of the comments he'd made, and the time he spent in the practice field, I would not have been surprised if he'd mentioned something to Pirithous.

"I suppose I will be returning from Egypt with your bride. Shall I find a suitable slave in the market before I set sail? We can parade her in through the gates of the palace and smuggle her right back out again, leaving Helen to take her place."

"Dark-haired and as close in body as you can find," Theseus agreed. "You can keep her veiled while you ride in. Blame it on foreign custom, and no one will know the difference."

"Meryet," I said. It was the simplest name I could think of, and much better than being named for a god in the common Egyptian fashion. Alcyoneus's gods may have been less terrible than ours, but I wanted nothing to do with them just the same. "Call her Meryet."

"Are we really in a position to be naming the pharaoh's supposed daughter?" Pirithous picked up his cup and leaned back in his seat. "Don't we need his permission first, before we jump to naming conventions? For that matter, what do you intend to do if he says no?"

I shrugged. "Pretend I'm a Hittite instead, I suppose."

"And do you speak the language of the Hittites as well?"

"No. But how many Athenians can tell the difference between Egyptian and Hittite?"

Pirithous grinned. "I'll be lucky if I can make myself understood in Egyptian. I don't suppose you'll make it easy and just send me with a clay tablet inscribed with your request?"

I frowned. "It will take more than one, and I cannot promise it will be perfect."

"I'll have Aethra bring tablets and a stylus in the morning," Theseus said, taking my hand. His thumb caressed my skin, and when he looked at me, I could hear the sea washing against the beach in soft waves. "The sooner the better. It will be a month's journey by ship to Egypt, perhaps weeks before the pharaoh will see them, and another month to return."

"Pray to Poseidon we're not smashed to pieces in either direction," Pirithous added cheerfully. "If we return within three months, it will be by his grace alone. Unless Athena will help you in this, too?"

Theseus sighed and tipped a portion of his wine into a golden bowl. "May she remember her promise and give us her aid."

Pirithous added his own libation to the bowl, and I did the same.

"I'll offer a bull to Poseidon tomorrow for good weather and gentle seas." Theseus rose from the table and poured the wine into the hearth fire with a few more words under his breath. The flames burned more brightly for a moment, accepting the gift. "Perhaps he'll grant me that much of his favor."

"Be sure to say it is for his grandson," Pirithous murmured. "Even if he has no love for you, surely he would not see Demophon suffer after what happened with Hippolytus."

Theseus nodded. "Perhaps you're right."

"I usually am. And if your wedding to Helen is accomplished without incident, I'll claim all the credit for that, too. You will owe me, Theseus, and do not think I will forget it."

"A debt I will be happy to repay. Shall we make it a wife for a wife?" Some of the tension had left Theseus's face, and he offered his friend a smile, though not his most charming or his most genuine.

Pirithous's eyes narrowed, his lips twitching. "Sworn upon the River Styx?"

My own gaze shifted to Pirithous, for to ask such a thing—a prickle of unease slipped down my spine. Oaths upon the Styx were never to be taken lightly, and to break them meant worse than dishonor. A half-life, if one survived at all.

"Are you truly so lonely as to demand such an oath?" Theseus asked, laughing.

"Only when I am forced to bear witness to your love," Pirithous said. "Now, will you swear, or won't you?"

"A wife for a wife," Theseus agreed, much too easily for my taste. "Upon the Styx. And once Helen is queen, she will help me in the search for such a woman, will you not?"

"I will have no trouble discerning which women he should *not* marry, in any case." I held out my hand to him, and Theseus returned to the table, taking it and sitting down beside me once more. When he was in such good spirits, I could not bring myself to frown at him over a promise made to his friend. And it was true that we would owe Pirithous a debt.

Pirithous snorted. "How do you even make it through the day's business when you have her waiting for you?"

"With determination," Theseus answered, grimacing. "And it will be harder yet if Demophon chooses to accompany you. I suppose I'll have to make more use of Menestheus."

Pirithous looked up from his plate, his eyes sharp. "The son of Peteus?"

"Who else?"

"Watch that one," Pirithous said. "He's hungrier than the rest for power. Thinks he has something to prove as a grandson of Erechtheus."

"We are blood, and he is loyal, as his line has been, always. Whatever he feels he must prove, he'll accomplish it as an able administrator, as his father did before him. Why should he want more when I have given him peace and prosperity?"

"Peace is all well and good in theory, and I grant you it is much better for our women, but the younger men need something to put their muscles to. Even a minor border skirmish would serve them."

"And shall I wage war against my allies just to appease them?"

Pirithous shrugged, but he glanced at me. Another chill went down my spine. "It isn't as though Menelaus and Agamemnon would have a hope of winning. And once you had won, Helen could walk freely under her own name without any need to disguise herself."

"Had I only the smallest excuse, I would see Menelaus dead," Theseus said, his voice low and tight. "But he is too much a coward to give me reason for war, and I will not betray my people by inventing one."

My heart beat hard and fast in my chest, my whole body growing cold. Pollux would come, if a war began, whether Tyndareus wished it or not, for he was as eager to test himself as any of the Athenian men, and Castor would not be left behind. And if they fought in my name, Tyndareus would have to send an army or be shamed.

I shook my head, trying to fight the image of my brothers' bodies broken below the Rock. I did not want to see them killed. Not because of me. I had come here to avoid a war, not drag Sparta into another. The losses in Athens would be nothing to what Sparta would suffer. And my brothers!

"Shh, Helen," Theseus said, and it was only then I realized I had made any noise, though I did not know what it might have been.

He turned my face to his and stared into my eyes until the panic that choked my breathing and made my ears buzz was replaced with the roar of the sea.

"It will not come to that," Theseus said. "I swear it to you. Your brothers will not suffer."

The tightness in my chest eased. "No war, Theseus. Promise me."

His jaw clenched, and he did not answer at once.

"I would have no more lives lost over me," I said, clutching at his hand and pressing it to my cheek. "Not even Menelaus's."

"I will not promise not to kill him, Helen." His eyes had turned the flat gray of a hurricane, and he pulled his hand away too carefully, as if he did not trust his own strength. "Do not ask it of me."

I turned my face away, that he would not see the words half-formed on my lips. Theseus had never spoken to me with a king's voice until that moment, nor truly refused me anything, and I was not so great a fool as to press him further. It was one thing to ask him to spare the life of the shepherd boy, innocent and too young to know what he meddled with, but I remembered then, what Pirithous had said, that day on the field before they had fought. Theseus would never forgive Menelaus for what he'd done. But it was more than that, and I had been a fool not to see it before now.

Theseus wanted Menelaus dead. And if Mycenae marched on Athens, he would make certain he had his way.

I did not speak of it again, and nor did Pirithous, within my hearing. For that much, I was grateful.

--- ❧ ---

The next morning, Theseus gave me clay tablets, and with Pirithous and Demophon, we argued over the language of the message that would be sent. In the end, I wrote three versions, each more specific than the last, with the third to be given only to the pharaoh himself, and Theseus pressed his owl seal into the soft clay.

Demophon and Pirithous left for Egypt three days later with two square-sailed ships and the most troublesome of the young men, spoiling for war. Theseus went to the port at Piraeus to watch them sail, and I practiced patience.

It would be a very long three months.

CHAPTER TWENTY-THREE

I stood on the palace walls to watch the procession, my hair and face hidden by a shawl. Most of the palace women had found an excuse to slip outside. Whether it was out of curiosity for their new queen, or simply to avoid being put to work by Aethra, I didn't know, but at least I would not be noticed. It was the nearest to freedom I'd been since arriving in Athens.

Theseus rode up from the port at the head of an honor guard, his chariot drawn by three shining horses, white as sea foam. A woman stood at his side in a flowing gown of pale yellow, her face and hair hidden. Even from this distance, I could make out the finery of her clothing and the glint of golden bracelets and necklaces. It seemed Pirithous had not spared any expense.

The women surrounding me whispered to one another. Theseus hadn't had a woman in his bed but me since he'd returned from Sparta, and few of them had been pleased with the development once they realized it would remain that way. Not that they knew who had displaced them, but the fact that they found his celibacy alarming told me more than I wished to know.

"Helen's curse," one of them hissed. "They say any man who looks upon her will never see another woman again. And now she has bewitched our king as well."

"Don't be foolish," another answered. "If he were bewitched by Helen, he'd hardly be marrying an Egyptian princess. It isn't as though he needs a wife, and Athens certainly has no need of a queen as long as Aethra runs his household and serves as high priestess."

The first woman sniffed. "Better for all of us if she went to Hades instead and Theseus remained unmarried. Then he would have to choose one of us to run the household at least."

"And you think it would be you?" The second woman laughed. "You barely lasted a month in his bed."

My face burned beneath my scarf, and I moved away as quickly as possible without drawing attention. Devoted as Theseus might be to me now, and as beautiful as I might have been to him, I was already nervous enough about our wedding night without hearing stories of the other women he had kept before me. Not when, in all the time I had slept beside him, he still had not yet done more than kiss my forehead and wish me pleasant dreams. I was beginning to fear he never would. Or worse. If a palace woman had only pleased him for a month, what hope did I have of lasting any longer? Perhaps he simply had not wished to tire of me until after we married . . .

The parade worked its way up the switchback to the palace gates. They had drawn near enough now that I could see Pirithous and Demophon, brown as the desert, riding on horseback behind Theseus's chariot. Demophon looked as though he had aged a full year, though they had been gone only four months.

"My lady?"

Acamas tugged on my sleeve, peering into my face. He kept his voice just above a whisper. Theseus had trained him so; whispers carried farther than low tones.

"Aethra says you should come in now, so that you might be waiting."

"Of course." I glanced about me to be sure no one watched. The others had eyes only for the procession.

Acamas led me across the courtyard in silence, and we slipped into the palace through the servants' quarters. He knocked on the door to the queen's room and Aethra pulled it open, a frown clearing the moment she saw me. I should not have left my rooms, but now was the safest time, and I had taken no unnecessary risks.

"Fortunate for you that Acamas knew where to find you so easily," Aethra said, pulling me into the room before I had time to respond. She shooed Acamas away. "Go greet your father and brother. It wouldn't do for you to be absent from the megaron."

Acamas bowed and sprinted back off down the corridor before Aethra had shut the door.

"Theseus should be at the gates even now," I said, unwinding the shawl from my face and hair.

Over the last months, Aethra and I had removed every extra footstool, tasseled cushion, golden wine cup, bowl, vase, and tripod from the room, and with the excuse of the princess coming from Egypt, we'd been able to repaint the walls as well. For appearances, I had chosen Egyptian images: reeds and water lilies and shining obelisks, painted in earth tones, with borders of olive wreaths for Athena. But I spent most of my time in Theseus's rooms, unless I was dressing or the servants were cleaning in his.

"What will you do with the slave girl?"

Aethra took the bone comb to my hair. We had needed to redye it nearly every month to keep the gold from showing.

"If Pirithous does not wish to keep her, I suppose we will send her to serve Athena. The goddess won't let a slave girl ruin Athens with a wagging tongue, especially if she favors you."

I didn't reply. Theseus had been sacrificing to the gods every day since Pirithous and Demophon left. We ate so much lamb and mutton, I did not know if I would ever be able to taste it again without the flavor of his anxiety. Athena, Aphrodite, Hera, Zeus, Poseidon, even Hermes, all received offerings at least once a week. He spent nearly as much time on his knees in the temples as he did in the megaron, and all of it, by his own word, to secure our marriage. And, I thought, because he still feared Zeus's price.

Everything that could be done, every blessing that could be obtained from the priests, he had seen to in preparation for this day. Theseus had even gone to the temples before leaving for the port of Piraeus to ask the priests when we might be married, now that the false Egyptian princess had arrived. I worried more about Menelaus, though we had heard nothing from Mycenae or Sparta since we had sent Pirithous away.

Aethra dressed me in the finest clothes I had ever seen. The flounced skirt was made entirely of rare silk and dyed in brilliant blues and yellows. Chiming gold ornaments, sewn to each tier of fabric, tinkled when I moved. The shift beneath was all but sheer and pure white, so light I barely felt it on my skin, but I did not feel exposed, and the blue silk of the bodice fit me perfectly with a gold-accented belt at my waist.

Aethra insisted that I let her powder my skin with umber and ocher, both, to darken it, and I endured the application of kohl and malachite to my eyes without complaint. Even the least informed knew the Egyptian style, and the paint would further obscure my features. "You can't hope to paint me this way every time I step out of these rooms," I objected.

She stepped back to study her work. "It is the first impression that will matter most, Helen. If we paint you brown from the sun tonight, the people will remember you that way later no matter how pale you become."

I swallowed my aggravation and closed my eyes obediently as she touched up the face paint around them.

Acamas burst through the door, making me flinch, and Aethra cursed as she smeared a line of kohl.

"Father," he gasped. I had no doubt that he had sprinted all the way from the megaron. "And the Egyptian."

"Catch your breath, Acamas," Aethra said, licking her finger to fix the smudge on my face. "And then stand outside. When the woman arrives at the door, show them in. No one else."

Acamas disappeared, and Aethra stepped back to look at me again, her eyes narrowed. "Well, it will have to do. Between your hair and the paint, I can't imagine anyone would recognize you when they expect an Egyptian princess. Even Theseus will have to look twice."

I grimaced. "He won't like that."

"If it means your freedom, he'll say nothing against it." She twisted a lock of my hair into place. We had dyed it as close to black as we could that morning, when word of the ships had come to the palace. "You look beautiful no matter how you are dressed or adorned, my dear."

A knock on the door warned us, and I rose to stand out of sight. Aethra wiped her hands on a towel, then turned to welcome her son and his false bride.

"Welcome!" Aethra kissed the girl's cheeks through the veil that covered her face and drew her inside.

Theseus followed, his gaze searching the room. He found me, and shut the door on the nobles and servants who loitered in the hall. I did not dare to greet him in front of the woman. The less she knew of her role, the better, though I imagined she must have been flummoxed to be greeted as nobility.

"Pirithous says she is called Layla," Theseus said, his voice low. "And he kept her veiled and hooded during the journey. None but he and Demophon know her face."

"Thank the gods Pirithous has that much sense." Aethra stripped the gold cuffs from Layla's arms and passed them to her son. "Come with me, my dear, and we'll have you bathed and dressed in something a bit less stifling, shall we?"

The girl ducked her head. "Thank you, my lady. If it pleases you."

Theseus shut the door to the bathing room behind them, hesitating for a moment before turning back to me. His eyes devoured me, as if cataloging every detail of my appearance. My face burned beneath his scrutiny.

"You make a splendid Egyptian," he said, just when I felt as though the silence would smother me.

I let out the breath I had been holding and dropped low in a *henu*. "My lord honors me."

He crossed the room, and his hand found my fingers, urging me to rise. I glanced up into his face to see he searched mine even as he slipped the gold cuffs up my arms. I traced the patterning of the olive leaves in the gold without looking. The cuffs had been Aethra's until now.

"And when this banquet is over, and we are left alone to our marriage bed, will you honor me?"

I swallowed, though my mouth seemed filled with sand and an ocean roared in my ears. "We marry tonight?"

Theseus nodded once, our eyes locked together. "The priests say the day is auspicious enough. If you will have me?"

"Yes," I said, my voice rough. "My answer will always be yes."

He drew me against his body, his forehead falling to touch mine. I closed my eyes, breathing him in. Dust and sweat from his journey mixed with the scented oils from his bath that morning, filling my head. Our noses brushed.

"Helen—" His voice broke, and I felt the tension of his shoulders beneath my hands.

He tipped my face up with a gentle finger beneath my chin, and our lips met for the first time. His mouth, warm and confident, tasted of pomegranate. My hand closed into a fist around the material of his tunic, drawing him closer as my lips answered his.

I clung to him when he pulled away, wondering if he felt my body trembling the way his did. My arms slipped around his neck, and my fingers twined themselves into the close curls of his hair.

Theseus sighed, one of his hands sliding up my arm, our foreheads pressed together once more.

"Helen, I—"

I stopped him with a kiss.

Whatever he had to say, I felt sure it would wait.

Aethra scolded us for it later when she found the paint on my mouth smudged and marking Theseus's lips, but Theseus ignored her to repeat his error one more time before she managed to tear us apart.

"The king of Athens cannot arrive at his wedding feast covered in dust from the road," she said, all but shoving him into the bathing room.

A strangled noise came from my throat at the loss of his touch, but Aethra only glowered at me and shut him from the room.

"You would think he had not been king for thirty years and married twice in that time, fool as he is for you."

She pushed me down onto a stool and went about fixing the damage Theseus had done. I stared at the door to the bath and wished he would hurry.

"There. And by the look of you, no one will ever say that Athens did not treat a princess of Egypt with all due courtesy. The court will be stunned into silence at your banquet."

Our wedding banquet. My stomach twisted into a knot, and the woman from the palace wall came to my mind. No more than a month in his bed and he had tired of her. How long could I hope to please him, once we were wed? I wished I had thought to ask if he had kept women other than his wives while he was married, but even thinking the question caused my heart to ache. I could never force the words past the lump in my throat to voice it.

Please, let him be pleased by me tonight.

I had scarcely finished the thought when Theseus returned, his hair still damp beneath the olive leaf circlet and his skin gleaming bronze with oil. He pulled me up, looking on me with eyes brighter than sunlight on the sea. His long tunic was blue silk like my gown, and I wondered whether Aethra had chosen his clothing to match or whether he had done so himself.

"Washed and dressed, you look very much the king." I smiled.

"And that is the difference between us, for you never look less than a queen." He kissed my forehead, careful of the paint on my face while we stood under Aethra's eye. "Are you ready to wear your crown?"

"For as long as you will have me as your wife."

"Acamas!"

The boy opened the door so quickly at his father's call, he must have been standing with his ear pressed against the panel. "Yes, Father?"

"Tell Menestheus it is time, and have the queen's circlet brought to the megaron."

Acamas bowed, grinning, and ran off before Theseus led me out on his arm. For the first time since I had arrived, we walked together in daylight.

For a wedding gift, Theseus, Hero of Attica, king of Athens, had given me freedom.

CHAPTER
TWENTY-FOUR

Helen hesitated at the entrance to the megaron, and Theseus paused with her, covering her hand on his arm. He smiled to see her biting her lip, and squeezed her hand.

"If Aethra were here, she would tell you to mind the paint on your face that took her so much time to apply," he teased.

Her face flushed beneath the umber, and she looked up at him, the lines around her eyes smoothing as some of the tension left her. "Then I am lucky that Aethra is not here to scold me. Won't she be at the banquet?"

"Aethra will bless our marriage herself," he assured her. "And Pirithous will be there with Demophon. You'll meet Menestheus tonight and most of the important nobles. But fortunately, you speak Egyptian, not the tongue of these lands. You need do nothing more than smile politely and mark their faces."

She pressed her lips together and inhaled deeply through her nose, then let it out with a sigh. Whatever her answer was, she spoke it in Egyptian, but he did not mistake her wry smile or the flash of amusement in her eyes. And in that moment, he did not care what the cost would be when it came, only that Helen was at his side, and she would be his queen, his wife.

She stepped forward, her chin raised high, and every line of her body filled with the confidence of a woman who knew she was the child of a god. Just as any child of the pharaoh would. As any daughter of Zeus might, though until this night he had never seen her adopt such a pose.

Acamas grinned and knocked on the door, signaling the guards inside to open them. Helen's eyes widened, and he thought he heard her gasp when she caught her first sight of the megaron in daylight.

Theseus hid a smile and cleared his throat. "I'm sure it is nothing compared to the pharaoh's palace."

She stared at the walls, covered floor to ceiling by frescoes of the heroic deeds of his youth, flowing together from one section to the next and bound between the twists and turns of a golden labyrinth. On the wall straight ahead, a bullring and his team of bull dancers leapt over the charging animal; on the left, his labors along the Isthmus road as he confronted and vanquished the twisted men and creatures at the gates to the Underworld; and to the right behind his throne, at the heart of an intricate maze, his battle against the Minotaur, though by all rights it ought to have been griffins instead.

It hadn't been his idea to have it painted, but Aethra had insisted it would be a reminder to his people that it was by his power that Athens had been freed. More than once it had served to silence a noble who might otherwise have argued with his ruling in a dispute. Everything had a purpose, he supposed, and if the labyrinth of his life had led him to Helen, he could hardly complain of the trials he had suffered along the way.

Pirithous met them at once, breaking Helen's stare by bowing over her hand. "My lady, you are transformed. Never have I seen anyone so beautiful."

Helen inclined her head, but her eyes lit at his performance.

"You know Pirithous, of course, king of the Lapiths," Theseus said, clapping his friend on the shoulder. "And my son, Demophon, prince and heir of Athens."

Demophon bowed, kissing the back of her hand with all Pirithous's charm and none of the other king's flirtation. "My lady, might I introduce to you my brother Acamas, prince of Athens."

Acamas stepped forward, frowning to smother his smile, and offered her the Cretan salute. "My lady."

"And this is my cousin and one of my advisers, Menestheus," Theseus said.

"Princess," he said, bowing low. "All of Athens is honored by your presence, and by the pharaoh's favor."

Helen smiled politely and said nothing, but raised her eyes to meet Theseus's as if looking for some kind of guidance he knew she didn't truly need. Her performance was flawless.

"Thank you, Menestheus," Theseus said. "On behalf of the princess."

Before anyone else could approach, Theseus guided her around the great round hearth to the table set before his throne. The gallery above was filled to bursting with men, women, and children, all eager for a glimpse of their new queen. It was a compromise to Menestheus to allow them. Not that he begrudged his people the right to see her crowned, but after these months together, the idea that Mycenae or Sparta might come to reclaim her brought him too much pain, and every man or woman who saw her risked recognition. This wife, he meant to keep.

"I'm sure you're hungry after your journey," he said, more for the benefit of the others than hers. "Some wine, perhaps?"

He seated her and poured the wine himself, offering the first drops to the gods, though he had already offered a true libation when he had arrived with the slave earlier. He raised his cup, and the conversations in the hall dwindled to silence.

"We celebrate today the coming of our bride, Meryet, princess of Egypt, daughter of the pharaoh." He allowed his gaze to sweep over the men in the hall, taking in their expressions. Most had eyes only for Helen, and for that he could not blame them.

He nodded to Aethra, who stepped forward with a cloth bundle in her hands. Theseus unwrapped it, lifting up the circlet of braided gold, a single emerald nestled within the overlapping threads. He'd sent all the way to Troy for the jewel, but when he placed it on her head, he thought the wait well worth it.

"With this crown, we make you our wife and queen of Athens."

Moisture dampened her eyes, and she touched the circlet on her brow, her fingers brushing across the gemstone. Helen met his gaze and rose from her seat before falling gracefully into the *henu* that never failed to impress him. He could have sworn he even heard the barest click of the gold band against the stone tile of the floor.

"My king honors me," she said in halting Achaean. "Thank you."

"To the new queen!" Demophon called out, raising his cup. "May the gods smile upon her and rain blessings down upon our city."

"To the queen!" the others answered. "To the king's bride!"

Theseus offered his hand and helped her to her feet. Her eyes matched the stone on her forehead, bright with joy.

She lifted her cup and offered the most brilliant of smiles, turning to the nobles who filled his hall. "To the king!"

When they had offered Theseus their salute, she drank as well, and they both retook their seats with the cheers of his people ringing in their ears.

Because Helen pretended ignorance of the language, Theseus's greatest challenge was reminding himself not to speak with her as he would have if they had been alone. Demophon and Acamas sat beside her at the table, engaging with her in stumbling Egyptian, but he did not remember enough of the tongue himself for even that much, and having her beside him in his hall at last, without the pleasure of telling her its history, was almost worse than not having her at all.

"Stop glowering at your sons, Theseus," Pirithous said, halfway through the meal. "The last thing your people need is to fear their new queen will be another Phaedra."

Theseus ground his teeth, transferring his glower to Pirithous instead. "This is my wedding day, Pirithous. Can you not watch your tongue for this one evening?"

His friend smiled. "Shall I make it my gift to you? I thought you might prefer something made of gold, or perhaps a sacrifice to the gods for the health and happiness of your bride."

"Gift me with whatever you like. As long as you don't mention my ill luck, I will be content." He poured more wine and forced himself not to show his jealousy that Demophon and Helen were laughing together over some Egyptian joke. His son spoke the language easily after his journey.

"Perhaps a distraction, then." Pirithous reached for more grapes.

Bowls of fruit, nuts, and bread, dishes of olives, platters of roasted wild boar, and plates of honeycomb covered the tables in quantities that would serve twice the number present, though Pirithous seemed determined to make up for the lack of guests, his appetite as hearty as ever. "The pharaoh bid me give you a message from his god, and since I do not expect anyone will see you for days once you take your bride to bed, now seems the best time to deliver it."

"From his god?"

Pirithous nodded, and though he smiled, lines had formed around his eyes. "It was by the order of Amun-Ra, their highest god, that the pharaoh agreed to this marriage at all."

"And his message?"

"Amun-Ra has taken interest in the affairs of your bride, as he does all those who are troubled. He says that if her future comes to find her here, she must be sent into his hands. Egypt will grant her its protection, in the pharaoh's own house."

Theseus glanced at Helen, and she turned her smile on him. The emerald of her diadem flashed fire in the lamplight, and her skin glowed bronze. Aethra had outdone herself.

"I do not know how he knew, Theseus, but he did. When she spoke of war before, I thought perhaps her fears were unwarranted, just a woman's worry over men's affairs. But if the Egyptian gods concern themselves . . ."

"Only fools do not listen when the gods speak," Theseus agreed.

"What will you do?"

He shook his head. "Keep her hidden and safe as best as I can. Listen, if she dreams again. Honor her for as long as she is my wife, and hope what has been done already will be enough to stop what she feared would come." He swirled the wine in his cup, staring at the ripples that played along the surface. "And I will turn to Egypt if her future, whatever that may mean, seeks her out. But if the pharaoh helps us only at his god's command, I wonder what reception we will be given."

"A warm one," Pirithous said. "From the moment Amun-Ra showed his favor, Demophon and I were given a most royal welcome. The pharaoh took us into his palace, gave us skilled women for our pleasure, and showered us with gifts of every kind. Your son has a strong start on a treasury of his own thanks to the pharaoh's kindness. The hold was stuffed so full of guest-gifts, we hardly had any need to raid."

Theseus nodded, but when he looked down the table, Demophon was absent and Acamas had taken his place. A quick survey of the room showed his son moving among those seated at the tables below, slapping the backs of the men he had fought with and speaking to the older nobles who had stayed behind. Menestheus watched him sourly, jealous no doubt. Demophon had become a favorite of the Athenian nobles even before he'd proven himself on this journey. But that was as it should be, and Menestheus knew better than to hope for anything else.

"How many were lost?"

Pirithous shrugged. "A handful in all, a couple to wounds that Apollo did not see fit to heal and a few in battle who were too eager for booty to keep to the line. None of any importance or real skill. You should be proud of Demophon. Had I not known who stood at my side, I would have thought he was you, the way he fought."

Theseus grunted, drinking his wine and waving to a servant for more water. "Let us hope he was gifted with all my strength and none of my youthful foolishness."

"You're too hard on yourself, Theseus. The bards will sing of you long after you've gone to Hades for what you did as a young man alone. How is that anything to be ashamed of?"

"I had my father's favor then, or I would have died a hundred times over. Poseidon does not take such a personal interest in Demophon."

"He took enough interest to see him delivered back from Egypt with only the barest of scratches. You worry too much, my friend. You raised a fine boy into a finer man, and when you are gone, he will be a great king. Certainly those who sailed with us found much to admire in him, and those who heeded him always returned to the ship without meeting any real harm. You could make him a leader of the host now, and no one would object."

Theseus shook his head. Helen's haunted eyes, when she told him the story of her nightmares, rose in his mind. He had practically heard the swords clashing and the screams of the dying when she spoke. It would be a bloodbath if it came, and little honor in it. That was not the legacy he wished to leave his son. And there was still Zeus's price to be paid.

"With what might come, I don't dare. Not until we know for certain what the future holds."

Pirithous snorted. "The future is never certain, Theseus, not even in the eye of the Fates. What comes depends as much on our choices as the determination of the gods. Obedience, disobedience, prayer, and sacrifice, all of these things change the course of our lives. The only certainty in life is death. Let your son die with honor, and he will thank you for it."

"There is no honor in this, or she would not fear it." Helen had offered the same arguments, but he knew the gods, had witnessed firsthand how they could tear lives apart and strip them of glory. "Content yourself with raising your own son, Pirithous, or distract yourself with finding another bride, and leave me to see to mine."

Pirithous grinned. "Name a woman worth winning and I shall claim her as my own, but even with your help, I cannot hope to be half so fortunate in choosing a second wife as you have been with your third." He raised his cup. "I wish you a very long and happy life together, or if not, that you will at least let me have her when you're through."

He glared, but Pirithous only laughed, then stood to toast the new queen of Athens in front of the entire hall. When he had finished, Aethra gave them Hera's blessing and announced that their rooms had been prepared.

The desire to finish his conversation with Pirithous fled the moment Theseus was freed from the banquet to take Helen to their marriage bed. More than half a year he had waited, and now he took her by the wrist, leading her from the hall as her husband.

Nothing else mattered but that.

CHAPTER
TWENTY-FIVE

During the feast, I had not thought the evening could go quickly enough, but now that Theseus shut the door to the bedroom, my stomach twisted into knots. I stared at Theseus's bed. It was the same bed I had slept in every night for half a year, but tonight, Theseus would do more than stroke my hair and kiss my forehead. Tonight, he would claim my body as he already had my heart.

The price of the crown on my head and payment for the risks he had taken. He had not said it, had never suggested it, yet the words played through my thoughts, and my heart picked up speed. I owed him this, after all he had done.

Menelaus's words wormed through my thoughts, haunting me now.

I shivered. Menelaus was the last thing I wanted to remember, but how could I not think of him when he had taken the same payment in kind?

A hand touched my shoulder, and I bit back a cry before it left my throat. Theseus dropped his hand at once, but I turned to him and hid my face against his chest to keep myself from sobbing. For a terrible moment, it had been Menelaus's touch I had felt, but even as understanding as Theseus was, I could not tell him that. I would not let Menelaus poison this night for either of us.

Theseus kissed the top of my head and stroked my hair, the weight of his arms around me enough to drive the memories away.

"What's the matter?" he said into my hair.

All night, I had waited to be alone with him. During the length of the feast, I had dwelt in his kiss, anticipating the next to the point of distraction. I had barely thought even of eating, though the food filled the table before me. And then I had been too anxious for what was to come, my stomach roiling with nerves. Theseus, my hero, my king, my husband, at last.

"Nothing," I said, inhaling his warmth and waiting for my heart to calm. "I only missed you."

He laughed and I drew back, looking up at his face. His hand slipped from my hair, caressing my cheek instead. Then he stopped, staring at his fingers for a moment. The umber from my skin had darkened his fingertips.

"This will not do at all, Helen."

I shook my head. "I'm Meryet now."

He raised his eyes to mine, brilliant as the sea.

Theseus drew me toward a low table and reached for a linen towel, dunking it in a basin of water and rose petals. I had not noticed it before, but it seemed Aethra, or perhaps Theseus himself, thought of everything. He held my face in his hands and wiped the powder and paint away, his touch gentle.

"I had my heart set on taking Helen of Sparta to my bed, and making her Helen of Athens, my wife." He paused to dunk a dry portion of the towel in the bowl and cleaned the kohl from around my eyes. "Does Meryet have any objection to that?"

I shook my head, my heart skipping at his words.

Theseus finished wiping the paint from my face, brushing the cloth across my lips and making them tingle. He stroked my cheek again with his bare fingers, lighting a fire beneath my skin.

"Even with hair so black, you still glow golden."

He kissed my forehead, then each of my eyelids, and when I turned my face up to his, he kissed the corners of my mouth. I sighed, winding my fingers through his hair and pulling his head down again to kiss him properly.

His mouth tasted of mint, and one arm encircled me, drawing me closer. My body, flushed from head to foot, begged for his, aching with anticipation for what he had denied us both. How had we waited for so long?

Theseus stepped back, taking up the cloth again to wipe the umber from my throat and neck, then my shoulders, working the material of my shift loose to bare that strip of skin between my breasts. The light fabric clung to me but, even so, it threatened to slip from my shoulders. He paused to kiss my pulse and I shivered, the coolness of the wet cloth only making my skin burn with greater heat. After he washed away the color from my arms, he kissed my palm.

"This is the woman I missed," he said, his voice rough. "Pale and clean as moonlight on water."

I dropped my forehead to his shoulder and let him gather me into his arms again, my fingers tracing the lines of muscle beneath the silk of his tunic. "Will you love me still when I am sun-kissed from wandering the palace grounds?"

He laughed and caught my hand, holding it against his heart. "I will love you still when you are old and gray and stooped with age."

"Will you?" I looked up into his face. "Will you keep me in your bed, even then?"

He sighed and stroked my cheek again with gentle fingers, meeting my eyes. "I would keep you in my bed for eternity, and it would not be time enough. I would make love to you night and day if you wished it, and never let you rise. But let it be for your pleasure, Helen. Let me please you tonight."

I pressed his hand to my cheek and turned my face to kiss his palm, wondering at my fortune to have ever found such a man. When he kissed me again, my body formed to his like warmed honeycomb.

He lifted me in his arms and crossed the room to the bed. When he laid me down, I pulled him with me. Theseus hovered over me, his eyes searching mine. I could feel the effort it took for him to pause, the tension in every line of muscle, every surface of his face.

"Tell me this is what you want."

"Shh." I pulled his head down to kiss him. "Let me be your wife in body as well as heart."

The flash of sunlight in his eyes darkened as he brushed the hair from my neck and shoulder, his jaw tightening. When he lowered his head to kiss my throat, I shuddered at the touch, a whisper against my skin.

The warm metal of the circlet on his forehead brushed against my fingers, and I raised it free from his brow, then reached for mine. He stopped me, drawing my hand away and sliding the sleeves of my shift down my arms to bare my breasts. His lips followed the trail of the fabric, down the valley between them, his calloused palms grazing my sides, rough and warm at my ribs. His tongue teased me until my back arched, and I pulled him closer, moaning.

I did not need his encouragement to free the belt from his waist, but my fingers trembled, fumbling the tie. He chuckled, helping me, and then I pulled his tunic up over his head, forcing a sliver of space between us.

My breath caught, and I could not tear my eyes from his body. All these months we had spent together, I had never seen him less than fully clothed. Even when we slept, he had remained modest. Now I pushed him to his back, that I might see him naked. He pulled me with him, laughing as he rolled, but I didn't let him draw me down, sitting on my heels.

"Am I so fascinating?"

I ran my hands over the muscle of his chest, my fingers tracing the faded lines of scars and old wounds. Even marred, he was incredible, the planes of his stomach chiseled perfection and the lines of his body balanced to absolute symmetry. Looking at him, seeing the bronze of his body laid bare, I no longer wondered that when he called himself the son of a god, men believed him.

"You're beautiful," I whispered.

His hand slid down to the small of my back. My shift had bunched at my waist when I had rocked back to my knees, but he tugged at the belt that held my skirt in place atop it, and the fabric fell to my hips. I felt myself flush and turned my face away.

"Look at me, Helen." The gentle pressure of his finger beneath my chin raised my face to his. "I am nothing compared to you. Unworthy."

I shook my head, taking his face between my palms and pressing my forehead to his. "You are the most worthy man I have ever known."

The last of the fabric between us was pushed away, the gold ornaments on my skirt chiming against the tiles, and my shift following soon after. Theseus rolled me to my back, kissing me again while his hands moved over my body, fondling and caressing, tickling my stomach before sliding between my thighs. His touch at my sex made my heart stutter. When his fingers slipped inside me, I gasped.

His hand stilled, and he kissed my throat, then my collarbone. My body arched of its own accord, pressing against his hand until I moaned with pleasure. Palm flat against me, he matched his movements to mine.

I had never realized what pleasure a man could give this way, with just the touch of his hand. The wave built a roaring of the sea in my ears, and Theseus's lips found my throat, teeth grazing the flesh. My hands closed into fists in the linens, as though if I did not hold on, I would be swept away. And then the wave burst, and I cried out, my whole body shuddering with release.

Theseus's hand slipped free when I had stilled, and I heard him chuckle again, low and smug. He tickled the inside of my thighs. I shivered and he shifted, his hand persuading my legs to spread beneath him.

"Open your eyes, Helen."

I could not have denied him anything then, and did as he bid, meeting his eyes as the length of him pressed against my opening where his fingers had been. Anticipating the pain of his thrust, I bit my lip against it.

"I won't hurt you," he murmured, and then he kissed me, his lips parting mine as his body filled me with its hardness until I moaned with new pleasure.

My nails scraped his back for purchase, my legs spreading wider to let him in. His forehead falling to mine, he held still as stone above me for a long moment, his breath coming hard. I wrapped my legs around his waist, drawing him closer, and he groaned my name.

When he began to move at last, I thought I would never need to breathe again, that just this moment, and his body inside mine, would sustain me for the rest of my life. I raised my hips to meet his, finding his rhythm and echoing it with my own.

He swore something I didn't hear, for the ocean roared in my ears again. My heart beat so hard, my whole body throbbed, and his pace increased. Faster, and the wave built inside me again, slow and steady with his strokes. I wove my fingers into his hair, and let him carry me, let him fill me, let him hold me afloat, until I shuddered.

My whole body shook from the inside out, and I lost myself in the ocean as it crashed over me again.

Theseus groaned, one of his hands lifting my hips. Holding me tightly joined against his body, he shivered and stiffened with his own release, his seed spilling inside me. He collapsed against me on the bed, his weight somehow not crushing me against the cushioning, his breathing as ragged as mine.

With what seemed a great effort, he lifted himself up and rolled to his side. I sighed at the loss of his body in mine, feeling the absence like an ache. He smiled at me, stroking my cheek, his thumb tracing my bottom lip.

"Did I please you?" he asked.

I blushed, though my face must have already been flushed from our joining.

"Very much," I whispered.

His fingers moved to the circlet still on my brow, and I thought he traced the lines of the braided gold. He kissed my forehead, and though it was a gesture he had made a thousand times before, so soon after his lovemaking it made me shiver.

"You are everything I dreamed of," he said. "Everything I could have ever hoped for, in a woman, in a wife, in a queen."

I laughed and closed my eyes. "You are blinded by love."

"I was blinded before now." He brushed the hair from my face, tucking it behind my ear. "But you taught me to see."

I shook my head, not knowing what to say to such praise, and his every touch scattered my thoughts. He kissed my temple, then the pulse at my neck, his fingers trailing over my rib cage and making my body burn again.

But my stomach begged me for food, now that my anxiety had fled.

"Theseus."

"Hmm?"

His hand had reached my breasts, and I ached for his lips to follow. Another moment and I would no longer be able to think for the distraction he would give me.

"I'm starving."

He stopped, and in the silence I opened my eyes to look at him. He searched my face for a long moment, his forehead furrowed. And then he laughed. It was not the chuckle of our lovemaking or his self-satisfaction, but a full-throated roar that came deep from his belly, making him fall backward on the bed.

"Shh!" I said, feeling the blood rise in my cheeks again. "They'll hear you in the corridor!"

He did not quiet, but gathered himself enough to sit up and swung his legs over the edge of the bed. The laugh settled into a softer chuckle when he stood up and, naked as a god, he crossed the room and threw open the door.

"Food and wine!" he called, and by the sound of it, he had startled several loiterers with his sudden appearance. "And bring some of the oranges from Pirithous for my bride!"

We made love again after he had fed me, then fell into sleep, our bodies still twined together. I woke covered with a light blanket, cupped in the curl of Theseus's body, my back against his chest. The golden circlet lay on the bed beside me, its emerald reflecting sunlight and green fire into my eyes.

I had only to extend my arm to touch it, my fingers caressing the jewel and tracing the intricate lines of the braiding. It was a far cry from Theseus's own crown, and I could not help but wonder where this one had come from. The stone reminded me of something, though I could not quite remember where I had seen one like it before.

"I had it made for you," he said, startling me with his voice. I had thought he still slept. "The emerald reminded me of your eyes."

"It's beautiful." I rolled over to look at him, fighting a grimace at the stiffness of my body from the night before.

He kissed my forehead where the emerald would have sat and tucked the blanket up over my shoulder. "How are you feeling?"

"As well as I might expect to feel, I think." I smiled. "Thirsty, for the most part." Theseus shifted as though to rise, but I pressed him back before he could. "You're not going to throw open the door and start shouting again, are you?"

He grinned, his eyes crinkling at the corners. I had never seen him so pleased with himself. "If they're going to loiter in the hall outside my rooms, they can at least make themselves useful to their king."

"And all this time I thought you were a modest man."

"I believe I was more concerned with your modesty than mine." He stroked my hair from my face. "I never wanted you to be uncomfortable."

"I'm not uncomfortable now," I assured him, pushing the blanket back and stretching in the sunlight that poured through the open balcony.

"Mmm." His gaze swept over my body, his palm following down my chest, over my stomach, pausing at my navel. "Pirithous was right, you know."

I covered his hand with mine, guiding it lower, across my hips. "Hmm?"

"He'll be gone long before I can bring myself to leave you."

Then he kissed me, and we said very little else.

CHAPTER TWENTY-SIX

Aethra brought them a meal at midday, and Theseus left Helen asleep in the bed to open the door at his mother's distinctive knock.

"Ariston sent a potion, if she needs it." Aethra set the tray down on the table by the hearth, glancing at the bed. Helen hadn't so much as stirred. "I trust you took care to treat her kindly."

"I'm not a brute, Mother, and if I were, I'd hardly have waited this long to maul her."

Aethra sniffed, her gaze raking over him. "Perhaps you aren't a brute, but there's certainly a lot of you for that poor girl to take on, even if she wasn't a maiden."

"After everything I've done to protect her, do you really think I'd let her suffer at my own hands?" Theseus kept his voice low in spite of his irritation. "She's well loved, and I mean to keep her so for as long as she desires it."

"Your son is anxious to prove himself ever more competent now that he's returned, and he'll feel cheated if you do not allow him at least a sevenday to manage on his own," Aethra replied.

"And your opinion?" Theseus asked.

Aethra shrugged. "Give Demophon a month if you wish it. It isn't as if the nobles haven't lived without your constant presence in the past, and it's been a decade at least since you've run off on your own business. Some time away is long overdue, for you and your bride. Take Helen to see her new country if you think it can be risked. She needs fresh air and sunlight and a chance to stretch her legs after so many months cooped up in these rooms."

He shook his head. "All it would take is one man who had been in Sparta to notice her, and we would have Mycenae raining arrows down on our heads."

"Menestheus does not think it would be such a bad thing to give the young men a war."

"Menestheus does not know what I know, nor does he recognize the threat Helen's future brings if she is not kept tucked out of sight. One of many reasons the man is not a king."

Aethra studied him, her lips pursed. "I don't suppose you wish to share this knowledge with me."

He looked at Helen, still unstirring. She had not even whimpered in her sleep for months, not since he had taken her from Sparta and kept her in his bed. *Please, Father, Zeus, Athena, let it last.*

"Until and unless her dreams begin again, we are safe." Theseus picked a grape from the bowl and rolled it between his fingers. "But Pirithous brought word from the pharaoh, and even Egypt's gods fear what might come. I won't have the sons of Athens wasted when we may need every sword arm we can spare."

"Athena will protect Athens." Aethra poured a cup of wine and set a vial beside it. "Even if Aphrodite is against us. And do not think I have not seen those omens, Theseus. The goddess is not pleased with Helen, though I think it would have been so no matter whom she married."

He sighed, thinking of the oarsmen. War he could defend against, but men mistaking her for a goddess—he could not control that. The gods took offense where they willed. "If Athena is to be believed, Zeus may yet claim a price for Helen's freedom."

His mother looked up, her sharp eyes narrowed. "The goddess herself said so?"

"In Sparta, when she promised me her aid."

"Have you any idea what he asks for in exchange?"

Theseus shook his head. "Athena could not say, but I spilled wine on the altar, and it coated my hands like blood."

"And what did Helen say when you told her?" From the tone of her voice, Theseus felt she would thrash him if he had not shared the goddess's words with his wife.

He poured himself a cup of wine. "She believes Zeus means only to deceive us. She says he has never bothered with her before, and sees no reason why he should now. And perhaps I wish to believe it, too. Is it so wrong that we should keep that one small hope?"

"If she were anyone else, Theseus, and if any other god but Zeus were set against you, I would believe it possible. But I'm afraid hope will only bring you heartbreak, now. Better to prepare for the worst in this matter, and to prepare Helen for the same."

"There is no way to appease the gods?"

"We can make an appeal to Hera, but if it is Zeus's will, she must obey him just as we do. It does not help if Aphrodite whispers encouragements in his ear, either, but I do not think there is anything that can be done in that regard. You already shower the gods with sacrifices."

"How can I do otherwise?" Theseus picked an orange from the bowl on Aethra's tray. Helen's favorite, but for the wild strawberries. He had men searching every hillside, every valley, and every shaded spot in Attica for the plants, but they were impossible to find. "I have never loved anyone as much as I do Helen. And the love she has given me burns so brightly, it makes everything else pale. The heat of a bonfire against the smallest candle."

"Be with your bride, then. Enjoy this time for as long as it lasts. Demophon will see to the affairs of Athens for now." Aethra smiled and kissed his cheek. "Give Helen my love when she wakes."

He nodded and latched the door behind her to keep the servants from inviting themselves in on specious errands. No doubt Helen would be happy for the food and drink, but he hoped he had been gentle enough that she did not need the potion. Certainly he had not left any marks on her skin, which was more than could be said for Menelaus.

Theseus ground his teeth at the memory. Even with Helen safe in his bed, he still wanted to wrap his hands around the man's throat for what he'd done to her.

She had put on a brave face, but Theseus had not slept by her side for half a year without knowing something of her thoughts. His determination to give her an experience of joy and love and pleasure, already well formed, had grown even stronger after he had seen the look on her face at the touch of his hand on her shoulder. Her first time should have been a gift, and he had done everything in his power to make up for the loss of it, as he would continue to do.

He rubbed his forehead, trying to force the thoughts from his mind, and went back to the bed. Helen slept in the sun, her fair skin washed in gold. She had curled into a ball, her newly darkened hair even more startling against the canvas of her nakedness. Without the kohl around her eyes and her skin powdered to copper, no one would mistake her for an Egyptian, though umber still smudged her arms and shoulders.

More than anything, he wanted her to feel comfortable, safe, secure. More than anything, he wanted to reassure her that no matter what came, he would protect her and love her. No demand of Zeus would ever change that.

He loved her.

He stroked Helen's hair, fingering the soft strands, warmed from the sun. He didn't know how Aethra had managed to turn it raven black, but it shone brilliant and smooth in the light. Beautiful, no matter what color.

Helen's eyelids fluttered open, a lazy smile spreading across her face as their eyes met. She stretched her arms over her head, her back arching, and desire stabbed through him, though he would not allow himself to respond.

By the gods, he wanted her, and the feeling had not diminished with their coupling. Having her so near, being inside her and making her moan with pleasure, her nails digging into his back, had overwhelmed his self-control, and what he meant to make last had gone very quickly that first time. He had still struggled with his discipline after they had eaten, and only this morning had he managed to find his restraint. He had no intention of losing it again.

Helen caught his hand, bringing it to her face and kissing his palm. Then she pulled him down, and Theseus realized, when her mouth found his, that his wife had other plans of her own.

CHAPTER
TWENTY-SEVEN

For a full month, Theseus and I did nothing but celebrate our marriage. The sun would rise, washing us in gold, and we would turn to each other, unable to keep our smiles hidden for more than a moment. In the morning, he would reach for me, and I would answer, and we would spend our days in the happy glow of lovers. And in the evening, I would reach for him, and we would fall asleep after, our bodies still locked together.

He took me to the harbor at Piraeus by chariot, retracing in sunlight the road that had brought me to Athens. He showed me the woods where he had hunted as a youth before he went to Crete, and his favorite hilltop to climb after he came home, where he had gone to grieve for his father's loss and forget that he was king. And other days, we simply let the horses run, no destination in mind, for the feel of the wind against our faces, tugging at our clothes, and the joy of freedom.

I had never laughed so much in my whole life as I did then, clinging to the rail as he urged the horses to greater speed and the chariot jolted and bounced. I stood within the circle of his arms as he drove, his body braced behind me, warm and strong, and when we stopped at last, tumbling out into the grass, we made love in the open beneath the cypress trees, so absorbed in each other, it did not matter if anyone saw.

The month passed and half of another, before he took up his duties as king again. But this time, when he went to the megaron to hear petitions and complaints, I sat with him. For once my beauty served a purpose, for the men who came before the king without real reason flushed red, bowing and murmuring apologies instead. Full days became half days, then mornings, and the petitioners began bringing gifts instead of problems. The first came from Menestheus.

I stared at the basket of figs and nuts, unsure of what to do. Theseus relied on Menestheus, believed in his loyalty. I did not know what he meant by offering me such a gift, if he only wished for my favor as the wife of his cousin, or something more. But the look in his eyes reminded me of Pirithous just before he stole his kiss, and I knew that Theseus saw it, too. He stiffened on his throne, and I laid my hand on his knee to calm him.

"If you wish to honor me," I said, having been queen long enough for Meryet of Egypt to learn some Achaean, "make these offerings to the gods. Not for me, but for the peace and prosperity of Athens, and blessings upon its king."

"It will be done, my queen." Menestheus swept a bow as deep as a *henu*, but his eyes flashed and a chill went down my spine. "I will make it a gift to Aphrodite."

From the corner of my eye, I saw Theseus sit back, the tension in his body disappearing as his cousin backed away.

"Do any others wish to be heard?" he asked.

When no one else came forth, he rose, extending his hand to me. He smiled his approval, and I closed my fingers around his, feeling the warmth of his palm spread up my arm and down into my middle.

We left the megaron, and the moment the great doors shut behind us, Theseus caught me by the waist, lifting me up off my toes in his elation.

I clutched his shoulders, laughing. "What on earth?"

"You are the wisest queen Athens has ever known," he said, setting me back on my feet only to kiss me. "Did you realize what it would mean to them? To know you honor our gods over the Egyptians'? They will sing your praises from the walls! And the gods themselves cannot be displeased, as long as your admirers offer them gifts upon gifts. Aphrodite may forgive us yet!"

"What has Aphrodite to do with anything?"

"Nothing more, I hope, with so many men sure to bring her offerings now, out of love for you." He lifted me by the waist again to spin us both.

I laughed from the sheer joy of seeing him this way. It was as if all the weight of his years had been lifted and left him a youth again, because of his pride in me and the future he saw for us. A future he no longer feared.

I was glad of it. For him, for me, and for the baby that grew in my womb.

❈

The second month after I had stopped bleeding, I woke in a cold sweat, my heart racing and my stomach cramped. Theseus still slept, though the first tendrils of sunlight slipped over the balcony and through the open doors. A nightmare, and it had come with the same weight as the dreams of the burning city.

In it, I stood between Theseus and our child, lying sleeping in its crib. His face was ashen with grief as he spoke, but the words made no sense to me. I held tight to the wood, refusing to let him near. When he stepped forward, I lashed out, slapping him across the face.

His grief turned to sorrow, but he did not stop. Though I screamed and clawed and beat against him, he did not flinch. He caught my arms, then held both my hands in one of his, his strength so great I could only fall to my knees before him. He tried to speak again, but I could not hear over the roar of blood and despair in my ears. Aethra came in behind him at his shout, and though my throat was hoarse from screaming, I cried out again, begging. She was dressed in the robes of a priestess, her face painted white with red sunbursts on her cheeks and forehead. She took the baby, and though I threw myself after her, Theseus held me back.

"It is the only way, Helen," Theseus said, his voice hoarse but loud enough to pierce through my sobs. "Zeus's price must be paid, or the war will come. Athens will perish, and countless will die. If we disobey him now, it will be even worse than the nightmare you feared. How many would you see killed for standing in the way of your father?"

I did not need the priests to tell me what this dream meant. But it was early yet. I had time to act, time to stop it from coming. I pressed my hands against my stomach, imagining the life inside.

Theseus stirred, the sunlight having reached the bed. His hand covered mine, but I could not bring myself to face him. If he met my eyes, he would see my grief, and I would have to tell him of the dream and the baby he did not yet realize we had made together. To him, now, it would be nothing to give up if the gods demanded the sacrifice. But if I waited, perhaps he would come to love it enough to refuse.

And in the meantime, I would settle my own debt to the gods, without the blood of our child in payment.

Aethra helped me dress in the mornings, and she watched me with narrowed eyes as I tied the tasseled rope to cinch the cloth of my gown at the waist. I flushed under her scrutiny, knowing what she saw.

"It's been three months since your last blood," she said to me at last. "One we might discredit from excitement or distress, but three is a child, and you will not be able to keep it secret for much longer."

I sighed, pressing my hands to my stomach, still flat but thickening now. I had felt Theseus's hands pause there when he loved me, but I could not bring myself to speak of it. So often a child might be lost in the first months, before it had even formed, and with the threat of the gods hanging over us, I feared it even more. Theseus already had two sons. What if he did not want this child? What if he did not care if Zeus took it, or asked me to give it up even before its birth? I could not stand to know.

"It's so soon," I said. "Early still."

"If I have noticed, Theseus must have. He is no fool not to realize what three months of lovemaking might mean, besides."

I smoothed the material of my gown—linen today, dyed pale blue, but finely woven and embroidered with acorns at the edges. "Do you think he will be pleased?"

Aethra smiled, taking my face in her hands. "The only thing that pleases Theseus more than his children is you, Helen. He only waits for you to tell him he has not misread the signs, and you will see for yourself how he rejoices."

We drove to Piraeus that day, for Theseus had promised to take me to the sandy shore. While I had played in Sparta's river as a girl with my brothers and sister, it was not the same as the sea. I still had not had my fill of looking at it, as long as I had land beneath my feet.

He knew a secluded place where the horses might find grass to graze, and we would be undisturbed by ships and oarsmen. We left our clothes in the chariot and bathed in the salt water, exulting in the warmth of the sun and the waves until dolphins joined us in the cove. I had never seen them so close, and Theseus called them nearer.

They were immense, longer than Theseus was tall, their thick tails beating the water and propelling them forward with such speed, I thought they might knock us over when they came.

"It is a sign from my father," Theseus said when they swam in circles around us, nudging us with their smooth noses and clicking greetings I did not understand. "That he blesses our marriage."

A smaller calf had come to me, rolling on its side and staring with an eye above the water before diving beneath the surface again. Its body brushed against mine, its skin the texture of smoothed cork. Another of the creatures bumped my stomach, and I stroked its side, hope flaring bright and hot in my heart. Poseidon's blessing. Surely he would not give us such a sign if he did not mean to protect us. Zeus was king, but perhaps Poseidon, his brother, could intervene where the other gods would not. With a flick of their tails and splashing leaps into the air, they all swam off as suddenly as they had come.

Theseus smiled at me, catching my hand and pulling us toward the beach with easy strokes. I had never seen anyone so at home in the water. Even beside the dolphins, he was still graceful. We lurched from the sea, thick and heavy on dry land, and Theseus laid out a blanket beneath the shade of a stray oak. We had a lunch of figs, cheese, and bread, with a skin of wine that was mostly water.

After, I dozed, my head pillowed on Theseus's arm, and I felt his hand spread over my stomach, the touch almost reverent. I covered it with mine and pressed his palm to the place above my womb.

"Perhaps it will be a girl," I said, emboldened by Aethra's words, and Poseidon's sign. "A princess of Athens and Sparta."

Then he was kissing me, and I did not have the breath to say anything else.

Theseus frequented the temples, leaving me almost daily in the afternoons. I knew that he consulted Aethra often, for as high priestess, she knew much of what would please the goddesses, and Theseus was determined to slight no one.

For the most part, during those times, I kept to our rooms. I had given up painting my face as an Egyptian, though my skin had browned nicely even without the help of umber. But the night before, I had dreamed again, and when Theseus had gone to make his offering, I had gone to the megaron to make one of my own.

There was no fire more sacred than the hearth within the megaron, the heart of the palace itself, and in times of need or great distress, only the queen could make the proper offerings to the gods. In Sparta, it was believed that the gods would not hear the petitions of any other, if the queen did not do her duty first, but in Athens, it was different. There were some rites and rituals only a woman could perform, and Aethra saw to those mysteries still, but the king did not need a queen to speak to the gods, no matter the circumstances. Whether it was because Theseus was known as Athena's champion, or because of some king before him who had received the favor of the gods, I did not know.

I knew the ritual well, for Leda had made me follow her every gesture since I was old enough to hold my own cup. I poured the wine into a kylix from the small jug on the offering table, and then raised the two-handled cup high, taking my place before the fire, with the throne behind me. It was not that I wanted to pray, to beg for help from the gods who had caused my distress from the start, but rather, I could not shake the fear that every offering Theseus made might go unrecognized because I had not done as I ought. Because I had not done my duty first, as queen.

"Dionysus, hear us," I began, pouring a sip of the wine into the fire. "We are the vessel, and you are the wine. And so we drink to you, of you, with you, that we might know you, and you might know our hearts and prayers, and carry them up, to Olympus, to Zeus our king of kings, and Hera our queen in all things, that we might be heard and answered!"

And then I drank. One sip, then two, before I circled the hearth, pausing between each of the four pillars, to raise the cup again and drink, giving thanks to Dionysus with every touch of the wine against my lips. When I reached the position before the throne again, I finished what remained in the kylix and dropped to my knees before the hearth.

"Accept our offerings and all our prayers, we beg of you," I finished, lifting my arms and throwing my head back. My eyes closed. "Accept us as your servant, your vessel, in this."

"I had not realized the Egyptians worshipped Dionysus," a voice said, and my eyes snapped open, my head turning toward the door. Menestheus stood at the entrance, a clay tablet in his hand. "Forgive me," he said, a small smile curving his lips, "but I heard voices, and I wanted to be certain all was well."

"As you see," I answered, rising to give myself time to gather my composure. The second jug on the offering table held water, and I used it to rinse the kylix, then drank that as well, before replacing the cup. I felt as though I had been jarred awake from a dream.

"Dionysus is a son of Zeus," Menestheus said, still standing in the doorway. There was only one entrance into the megaron. "Or is he something else to your people?"

"I am Athenian now," I told him, keeping my voice even and cool. "Theseus's people are my people, his gods become my gods. And I will serve them as an Athenian queen should. It is a mystery you should not have seen."

"But it has been my understanding that it is Aethra, still, who serves as high priestess in Athens."

I lifted my eyes to meet his gaze, too sharp upon me, too focused. My hands shook, and I closed them into fists to hide my weakness.

It was a Spartan ritual, and if he recognized it—oh, I had been a fool to come alone. If I had asked Aethra, she would have helped me. She would have joined with me in the ritual, and what Menestheus had seen, he would not have questioned. Nor would he have dared to interrupt. I raised my chin, drew myself up, and looked down my nose upon him.

"Some rites yet belong to the queen. She has taught me what I must do, and I have done it. Do you object?"

He pressed his lips together, tilting his head to the side, like a bird examining a worm upon the stone, far from the safety of its burrow, unsure whether it should strike, or whether it was yet some trick. I held my breath and my gaze, refusing to look away first. Meryet or Helen, Egyptian or Spartan, I was queen, and he had no right to question me.

"You must forgive me," he said, offering a bow at last. "My curiosity has ever been a weakness. For a moment I feared—" But he smiled, stopping himself. "It is only that Theseus has devoted himself to you so utterly, or so his women tell me. I had not expected love from such a match, or at least not found so soon. But you are right, of course. It is not my place."

My heart twisted, even as relief flooded through me. I allowed myself to soften, and held out my hand to him in forgiveness. "I cannot be angry with you for loving your king," I said much more warmly. "But you need not fear for him. The love and affection we share is no bewitchment, unless we are both bespelled by the gods themselves."

Menestheus bowed again over my hand, kissing the back of it before he left with a mumbled excuse.

At least in that much, I had not needed to lie.

❧

My spirits lifted after that, the burden of guilt falling from my shoulders. I had done my part, my duty, and I had no need to fear that Theseus's offerings would be wasted.

"You worry too much about me, Theseus," I told him when he planned another sacrifice to honor Hera. We were alone in his room. "I am well, your baby grows, and your father himself has blessed us. What more could you wish for?"

His hands warmed my shoulders, then slid down my arms to take my own. "You are young enough to think yourself invincible, I know. And as a daughter of Zeus, perhaps even more so. But I have seen women die to bring children into the world, and I do not mean to see you suffer the same fate."

"You worry too much," I said again. It was not my life that mattered, and I would have traded it gladly for our child's if it would not have caused Theseus grief. "I'm young and strong, and even Aethra has said my body is made for birthing children."

"There is nothing else for me to do but this." He pressed his forehead to mine. "The risk of a child is not an enemy I can fight. Let me have this small comfort, that by some action of mine I might help keep you safe."

I sighed. Hera would never love me. I was a daughter of Zeus and proof of his faithlessness, but if it reassured Theseus to pray to the goddesses, I should not argue. And while he was on his knees, I could make my own offerings. For since we had seen the dolphins, and I had performed the ritual in the megaron, a thought had come to me. Just like Theseus, I had no wish to overlook any opportunity that might guarantee us peace, and there was more yet I might do about my dreams. But better that I not go about it without his help. Menestheus might not be the only Athenian worried I was some sorceress.

"I wish to offer a bull to Poseidon," I said, "for his protection and to thank him for his blessing. Even if he will not speak to you, perhaps he will answer me now that I carry your child. I would honor your father."

He pulled back, searching my face. He knew me too well, I feared, to think this came from nothing. I only hoped he would not press me for the reasons. "I will find you a black bull, then, and let it go consenting. Would you have a feast day as well?"

I shook my head. "If it is a feast, the people will expect the sacrifice by your hand, and I wish it to be mine. This is between me and the god."

His forehead creased, and his eyes crinkled in long-absent lines of concern. "You have had some sign from him?"

"It is not that." And I promised myself it was not a lie, for I did not know who sent my dreams, or why. "But if we are to be a family, I would not have strife between you and your father. Aethra has told me of Poseidon's kindness to her. Perhaps my beauty will serve us here. Give me this, and let me do it alone."

"You do not know what you ask, Helen." His hands fell from my arms, and his blue eyes darkened. "You might be safe enough from Zeus as his daughter, but Poseidon will have no reason to stay his lust. Are you so willing to give yourself up?"

"I have done it before," I said, though the reminder of Menelaus pained us both. "And for peace, I would do it again." For the child Theseus had given me, I would give myself up to the god and more if it meant protection from Zeus. "Please, Theseus. I do not mean to tempt him, and surely he would not betray his own son in such a cruel way. Poseidon is not Aphrodite, to spite you so."

He looked away, his jaw tight. "You are determined."

I touched his cheek, turning his face back to mine. "The last thing I was so set upon was my marriage to you. You trusted me then. Trust me in this now, too."

Theseus pulled my hand away and turned his back on me, busying himself pouring wine. I waited, even so slight a rejection stinging my heart, but it would not serve me to press him further. He set the jug of wine back on the table, the movement slow and careful, as if he feared he might shatter it with his hold. I had only seen him so cautious once before, after he had turned the handle of a water jug into dust at the banquet in Sparta. If he refused me, I would go to Aethra, but I did not want to act any further in secrecy than I already did.

"There is a shrine I know, dedicated to Poseidon Earth-Shaker," he said at last, his voice low. "A half day's journey from here, near a shepherd's fold belonging to one of the men who went with me to Crete. If it must be done, let it be done there, where it will truly be between you and the god if he claims more than the bull you would give him."

"Will you take me?" I asked, hoping he would see it as a compromise. "At least to the shepherd's fold, if not to the shrine."

He offered me the wine cup and met my eyes, his own still dark with emotions I could not name. "I would trust no other man with your honor, Helen. We will leave as soon as the bull can be found."

CHAPTER
TWENTY-EIGHT

For the journey, by chariot, with the bull plodding beside, I wore a simple shift, so as not to ruin fine fabric with the dust of the road. Theseus kept me before him in his arms, as he had during those first days after our marriage, his body tense behind mine. He said little, and even if we had not had the bull, I do not think he would have hurried the horses to anything faster than a trot. Nor would I have wished him to, for I needed the time to prepare myself for what I meant to do.

In a basket lashed to the chariot, I had finer clothes—a flounced skirt in shades of blue and brown for the sea and the earth, and a fitted underdress that covered my breasts, embroidered with horses along the edges. Theseus had made no comment on my choices, though Aethra had assured me I would not dishonor the god. I would change in the wood before entering the shrine, while Theseus tied the bull to the altar.

It was not only that Poseidon might want my body, but Theseus feared for the strength of the bull, which might fight me during the sacrifice. If the beast did not consent, I would have a hard time of it, to be sure, but Theseus had chosen the mildest animal he could find, and if I never trusted a god again, I must put my faith in Poseidon now.

Theseus muttered a low oath, just before the sun had reached its zenith, and drove us off the road. He leapt from the chariot before it had stopped and stormed toward a grove of olive trees.

I caught up the reins, tying the horses to a small oak nearby, then followed him.

"Theseus?"

He swore something I didn't hear, and his fist slammed into the thick trunk of an olive tree so hard, the wood cracked and olives rained down over his head. I stopped then, for I had never seen him strike at anything so violently, and I had no wish to test his restraint.

"You ask me to give you up to my father. To let you suffer another rape, if the god demands it! For what? My father's favor, when the child is born? His forgiveness? It is not worth such a price, Helen!"

"You do not know that he will ask it of me," I said quietly. "And it is worth it to me, to see our child safe from the other gods who might hope to do him harm. After everything you have told me of your past, how can you begrudge me this?"

He laughed bitterly, raising his head to look at me. He gripped the bark of the tree so hard, it broke off in his hand, turning to splinters and dust. "You should not have to sell yourself. Is that not what I said, when you came to me in Sparta? That I would not have you sell yourself for peace or protection. Not to any man and not to any god!"

I went to him, cautious but determined, and stroked his cheek. "In this, perhaps I must, but I do not do it lightly, and I do not wish for it. Don't you see? Poseidon is our best hope—" But I swallowed the rest of my words before the dream slipped from my tongue, and I hid my face in the curve of his shoulder. "Theseus, I must believe he will be your father now, and grandfather to our child. I must believe he will be more than just a god, this day. Please, do not make it any harder."

His arms wrapped around me, drawing me close, and if he held me tighter than I might have liked, I refused to complain. He buried his face in my hair, and then his lips found my neck. The roar of the sea filled my ears, and I felt his body hard against mine. My fingers coiled into his hair, holding him fast. If I must face the god today, I would go to him a wife. I would go to him with the feeling of Theseus's kiss still on my lips, and my body still aching for my husband's touch.

Theseus loosed the belt at my waist and pushed the fabric from my shoulders, letting the shift fall. Only then did he step back, gazing at me as though I were water in the desert and he near perishing from thirst. I let him drink his fill, first with his eyes, then with his mouth, before stripping him of his tunic and taking my turn at the well.

The spilled olives were crushed beneath our bodies, oil staining the fabric he spread to protect me from rocks and twigs. He teased me with clever fingers and urgent kisses until I writhed, moaning, and begged for his body inside mine. He did not answer me at once, but took his time.

"Look at me," he said, for my head had tipped back, my eyes closed with pleasure as our bodies joined at last. I met his eyes, then, and wrapped my legs tight around his waist.

"Love me, Theseus," I said, pulling him closer. "Make me yours."

I did not need to say anything more.

Theseus pressed a kiss to my forehead, holding my hands in his. We had come to the shrine just past midday, and the bull waited for me in the grove. "I will wait for you, near enough that if you shout for me, I will hear."

I squeezed his hands. "Only come if I call your name. I will try not to shout otherwise, but I can make no promises that my temper will hold."

He smiled at that, some of the shadow leaving his eyes, and kissed me again before going. I waited until he had left my sight, then smoothed my skirt over my hips and took a deep breath to steady myself before stepping forward into the grove. It had been years since I had sought the favor of any god, and I could only hope this would not end poorly, if it accomplished anything at all.

The bull cropped the grass around the stones, and Theseus had left the knife and bowl for me on the worn altar. This shrine, Theseus told me, had been ancient when he was young, and he had seen it kept up since his return from Crete. I knelt in the grass and bowed my head. My knees trembled.

"Lord Poseidon, father of Theseus, I come to give you thanks for your blessing, and beg your grace and protection for the child in my body. Accept this bull as my gift to you."

I realized then, it was not my knees that trembled; it was the earth, and when the sound of footsteps came, I held my breath, not daring to lift my head. It could be Theseus, still, come to check on me. The bull snorted, hoof scraping over stone as it pawed the ground. I waited, listening, but when no voice spoke, I began again.

"Lord Poseidon, lover of Aethra, father to my husband, forgive us for any offense we have given. Grant us the promise of peace in our future, and protect us from my father, Zeus."

"A bold request, daughter of Zeus."

I swallowed against the thickness in my throat, and kept my eyes upon the earth. The footsteps sounded nearer, but I did not wish to show him my face. I had promised Theseus I would do nothing to tempt the god, and to look upon one in the flesh—for one, sharp moment, I resented that Poseidon had come at all when my father had abandoned me so completely for so long.

"You offer this bull as gift rather than sacrifice. Do you think I am so easily trapped by sacred laws? I am not a king that you can make me your guest-friend and bind me to your protection."

"I come to speak to the father of my husband, my lord, not to the god."

"And yet, it is the god's favors you ask for." His sandaled feet were tied with seaweed instead of leather, so dark a green they looked black. He offered me his hand, and I had no choice but to take it, or risk giving offense. His fingers closed over mine, warm and dry and well calloused. "Rise, daughter of Zeus, ill-gotten wife of my son."

I did as he bid, keeping my gaze averted from his face. He wore a sailcloth kilt the color of sea foam, wrapped around his hips and tied carelessly with thick ropes similar to those I had glimpsed on the deck of Theseus's ship, but his chest was bare, and he stood taller than his son by a head or more. He was as brown from the sun as any oarsman, his body so thick with muscle, he made Theseus look sparely built.

"Make your sacrifice, Helen, for you surely need the god's favor more than the father's love."

Poseidon led me to the bull, his thumb caressing my knuckles. I snatched my hand away as soon as I could, feeling his laugh through the soles of my feet, more than hearing it. My hand shook when I took up the knife. The bull stood placid, Poseidon's hand on its shoulder. It tossed its head, but the movement was lazy. A good sign. I stroked its nose.

"Forgive me," I murmured, for even with the god beside me, the waste made my stomach churn. "Lord Poseidon, accept this sacrifice."

The god said nothing, but his hand did not move from the bull's shoulder, as though he held it still by his touch. I set the bowl on the ground beneath the victim's neck where I thought the blood would flow, then sliced its throat.

Hot blood covered my hands, sticky and wet. The bull dropped to its knees as its eyes dimmed, nearly knocking over the bowl. I picked it up to catch the rest of the blood, stepping around the bull's head so it would not fall upon me. Poseidon said something I did not hear, but the bull shuddered once more and toppled dead. When the flow of blood became a trickle, I set the bowl upon the altar and bowed my head.

"You begrudge us even this much," Poseidon said at my back. "Why should I grant you any reward in exchange?"

"For your son's sake," I said, closing my hands into fists. "And for his child."

Poseidon took the golden bowl from the altar, filled with blood, and set it before me. "Wash your hands."

"They have already been washed in blood," I said, unable to bring myself to look into the bowl.

"Wash your hands," Poseidon said again. "Or will you refuse to obey your gods even in so small a matter?"

I pressed my lips together and dipped my hands in the bowl. Instead of warm, sticky blood, I found cool water. My face flushed, and I scrubbed my hands clean without comment. When I had finished, Poseidon threw the water away into the trees and tossed the bowl back to the altar with a clatter.

"You try my patience, Helen. And your father's, besides." Poseidon gestured for me to rise again, and I did, though I kept my gaze upon the altar. "Look at me, girl."

I lifted my face, forcing myself to meet his eyes, ocean blue and liquid as the sea. I could almost see waves crashing against the shore inside them. I understood now, how Aethra had known Theseus as Poseidon's son. But Poseidon lacked his son's warmth when he looked at me.

"Your child belongs to Zeus," he said. "Not to Theseus, and not to me. Just as Hippolytus belonged to Artemis."

"But you are Poseidon the Earth-Shaker, lord of the land and the sea. Surely you have the power to claim the child of Theseus as your own. Surely you have the right to do so."

"Perhaps I would, were the child's mother not a daughter of Zeus, and Theseus not fool enough to steal you from Sparta." His gaze traveled over my body, his eyes narrowing. "Though I cannot say I blame him for losing his head. I would have taken you myself this day, but for the babe already in your belly. Later, perhaps, after it is born."

My stomach twisted and my face flamed. "I am your son's wife!"

Poseidon arched an eyebrow. "Not for long, if you continue in this fight against your father. Do you think he will leave you unpunished, insolent as you are? What will you do then, with Theseus's life traded for your child's, when Mycenae comes in the night?"

"I would have both," I said, raising my chin. "Theseus living, to care for our baby under your protection. I would have them live in peace!"

"It is no small favor, even for the sake of my son, and Zeus is determined."

"My lord, in this if nothing else, I am my father's daughter. I will have my way, even if I must sell myself to Hades. Will you have it said that your brother stood against Zeus when you would not? That the lord of the Underworld has more courage than the god of all the lands and seas?"

The ocean roared in my ears, and the ground shook beneath my feet. The gold bowl fell from the great stone altar, ringing loudly against the rocks.

"So be it." Poseidon spat the words, fury turning his eyes to hurricanes. "If my son will be bound by this, they will both have my protection. But when the day comes that your child is born, and Zeus's wrath falls upon you, do not call to me again, Helen, for you will have no more of my kindness."

Before I could respond, the god was gone.

It was not until much later that I realized what Poseidon had promised me. The lives of Theseus and our child would be spared, yes, provided that Theseus himself agreed.

But surely there was no reason he would not?

CHAPTER
TWENTY-NINE

I took offerings daily to Aphrodite and Hera for Theseus's sake, and to reassure his people. A queen should never be seen to slight the gods, no matter what I felt in my heart, and more than one king had lost his throne when the people believed the gods had cursed him. I had already angered Poseidon, though he had promised his protection. It would not do to offend the goddesses as well, much as I might dislike honoring them.

"You should rest," Theseus told me after I returned and we were alone together in his room for the evening.

He had spent the day with Demophon and Menestheus, counting ears of wheat and amphorae of olive oil. The musty smell of the storerooms still clung to his tunic, making me sneeze. He stripped it off at once and tossed it away before coming back to me in the bed.

"And if I'm not tired?" I propped myself up on an elbow, running my fingers through the fine hairs on his chest.

I may not have had the favor of Aphrodite, but watching him stretch out beside me, all bronze skin and muscle, had a predictable effect on my desires. Theseus had not asked what had passed in the grove, and I did not tell him, but I made certain he knew Poseidon had not touched me. If he came later, it would go poorly for us both, but as long as Theseus lived by my side, I would not fear it. Poseidon was not Zeus, to treat his son in such a way, even if he had no love for me.

The rumble of a chuckle rose from his chest to his throat. He caught my hand and kissed my palm.

"You should rest," he said again, meeting my eyes. "For the sake of the baby in your womb. We need not tempt the gods, and all it might take is a fall."

I sighed, rolling away to stare at the ceiling. He had repainted it with stars, when I had described my bedroom in Sparta, in the first days after I had come. But these were made of gold hammered into the thinnest sheets, and the play of light from the hearth fire gave them the illusion of twinkling.

"You worry still, and overmuch. Poseidon protects us, even if the goddesses will not. Whatever slight Aphrodite believes we have done her, it will not be solved with sacrifice. Aethra even says so."

He stroked my hair from my face. "Perhaps it is best if you stopped going to the temples so often, now that you are so heavy with child."

"And what will I do then? You will not let me sit with you in judgment, either. All I do is lie in bed when I am not on my knees. I am going mad, Theseus."

"Let me open the queen's megaron, and you may choose any of the women you'd like to join you while I cannot be by your side. Surely the company will keep any madness away, and I will know you are cared for."

"Surrounded by servants, you mean, waiting to sprint off to find you if I so much as twitch in discomfort."

"Would you deny me that small reassurance?" His hand found my waist, cupping the swell of my stomach. "Perhaps Menestheus's sister would join you, and I am certain Aethra could find other women, wives of the nobles, who would be honored to be chosen to sit with their queen."

Menestheus's sister was the last woman I wished to be near. Since that day he had found me in the megaron, I had seen the way he looked at me while I sat at Theseus's side, eyes narrowed and lingering. I had no doubt every action, every beat of my heart would find its way to Menestheus's ears if I took up the company of his sister, or any others. I would have to be Egyptian from dawn until dusk, never Helen, never myself, and I had already given him one reason for suspicion. It would endanger Theseus more to be so on display, and if I faltered and Menelaus heard of it . . .

I shook my head, covering his hand on my stomach with my own. "If you will give me a loom and yarn, weaving will keep me occupied well enough here." I forced myself to smile at him. "Will that do?"

He leaned down and kissed my forehead.

"If it will please you and allow you to rest, I'll have it done tomorrow."

Theseus lay back beside me, and I fit myself against his body, resting my head on his shoulder. I thought of the nights I had spent in Sparta, weaving when I could not sleep, and how the work had always calmed me. It had been a long time since I had used a loom. Aethra had always supplied me with so much fabric, and so many new gowns, I had never asked for a loom to be placed in the queen's room. And Theseus had distracted me.

I trailed my fingers over the scars on his chest, then rose and kissed each one. Beneath me, Theseus sighed.

"Helen," he pleaded, "that is not what I meant by rest."

But it was not long before his lips were too busy to object.

The following morning when I returned from my bath, a loom stood against the wall, the warp already threaded and weighted to the floor. A basket of yarn in every color I could want sat on a stool beside it, waiting.

Theseus did not return until evening, and from the sweet smell of his tunic and the blood beneath his nails, he had spent his day making offerings to the gods. I did not ask, and he did not tell me, but it would not be the last time he left me to pray.

We ate lamb stew, cold and hot, and lamb steaks, legs, and every other cut, seasoned in every way imaginable, sometimes with herbs I could not name. Theseus offered so many of the poor beasts to Hera, Aphrodite, Artemis, and Zeus, I wondered that there could be any left in the city. Still the months passed, and Aethra brought me lamb-stuffed breads in the morning and roasted lamb for the evening meal, while Theseus spent his days upon his knees.

I began to weave, planning a family scene as a counterpoint to so much gloom. The lands of Athens would be in the background, framed with olive leaves. It would not be a large work, more a wall hanging than anything else, and it would take considerable skill, for I meant to make the figures in our likeness, but it would keep my mind off the things I could do nothing about.

"I've never seen a woman so heavy with child so determined to stay on her feet," Theseus teased me one evening, watching me from the bed while I shuttled the last of the blue yarn through the warp for the sky.

"If every woman had a husband as kind as you to rub her feet, she wouldn't mind being on them nearly so much," I said, smiling over my shoulder.

"Is that so?" He rose and came to stand behind me, studying my work. "You've even put clouds in the sky."

"Mmm." I stepped back to look at it from the circle of his arms. The light from the hearth didn't do it justice. "I needed to stretch the blue, for there was not much of it, but I think it will do. Of course, I will probably need more of the white later."

"If I had known you enjoyed weaving so much, I would have given you a loom long before now. All those months you were locked away, why did you not ask for one?"

I leaned against his chest. "You had done so much for me already."

"Not enough." He kissed me behind my ear. "And so I pay my debt by seeing to your swollen feet. Will you come willingly to bed now that you can barely tell the colors of your yarn apart, or must I take you by force?"

He swung me up into his arms before I could answer, and I laughed, curling an arm around his neck.

"Tomorrow, Demophon will see to Athens, and you and I will spend the day in any way you desire," he said. "I only wish I could give you some greater gift for your birthday. A feast day for all of Athens to celebrate with us, perhaps. But I'm afraid it would be too great a coincidence for anyone to overlook if word got back to Sparta."

"You remembered," I said, blinking back tears. With as often as he had been gone, I had expected more of the same.

"How could I forget the day we first met, or the reason for it?" He laid me down on the bed, kissing the tears from my cheeks. "Aethra said she will prepare you a meal of anything you wish. You have only to whisper it."

"Anything but lamb." I pulled him down. "Please!"

Theseus laughed and lay beside me. "Nothing else but that?"

"Perhaps some dolmades, if she would be so kind." Aethra's stuffed grape leaves were the best I had ever tasted. Even when she used lamb.

"Wouldn't you like some of your strawberries?" he asked.

"It isn't nice to tease me with things I can't have." I frowned. "You'll hardly let me wander around the countryside looking for them."

"Why stray so far afield when they're growing in the garden?"

I sat up as quickly as my body would allow, which was not very, and stared at him. He wore the smuggest smile I had ever seen on his face, and his ocean blue eyes seemed lit by the sun of his humor, even in the dim light. It had been a long time since I had seen him so pleased.

"Is it true?" I heard myself beg but could not stop it. "Tell me it is!"

He chuckled and pulled me back down, tucking my head beneath his chin. "I had to send to Troy, and the plants and seeds cost me a goodly sum in gold and copper, but I thought perhaps it would be worth the price if it brought you joy."

"I haven't had them in years," I sighed, letting him soothe me. "Is there fruit on the vines? Truly?"

"I wouldn't have mentioned it if there were not. The merchant who brought them back said they came all the way from Elam. Where on earth could you have found a taste for them?"

"Once Pollux and Castor took me hunting, and we stumbled across a plant. I went back a hundred times, but I never found another, and I have been starving for the taste ever since."

Theseus smoothed my hair, smiling, and kissed the top of my head. "I'm glad you are pleased."

"I could only be more pleased if you had a basket of them beside the bed at this very moment," I said with a yawn. "Tomorrow for the morning meal, maybe?"

"First thing," he agreed. "Rest now, my beloved. May the gods give you peaceful dreams."

"Meryet," I said, only half-awake. Somehow when Theseus wished me to sleep, I never had any trouble finding exhaustion. "That's what it means. Beloved."

He chuckled again, and then his heartbeat, steady as waves against the shore, lulled me into sleep.

True to his word, a bowl of strawberries greeted me in the morning. Theseus fed them to me, and they were as sweet and refreshing as I had remembered, with just a hint of tartness on the tongue. I groaned my contentment with every bite, and Theseus laughed, clearly satisfied with himself for devising such a gift.

After our morning meal, he took me to the sheltered garden where he had planted the berries, so I might find them to pick more on my own if I wished.

"I do not know much of their growing, nor does the gardener, but Demeter at least we have not offended, so perhaps she will smile on us in this small thing." Theseus covered my hand on his arm with his, half frowning at the heart-shaped berries before us. "Perhaps I should make her an offering."

"If they grow wild in the woods, I hardly think they'll fail in the shelter of the palace." I forced myself to smile, but the last thing Theseus needed was to sacrifice to another god. It stole too much of our time already, now that he would not let me go with him.

He laughed and kissed my cheek. "As you say, Meryet."

One of the servants tittered and slipped inside. Theseus's smile faded as he watched the girl go, and I wondered what gossip she would spread about the king and his queen's fascination with strange fruits.

I heard less gossip now than I had during the months I was hidden away, but I suspected it had more to do with the company I kept than anything else. Aethra did not gossip, and though Pirithous might have, he had long returned to Thessaly and his own affairs. As for Theseus, neither he nor his sons would ever repeat what little they might hear in reference to their queen, and Acamas did not visit with me as often as he once had. If I had kept servants of my own, I had no doubt I would have heard much more. That was one more reason I was grateful Theseus had not forced any upon me.

"Do they find it odd that I love you?" I asked, for Menestheus's fear that I had bewitched him was never far from my thoughts, and I had often wondered if they saw my affection for him with the same concern.

He shook his head, his eyes falling on another servant tending to the plants. A jerk of his chin emptied the little garden, and he walked me to a stone bench beneath a fig tree.

"Odder that I am so clearly in love with you," he said. "It would never occur to them that a woman would not love their king and hero, but there will always be talk about any man who shows too much devotion to his wife."

We sat together, and I chewed my lip to keep from asking imprudent questions too specifically. "I was under the impression that the king of Athens did not hide his feelings in these matters."

He grimaced in spite of my careful phrasing, and the shadow of Phaedra and Hippolytus darkened his eyes. In truth, it was never far away, even all these years later, and I had seen it in his face more than once before now.

"I saw no reason to before, and now I do not think I could hide my love for you if I wished it." He forced a smile for my benefit. "Athens has seen its share of foreign queens before mine, but when *this* king found himself too much in love, it never ended well. It makes the people nervous, but the only reassurance I can give them is by continuing to love you without incident."

"Is there something I might do?" I did not like the way his forehead had furrowed while he spoke. Why had he not mentioned this before now if it weighed upon him so heavily? "Some way I might reassure your people that your love is not misplaced?"

He squeezed my hand. "It is not so great a concern that you must do anything you do not wish to, and the only help you might offer is to put yourself on display and take up spending your days with the wives of others. But if you are happy as you are, I will not ask it of you."

"The queen's megaron." My stomach churned at the thought. The more time I spent with Theseus, the harder it was to remember I played the part of an Egyptian. But a queen had an obligation to serve, and if it would help him in any small way, I owed him as much. "That would help, wouldn't it? They would not think me a sorceress if I spent my days more in their company. They would see I could not have bewitched you, after all."

"Who has said such a thing to you?" he asked.

I pressed my lips together, chiding myself for mentioning it at all. It had been months ago, and Menestheus had kept his distance since, even if he watched me more closely than I would have liked.

"You cannot expect me to believe you imagined so specific an accusation," he said when I did not answer. "If it was one of the palace women, I will have her dismissed at once. They have no right to speak so to their queen, and I have made my feelings clear on the matter."

I shook my head to stop him before he went on at any greater length. That he'd had to speak to them at all made my heart ache, and heavy with child as I was, I did not want even to consider that he had gone to them lately for any reason.

"I had not realized the palace women found me so troublesome, though I suppose I should have known they might," I said stiffly. I would not ask him if he had availed himself of the pleasures they offered after we had been married. I did not want to know. "By all accounts you made good use of their favors before you brought me to Athens, as was your right. It is only natural they might find reason for jealousy when I replaced them. But as it happens, I did not hear it from any of your women. Indeed, it has always been my preference to avoid their company altogether, and I confess I hoped you shared it."

"I do," he said at once, his voice low and rough with emotion. His fingers tightened around mine, and my eyes closed, my relief so strong, I trembled. "I would not have you believe for a moment that I have been unfaithful to you in body or spirit. But if it was not one of the women, then I would know who spoke so disrespectfully of their queen. Of my wife!"

"I have no desire to tell tales," I said softly. "It was months ago, and there is no purpose in punishing a man simply because he shows concern for his king, and I am certain that is all it was." Perhaps that was all it had ever been. Menestheus's protectiveness of Theseus, of his king, made more sense the more I thought of it. He only wanted to be sure Theseus was not bewitched, and I could not fault him for it.

Theseus studied my face for a long moment, but queens wore their own masks at times, and mine was set in place. At last, he kissed my palm. "Today is for your pleasure, my love. Not for affairs of court. We will not think of it any further.

"Come," he said, drawing me up. "I'll pick you more strawberries."

CHAPTER THIRTY

"My lord!"

Theseus looked up from the altar in time to see the woman throw herself gasping at his feet. The further along Helen's pregnancy, the more time he had spent in prayer, begging for some sign from Hera or Zeus that all would be well, and it was not uncommon for attendants to come in search of him. He helped her up, noting absently that she was one of Aethra's servants.

"Catch your breath," he told her, removing them both from the temple and seating her on the stone steps outside. Though his heart raced in his chest, it would not do to show his own fear. He was a hero and a king, and he was bound to behave as such. "Now speak."

"The queen goes into labor! My lady Aethra says that you should come at once."

His stomach twisted, and he set his jaw. "She is in her rooms?"

"In yours, my lord. The pains came upon her while she stood weaving."

Without another word he turned and left her, holding his pace to less than a run by force of will alone. Theseus was certain Aethra would have had Ariston called just as swiftly as she had sent word to him, but it did not make him less anxious to see to Helen himself.

He shoved the door open, and Aethra glanced up at him from the bed only briefly before turning her attention back to Helen.

"Clear the room!" he commanded.

The women who buzzed about without real purpose fled past him. Ariston did not remove himself from the bedside opposite Aethra, and his mother had ignored him altogether. Theseus shut the door on the faces of the rest of the curious who lingered outside, absently noting Menestheus among them, and crossed the room.

"Breathe, my dear. Deep breaths. Let your body do its work." His mother held Helen's hand and smoothed damp hair back from her white face.

Helen sobbed, choking on a scream, and Theseus went to her side, taking Aethra's place. Helen's fingers closed on his so hard, his bones pressed together.

"Helen." He stroked her face, and she opened her eyes, turning toward his touch. "Is there anything I can do?"

She gritted her teeth on a cry as another spasm took hold, and her grip became even fiercer.

"Please," she gasped. "Just stay with me."

"Not even the gods could pry me from your side," he promised, ignoring Aethra's scowl.

She looked so pale. How long had she been in labor before he had been called? He glanced up at Ariston. The man's face looked gray, his mouth a thin line of stress.

"Why did you not send for me sooner?" Theseus asked his mother.

"The moment I knew, I sent a slave," Aethra said, her eyes on Helen's face. "I have not the time to reassure you, Theseus, and your fretting does no one any favors. If you stay, bite your tongue."

"Drink this." Ariston nodded to Theseus to help Helen sit up. The physician held a cup to her lips. She pressed them together stubbornly. "It's only water."

She drank, then sighed and lay back against the cushions and blankets piled behind her. Theseus smoothed her hair as Aethra had done, and her body relaxed.

"It might help her to walk," Aethra said, not even glancing at Ariston for his opinion. "One of you on each side to support her, if Theseus will ease her from the bed."

Helen groaned, but she let him help her up, leaning heavily against him. Ariston stood ready on her other side, but she did not reach for the physician.

"I am a whale," she complained, then gasped and almost doubled over but for his hold on her body. She cried out, clinging to him, her nails digging into his arm.

"Let it pass." Aethra pressed her hand against Helen's rounded stomach. "Just breathe."

Helen breathed through gritted teeth, her jaw tight, but another sob escaped, rending his heart, and her nails bit deeper, drawing blood.

"Are you certain this is better?" Theseus asked, watching her face. All the color had drained from it, and she moaned another cry before the moment passed and her body stopped shuddering.

"Easier for the baby, to be sure," Ariston answered. "For as long as she can stand it. But her pains are coming more quickly than I would have expected for her first birth—"

Aethra's glare stopped him abruptly. Helen did not seem to notice, but Theseus's chest tightened. Surely if there was nothing wrong, Aethra would not silence him.

"She's doing just fine for her first birth. And, Eleithyia and Artemis bless her, all the more fortunate if it comes quickly," Aethra said, though he did not think it was for his benefit. "Now, walk, my dear. Slowly. For as long as you feel able."

Helen walked, alternating between easy movement and agonized labor, sometimes so bad it took both himself and Ariston to keep her upright. But she refused to return to the bed, and Aethra and Ariston insisted that keeping her on her feet for as long as possible would help the baby to come faster. By the time Helen could no longer stand for stumbling, even Theseus was exhausted, and when the next pain struck her, Helen barely had the strength to cry.

It did not seem to Theseus as though the baby had traveled at all.

He met Aethra's pinched eyes while he helped Helen into the bed, for it was clear she was not ready for the birthing stool. His mother shook her head just slightly, her lips pursed. Theseus's stomach turned to ice, but he said nothing. Nor did he have the time to consider the implications before Helen was caught by another long spasm. He gripped her hand; Helen did not return the pressure.

❦

As the night wore on, Aethra dozed, leaning against the bedpost, and Ariston sat slumped at the table, staring at the hearth. Helen slept fitfully between her pains, and though Aethra had food and drink brought, none of them had any appetite for it, Helen least of all.

Lying beside Helen, who had curled up on her side, Theseus cradled her body and rubbed the spasms from her back when they came. At least it gave him something to do, however meager, for he could not sleep, afraid he might wake to find Helen's spirit gone.

Morning came, then midday with still no progress, and Helen growing weaker and weaker with every pain. *Artemis, spare her. Let her live.*

"I am young," she said, so softly that he barely heard her. "You need not worry. Zeus would not birth so frail a daughter."

He hushed her, stroking her hair. "Conserve your strength."

"But you worry," she said, her voice breaking. "Poseidon will keep his word, Theseus. He must."

"Shh." He kissed her head. "Rest, now."

Her breathing halted, and his heart stilled, his body stiff with fear, waiting for her chest to rise again.

A ragged sigh escaped her lips, and she drifted back to sleep.

It did not last, and she woke moaning as her body shook once more. Helen bent double over her stomach, wrapping her arms over the bulge, and cried out as though she had been kicked.

Aethra jerked awake, coming to her side again. She pressed her hands against Helen's stomach.

"We must get her to the stool. It will be now, or not at all."

It was difficult to manage while she fought against the pain, and had he not been half-god, he wondered if he would have accomplished it at all. He had never realized her strength.

Helen sobbed, clutching at her stomach, and then collapsed back against him. He steadied her, for she was far too weak to sit up on her own.

"Hold her still with the next spasm," Aethra ordered.

Ariston rose from the table, coming to help, and at Aethra's direction he supported Helen's other side, to keep her from twisting away. Not a moment later the next pain washed over her. Theseus struggled to keep her still while Aethra leaned on her stomach.

Helen screamed.

"Once more, Helen, push as hard as you can," Aethra said. "Do you hear me?"

Helen shook her head violently, sobbing and gulping.

"Please, Helen," he said.

Her body shuddered, and she cried out. Aethra leaned again and the cry turned into another scream of agony. It cut off as suddenly as it had come, and Aethra sighed. But the baby she pulled from between Helen's thighs did not cry, even after she had cleared its throat.

One arm flailed, and a tiny foot kicked. Aethra wiped it clean while Helen lay limp against Theseus, all but slipping from the stool had he not held her. That it lived at all was a miracle, but the space between Helen's breaths grew longer, and a chill settled in Theseus's bones.

"My baby," Helen whispered. "Please."

After swaddling the child, Aethra laid it in Helen's arms. But the baby did not seem interested in its mother.

"A girl," Aethra said.

She did not have to tell him the child was unlikely to survive. He could see it already in the pinched face, lips cast blue, and wide milky eyes. Helen offered her breast, but the baby turned her head, slapping at Helen with a tiny fist and trying to squirm away.

"Ariston, have the wet nurse called. Helen has work to do yet before she might sleep, and I think our senses should be spared a squalling child."

"Yes, my lady."

Helen's arms tightened around the baby. "I never asked for a wet nurse."

"Just for tonight," Aethra soothed her.

The baby blinked, and when she opened her eyes again, they had turned emerald green like her mother's. Theseus shook his head. Surely it was only his fatigue, for they had spent a long night and an even longer day.

At the sound of the door opening, Aethra took the baby back from Helen's arms, and passed the child off to the woman who entered, shooing her out again.

Too weak to protest, Helen sighed. Her body trembled beneath his hand where it rested at her waist, and then she shuddered harder.

"Help me move her back to the bed, and then you must leave us for a moment, Theseus," Aethra said. "The last of this should not be seen by men's eyes."

He did as his mother asked, settling Helen comfortably within a nest of cushions and furs, even as Aethra slipped a rag of sailcloth beneath her hips to protect the bedding. And then he squeezed Helen's hand, leaning down to kiss her forehead. "Wait for me," he said.

Helen's lips twitched in what might have been a smile if she had not been so weak. "I haven't the strength to move without your help, but I'll be fine, now. Go."

Allowing himself to be persuaded, Theseus left the room, glancing back only once as he closed the door behind him.

CHAPTER
THIRTY-ONE

Theseus was shouting.

The realization brought me out of sleep, but the words—
The words burned through me like fire, and my eyes
flashed open.

"Was Hippolytus not enough!" he roared. A crash of the sea
quenched the flames in my stomach, but my breath still caught. "Now
they would take Helen's child, too?"

Aethra stood unflinching before him, though the knuckles of
her hands were white behind her back. Theseus held a silver cup, all
but forgotten.

"If you do not obey them, you know what will come. The bargain
she struck with Poseidon will be kept if you agree to it, but the price
is terrible. He cannot protect Athens, too, or stop your people from
turning you out. Nor will he defend Helen against Zeus, and that
god is most displeased."

"Has Helen not suffered enough by her father's will?" The cup crumpled in his hands, wine spilling over his fingers and leaving trails like blood. "Even now she lies bleeding, on the edge of death! Taking the child now will kill her!"

"No!" The word burst from my throat before I could think, and Aethra moved as if to come to my side.

Theseus caught her by the arm, jerking her back.

"Go," he told her as he opened the door to the hall. "Go to the temples and find another way."

He shut the door behind her, but he did not turn to me. The lump of metal he held was no longer recognizable as a cup. He set it down on the table and wiped his hands.

"Theseus." My voice was rough, my throat thick with fear. "Theseus, what's happened?"

His jaw tightened, his hands closing around the edges of the table. And then he threw it.

The table and all its contents flew across the room. The wine jug shattered against the hearth, and the cups chimed as they bounced on the tile floor long before the table hit the plaster wall. It cracked like thunder, and if it had not been the external wall, lined with brick and stone, I did not know that it would have stopped there.

My heart pounded in my ears, and I struggled to sit up. Every muscle in my body felt stretched to breaking, and my breasts ached, too full of milk for the child Aethra had torn from my arms.

"Theseus," I gasped through the pain of being upright. It could not be. Poseidon had promised me. "Please. Tell me."

I did not see him move, but he was beside me, tucking cushions and furs behind my back and easing me against them.

"It doesn't matter," he said, his voice flat.

"My baby—"

"Our daughter is warm and fed, sleeping in the queen's room even now. I have seen it so myself."

"Then why?"

Theseus sighed, searching my face. What he saw there, I do not know, but the lines around his eyes fanned into deeper creases. He took my hand, his grip too tight.

"There has been a sign."

"You saw it?"

He shook his head. "Menestheus had a dream while you gave birth that Athens would be turned to rubble, the world laid to waste. He told the priests, and the auguries confirm it. They say we must leave the baby exposed to die."

"No!" I tried to sit up again, but he pressed me back down.

"I have forbidden them from touching our daughter, as yet. That is why Aethra came, to persuade me."

"Promise me." His face blurred, and my nails dug into his hand. "Promise you will not do this. We need only wait. Poseidon swore to protect us. That is why I went to him, Theseus! To stop this!"

"Shh," he said, stroking my hair, my cheek. "You are so weak, still. Rest now."

"I can't," I murmured, my eyes closing without my permission. "I won't."

"I know," he said.

And then I slept.

I woke again with the dawn, my hand going to my empty stomach. I had dreamed of my baby, and Apollo, with an arrow drawn, his face a mask of fire. My legs trembled when I stood, and my belly ached, but I was strong enough for this.

The door to the bathing room had been left open, and I picked my way through shards of pottery on the floor. Theseus must not have allowed the slaves to clean while I slept. The baths were empty, and the door to the queen's room stood ajar. I smiled to think Theseus might have been listening for our daughter's cries, and I pushed it open.

Hippolytus's cradle had been brought out of the storerooms and polished to gleaming a month before, the olive wood inlaid with gold and silver horses. It had sat by my bed, waiting for the child that might come. I went to it now, desperate to hold my daughter and know her safe and well, to feed her from my own breast and feel the weight of her in my arms.

But it was empty.

"No."

I threw open the door to the hall, searching for a servant, the nurse who must have fed my baby, waiting outside for her cry, but there was no one on the stool. No one in sight.

"No!"

"Helen?"

Theseus! Theseus had done this. Allowed our child to be taken. Perhaps he had even taken her himself! My legs shook, but I refused to fall. I knew where they would take her—to the stone from which Aegeus had leapt, when he believed Theseus would never return home from Crete.

I ran.

"Helen!"

Theseus's call did not slow my feet, and I sprinted through the corridors faster than I had ever run in my life. Shadow and torchlight should have tripped me, but they didn't, nor did the cold stone on my bare feet make me so much as blink. I heard Theseus behind me, shouting, begging me to wait.

I leapt down the stairs from the porch and sprinted across the outer yard of the palace, around the slaves' wing, and the kitchens, through the practice field and past the stables. I could see it now, rising above the massive stones of the wall. And I could see the bundle atop, still as death.

"Stop!"

Theseus's hand closed on my arm, and we both tumbled to the ground. I clawed myself free, biting at his fingers, and struggled toward the rocks. Up the steps, carved in the stone and worn smooth with age, on my hands and knees, even, as my legs grew weak.

"Wait!"

There. The small bundle of our daughter, swaddled in blue cloth. I reached for her, everything inside me shattering at the stillness of her body. She ought to have twitched and squirmed. She ought to have cried, wailed at the cold. A sob tangled on the back of my tongue, turning to a keen, long and raw, my throat torn by the sound. I hugged her to my breast—my daughter, still and silent and lost. Lost to me, forever.

"I had no choice," Theseus said, behind me. "She would have destroyed everything if she'd lived. The gods saw it. Wasted lands, Athens in ruin, and you dead, Helen."

I whirled, still cradling our daughter to my chest. "She is my daughter! An innocent baby!"

"She is a princess of Athens."

He reached for her, to take her back, and I tried to strike him, to bite, to scratch, while I held her tight, but Theseus was stronger. His hand turned to iron on my flailing arm, my worthless, strengthless body, and with a deft twist, he defeated me altogether, our child's body tucked in the crook of his arm as he turned away. I hugged myself, shivering, tears streaming down my cheeks, though everything inside me felt numb and broken and so twisted.

Theseus set her down again upon the rock, so carefully, so reverently, and when he turned back to me, I could see every line of his age so clearly. My gaze slid away, back to the small, cold bundle of our daughter. I did not want to see his pain when I held so much of my own, already. Too much, filling me up with bitterness and rage.

"Listen to me, Helen," he said, shaking me until I met his eyes. "In this, she serves her people, if nothing else. Would you have let her live, if it meant death to all who look to you? This was Zeus's price. Her life, or the lives of every man, woman, and child; a thousand times worse than the war you dreamed of, and no glory, no honor, nothing but death! This is why they did not want me to have you!"

I shook my head, my eyes blinded by tears. "We were supposed to be free, Theseus. You and I. We were going to be free! Poseidon promised me peace. We could have saved her from it. We could have stopped this, too."

His hands gentled, and he pulled me against his chest, tucking my head beneath his chin. For the first time, I realized he was naked, and his skin burned against mine, blazing even in the chill of dawn.

"Not this time," he murmured. "Don't you see, Helen? The bargain you struck was for your life in exchange, and Apollo had the arrow strung. I could not bear to lose another wife in such a way, not even for our daughter. I could not let them take you."

"Better if they had." I shoved him away, and he stumbled back. "I would rather have been dead than give my daughter up to Zeus."

I left him there, atop the rocks, and I didn't look back.

CHAPTER THIRTY-TWO

In the queen's rooms, the sight of the cradle brought the image of the bundle above the wall, and the room blurred, my eyes burning. I fell to the floor beside it and pressed my face against the wood, the metal inlays cold against my burning cheeks.

My daughter. My girl. We had not even named her, yet.

I did not hear Theseus over my own weeping, but I felt his hand on my shoulder and the warmth of his body beside mine. He tore my fingers from the wood and drew me away from the cradle, pulling me into his arms instead.

"I am so sorry, Helen," he murmured. "I am so sorry I could not stop this."

"You left her," I sobbed. "You left her in the cold. Left her to Zeus."

"Not Zeus," he said, smoothing my hair beneath his chin. "The dead belong to Hades, and that is where her shade flies. Zeus will never touch her. Never know her. Never look into her eyes. She is safe from him, more free now in death than she could ever be alive."

I clung to him as my thoughts clung to his words.

"It's over," he said, his voice hoarse with his own pain. "The price is paid, and the world is safe. Mycenae does not know you as anything but a princess of Egypt, and Sparta has given up the search for its missing daughter. We need fear nothing now."

"Nothing but the gods," I said.

He pulled back and caught my chin, forcing me to meet his eyes. "Nothing, Helen."

Waves against stone, and the cliff face crashed into the sea. Theseus was the ocean, and in his face, the gods were only rocks, to be worn away and drowned in time. Looking at him, I almost believed it.

But it did not bring back my daughter.

⁕

Theseus did not leave my side for days, refusing all requests for his presence to see to my needs. For the most part, his people mourned with us, respecting their king's choice. The bright hope of a princess of Athens had left the city in shadow with its loss, and Theseus and I grieved in peace.

Mostly, I slept, not wanting even to look at Theseus but needing him all the same. Even rising from the bed to relieve myself took more fortitude than I had. My run to the wall had sapped me of what strength I had gained, and I still cried in my sleep for the baby I had struggled so hard to birth.

And I still feared the gods. But more than that, I hated them. So much for Poseidon's kindness. He was no better than Zeus, slippery and deceitful, offering hollow promises we could not have risked letting him keep.

"Can you mix me a potion?" I asked Aethra while she helped me bathe. I did not have the strength to do it alone, and I did not want

Theseus's help. I was too sore and too bitter to make love and did not want to tempt him. "One to stop me from conceiving?"

She paused in the motion of scrubbing my back, and I turned my head to look at her.

"I will not survive this a second time, Aethra. Even now, I wish he had let me die more often than not. And he will always do as the gods ask. He is sworn to it, and no matter what he says, I know he will not break the vow."

She sighed, dunking the sponge in the water and taking up where she had left off. "I will speak to Ariston. Perhaps he knows of something that will be better than what I can make, for the potion I know of does not always work."

"I do not know what else to do." My throat tightened, and I splashed my face with water to hide the tears that pressed behind my eyes. "I want nothing more than to forgive him, to put this behind us and never think of it again. But sometimes I look at him, and it is all I can see. I have to close my hands into fists to keep from scratching his eyes out. I know I should not blame him, that it is the gods who made this happen, but it was his hands that carried her to the wall. If I had told him when I dreamed of it, perhaps we could have stopped it. Perhaps if I had not gone to Poseidon . . ."

She hushed me, stroking my hair. "You must cleave to each other, and in time, it will be easier to go on."

I shook my head. "He warned me, before we married. But when he told me the story of Hippolytus, I never dreamed it could happen again. I saw the pain in his eyes, Aethra, and it has never left him. You say to give it time, but he has spent more than ten years mourning. I should have listened, then."

"Did you love him?" she asked.

"Yes."

"And do you still?"

I swallowed against the lump in my throat. "Yes."

"Then you will heal together." She squeezed the water from the sponge over my shoulders. "And I will find you any potions you require."

~❦~

Theseus watched me recover, occasionally chiding me to let my body mend as it must. The worry I had felt from him during my pregnancy had been replaced with a calm certainty I could not share, no matter how much I wished to. But I remembered what Aethra had said, and so I had begun to let him help me when I hurt, and in the night when I cried, I turned into his arms for comfort. I think we both felt the stronger for it.

But I was still not strong enough.

"You are more patient than I am." I leaned heavily on Theseus's arm while I walked about the room. No matter how I lay in the bed, my body ached from it.

"After seeing you struggle for every breath, this is a marked improvement." But he smiled as though he knew my thoughts. "A wound on my thigh kept me in my bed for near a month, once. Every time I rose, a fever would grow. Aethra almost killed me herself to keep me off it in the first days, but then I became too miserable to argue."

"What was it from?" Theseus was so filled with life and vitality; I could not picture him crippled by anything.

"A bull gored me at Marathon. A furious beast rampaging on the shore."

"Pirithous said you charmed bulls not to gore."

Theseus smiled again, looking down at me. "And if you believe everything Pirithous tells you, you will think I can breathe water and ride dolphins across the sea with no need of a ship."

"Can't you?" I had missed his teasing, though part of me hated missing anything from him. I understood what he had done, even why, but how could I forgive it? How could he have forgiven me? I hated myself as much as I hated him.

He twitched a shoulder. "I have never been shipwrecked, no matter how terrible the storm, and often enough I have sailed distances in half the time it might take other men on a similar ship, but I hardly ride dolphins even if I swim like a fish. How I escaped serious injury in the Cretan bull ring, I can only attribute to my father's protection."

Poseidon's protection. I fell silent for several heartbeats. I should have known better than to trust any god, no matter how Theseus and Aethra spoke of them. And I had thought myself so wise, but I had not believed the gods would give Theseus so great a reason to object. A kingdom of people for the life of one child, and my death as well. I should have known. "I cannot do this again, Theseus. To myself. To you. To the child who might die for it."

He squeezed my hand. "I would not ask it of you, though I am sorry for it. I wish I had known to warn you before we married. I wish I had known not to give you a child at all."

I tried to smile. "It would not have stopped me from trying to thwart them."

"Perhaps not," he said. "But we both would have been more prepared for the loss. We could have guarded our hearts against it, even if we hoped for something different."

"Was this what it felt like, before?" I asked, unable to stop myself.

Theseus sighed. "Hippolytus, you mean?"

"Yes."

He shook his head. "I was alone in that grief. For a long time. It made it easier to dwell on my sorrow when I had no one to share it with. I picked at it like a scab, never letting it heal. Until I loved you."

I did not know what to say, so I said nothing. But Theseus stopped me and turned my face up to his.

"Even if we can have nothing more, it does not matter to me, as long as we have each other. I do not think my heart can beat without yours."

I brought his hand to my chest, over my heart. "Then I will have to make sure it never stops."

He leaned down and kissed me, for the first time since before our daughter had been born. Nothing more than a soft brush of his lips against mine. But even so, even after all that we had been through, and in spite of all our pain, my pulse quickened in response.

I knew then that Aethra had been right.

"Come," Theseus said, lifting me up into his arms. "You've time for a nap before Aethra brings the evening meal, and you are white with exhaustion."

—❈—

The next morning while he bathed, I tore all my weaving from the loom and began again, unable to bear the reminder of the future I had envisioned, of the family we might have been. If Theseus noticed, he did not comment, but the basket never emptied of yarn, and the colors I needed always sat ready.

It was days before I realized what I wove, my mind too distracted to make sense of what my fingers did. Fire and smoke leapt from shining gold towers into a purple sky.

The burning city of my nightmares.

Theseus stared at it over my shoulder for a long moment, and for the first time since our daughter's birth, he left me to pray.

I wished I were well enough to do the same.

CHAPTER
THIRTY-THREE

Pirithous arrived by sea and rode through the gate with the last of the sunlight.

"You should have sent for me sooner," Pirithous said in greeting. "To celebrate if not to mourn."

Theseus shook his head. "It happened too quickly to think of it, and my wife has not been well." He clasped hands with his friend. "It is good to see you."

Pirithous grasped his shoulder. "I only wish I brought you better news. We must speak, and better it be done in private."

"My rooms—"

"You will not wish your wife to hear what I have come to say. Not after what's happened. I am not sure you will wish to hear it yourself, but it must be said."

Theseus studied his face, noticing the lines of strain. "We'll go riding."

Pirithous nodded.

Theseus caught a servant by the arm. "Have fresh horses brought. And send a message to my queen. We'll return to her before the evening meal. A feast in Pirithous's honor."

"Yes, my lord."

Theseus glanced up at the balcony of his room. More than a month after the loss, Helen still spent much of her day there, weaving and resting. He did everything he could to raise her spirits, but it was clear her heart still ached. He could not blame her for it. But he wished she had not begun weaving a burning citadel. It did her no good to dwell on the futures she had abandoned, and it made his heart break to think she might be wishing she had not left Sparta to be his wife. Would she have preferred that war to the loss of her daughter? He could not ask. He did not want to hear the answer.

Helen stood at the rail, dressed in a simple chiton of red linen. She had wrapped the golden cord belt in a crisscross pattern from her hips to her rib cage, tying it beneath her breasts. The sunset gilded the bare skin of her thigh where it showed, and he closed his hand into a fist to keep from imagining the softness of it against his fingertips.

It had been too long since he had loved her, but he worried she would not welcome his touch the way she once had. It was another question he feared the answer to.

"She is still as lovely as ever, Theseus."

"Yes," he agreed. "And she will be pleased to see you, no matter what news you've brought. If only because you had no part in her sorrow."

Pirithous snorted. "Then perhaps I should give thanks to the gods, because until now she has barely tolerated me but for love of you."

The horses were led out to them and they mounted. There was not much light left for the ride, but the distance from the palace would keep them from being heard. Theseus pressed his fist to his forehead, offering Helen the salute, and was rewarded by a smile before they left.

When the palace and the city were behind them, they dismounted. Theseus led the way to a small spring in a grove of olive trees where the horses might drink, and Pirithous could wash the dust of his trip from his arms and face. He had taken Helen here, once. And he had made love to her in the dappled sunlight, on a bed of olive leaves and their cloaks.

Pirithous crouched by the stream, staring into the water. "You know that I sent men out, after we learned of the unnamed price, and again when the Egyptian god sent warning."

"Of course," Theseus said. "And you have learned something from them, after all this time?"

Pirithous splashed water on his face, turning the dust on his skin into mud. "Zeus fears the child of two demigods will unseat him from his throne. You birthed a goddess between you, Theseus, and Zeus wanted no threat to his power."

Theseus let out the breath he had been holding, but the ocean roared in his ears, and he steadied himself against the flank of his horse. "Zeus lied."

"I am sure the threat to Helen was real enough. If you had refused them and born a second child with Helen, and those children united against the gods . . ." Pirithous shook his head. "Perhaps if Helen had been more devout, more obedient to their commands, as you are, it would have been different, but I doubt Zeus would have risked it. If his daughter hates him, it is no one's fault but his own." He paused, his lips curving. "And perhaps Leda's. That woman was filled to bursting with venom."

"Helen was right," Theseus murmured. The words settled like stone in his stomach. All those times she had accused Zeus of accomplishing nothing without deceit. She had never trusted the gods, and even when she had tried to, with Poseidon—his father had taken advantage of her desperation, even if he had not lied outright. He could not imagine Helen agreeing to the terms, otherwise. She was queen, and Spartan besides, too aware of her duty to throw away the lives of so many, even for her own daughter.

"You cannot blame yourself, Theseus. You did what you had to do to save your wife, perhaps even your city. If you had not obeyed, your nobles would have seen to it that you no longer wore your crown. You would have lost everything. Helen would have lost everything."

Theseus laughed, but the sound was broken and hollow even to his own ears. "The gods would have taken everything, you mean. Everything I had built in their service, to honor them above all, struck down because they could not trust me to raise a child who might love them."

Pirithous gave him a look filled with pity. "After everything the gods have done to you, Theseus, what reason could any child of yours have to love them? Even the blindest man can see the injustice, the cruelty with which they've treated you. Your children would have loved you, as Acamas and Demophon do, but they could not have loved the gods who caused you so much pain, and took their mother, even if you insist upon your own loyalty."

"No longer," he said, his hand so tight a fist at his side that his knuckles ached. "I have done my duty and then some, and this is how they have repaid me. With deceit. With betrayal. The gods will have nothing more from me. Zeus will have nothing more from either of us."

"And what of your father? And Athena?"

Theseus shook his head. "If they do not answer me now, they will find I no longer answer them."

Pirithous wiped his face on his arm, smearing dirt more than cleaning it, and rose. "Will you tell Helen?"

"It will only give her more pain when she has not put the worst of it behind her yet. I still wake to find her crying in the night, though much less frequently now. On her good days, you would not know she suffered, and she behaves toward me as if nothing happened between us. But on other days . . . She still has not forgiven me, I think, for letting her daughter die in her place."

They led the horses from the grove and mounted again, turning them back toward the walls.

Pirithous pressed his lips together, studying the horizon. "She will," he said after a moment.

To Theseus, it sounded like a threat, and he glanced at his friend, sidelong. "She is not some servant to bend to your desires, Pirithous."

He shrugged and offered a smile, too artful to be reassuring. "I would never dream of toying with her thoughts, of course. But leave it in my hands, all the same. She will gaze upon you with adoration before the night is through, Theseus. I promise you."

He wanted it too much—this rift between them healed. His heart had ached for too long, and so had hers. Whatever Pirithous had in mind, it was better if he did not know.

⬥

Coated with dust and horse hair from the ride, they both needed a proper bath before the feast, and Theseus sent word ahead to have it prepared. Helen met them in his room, overseeing the maids while they heated the water and laid towels for their guest.

"My lady." Pirithous bowed over her hand. "Theseus said you would be pleased to see me, but I confess I did not believe him."

She smiled. "I assure you my presence was simply a question of expedience. I'm too hungry to wait for you to dally with the maids."

He laughed and swept her another bow. "I promise that if I do dally, it will be quickly done."

Helen waved him away to the bath that had been drawn for him, and the maid shut the door only far enough for modesty, not privacy.

Theseus smiled. "You make a very wise queen."

Helen sighed, raising her eyes to the ceiling when Pirithous began making exaggerated noises of pleasure. She crossed the room and poured three cups of wine before passing one to Theseus and taking up another for herself.

"If he wanted to take his time, he should have considered that before making off with you on a sunset ride."

"He needed to speak to me privately," he told her, though she would not have asked directly. "It seemed the best way to keep it from the servants' ears at the time."

"The servants' ears? Or mine?"

Theseus stroked her cheek, his fingers finding their way into her hair. Soft as silk. Her eyes dropped and her face flushed. Tonight, he thought. He would not spend another night as a coward in his own bed. He had to try. And perhaps it would help her to find room in her heart to forgive him if her body remembered the way.

"He wanted to give me his personal regrets, and feared upsetting you with the mention of it." It was not entirely a lie, and in the service of her health, he felt it warranted.

"Oh," she said.

He kissed her forehead. "Thank you for this. I know it was not only to hurry him, for Aethra might have accomplished the same goal."

"Pirithous was kind to come so quickly," she murmured. "He honors us by it, and it is only right he be shown the same respect. But do not tell him I said so. He does not need any encouragement."

One of the maids squealed in obvious delight, and Helen wrinkled her nose.

"With us standing right here?" she asked.

Theseus chuckled. *"Because* we're standing right here."

"I gave the maids strict orders."

"Yes, and I'm sure Pirithous has driven those orders right from their heads, or fogged their minds with enough lust that they've forgotten at least."

Helen's eyes widened, the blush in her cheeks draining away. "He can do that?"

"Just as he encouraged the guards to look the other way when you left Sparta. I've used the same power to help calm you, when you wake in the night, though I cannot say I have ever used it to get a woman in my bed." He grimaced. "Gifts from our fathers."

Helen fell silent, her lips pressed into a thin line and her body going stiff.

"Helen?" Theseus frowned, dismayed by the transformation. "What's the matter?"

Her jaw tightened, and she shook her head as if to clear it. "Can any god gift it? Or must you be born with such a talent?"

"The gods can give any gift they please to any man. But Pirithous and I were born with it in our blood." He smoothed the crease from her forehead. "What's upset you so? If you fear I abused you, I swear upon the Styx, I have never sought to influence your thoughts or change your mind. Nor has Pirithous. I thought you knew—that everyone knew."

She shook her head again, her gaze shifting over his shoulder. He turned to look, his eyes falling on the loom, with its flame and smoke rising over a city.

"I always wondered how I could have gone with this prince, knowing what I do. Even to escape Menelaus, it seemed impossible. And in the dreams, sometimes, I wanted him. But how could I have betrayed my people? But if what you say is true, if some men are blessed by this—this power, and I have succumbed to it already, even in so small a way as you have described . . . What if the prince shares it? What if that is why I followed him?"

He lifted her chin, catching her eyes with his and trying desperately to ignore the chill that settled in his heart with the words.

"It does not matter now," he told her. "He will never take you. Not as long as you are my wife."

"Well then," Pirithous said, announcing his presence. "I told you I could dally quickly enough."

Theseus dropped his hand from her face and she turned away, busying herself with the wine jug at the table. He dragged his attention to Pirithous, who was dressed only in a towel.

"I suppose you did not think to bring any clean tunics in your haste," Theseus said.

"I supposed you had more clothing than you'll ever wear and wouldn't begrudge the lending of it to your cousin. Or am I your brother now, since you've married my half sister?"

He sighed. "The chest to your right, Pirithous, and be sure you don't expose yourself to my wife."

"Of course." Pirithous grinned, taking the wine cup from his hand. "You'd better hurry, Theseus. I have it on good authority that Helen is starving."

Helen rolled her eyes and crossed the room to the chest Theseus had indicated. Theseus's last sight of Pirithous included the tunic she had thrown at his head.

CHAPTER
THIRTY-FOUR

Pirithous sobered at once after Theseus disappeared into the bathing room, and for the first time, when he looked at me, I did not feel as though he imagined me in his bed. I turned my back on him to let him dress, and tried not to be bothered by the lack of humor in his eyes. I had never known Pirithous to be serious, and I did not want to think what it meant now.

"Theseus said you would not be offended if I offered you my sympathy," he said quietly, coming to the table after he had dressed. "But there is more that I would say, though he would not wish me to."

"If Theseus thinks you are better served by keeping it to yourself, perhaps you should listen." I took a long drink of my wine, already unsettled by what Theseus had told me, echoing as it did the dream I'd had the night before.

It was the nightmare I had hoped never to have again. I could still feel the strange prince's hand at my waist, and taste the dust rising from the movement of so many men. I had felt his desire, thick in the air, infecting me, and I wished for Theseus to take me away.

"It is something you should know, and I believe it will give you comfort. Theseus has only kept it from you this long out of fear that the people of Athens will learn the truth."

I looked up at him then, searching for some hint in his features. "Why should Theseus fear his people? He only serves them."

"Not in this," Pirithous said, stepping so near to me, I could feel the heat of his body and his breath against my ear. "And if they learn of it, he would lose his kingdom, and all he has done will be for nothing. You will be lucky to escape with your lives."

"Pirithous—"

"Your daughter lives," he breathed. "He exchanged her with another, stillborn, and secreted her away."

My heart stopped and my breathing with it.

"You must not tell him what I've said, Helen. If even for a moment the people of Athens suspect, through a look exchanged between you or a whisper at the wrong moment, they will find her and kill her, just as surely as if he had left her to die. Do you understand me?"

I nodded, not trusting myself to speak. I did not think I would ever have air in my chest again. My daughter. Our daughter. And Theseus, forced to let me grieve, unable to even tell me what he had done, knowing it would bring me too much joy. Suffering my anger, my pain at his betrayal, though he had never betrayed me at all. Though he had chosen me and our daughter over the gods. Even over Athens.

Pirithous stepped back, and I stared into his face. His lips curved as he raised his cup to drink. It was as if he read my mind.

"Thank you," I managed to say, grasping his hand.

He set aside his cup and kissed my fingers before letting me go.

When Theseus came from the bath and we descended to the feast below, I clasped my husband's hand, hoping that in my touch, he would feel everything I could not say. He raised his eyebrows, looking down at me, before his gaze shifted to Pirithous, who had donned a mask of innocence almost at once.

Perhaps I could not mother her myself, but it was enough to know she lived, and Theseus had made it so.

More than enough.

⊰※⊱

I did not stay long at the feast, too distracted by my thoughts and not trusting myself to keep from my eyes the secret Pirithous had told me. When Pirithous began boasting about the woman he hoped to win as his wife, I excused myself, leaving Theseus to drink with his friend.

Weaving kept me occupied while I dreamed of the daughter I had thought lost. I let my mind wander while I worked, trusting my fingers to draw what they wished in the fabric. Since it had begun that way, I saw no reason not to finish it in the same manner.

The sun set, but the full moon and the hearth fire gave me light enough to weave, so I continued. The tapestry grew, the skyline of the city clear now, even engulfed in flame.

Flame that would never consume me, if last night's dream was true, though the city itself would perish. And now, knowing my daughter lived, I no longer wished to be devoured by such a fire.

"You're still awake?" The door shut, but Theseus did not come to stand behind me as he often did, nor did he kiss me in greeting.

I glanced back to see him seated on the edge of the bed. He dropped his head into his hands, his shoulders bowed under an unseen weight. I abandoned the yarn in my hands. The pinched look around his eyes disturbed me. An evening spent drinking wine with Pirithous should not have upset him so.

"Did Pirithous outdrink you?"

Theseus snorted and rubbed his forehead. "If it were only that, I would sleep easily."

"Then what?" I knelt between his knees, that I might see his expression more clearly.

His fingers traced the line of my jaw from my earlobe to my chin. I closed my eyes, leaning into his touch. When Theseus pulled me up from the floor and into his arms, I did not resist. For too long I had refused him, unwilling to love him, insisting that I was not yet recovered. Now more than ever, I missed my husband's love.

He drew me into his lap and hid his face against my neck. I stroked his hair, determined not to show my frustration, though my cheeks had flushed hot with anticipation.

He sighed into my hair. "I don't know how I will ever leave you."

My blood ran cold.

"Why?" I asked, barely able to speak the word.

"Securing Pirithous his bride will require a journey," he said.

"Let me come, then. Bring me with you. I promise I will not slow your travel. I'm a good rider. Castor and Pollux saw to that."

He lifted his head, and the brief hope that he would grant me such a concession turned to ice in my stomach.

"A journey to the house of Hades, Helen," he said quietly. "And that is no place to bring a wife, even if she is the daughter of Zeus."

My forehead furrowed. But when I opened my mouth to ask, he pressed a finger to my lips.

"A trip to Hades's realm is not without risks, I know. But I cannot turn my back on Pirithous in this after everything he has done for us, even if I had not sworn myself to it with that foolish oath—and I do not think for a moment he did not know what he was about, then, asking me for my oath upon the Styx. He would have me show him the way to the gates of the Underworld, but that is only the beginning, the easiest piece of this quest. He means to steal Persephone, and for that he will need the help of another demigod."

I pulled his hand away, searching his face. "You can't be serious. Even if you find the gates, Pirithous cannot take the wife of a god!"

"I know the way. As a youth I passed the gates and destroyed the monsters set before them. As for what Pirithous can or cannot do . . ." Theseus shrugged. "He claims Persephone has called to him in his dreams, begging him to free her."

"His dreams!" I launched myself from his arms and turned away, hugging myself.

"It is the same proof you offered, Helen, when you begged me to take you from Sparta. The same proof you acted upon, in seeking Poseidon's favors. Am I to trust you, and not him?"

I shook my head, ignoring the reproof. He could not mean it. He could not do it! How long would Pirithous drag Theseus through the Underworld, and how far? Too far. Even if they succeeded, and I did not see how they would steal a goddess without being caught, Theseus would still be lost to me. For months, possibly for years.

"Is Pirithous's bride more important than the world? You said he would not have left me to Menelaus, before. He must see reason now. He must know what it will mean. You would give me up to Menelaus, and then this strange prince, if you go."

"I will leave you well guarded in Demophon's keeping. And surely if Menelaus knew you were here, he would have come already to take you."

I could not bring myself to look at him, for fear he would see the tears I fought. A moment's peace and joy, shattered already. "If you leave, they will find me, and then the city will burn. I've seen it, Theseus. In the dream, you are lost, and I am trapped by a foreign prince."

"Shh." Theseus caught me, pulling me into his arms. "Helen, you will be safe. I swear it. You have no need to worry over this old fear. You are Meryet, now, queen of Athens. You have not had a nightmare in more than a year!"

I shoved at his chest to free myself. My eyes burned with tears. "The dream came last night!"

He stumbled back, though I was not sure if it was because I pushed him, or the shock of my words. "Last night?"

"I did not want to worry you. I thought perhaps it was only my own fears. Too much time spent at the loom."

Theseus dropped back to the bed and stared at the hearth fire. "Then you do not know for certain."

"This is a fool's errand, Theseus! I know that much, without a doubt."

Yes, we owed our marriage to Pirithous, but now he asked too much, trapping Theseus within a cage of honor and oaths. I would never forgive him for this. Theseus had already suffered. We had both already suffered more than our share. How could Pirithous in one moment bring me so much hope, and in the next strip it from us? A true son of Zeus!

"The gods will not forgive it," I said. "Even if you succeed, they might take me from you out of spite. You know Hades will not let this go unpunished, and the gods have little love for you already and even less for me. Athena cannot protect you in Hades's own house!"

He dragged his fingers through his hair as if he would rip it from his scalp. The silence choked me, filled as it was with his determination. His gaze shifted over my shoulder, and his face grew even more lined. I did not have to look to know what he saw.

The loom and the citadel in its threads, set aflame.

"Persephone can be found in the Underworld only during the winter months," he said at last. "There are two months still before solstice. If you dream again, perhaps more will be made clear, and Pirithous might be persuaded."

Two months.

Two months until I lost everything.

CHAPTER THIRTY-FIVE

The nightmare came again.

Menelaus himself breaks down the door, his sword drawn and murder in his eyes. He grabs me, twisting my arm behind my back to pin me against the wall.

"Tell me why I should let you live," he growls in my ear. His body presses against my back, trembling with his rage.

I close my eyes, my face forced against the cool plaster wall. "Kill me, then. Better if you had done that than taken me as your wife."

He twists my arm harder, making me cry out. "You think that if you beg me to kill you, I'll show you pity?"

My shoulder feels as though it will pop free from its joint, and I choke on a sob.

"Do you think I did not hear the rumors of Meryet? Menestheus told me it was you! Theseus's wife! And where is that great hero to save you, now? I'm sure you didn't hear of his death while you were locked away inside these walls, sheltered and safe while men die for your love."

Tears fill my eyes, streaming down my cheeks. I cannot ask about Theseus without enraging Menelaus further. Nothing I say now will help me.

"Or maybe you did hear of it, and that's why you beg me to kill you now. So you can return to your lover in the Underworld. Your noble hero. Do you know how he died?"

When I do not answer, he twists my arm again, and I can no longer hold back the sob in my throat. Theseus. My love. My hero. My chest feels as though it will burst with sorrow.

"He was so crippled, he could not even walk without aid." Menelaus sneers. "Your famous husband slipped and fell off a cliff, and Poseidon let him drown in the sea. The gods did not even let him die with honor after his betrayal."

"No." My voice cracks on the word. The image of the man I loved so weakened is too much. Dead now. Drowned. I have nothing left.

"Menestheus made sure of it. He could not risk Theseus returning to Athens, after all, while he was absent, waging this war. Just as I could not risk Castor and Pollux taking Sparta after you had gone."

My brothers. My brothers, too. "I don't believe you."

Menelaus laughs. "What else could keep them from fighting for you, Helen, if not their deaths?"

My body shook with grief even as the hand holding my arm fell away. Another touched my shoulder, gentle and kind.

"Helen," a different voice called. "You're dreaming."

Theseus. My living, breathing Theseus. I opened my eyes and stared into his.

He sighed with relief and caressed my cheek, wiping the tears away with his fingers. "I did not think you would ever wake."

"You can't go."

"Shh." He gathered me into his arms, tucking my head beneath his chin.

I hid my face against his chest. "Please, Theseus. You cannot go. I'll never see you again. And Pollux! He'll kill Pollux and Castor!"

"Shh," he said again, kissing the top of my head. "Put it from your mind. The morning will be soon enough to discuss it. Rest, now."

"Menestheus." But my eyes were already heavy, and the words were difficult to find. I grasped for them, desperate to warn him of his own death, if nothing else. "You'll slip . . ."

When I woke again, Theseus was already gone.

I sought out Pirithous that morning, and it did not improve my mood to find him flirting with a kitchen maid. The girl on his knee rose at once when she saw me, and Pirithous grinned.

"My lady." His gaze swept over me, and his smile widened. "I'm honored."

My eyes narrowed, and though I had not made it my business to interfere with the running of Aethra's kitchens, my glance at the other women sent them from the room faster than any order I might have spoken.

Pirithous chuckled. "You make a fine queen, my lady."

I slapped him across the face so hard, my hand stung. He had me by the wrist before I had even thought to step back, rising from his seat in the same fluid motion.

"Once, and deservedly, I might accept violence from your hand, Helen." He towered over me, and his jerk on my arm nearly lifted me off my feet. "But it is not my habit to ignore such an offense a second time."

I raised my chin. "You've earned it this time, too, coming here with such a favor in mind. To think I welcomed you as a friend!"

"I am owed!" He released me, and I fell into the counter, the stone bruising my ribs. "You would not even be here if not for me and the help I gave you both. Now you take offense when I ask for repayment of that debt?"

"To steal the wife of a god, Pirithous, yes! You know how much the gods have already hurt him. He spends more time on his knees than he does on his feet!"

"All the more reason!"

"More reason for what? For him to castigate himself further? You cannot think you will succeed in this. Even if you reach the Underworld, do you really think Hades will let you leave alive? You said yourself men like you are not meant to marry goddesses, but to serve them!"

"And so I do. Persephone calls me and I answer. Just as the gods called you to leave Sparta. Just as Poseidon called Theseus to Crete! I have helped him more times than I can count, and now I ask one favor in return. One! Theseus knows the way better than any mortal, and he has already fought against these demons and won."

"In his youth!"

Pirithous stepped forward, crowding me against the counter. "Theseus is my only chance at this. Without him, I will fail before I begin."

"With him or not, you will fail." I glared up at him. If I had not been so furious, the flash in his eyes would have terrified me, for there was no kindness left in his face. "Do you have any idea how many men will die for this, Pirithous? He will never forgive himself for what will come because he left with you, and in the end it will mean his death as well!"

"Theseus has already lived a longer life than most," Pirithous said. "At least if he dies in this, he will have some kind of revenge for everything he has suffered at the hands of the gods."

"Then we will never be free," I shouted. "After everything he has done to give us that, you would waste it!"

"Love is never a waste." His fist crashed into the table behind me, and I flinched at the crack of stone. "You should know that better than anyone!"

"You think a goddess will ever love you? Will ever live at your side? We are nothing to them, Pirithous. Nothing but dirt to grind beneath their heels. You know it as truth. You've witnessed it in everything Theseus has suffered. They deserve nothing from us, least of all our love!"

"Don't you understand?" He grabbed me again, his fingers digging into my arm. "Your daughter did not have to die! If you had believed, if you had trusted, they would have let you keep her, to be raised to serve them. You brought this down on him, Helen. You did this, not the gods."

He threw me away from him then, sending me into the wall. I slid down it, his words a knife in my stomach, poisoning my blood. I was too stunned even to weep. "But you said . . ."

"I lied," he snarled. "Because Theseus deserved some happiness, after everything he had suffered. You are not the only one who lost a child in all this, and if you had only trusted him instead of going to Poseidon behind his back—" He snapped his mouth shut on the rest of what he would say, and turned away. "You had no right to punish him for doing his duty. Not then, and not now."

And then he left me there, with his words spinning through my mind.

He had lied to me. He had lied, and the truth was so much worse.

Our daughter was dead because of me.

⊰❋⊱

I returned to our rooms midday, only to find him sharing a private meal with Pirithous. Theseus saw me before I could withdraw, and he rose to welcome me.

"I had the last of the strawberries brought for you, in the hope that you would return to eat them," he said, pouring me a glass of wine. "And Pirithous brought you oranges."

"The least I could do," Pirithous said, "considering that I must ask you to part with your husband."

"Am I asked?" I sat down beside Theseus with ill grace. "I was under the impression you had made up your minds without me."

Pirithous smiled, but his eyes were hard. His gaze shifted over my shoulder, and he frowned. "Is that your weaving, Helen?"

"Who else?" I turned my attention to the table. A cold haunch of boar sat on a platter, and Theseus deposited several slices on my plate.

"I had not realized you had been to Troy itself," Pirithous said.

I glanced back at the loom. "Troy?"

"The golden towers are impossible to mistake. I'm surprised you did not recognize it, Theseus, as often as you trade with them." Pirithous poured himself more wine. "Is that the city you see in your dreams?"

"Yes." My mouth had gone dry.

Pirithous laughed and raised his cup in a toast. "If Agamemnon calls for war against Troy, he may count on me to fight. The sack of Priam's city will bring glory and riches beyond even what Heracles has attained. To have my name included among those who won it would be as good as immortality, whatever the price."

Theseus's frown told me he did not share Pirithous's enthusiasm. "The man who comes for you, Helen, he is a prince?"

I nodded.

"One of Priam's sons, then," Theseus said.

"He has a brother. Tall and grim, broad across the shoulders. He leads the army."

Theseus exchanged a glance with Pirithous. "Hector. Priam's oldest son and Troy's future king. But I would have thought the man had more sense than that."

"He's young enough yet to reach for glory over reason," Pirithous said.

"But which of the sons would be foolish enough to steal another man's wife?"

Pirithous shrugged. "Wasn't there a prophecy? Something about a son of Priam bringing fire to Troy? But they had the child exposed as a babe. It is done with."

Just as Theseus had exposed our own? I bit my tongue on the words. I would not pain Theseus further. Not when the blame was mine. Pirithous had not lied about that much.

"Besides," Pirithous continued, "Helen cannot be stolen from Menelaus while she is not Menelaus's wife. As long as she is in Athens, none of this matters."

"And when you and Theseus leave, who will stop Menelaus from reclaiming me?"

"Demophon and Menestheus will see to your safety," Theseus said.

Menestheus. I shivered at the name. "In my dream last night, Menelaus told me Menestheus had you pushed off a cliff to your death."

Pirithous snorted. "I would give chests of gold to see the man attempt it. To think that anyone could topple Theseus with a push is absurd."

Theseus searched my face, and I went on, though it hurt my heart to do so.

"He said you were crippled." The words came out as a whisper. "You fell into the sea and drowned."

Theseus touched my cheek. "I am born of the sea. Returning to it does not frighten me. I would simply swim to safety."

"At least we know it will not be our journey to the house of Hades that kills you," Pirithous said. "I find it a great reassurance to know you are pushed off a cliff to your doom."

Theseus smiled. "There, you see? You've nothing to fear about my going with Pirithous. Your own dreams have said as much."

"But if Menestheus is your enemy—"

"Menestheus is my cousin, my blood, and he has served Athens loyally for decades. He would not act against her interests, and if he did, the people would not allow him as their king. Can you imagine any Athenian turning a blind eye to a plot against me? You have seen the devotion of my people, Helen. That will not change because I have honored a promise to a friend. And why should Menestheus want the kingship when he has done so well as my steward and adviser? He has been rewarded, time and again, and he knows his place. Kingship is not an easy burden to bear."

"If you are gone, Menestheus will take advantage," I said.

"Even if such a threat existed—and I do not believe for a moment Menestheus would reach so far—Demophon will not permit it. Just as he will not permit any harm to befall you in my absence." He passed me the bowl of strawberries. "Eat, now. If there is more to discuss, it will be done later."

Ignoring the bowl, I stared at him, half-tempted to take my meal elsewhere. Something of my feelings must have shown in my face, for Theseus set the berries aside and took my hand. He kissed my knuckles.

"I had hoped you would be pleased with the meal after all the lamb, and I never meant for it to be spoiled with the politics of the city. Humor me in this?"

I exhaled my frustration and nodded. With the excuse of reaching for my wine cup, I pulled my hand away. Theseus let me, though I knew he was not fooled.

For the rest of the meal, I did not look at Pirithous, but at least he had the grace not to speak of the plans to steal his bride.

CHAPTER THIRTY-SIX

Theseus stripped off his tunic and dropped it to the floor where one of the servants would find it. Helen had gone to bathe, preferring to do so in the evenings and braid her hair before sleeping. He sat on the edge of the bed and rubbed at his face. Helen had been polite enough during the day, but Theseus had not had two wives before her without learning that women did not forget arguments so easily.

She would not like what he had to say. Not at all. But she could not truly have expected Pirithous to change his mind.

The door to the bathing room opened, and Helen crossed to the hearth, toweling her hair as she went. At the fire, she let it down, running her fingers through the strands to help them dry. The flames lit the outline of her body beneath the thin robe she wore, and Theseus could not bring himself to look away. He wanted to remember this moment, the warmth of the light on her skin, the swell of her hips and breasts beneath the linen.

She glanced up, a crease in her forehead clearing into something nearer to a smile. "Am I so fascinating?"

"Always," he said. "You are sunlight after the storm, clear and bright, leading me home."

The crease returned, making a line between her eyebrows. "And yet."

"And yet your own dreams tell you that I will survive this journey. As long as I do, I will return to you, no matter where you are in the world. I give you my word."

"Then you admit there is a risk in leaving me?" Her fingers stopped moving through her hair, her eyes meeting his.

"As long as you live, there is a risk. As long as Menelaus breathes and we remain within marching distance of Agamemnon, there is a risk. But the Rock will not fall, even if the gods turn against us. Athens will defend you if need be, led by Demophon. Pirithous did not exaggerate when he said the men needed a war. If Mycenae comes, they will fight with joy in their hearts. And if by some cruel trick, you are taken, I will hunt for you. Anywhere in the world, I will find you. Troy or Egypt or Sparta, I will come and carry you away. On the Styx, I swear it."

She combed her fingers through her hair again, and the silence weighed heavily between them. He did not think it would come to war, but it would be no use to tell her so.

She began to plait her hair, but her movements were slow, as if she had forgotten how it was done. "You risk Athens in this. You risk the war we have fought so long to stop from coming. You might as well leave me in Mycenae on your way."

His eyes narrowed. "That is not fair, Helen."

"You trusted me once, Theseus. Why not now?"

"After everything that's happened, you ask me that?" The sea roared in his ears, and he could not keep his hands from balling into fists. "You did not even trust me with our daughter's life!"

Her face paled. "You serve the gods first. How could I have known you would fight them?"

"How could you have believed I would not do everything in my power to save her?" he demanded, all the anger and frustration of those days surging through his heart. To have heard the gods' commands from Menestheus of all people, and then learn Helen had known of it from the start! "If you had not gone to Poseidon and traded your life, we might have found a way. Even if it meant sending her away, to be raised by Pirithous among the Lapiths or by the pharaoh in Egypt, she might have lived at least. You tied my hands, Helen, and look what came of it. You did not trust me, and we both suffered for it."

"To save our family," she breathed. "To save our daughter."

"And what came of it, Helen?" he demanded, his voice cold even to his own ears.

She dropped to her knees before him, grasping his knee in supplication and pressing her face against his leg. "Forgive me," she said, her voice broken by tears. "Forgive me, Theseus, please."

She had never wept before because of him, and every sob made him ache. He hadn't meant to fight with her this way. He had not wanted to make this any harder for either of them. And in truth, if Zeus had feared their child, it was not likely he would have succeeded where Helen had failed, but he had only wanted the opportunity to try. That he might look back and know he had done everything within his power.

"When I took you from Sparta, I knew what you wanted, and how far you would go to see it done. I knew what you were, Helen." He drew her into his lap and wiped her tears away. "I loved you for it. Then and now."

"All I have done is bring you pain. And now, this threat of war again, when we thought we were free at last."

"You said yourself you thought these dreams were nothing, at first. Just too much time spent at the loom." She shook her head, but he caught her by the chin and held her eyes with his. "Put all of this from your mind, and set your weaving away. Let us see what comes when your thoughts are distracted by other things."

"That is easy to say," she said, "but so difficult to do."

He wound his fingers in her hair, remembering the color it had been in Sparta. Bright as sunshine and just as golden. He did not think he would recognize her now if she came to him so honey blond. He kissed her throat, where her pulse beat beneath smooth skin.

"With this at least, I can help," he murmured. "If you would let me."

⚬

He made love to her until she slept, and watched her face while she dreamed. Over and over again, as often as she was willing, and when she tired of his bed, he drove them to Piraeus and the small cove where they had seen his father's sign, letting her swim herself into an exhaustion just as complete.

Every crease of her forehead, every line of her face, he studied for some sign that the nightmares she'd had were truth and not just old fears coming back to haunt her mind. And when he kept her so distracted, so well loved, they did not come with any regularity. Once in four days, then once in seven, then two nights during the entire rest of the month, and the fear that had made crow's-feet in the corners of her eyes slipped away.

She laughed again, as she had in those first days after their marriage, and when she looked on him, it was not with the echo of loss and pain, but with love so bright and full, he thought he might be lost in it. During those days, for the length of those moments, he wondered if he could bring himself to leave her.

"Solstice is not far off, Theseus," Pirithous said to him after that first month, during an evening banquet, in honor of Dionysus and

Demeter. "I trust the reason you make love to your wife is to remember the feel of her in your arms while we travel."

Theseus dragged his gaze from Helen, her lips stained red from pomegranates and wine, and her green eyes shining with the fire of the emerald in her crown. He wanted to take her back to bed, though they had barely risen from it.

"I hoped the distraction would ease her fears and her dreams."

"And?"

"And she no longer begs me not to leave with tears in her eyes for what will come in my absence."

"You can't really believe you'll fall from a cliff, can you?"

He smiled. "As long as you aren't planning to push me, I have no fears. But you had better be certain about this, Pirithous. Perhaps you ought to find distraction yourself and be sure that you are not just dreaming to dream."

Pirithous smirked. "I think you'll find half a dozen of your women showing the proof of it before we leave. I expect to hear Aethra chiding me before long, but it simply isn't a proper visit if she hasn't. Whatever happened to Menestheus's sister, anyway? I have not seen her since I arrived."

"Aren't the women in the palace eager enough? I am told they still complain bitterly that I sleep with no one but my wife."

"Who can blame you?" Pirithous's eyes followed Helen as she rose to reach for more bread. "If she weren't your wife, I'd have taken her to bed by now, too."

"As she is my wife, I would thank you to stop ogling her before I can no longer ignore it."

Pirithous sighed and redirected his gaze. "Soon enough, Theseus, you will be ogling my bride, instead. Only I won't be so miserly that I do not let you."

Theseus shook his head. "I'm afraid I have no interest in any goddess. No matter how beautiful she is. All they have ever brought me is pain. I hope for your sake, your experience is different."

Pirithous clapped him on the shoulder. "You need not worry, my friend. Once we find her, she will be so pleased to be brought back into sunlight, she will bless us both."

"It is not exactly something I can pray for, Pirithous, but I hope you're right."

"Theseus?" Helen touched his arm, her lips curving in a smile he knew well. "Might I steal you from your friend?"

Pirithous snorted. "Yes, of course. Go enjoy the pleasures of your wife while you may. We leave before the next full moon, Theseus. I hope you will be ready."

He would never be ready to leave her, no matter how many days and nights he spent in her arms. But perhaps, if they succeeded in this, the gods would understand.

Theseus would never again serve as their champion.

CHAPTER
THIRTY-SEVEN

I stood on the walls to watch Theseus and Pirithous ride out, my heart flying with them. What little sleep I had managed, wrapped in Theseus's arms, had passed dreamlessly, and relief made me giddy. Theseus would return.

Theseus would return to me.

I had to believe it.

They disappeared over the horizon by midday and Acamas came to fetch me from the wall. "Aethra says Father will not forgive her if you catch a chill while he's away."

I laughed and followed him down the stone steps. "He would not forgive me, either, I think."

"Father said we should not expect him back before the weather warms. That is how we will know to look for him, for Persephone's return to the earth will bring Demeter joy."

An early spring would bring them home regardless, and perhaps it would be enough to convince Pirithous to give up on his quest. After all, there was no point in traveling to the Underworld if Persephone had already returned to the surface and her mother, Demeter, as she did every year. They would have to wait for winter to fall before they could try again, for there would be no reaching her on Olympus.

I sighed. The idea of spending the winter in an empty bed did not appeal to me in the slightest, but I could not bear to try persuading Theseus of the fruitlessness of his journey any further. He was set upon it, and it would have only caused us both pain.

"We'll have a feast for them," I promised Acamas.

"A wedding feast for the new queen of the Lapiths!"

I smiled and let him dream. He was young enough still to believe his father capable of any feat, and when it came to Theseus, it would never be far from the truth. But he was no god, to fight them this way. Perhaps one day Acamas would understand that some powers should not be tested, but I would not be the one to spoil his childhood with such a lesson.

At that moment, I wanted too much to believe Theseus would win.

A week later, the dreams returned. Aethra shook me awake when the city began to burn, the prince's hand a fetter on my wrist. I sat straight up in the bed, the scream still in my throat. She caught me by the shoulders and eased me back, searching my face by the lamplight.

"The servants thought you were being murdered in your bed," she said.

I closed my eyes, but fire licked at the inside of my eyelids, making my stomach churn, and I opened them again. "Something has changed."

"I imagine it has." She smoothed my hair back from my forehead the way Theseus always did. "By now they've passed through the gates to the Underworld, and what they meet there, only Hades knows."

"He won't return." Saying it aloud brought fresh tears to my eyes. My bedding was already wet from them. "Menelaus will come, and then the prince."

"Hush now, Helen." Aethra squeezed my hand. "Theseus will find a way. He has not conquered so much to be struck down now. Athena will bring him home, no matter what trouble they meet. She will not let Hades take her champion."

I turned my face away, and the room swam with screaming women and crying children. Theseus had always soothed me to sleep after my nightmares, but in his absence, I had little hope of anything but sleeplessness. My heart still raced in my chest, and the echo of the dream rang in my ears.

"You are queen of Athens, Helen. You must give the people hope."

I swallowed the lump in my throat and nodded. "Thank you for waking me."

"Should I send you a maid?"

"Not if you wish the people to have hope."

She frowned. "Perhaps a potion of Ariston's?"

"For tomorrow night, though I can make no promises as to its effect."

"We'll try it." She sighed. "When Theseus told me you might dream, this was not at all what I expected. Crying we might explain as lovesickness, but screaming is another matter entirely. There will be talk."

"Theseus's beautiful queen, suffering from nightmares." I did not like to think what might happen if word of it spread. "Pollux and Menelaus both knew I dreamed this way, and Clytemnestra, too. If rumor flies to Mycenae, they will come."

She pursed her lips, staring into the darkness. "Then we will pray Theseus returns swiftly."

I did not reply. The gods would not help Theseus betray them, no matter how much we prayed for it.

Aethra patted my arm and rose from the edge of the bed. "Sleep, now, my dear, if you can. I'll send for Ariston in the morning."

She left me the oil lamp, and when the door shut behind her, I swung my legs over the edge of the bed. Going back to sleep would only bring more nightmares. I took the lamp with me and went to my loom. Theseus had set it up again before he left, knowing the comfort weaving brought me when my heart was troubled.

I worked the yarn through the warp, focusing on each thread with all my attention. I did not even notice when the sun rose until a slave came with my morning meal.

After that night, even with Ariston's potions I did not sleep much. The nightmares only grew worse.

❦

Aethra sat a servant by my door at night with orders to wake me from my nightmares, but word spread from the palace to the city all the same. Menestheus came to see me more than once, his dark eyes searching my face. With Aethra's help, I made certain to keep my hair dyed. Whatever Menestheus searched for, whatever ideas he might have, I would not give him any help.

He wasn't the only one who came. Many of the younger nobles took to calling on me in Theseus's absence, their hungry gazes sweeping over my body when they thought I would not notice. All those days they had come to bring me gifts, I had not realized how much Theseus's presence had protected me. Now that he was gone, the men of his court circled like wolves, waiting for the first sign of weakness, so they might offer me false comforts and worm their way into my confidence.

I kept Ariston and his wife close, and even allowed Aethra to assign me a maid during the day. Rumors of nightmares were one thing, but I would not give anyone in the palace reason to suggest I had been unfaithful to my king. Even when I walked the walls, I kept a woman near, and if that failed, Acamas could often be persuaded to join me.

Demophon, of all the men, kept his distance, busy with the affairs of a king, and mindful of the specter of Phaedra that still haunted Athens. When he wished to consult with me, it was always done under Aethra's eye, and with Acamas's presence. If he had not insisted upon it, I would have, and when I sat beside him in judgment, listening to petitions and complaints, we exchanged no smiles.

The weeks turned into a month, then nearly two, and no word came from Theseus or Pirithous. Aethra took my place in the megaron when the dark circles beneath my eyes could no longer be hidden by paints, and the men began to watch me with open desire.

"It is better this way," Aethra assured me one afternoon. We often shared the midday meal privately, with Demophon and Acamas, too, in council.

Behind her, Demophon poured us both wine, his expression carefully blank. It was the king's mask I had seen Theseus wear so often. What I would have given to see him look upon me even so coolly, now, when he had been gone so long.

"Let them forget the sight of you, for a time, and perhaps their ardor will cool."

"Then I am to be locked away again, after all," I said, forcing a smile I did not feel. But nor was it bitterness that weighed so heavily in my heart. No wonder Demophon wore such an expression, if this was what he had decided. I did not blame him for it, and in truth, I was worn thin with exhaustion and worry. My nightmares were neither restful nor reassuring.

"Not wholly," Demophon promised, passing me a wine cup. "Though you might consider wrapping your hair and covering your face if you wish to leave your rooms. The way the men talk—I would not ask it of you if I did not have reason, Helen. Were it not for

Phaedra, I might have pretended my own claim to you if the worst comes to pass, but as it stands . . ."

He did not need to say it. We both knew too well. If the people believed he had fallen in love with me, or I with him, we would both be in danger of exile. "Do the guards suffer from the same affliction?"

Demophon shook his head. "Father set the bull dancers upon the walls, the men he rescued from the Minotaur in Crete. They would sooner die than betray their king in such a way. We need not question their loyalty."

"Then I will limit my wanderings to the wall and remain in the king's rooms, otherwise," I said, staring into my cup. "It will hardly last forever, either way."

And so another month passed, and I spent my days at the loom, the burning city weaving itself into the warp no matter how many times I tore it free. I tried to sleep, but even with Ariston's potions, the dreams came.

I call for Theseus to save me, to protect me, to rescue me, but he does not come. The prince takes me through the market of Troy, laughing and eager to please me. I stare at an emerald, laid out for my inspection. My fingers caress the stone, thinking of the crown Theseus made for me.

"Do you like it?" The prince's fingers lace through mine, just tight enough to keep me from being able to pull free.

"It's lovely." I drop my hand and step back. "But I have no need of it."

The prince laughs. "With you it is always about need. Do you never wish for something just to have it, to show the world that it is yours?"

"There is only one thing that I wish for," I say, thinking of Theseus.

"And what I wish for," the prince says, turning my face up to his, "is to have you willing as my wife. Think of the freedom it would give you. Menelaus barely allowed you to be seen, he was so jealous.

But I will shower you with gold and fine cloth and jewels and share you with the world."

"And all the world will see how splendid you are, to have found yourself such a wife," I mock him. "I have no wish to be one of your things, to be put on display."

His fingers squeeze mine painfully. "I'm offering you a better life."

"You're offering me death."

The prince jerks me into his arms, his heat flooding through my body. "There is nothing cold or lifeless about this."

He kisses me, and the city bursts into flame.

My own screams woke me, and when the servant girl opened the door, I waved her away.

"I'm fine, I'm fine."

Korina came to the bed anyway, pouring me wine. "Another draft, my queen?"

"No." A glance toward the balcony told me dawn was not long off. I had not meant to fall asleep at all, only to doze for a moment. I sat up and rubbed my eyes. "Perhaps just a walk."

She helped me dress, and I wrapped myself in one of Theseus's cloaks. The smell of him still clung to the fur. Korina followed me dutifully up the stone stairs.

The guard at the top knew me well and offered a hand to steady me as I climbed the final steps. So early in the morning, I had not expected the number of men on the wall who greeted me. Demophon stood not far off, staring at the northwest road by which Theseus and Pirithous had left. He glanced at me, and from the circles beneath his eyes, I did not think he had slept much more than I did.

"My lady." He bowed.

"You are not often on the wall," I said. Surely he would have sent for me if it were Theseus. "Has some news come?"

He met my gaze, his mouth a thin line, and I knew it was not good. "A runner came late with news of an army marching from the Isthmus road."

"Is that not the way Theseus meant to travel?"

A jerk of his chin made space for me at the stonework beside him, crowded by broad-shouldered men. The sky was deep purple still with night, and darkness fought against false dawn. Demophon pointed to a smudge on the horizon.

"How long?" I asked.

"An army is slow, weighted by armor, swords, and shields, but they will be here before midday if they do not change direction."

My stomach sank. "Who leads them?"

"The runner did not know for certain." Demophon glanced at me again and dropped his voice. "If it is Mycenae, I will not give them more proof by asking. Why should I expect the brothers Atrides if I have nothing they might seek?"

"Wise."

"At least they will not glean much from the fields. Any attack on Athens means a siege, but if we cannot plant come spring, it will be a bad year for everyone."

"Perhaps they do not mean to march on Athens?"

"We'll find out by midmorning. I cannot bring those below behind the palace walls before I'm sure. There is no reason why anyone should want to attack us, even with Father gone."

"But for me," I said softly.

Demophon nodded, stiff, his gaze fastened on the threat below. "Even rumor does not travel so swiftly without help."

"Who?"

He shook his head. "The youngest of the nobles are too enamored of you, even if they had suspicions. The oldest are wise enough not to wish for war on any count, and of those who know the truth for certain, none would benefit from a siege, and all are too loyal to Father, regardless."

Politics and court maneuvers. Had I only opened the queen's megaron when Theseus suggested it, I would have known more. Wives often spoke more freely among themselves than their husbands might wish. A second chance was unlikely now. If Demophon doubted who marched, I did not. They came for me.

"Have you woken Aethra?"

"Perhaps you might do me that service?" Demophon frowned at the smudge. "Better, I think, if you are not seen on the walls if any scouts are sent."

I wrapped the cloak more tightly around my shoulders, suddenly chilled. In the dark, we would not see a single man on foot, but with the torches lit, he would see us. "I'll be in Theseus's rooms."

Demophon did not even look up when I left him. I called to Korina, and though I wanted nothing more than to run to Aethra, I forced myself to walk.

Meryet, princess of Egypt, need not worry about an army that would break against the Rock, from Mycenae or elsewhere. Departing from that role now would only cause more trouble for Demophon. If someone had betrayed us, we might still deny it. As long as I remained out of sight, they had no proof. And if they did see me, even Pollux would look twice under the right circumstances.

I had stopped painting my face in the Egyptian style long ago, taking up the Athenian fashions instead. No longer. The people of Athens needed a reminder before any messengers arrived looking for a Spartan princess.

"Wake Aethra and tell her I have need of her, if she would be so kind as to attend me. Ask her to bring her supplies from my wedding feast. I will want to look my best to reassure our people."

Korina bowed and ran off down the hall as I slipped into Theseus's room.

Alone at last, I sagged against the door. The Rock had never fallen, I reminded myself. There was no safer city in all of Achaea. If Demophon could only hold them off until spring, Theseus would return.

I had to believe it.

CHAPTER THIRTY-EIGHT

S partans!" Acamas gasped, catching himself on the door frame of the king's rooms before he fell over. "Castor and Pollux lead them!"

"And their demands?" Aethra poured him a cup of watered wine and beckoned him inside. She had brought me bread and cold meats along with the paints, and made me eat though my stomach churned.

I shut the door, unsure of my own feelings. Castor and Pollux were sure to be more reasonable, but they would not be turned away until they were satisfied. If keeping my secret meant their deaths, what then? I did not know if I could let Demophon hurt my brothers. Or allow my brothers to harm Demophon.

Acamas collapsed onto a stool. "They wish to see the queen. They say if we do not allow it peaceably, they will lay siege. Demophon does not think it is an idle threat."

"After they've come all this way with an army, of course it isn't," Aethra said. "What does Demophon intend?"

"I'm to bring Helen to the wall, in all her finery. He hopes that will do."

They both looked at me, Aethra's sharp eyes taking in my appearance. She had dusted my skin with ocher and painted my eyes with kohl and the blue malachite.

"Well?" she asked.

"From a distance it should be easy to fool them for a time. But if I speak to them for too long, Pollux is bound to know me, and if I reply in Egyptian, feigning ignorance, those inside the walls will know I lie."

"Then we will let Demophon answer for you as much as possible." Aethra nodded to Acamas. "Run ahead and tell your brother. It is not unheard of for men to order their women not to speak. It should not be questioned."

Acamas wasted no time and left his cup half-full on the table. I barely had time to open the door for him on his way out.

"We'll wait." Aethra poured me a cup of wine, and I noticed she did not add any water at all. "The queen should not come running at the least demand of a strange army."

My hands shook when I took it from her. It was Theseus's cup, embossed with the depiction of his battle against the Minotaur. "They are my brothers."

"They are not Meryet's brothers," she said, pressing my hands to the cup when my fingers slipped. "You are a princess of Egypt, now. Remember that."

"They would not have come without a purpose, Aethra, even if they are not certain I am Meryet. If I can speak to Pollux, tell him I am happy here, perhaps he will see reason."

"Demophon has decided how we will begin. If seeing you on the wall is not enough, there is time to discuss our other options. And one way or another, Theseus will return with the spring."

The warmth of the wine steadied my hands, but my mind found no comfort in it. I held the cup out for more, and Aethra refilled it without comment. By the time I had finished the second cup, she judged our delay effective and walked me to the wall.

"Keep your chin held high, my dear, and glare at them as if they were nothing but desert sand." She smiled and squeezed my hand. "It's been nearly two years since you came to us, you know. Even without the paint on your face, you've changed."

I took a deep breath and climbed the stone stairs, Aethra following a few steps behind. A guard announced my approach, and Demophon met me at the top, his expression impassive. He guided me forward. From the height of the wall, it was easy to look down my nose at those assembled below. I stared diffidently at the army beyond the outer walls first, most of the men armored in leather, hide shields strapped to their backs. Sunlight flashed off bronze swords and spear tips, and those wealthy enough for bronze armor stood behind impatient horses in their chariots. I could not see their faces from the palace, but I had no doubt I would recognize most of them. After a moment to survey the others, I deigned to glance at the men waiting at the palace gate.

Pollux met Theseus in height now, and Castor was not far behind him. They stood in full armor, flashing bronze beside matching white horses. Another man remained mounted, flying a flag of truce. Seeing my brothers again sent a stab of longing through my heart, but I could not let them know it, and if I looked too long, I feared it would show.

"Queen Meryet of Athens, princess of Egypt," Demophon said.

Pollux studied me, and I affected a sniff of irritation, dismissing him with a lift of my chin.

"If she is as you say, then you will have no reason not to invite us in as your guests," Pollux called. "We have no interest in anything that is not ours."

My jaw tightened at his phrasing. It sounded too much like something Menelaus would say. I swept my gaze over the army again, looking for the telltale red of his hair. Boar's tusk, leather, and bronze helmets covered their heads, obscuring my view.

"Athens does not turn away its friends, so long as they come in peace, but in winter I cannot entertain all your men." Demophon nodded to the guards manning the main gate in order to prove his words.

Pollux frowned, still staring at me. I met his gaze, hoping he saw only irritation and not my worry.

Castor smiled. "We would not ask it of you. Give my brother and me beds for the night, and in the morning we will march on, once we are satisfied, of course."

"Of course," Demophon said, his tone light, though he spoke through gritted teeth.

He turned from them, and I took my cue, giving my brothers one more contemptuous look before leaving them behind.

"Let us hope that Athena is with us tonight," Demophon murmured in my ear. "If you would not mind returning to your rooms, I will see our guests welcomed with all due ceremony. Once the formalities are observed, they can hardly make off with you, whether they recognize you or not."

"If they catch us in the lie, hospitality will no longer bind them," I said. In my hurry, I nearly tripped down the steps, but Demophon caught my elbow before I lost my balance. "Let me speak with them privately."

He shook his head. "As a last resort only, my lady. The more people who know, the greater the risk. A siege now will hurt no one, as long as it ends before spring. A siege in full summer will see the fields razed and a lean winter."

"Theseus will be back long before then."

"If Mycenae comes, I am to send you to Egypt by my father's orders. Whether he is returned or not."

"Egypt!" That time I did lose my balance, but fortunately we had already made it to the ground, and Acamas steadied me. I had not even realized he was there.

Demophon hushed me, glancing to see if anyone heard. The guards had remained on the wall, and the gate had only just begun to open, the heavy panels groaning.

"Acamas, see the queen to her rooms. Quickly."

We had just made it into the shadows of the main porch when I heard Pollux's greeting. "I had hoped to give the queen my thanks for her tolerance."

"My lady will join us for the meal, but she does not care to socialize much in my father's absence."

I slowed my step, ignoring Acamas's hiss. They would not see me here, not yet.

"We had heard that King Theseus met trouble on his journey." My blood ran cold at Castor's words. "On the way here, we were told he passed through to the Underworld at Eleusis, months ago."

"A delay only, I'm sure." Demophon spoke with more confidence than I might have had in his place. "We expect Theseus and Pirithous with the first days of spring."

"My lady," Acamas whispered. "Please. You cannot be seen."

I picked up my skirts and let him pull me away, but the news made it difficult for me to breathe. Just a few more weeks, I told myself as Acamas pushed open the door to Theseus's room.

But why would Theseus want me sent to Egypt?

<hr />

Aethra fussed over my appearance, touching up every line of kohl and tucking every strand of my hair into its place until I lost patience and waved her away.

"There is nothing more to do, Aethra, except smudge what you've already fixed."

She scowled at me, but stepped back. "I'm not sure you should wear that circlet. It brings out your eyes."

"No matter what I wear, my eyes will not be well enough hidden if Pollux is seated beside me at the table."

"He won't be. You'll be at Demophon's right, and Acamas will sit on your other side. Pollux and Castor will have to crane around Demophon to see you at all. I've already seen to it. Theseus would never allow guests in his hall for the sole purpose of ogling his wife, and under the circumstances, I have no intention of making it easy for them to do so."

I sighed, caressing the emerald in its golden setting. I tried not to think of the Trojan marketplace of my dream. "If Demophon hadn't let them in, Pollux would have seen the lie, and we'd be preparing for a war."

"That brother of yours is too sly by half."

"Not my brother." I raised the circlet and let Aethra settle it on my head. "I'm Meryet of Egypt."

"Just so." Aethra smiled.

A persistent knock brought me to my feet. I smoothed my skirt. Aethra and I had debated for some time over the gown, but in the end she had decided the greater temptation of baring my painted breasts to the young nobles of Athens would be too much, and we had both dressed conservatively.

"That will be Acamas, no doubt," Aethra said, waiting for my nod before she opened the door.

Menestheus stood in the corridor, his dark eyes darting about the room before stopping on me. He bowed. "My queen, I beg the honor of your company. It would not do for you to be escorted by a child."

Aethra sniffed. "I'm not certain it's any greater honor for her to be brought in on your arm, Menestheus, but if that is Demophon's wish, I suppose it is too late now."

The man stiffened, but surely I only imagined the curl of his lip as he glanced at Aethra. I forced myself to smile at him, though taking his arm made my skin crawl. I hadn't been able to look at him without thinking of Menelaus's words in my dream. But perhaps this was for the best. If trouble came, it would be good to know where Menestheus's loyalties lay, and Theseus would have the proof of it, one way or the other.

"You are the jewel of Athens," Menestheus said, sweeping me away from Aethra. "Theseus is a most fortunate man."

"I am most fortunate in Theseus," I replied. "He is practically Egyptian in his sensibilities."

Menestheus snorted, and his arm pinned mine to his side. "Pretty phrases. Was it Pirithous who taught you, or Theseus himself?"

I looked up, startled by the savagery of his words. His fingers dug into my arm when I tried to pull away. That was when I noticed the guards were dressed in bronze, not leather, and I recognized none of them as Athenians. I tore at his fingers, jerking harder against him, but he only twisted my fingers cruelly.

"Get the old woman," he barked to one, but he did not wait to see the order carried out, lengthening his stride. I set my heels, clawing at his arm, his hand, his face. He growled, tightening his grip.

His hand slipped on my forearm when I moved to bite him. Enough for me to break free, and I spun, running back toward Theseus's room.

"Aethra!"

Armed men already stood in the doorway, blocking it from view. Menestheus tackled me from behind, sending me sprawling on the floor. My wrist twisted beneath me, and my palms skidded against the polished stone, burning.

Aethra's shriek echoed down the corridor, and Menestheus cursed, hauling me back to my feet and dragging me down the hallway again, this time with a knife pressed against my ribs. The blade stilled me, the bronze digging harder into my side with every breath.

"You!" I gasped the word. "How—"

"How did I know?" He jerked me forward, faster, harder. "All that dye Theseus kept trading for, and that Spartan ritual in the megaron, to say nothing of the stories that came back with him from Sparta. Perhaps others might have been fooled by his Egyptian ruse, but if Theseus was so in love with Helen of Sparta that he set guards beneath her window and bargained for her hand in marriage, he would never give her up so easily for some Egyptian princess he had never met. Nor would he be so devoted."

I stared at him. "He trusted you!"

"Not enough to tell me the truth about his bride." The blade pricked me through the fabric of my gown. "And you, behaving as though you were too good to even look on any of us. Unwilling to even give audience to any of his people after he had gone. Hiding away in his rooms."

"For that, you would do this?" I did not care that I shouted, nor did the trickle of my own blood give me pause. "You would betray his sons! Athens itself! Theseus has been nothing but good to you, to Athens!"

"Athens should have been mine! I thought for certain he would refuse to give up your child, and I would have the throne then, but no." He sneered. "Aethra persuaded him, and of course Athena favored him with counsel. She took the crying baby from his arms herself! But I am done waiting now."

His words stabbed through me more keenly than any blade. My daughter. How could he speak so cruelly of an innocent child? As if she were worth nothing, but for how he might use her for his own purposes. Oh, Theseus! I should have warned him. He should have heard of the dream from me, not Menestheus, who did not care what blood was spilled, only how much closer it brought him to the throne.

Menestheus threw me the last few paces into the megaron. I landed on my hands and bruised knees on the tile before two pairs of sandaled feet. They did not belong to Demophon or Acamas.

Pollux crouched down to help me up, but I ignored him, glaring.

My brother straightened, his usually good-humored expression filled with hurt. "Forgive me for thinking you might prefer to be found by your brothers over Menelaus."

I rose to my feet, forcing the pain from my heart and raising my chin. If Theseus had not defied the gods, then they must stand with us now. We had paid Zeus's price. Athena had given us her word. And Theseus trusted her, above all. Theseus would come. The goddess would bring him home.

"A princess of Egypt has nothing to fear from any Achaean prince," I said. "We have no enemies here, and you have no right to me. I belong to Theseus. To Athens!"

"Enough of your lies!" Menestheus snapped. "Take her. Perhaps if I'm lucky, Theseus will be so distracted by finding his wife that he won't bother with trying to reclaim Athens. If he returns at all."

"*When* he returns, Menestheus," I said. "And his people will rise to his call and throw you to your death from the Rock! Zeus himself will curse you, and all your children."

He grabbed my arm, the bronze blade, cold and stinging, finding my throat. "I warn you, Princess. Still your tongue, or I will cut it from your head."

Pollux stepped forward, his hand closing around Menestheus's wrist. "You will not touch our sister again."

For the first time, I realized how impressive he had grown in my absence, for he towered like Pirithous over the man. Menestheus seemed to realize it, too, for he dropped the blade, his lip curling as he glared at me.

"Demophon and Acamas will wake rudely aboard ship come morning, and the island of Euboea will keep them well away for some time," Castor said. "I trust you can handle any trouble that might come if they return?"

"Why should anyone want to be led by a son of Theseus after this betrayal?" Menestheus said, his gaze flicking over me before he turned away. "Clearly they can't be trusted if they would help their father break even the most sacred of laws."

"Then the city is yours," Castor said.

"Come." Pollux took me by the arm. "The sooner we are on our way, the less likely Menelaus will hear of this and follow."

I tore my arm free. "I won't leave."

"Tonight with us, in peace, or later by force and with blood-shed, Helen. How many do you want to see dead now, if war threatens later?"

"There would be no threat of war if you had not come. If you had not helped this usurper—this dog! We paid the price in blood, Pollux!" *Zeus, I beg of you. You have our daughter. Strike Menestheus down, and bring Theseus to my side!* I screamed the words in my mind as tears filled my eyes. *Father, help me now!*

Castor swore. "We haven't the time for this, Helen."

I spun, glaring at him. "My place is here, as queen of Athens. I will not abandon Theseus or his city."

Pain exploded in my skull, and Pollux shouted something I couldn't understand, his expression livid.

Warm arms caught my body, but my mind fell into darkness and flame.

CHAPTER
THIRTY-NINE

The ocean roared in my ears, pressing down upon me, pinning my arms to my sides. I struggled to free them, to swim for the surface, my lungs burning for air. A wave crashed, knocking me back, and then an arm wrapped around my waist, catching me and pulling me up. Theseus, I thought. Theseus, who would never let me drown.

I gasped for breath, my eyes opening to the scrub brush of the Isthmus in winter. The ocean restricting me was only a cloak, wrapped so tightly around my body that I could not move my arms. Theseus's cloak, though I did not understand how that could be. My head ached, and I groaned at the jarring hoofbeats of the horse beneath me.

"Careful," Pollux said in my ear when I sat up straight and struggled against the fabric. We rode beside the sea. "If you fall off, you'll only be more miserable for the rest of the journey."

"I can't move."

"I couldn't have you flopping about like a fish while I rode." He helped me to free my arms. "After what Menestheus did, I didn't dare ask to wait until you woke. The man has no patience. I demanded your cloak at least, and one of the palace slaves brought this."

I rubbed the lump at the back of my head. The skin was tender, aching just from the weight of my hair. I wore the circlet still.

"Korina," I mumbled. Then I remembered Aethra. My eyes filled with tears. After everything she had done for me, to keep me safe. "What did he do to Theseus's family?"

"Exile." I sagged with relief, and Pollux wrapped his arm around me again, holding me steady. "Demophon and Acamas are well on their way to Euboea by now, and Aethra was sent back to Troezen. Menestheus would not do her any real harm, fearing Poseidon's wrath. I did everything in my power to be sure it would be bloodless. I'm sorry. I'm sorry that it came to this at all."

"You shouldn't have come!" My throat tightened, and I strangled a sob. Everything for nothing. Our daughter given up for nothing! "When you knew I was here, why did you?"

"Because if we did not treat with Menestheus, he would have gone to Menelaus! At least this way, Theseus would not return to a ruined city. I owed the man that much for keeping you safe this long."

"The Rock has never fallen," I said. "Menelaus never would have made it inside the walls."

"By the gods, Helen!" His arm tightened, making me cry out. He inhaled deeply, and his hold softened even if his tone did not. "Do you think Menestheus would have hesitated to let them in the same way he let us? Only if it had been Menelaus he invited, Theseus's sons and mother would be dead, along with any man who got in his way. What he would have done to you had you fought, I do not even want to imagine."

I fell silent, grieving for things Theseus did not even realize he had lost. Athens in Menestheus's hands. The daughter he had sacrificed for betrayal. Oh, Theseus. I did not deserve his forgiveness. Everything he had built, lost because of me. Even our child. Because I had not believed, had not shown faith, and now it was too late.

"He deserved better than this," I murmured.

"I doubt very much he'll ever return to see it," Pollux said. "Aphrodite has led Pirithous on a merry chase and Theseus with him."

"You can't know that." My hands balled into fists in the fabric of the cloak. "Theseus will return! He swore it. We've only to wait until spring, and then he will come for me. You'll see."

"Helen." Pollux's voice was gentle. "Very few have ever returned from the Underworld, and he has been a long time gone. Longer than he meant to be, according to Menestheus. Perhaps it would be best if we considered what you will do if he does not arrive. And even if he does, what good will it do? He is no longer king."

Egypt, I thought. We could flee to Egypt together and live the rest of our lives in peace if he did not win Athens back. That must have been what he intended, why he had meant Demophon to send me there. Pollux should have let Menelaus march. I would have been sent safely away, and Menestheus would have had nothing to offer. The Rock would have stood, and Theseus would have returned home to his crown.

"He would be king still, if it weren't for you," I said.

At my back, Pollux only sighed.

⚬

We camped on the Isthmus road beyond Eleusis, though Pollux had hoped to make it to Megara before nightfall. Castor called the halt, ordering several men to the first watch before riding back to us.

"You and Helen may have the constitution of gods, but the rest of the army has spent a long day on the march."

Pollux grunted. "You can hardly blame me for wanting distance from Athens."

Castor dismounted and helped me down from Pollux's horse. "No. But exhausted men will do us no good, and the lands on the Isthmus will not take kindly to the news out of Athens when it spreads."

"Attica loves Theseus," I said, not looking at Pollux. "Menestheus can barely throw a spear."

"If he is so poor a leader, I doubt he'll last very long as king," Pollux said gently. "Demophon will have no trouble finding allies to take back his throne."

"No." I frowned, the burning city rising in my mind. Remembering Menelaus pinning me against the wall, speaking of Theseus's death, I shuddered. "Menestheus will rule until the war. And when Theseus returns, Menestheus will have him killed."

Castor's expression filled with pity. "We heard rumors that Theseus's queen suffered from nightmares in his absence."

"But it made no sense," Pollux said. "If you were safe with Theseus, why would you dream of the war?"

"Perhaps because my foolish brothers meant to rescue me."

"Theseus can't protect you if he's lost in the house of Hades!"

I whirled, and Pollux fell back. "And how do you intend to protect me, Pollux? By allowing Father to marry me to Menelaus? Agamemnon's brother does not care for anything but his own interests!"

"I know." He raised his hands, palms out, his back against his horse's flank. His eyes were dark with pain. "I heard him speaking with Leda, after you disappeared. And if I had known then, Helen, I swear to you I would have helped Theseus steal you from the city myself."

"Leda?"

He clenched his jaw and looked away. "She helped him."

I shook my head, stumbling back. Castor reached for me, but I pushed him away. My own mother. The night rushed back to my mind, and I swallowed hard. Menelaus's hands on my body, rough and determined and cruel. My own mother had done that to me, after everything she had suffered at the hands of Zeus? She would do it again. If she had promised me to Menelaus, she would not go back on her word now.

"Helen, wait," Castor said. I turned from him, from both of them. They would take me back there. Under my mother's eye, into Menelaus's reach. Theseus. *Theseus, where are you?* My husband. My hero. My protector. Theseus. He did not even know. He could not come if he did not know, and he had to come. He had to.

The crashing of the sea filled my ears. Calling to me.

"Where are you going?" Pollux shouted.

I didn't care. I had to tell Theseus. I had to let him know what had happened so that he might come home. Anywhere in the world, he had promised me. He would find me. He had to find me. Theseus, Poseidon's son. "Theseus."

I scrambled through the scrub to the cliff, dimly hearing the snap of branches behind me. Pollux and Castor, following.

The land sloped up, but the cliff stood low enough that I could feel the sea spray bouncing off the stone with every strike of the waves. I paused at the edge, ignoring the shouts of my brothers. The smell of salt and brine thickened with the wind blowing into my face. "Theseus!"

But Theseus was not in the sea. No ship stood on the horizon, waiting to take me aboard. No dolphins leapt, showing Poseidon's last favors. I might have believed they could swim even the River Styx, fighting their way through the Underworld to give Theseus word of me, had they only shown themselves. I would have thrown myself into their midst and begged them to carry me with them.

I dropped to my knees on the hard rock, pressing my palms to the earth. "Theseus," I said again. Poseidon was lord of more than just the ocean. Of the land, too, and what of his son? I closed my eyes, breathing in the salt and the sand and the stone, digging my nails into its unyielding surface until they ached. "If you could only hear me. If you only knew. You swore! On the Styx, you swore to find me!"

Pollux crouched beside me. "In two days, we will reach Mycenae. Agamemnon will insist we spend the night within his palace, if only to appease our sister. Clytemnestra is queen there now. Menelaus will, no doubt, be present."

"Does Tyndareus know?" I could not take my eyes from the sea. "Was he part of it?"

"You are his heir, Helen. He would not treat you so cruelly, not even for Menelaus. But he will want you married as soon as the priests allow."

"I already have a husband."

Pollux took my hand, brushing the dirt from my palm. When he rose, he pulled me with him. My arms felt weighted by stone, like my heart. He framed my face in his hands when I tried to look away, ducking his head to catch my eyes.

"If Menelaus learns you were in Athens, that Theseus made you his wife, it will mean a war. And you can be sure that if Theseus is not dead already, Menelaus will not rest until it is so." His hands braced my shoulders when I did not respond, and he searched my face. "Do you understand what I'm telling you, Helen?"

I closed my eyes again, wishing I could shut out the images he had painted as easily. My legs did not seem strong enough to support me, and my shoulders drooped beneath the weight of my brother's words. Pollux pulled me into his arms, and I pressed my face into the curve of his shoulder, wishing it were Theseus who held me.

Theseus, who might never hold me again.

"We will say that your abductor hid you away," Pollux went on, his voice low. "That you escaped from his hands and went to Athens for help, where Menestheus, in Theseus's absence, sent word to us. And then we will marry you to a suitable husband as quickly as we can."

To Menelaus, I thought, clinging to Pollux as the first sobs ripped through me. My mother would see to that.

CHAPTER FORTY

*T*heseus.

At the call of his name, the desperate shout, he twitched against his restraints. Dark shadow burned against his skin, holding him in place, but his eyelids fluttered, fighting against the weight of his dreams. Over and over again, Aethra came to him, Menestheus at her side. Over and over again, he took his child, his daughter, from her bed, his heart shattering with the knowledge of what he must do. Over and over again, Athena took the baby from his arms, laying her upon the rock, and he stood vigil, each wail, each cry piercing him like an arrow, a spear, a sword through his soul. But the silence, the stillness that came after was even worse. And it always came. It always came, and he could do nothing but watch, but stand witness as her small, fragile life drained away.

Theseus!

Helen. Helen called to him, but how? He had left her in Athens, safe and protected. He had left her safe, though he had dreamed of that, too. Of Helen, stolen from Athens, torn from her chambers by Menelaus, screaming and struggling and clawing against him until he held her down, reclaimed her as his. He had dreamed of it, knowing himself trapped by Hades, incapable of reaching her.

How long had he been bound this way? Dimly he remembered Persephone's chiming voice, the smell of roasted meats and fresh breads that had drawn them. His eyes finally opened, and he saw the banquet, still, spread out before them, Pirithous still entrapped within the chair at his side. So much food, the aroma torture enough, even without the dreams and the shadow. Hades sat at the head of his table, dressed in blinding robes of silver and gold. A black beard covered his jaw, and his eyes flashed with the fire of diamonds. Beside him sat Persephone, her hair the deep brown of fertile earth, white flowers forming a royal circlet upon her brow.

"Ah," Hades said, his voice liquid and echoing in the vaulting cavern. "The hero wakes, Athena's well-chosen champion. Even the powers of Lethe cannot match his strength of will. But tell me, Theseus. Do you remember the vow you made to Athena, in the temple? Do you remember swearing you would never turn from us, your family, your gods?"

Theseus. Helen's voice again, a whisper now, filled with such impotence, such despair. He had never known her to despair, not truly. Not so long as they were together.

If you could only hear me.

Persephone's head tilted, her eyes narrowing as if she heard, too. "Not only his will," the goddess said, her gaze warm when it settled upon him. "Poor Helen. She has waited ever so faithfully, all this time. I cannot help but feel for her, knowing what it is to be torn from that which has been chosen, nurtured into life and love, peace and beauty. Every spring, I suffer the same, forced to leave my husband for the sake of my family, my duty."

The goddess laid her hand upon her husband's arm, lifting her face to his, so beautiful Theseus could not breathe, to look at her. But there was so much affection, so much intimacy even in so small a gesture. How could Pirithous have ever believed she would want to be freed?

If you only knew.

Theseus jerked against his bonds. Helen called to him, and he must answer. He must go to her, whether the gods willed it or not. But the shadow held, the black forms tightening around his chest and legs.

You swore! On the Styx, you swore to find me!

He groaned, throwing himself against the bindings. Stone cracked, dust and dirt raining down, as the cavern shook. He had never realized the power, never known he might draw from his father's strengths upon the land as well as the sea. He fought again, though the shadow had begun to sizzle against his skin, burning into his bare legs, his arms, cutting like ropes. The room shook again, rock crumbling, rubble cascading down the far wall, but still he could not tear himself free. And he must, by the Styx, he must, if Helen needed him, if Helen had been stolen. If only he had the strength . . .

"Peace, Theseus," Hades said. "You will not hear her once she is dead. And then, once your vows are broken, you will belong to the Styx, forevermore."

"You will not keep me from my wife," Theseus growled. "I will not let you keep me!"

Persephone rose and came toward him. Tiered with cloth of gold and emerald silk, her flounced skirt flashed with gems and tinkled with silver. He clenched his jaw against the gentleness of her touch, the chill of her fingers upon his brow. Helen, he must remember Helen. He must remember her call, her cry. But with every beat of his heart, her voice grew more distant, her warmth farther away. But he would find her.

"Go back to sleep, Theseus. You can do nothing more to help Helen now."

He must find her.

He must find.

He must.

Helen.

CHAPTER FORTY-ONE

I slept fitfully on the cold ground, even wrapped in Theseus's cloak with several furs beneath me. The nightmares almost felt like old friends, promising that whatever marriage I made to Menelaus, it would not last. Leda's betrayal, Menelaus's lies—none of it would matter for long. The war would come, washing it all away.

The sun touched the scrub grasses with fire, and I turned my face toward it. Castor had already risen, and Pollux lay sleeping in his place, one hand clutching the hilt of a knife. He looked so much like Pirithous in that moment, the creases of worry and determination relaxed in rest. But if Leda had her way, even if Pirithous was successful, I would never meet with him again, either.

I closed my eyes. True sons of Zeus, the both of them, set upon wiles and deceit to accomplish their goals. Always reaching to take that which was not theirs. To have their way at all costs, as if they ruled as kings.

But I was Zeus's daughter. They could not hold me if I did not wish to be held. The gods had already declared it so with these nightmares. And perhaps that was the truth of it all. Perhaps this war, this destruction, this death, was all mine. Because as much as I did not wish to see my people suffer, my brothers die, and the golden city turn to ash and smoke and blood, Menelaus would never have my loyalty now.

"Helen?" Castor's voice was low, and I opened my eyes to find him crouched beside me, offering a strip of dried goat. Pollux had already risen. "We should not linger," he said when he saw I was awake.

Around us, the other men were stirring, shaking out their cloaks and cinching sword belts over leather armor. Sparta's men, their lives in my hands.

"Here," Castor said, nudging me. A small white crocus, barely blooming, was pressed into my hand. I met my brother's eyes, my mouth suddenly dry. Castor busied himself with my extra furs, dropping his gaze. "I found it when I was checking on the horses. I'm sorry, Helen."

The first sign of spring. Nearer than I had realized. Nearer than it should have been. I stared into the soft white heart of the flower, turning it between my fingers. The seasons changed, I knew that. As constant as they were irregular. But I had been counting the days, anxious for Theseus, and even for an early spring, the crocus should not have budded so soon.

"Persephone is freed," I heard myself say. "She hurries from the Underworld."

My brother's mouth firmed into a hard line. "Even so, it does not mean Theseus or Pirithous has survived the journey."

I caught him by the arm when he tried to turn away. "Castor, please. If there is any hope, any chance at all that he might yet return—it is not so great a delay." He was shaking his head, but I dug my fingers into his forearm, forcing him to look at me. "A few weeks, Castor. If Tyndareus will only send word, keep his promise that I will not be married without the proper rites, Theseus will hear of it, and there will be time enough for him to reach me. And if he wins me fairly . . ."

"He won't win, Helen. Even if he comes, he will not win you. Leda will see to it."

"And what power does Leda have that my brothers do not? Tyndareus will want your counsel. Yours and Pollux's. If you speak against Menelaus, Father will listen!"

Castor sighed, his hand covering mine. "You truly believe Theseus still lives?"

"It is not his fate to die this way," I said, desperate to assure him. "Athena would not forsake him so easily. Not after—" I swallowed back the words, my throat too tight. What had happened to us, what had become of our daughter, I could not speak of it. "He has been her loyal servant, and she will not leave him to Hades's mercy."

He searched my face, and I could only hope he saw my determination, and the confidence I could not wholly feel. Perhaps Menelaus had spoken truly in my dream. Perhaps Theseus might yet live, but nothing in my dreams had proven he would not still be lost to me.

"I cannot promise you it will work," Castor said at last. "But you will have my help, all the same. If Theseus lives, if he escapes Hades even now, we will give him time enough to come for you, and if Tyndareus will not hear reason, your husband will have my help in stealing you away. I swear it by Zeus."

I threw myself into his arms, my brother, my sweetest, kindest brother, and in that moment, hope blossomed inside me like a sea of spring flowers.

Because I was a daughter of Zeus, and I would not be held against my will. Not by Menelaus, or Leda. Not by Tyndareus or my brothers. Not by the gods or the fates, with their burning city and their strange Trojan prince, and their war. Not even by my own father.

Perhaps Zeus was king, but I was Spartan, a princess twice over, and queen of Athens besides. I knew my duty.

And I would rule my own fate.

And so Theseus rightly felt love's flame, for he was acquaint with all your

charms, and you seemed fit spoil for the great hero to steal away, [. . .]. His

stealing you away, I commend; my marvel is that he ever gave you back.

—*Ovid,* Heroides, 16

ACKNOWLEDGMENTS

First and foremost, thank you so much to Michelle Brower for believing in *Helen*, and never giving up on finding her a home, and to Jodi at Lake Union, for giving me the chance to share *Helen* with readers, at last! And thank you, also, to Stephanie Thornton and Gary Corby, who have been so supportive of my historical fiction writing endeavors, both as Ancient History blog friends and author friends.

I absolutely owe a mountain of thanks to the usual suspects, including Diana Paz, Zak Tringali, Wendy Sparrow, L. T. Host, Natalie Murphy, Tina Lynn, Mia Hayson, Nick Mohoric, and Valerie Valdes, for reading (and in some cases rereading), and talking me down off those writing ledges along the way. Also to Hannah Wylie for a very complete and in-depth critique that helped me to make *Helen* so much stronger! Without your generosity, I am not sure this book would be where it is today. Thanks, too, to Katie M. Stout for being as passionate a beta as I could ever ask for, and tackling my grammar like a pro. I'm also grateful to Aven McMaster, for our countless chats and discussions regarding the academic interpretations of Classical myth.

And to my friends and family, for sticking with me on this roller-coaster ride of crazy-making, and/or providing fantastic critique and notes from the reader perspective: Karen, Dan, Tom, Denise, Aunt

Rose, Aunt Tommi Lou, Uncle Joey, Emi, Mattias, Connor, Drew the Third, Kevin, and John. I can't begin to tell you how much I appreciate the time you've invested in me and my work!

Lastly, thanks to my brother Don, for bringing home his copy of *Bulfinch's Mythology* from college and telling nine-year-old me that Hercules's real name was Heracles. I don't think either one of us expected that small moment to bring me here, to this book, and this authorial adventure, but it did, and I am forever grateful!

DRAMATIS PERSONAE

Acamas: Youngest son of Theseus, by his second wife, Phaedra; prince of Athens

Adrastus: King of Argos; grandfather of Diomedes; guest of Tyndareus at Helen's banquet

Aegeus: Previous king of Athens; one of Theseus's fathers, by Aethra; deceased

Aethra: Mother of Theseus; high priestess of Athens; consort of Poseidon and Aegeus

Agamemnon: King of Mycenae; son of Atreus; older brother to Menelaus; close friend of Tyndareus and his family after spending several years in exile at Sparta as part of Tyndareus's household

Ajax the Great: Prince of Salamis; older half brother of Teucer; great-grandson of Zeus; friend and guest of Tyndareus at Helen's banquet

Ajax the Lesser: Prince of Locris; guest of Tyndareus at Helen's banquet

Alcyoneus: Helen's Egyptian tutor

Antiope: Theseus's first wife; former queen of the Amazons; devotee of Artemis; mother of Hippolytus, Theseus's first son; deceased

Aphrodite: Goddess of love and beauty; daughter of Zeus

Apollo: God of music, poetry, oracles, plague, medicine, and the sun; twin brother of Artemis; son of Zeus

Ariadne: Daughter of Minos of Crete; goddess of the labyrinth, freed by Theseus; wife and consort of Dionysus

Ariston: Athenian physician and friend of Theseus

Artemis: Goddess of the hunt, virgins, and the Amazons; twin sister of Apollo; daughter of Zeus

Athena: Goddess of wisdom and war; daughter of Zeus; patron goddess of Athens; appointed Theseus as her hero and champion in Attica

Castor: Prince of Sparta; mortal twin brother of Pollux; son of Tyndareus by Leda; older brother to Helen and Clytemnestra

Clymene: Helen's maid in Sparta

Clytemnestra: Princess of Sparta; mortal twin sister to Helen; daughter of Tyndareus by Leda; younger sister of Pollux and Castor

Demophon: Prince and heir of Athens; son of Theseus by his second wife, Phaedra

Diomedes: Prince and heir of Argos; grandson of Adrastus, king of Argos; favored by Athena; guest of Tyndareus at Helen's banquet

Dionysus: God of wine, ritual madness, religious ecstasy, and epiphany; husband of Ariadne; son of Zeus

Hades: God of the Underworld and the dead; brother of Zeus and Poseidon; husband of Persephone

Helen: Princess of Sparta; daughter of Zeus (in the form of a swan) by Leda; demigod twin sister of Clytemnestra; younger sister of Pollux and Castor

Hera: Queen of the gods; wife of Zeus; goddess of women and marriage

Heracles: Son of Zeus by Alcmene; hero; blessed with tremendous strength and ability; friend of Tyndareus; helped Tyndareus to reclaim the throne of Sparta

Hippolytus: Theseus's first son, by the Amazon queen Antiope; devotee of Artemis; deceased

Leda: Queen of Sparta; wife of Tyndareus; consort of Zeus (who came to her once in the form of her husband, and the second time in the form of a swan); mother of the twins Castor and Pollux, and Clytemnestra and Helen

Menelaus: Prince of Mycenae; younger brother of Agamemnon; son of Atreus; close friend of Tyndareus and his family after spending several years in exile at Sparta as part of Tyndareus's household

Menestheus: Cousin of Theseus; steward of Athens; great-grandson of Erechtheus, founder of Athens

Minos: Former king of Crete; father of Ariadne and Phaedra

Nestor: Elderly king of Pylos; minor hero; guest of Tyndareus at Helen's banquet

Pallans: Athenian; oarsman for Theseus

Paris: Adopted son of Agelaus; shepherd boy living in the lands surrounding Troy

Patroclus: Guest of Tyndareus at Helen's banquet; Myrmidon and neighbor to King Pirithous and the Lapiths people, in Thessaly

Penelope: Cousin of Clytemnestra and Castor; niece of Tyndareus

Persephone: Queen of the Underworld; wife of Hades; daughter of Zeus by Demeter; goddess of spring growth

Phaedra: Theseus's second wife; mother of Demophon and Acamas; daughter of Minos; sister of Ariadne

Pirithous: King of the Lapiths, in Thessaly; son of Zeus by Dia; cousin and friend to Theseus

Pollux: Prince of Sparta; son of Zeus by Leda; demigod twin brother to Castor; older brother to Helen and Clytemnestra

Poseidon: God of earth and sea, earthquakes, and horses; brother of Zeus and Hades; father of Theseus by Aethra

Teucer: Younger brother of Ajax the Great; guest of Tyndareus at Helen's banquet

Theseus: King of Athens; Hero of Attica; son of both the god Poseidon and Aegeus, previous king of Athens, by Aethra; father of Hippolytus by Antiope; father of Demophon and Acamas by Phaedra; cousin and friend to Pirithous

Tyndareus: King of Sparta; husband of Leda; father of Castor and Clytemnestra by Leda; adoptive father of Pollux and Helen; uncle of Penelope; friend of Agamemnon and Menelaus; friend of Heracles

Zeus: King of the gods; husband of Hera; father of Helen and Pollux by Leda; father of Apollo and Artemis, Athena, Aphrodite, and Dionysus; brother of Poseidon and Hades; god of the sky, thunder and lightning, order and justice

IMPORTANT PLACES

Sparta: A landlocked city in the southeast of the Peloponnese, within the region of Laconia, ruled by King Tyndareus and Queen Leda. Helen's home.

Gytheio: A port city south of Sparta.

Mycenae: A very rich and powerful city in the eastern region of the Peloponnese, near the Isthmus that connects the Peloponnese to the greater mainland. Ruled by King Agamemnon and home to Menelaus.

Athens: A very rich and powerful city with influence over the greater part of a region called Attica, in the southernmost area of the mainland, and also over pieces of the Isthmus. Ruled by King Theseus, with the protection of its patron goddess, Athena.

Piraeus: The port of Athens, west of the city, and the main port of Attica. Part of Theseus's kingdom.

Thessaly: A northeastern region of the mainland, in which a number of independent peoples reside, such as the Lapiths, ruled by King

Pirithous; and the Myrmidons of Phthia, ruled by King Peleus (father of Achilles).

Troy: A wealthy kingdom across the Aegean Sea, ruled by King Priam.

Crete: A large island kingdom south of Attica and the mainland, once ruled by King Minos, but since brought into alliance with Athens by Theseus, via his marriage to Phaedra, daughter of Minos.

HISTORICAL NOTE

Reconciling mythology and legend to historical times and places sometimes requires compromise. The nature of oral storytelling and oral history is one of constant adaptation and alteration through retelling. The Homeric epics of *The Iliad* and *The Odyssey*, for example, create a world in which there is a strange mishmash of Bronze Age and Iron Age technology, custom, and religion—a world that does not seem to exist in the historical and archaeological record. We see the same kind of confusion and blending again in the myths themselves, where a hero is sometimes considered the son of a king, and other times believed to be the son of a god, and in yet another source, may be the son of *both* a man *and* a god. A good example of this is Theseus, who is sometimes a son of Aegeus alone, other times a son of Poseidon and Aegeus both.

These issues make retelling the myths in a historical setting a tricky business, requiring a careful balance of history and legend. In some cases, a strict adherence to the historical and archaeological record does more harm than good, warping the heart of the story or the characters into something unrecognizable. One cannot always stay true to the characters of myth, for instance, if one completely excises the living presence and manipulations of the gods, and in my opinion, this is *particularly* true in the case of the cycles of stories surrounding the Trojan War.

As Helen's story launches those thousand ships, I felt it was most appropriate and authentic to maintain that element of living divinity in *Helen of Sparta*, so it seemed fitting, too, to allow Theseus to have a more personal relationship with his patroness, Athena, and a recognition of Poseidon and Zeus as forces in his and Helen's world. I wanted to write a book that stayed true to history as the ancient Greeks—from Homer to Herodotus, the father of history—might have perceived it, while at the same time balancing the more definitive evidence uncovered in the modern historical record.

And that historical record is fascinating, all on its own. As I discussed briefly in the foreword, the archaeological evidence is rich and complex, but the scholarship (until relatively recent times) has also been plagued by bias. Heinrich Schliemann, the excavator of the Bronze Age sites of Mycenae and Tiryns, and what we now presume to be Troy, did his work before archaeology had developed as an academic and professional field of study. Methods of excavation were haphazard, and often more destructive than constructive to the gathering of historical evidence—perhaps even more accurately described as looting, at times. In addition, Schliemann and, later, Arthur Evans at Knossos in Crete, seemed intent upon finding proof of legend, and therefore interpreted their findings to match their assumptions, rather than reshaping their conclusions to match their discoveries. As a result, early scholarship on Troy and Mycenaean Greece, built from their records and findings, was all blurred through a Homeric lens at best, and in the case of Crete, even fabricated at worst.

But today, the continued research and scholarship by academics such as Dr. Dimitri Nakassis have begun to reinterpret the old data while gathering new without these kinds of issues and biases. The Linear B tablets found at Pylos have offered a wealth of information in regard to the structure and organization of the palace centers in

Mycenaean Greece, offering glimpses of the people who lived and worked within these societies through inventories and assignations of labor or resources. Smiths, shepherds, farmers, soldiers, landowners—the array of titles and names, according to Dr. Nakassis, suggests an even greater complexity and organization than previously believed, and while Helen and Theseus would have belonged to the highest tier of that structured life, there is the suggestion of professional men and local elites existing outside of the palace. Surrounding Theseus (and Tyndareus, and Agamemnon), there were nobles—these potential local elites—who had land and influence of their own.

And this interpretation of data also melds neatly with the ideas expressed by M. I. Finley in *The World of Odysseus*, which, through the examination of Homeric texts, offers insights into the society of the Greek Dark Ages. This possible continuity influenced my interpretations of Helen and Theseus's world—one in which a man was not king only because he was born a prince, but also required the goodwill and consensus of the local elites he might have ruled over. Perhaps that goodwill came from the perceived blessing of the gods, or some proven ability in battle, or able administration, wide travel, and accrual of wisdom, or even through marriage to a particularly important and valuable daughter. Perhaps it came from all of these elements and more. That isn't something we can know, but it's absolutely something we can explore in fiction.

There are some small historical elements I'm guilty of fudging through this same kind of elision and blending of periods, without the scholarship of academics to back me up. Citrus, for one, and sweet citrus in particular, were absolutely not in cultivation in Greece during Helen's time; but because there is so much evidence for trade and wide travel both in the archaeological record and in the existing mythology, particularly Homer's *Odyssey*, including the possibility of silk worn by Odysseus himself, I thought it not impossible to include citrus, as well as cultivated strawberries, as a traded specialty item, brought to

Athens or Sparta at great expense for a special gift or occasion (like winning the favor of the most beautiful woman in all the world). By that same token, I included silk garments as a luxury that Athens might have had access to, as a city with wider influence and trade, as well as green-dyed fabrics, the double-dipping process for which does not seem to have been discovered yet in Greece during Helen's time.

Also, the shapes and characters of the gods themselves are inspired by Homer and projected backward in time with a few nods to the possibility of goddess worship and mystery cults. The myths surrounding the Trojan War and Theseus's own stories have set these more familiar ideas of the gods in our collective cultural mind, and inform so much of the narrative, it would have disrupted too much of the myth to reconcile them to what little we know of Mycenaean ideas. There are some mentions of the gods in the Linear B tablets (Poseidon the Earth-Shaker, Persephone/Kore, Demeter, and Dionysus, for example), but the information we have regarding worship is scarce. A few Minoan and Mycenaean images of women seated on thrones in what might have been the megaron, receiving offerings and honors, seem to indicate the role of women might have been critical, though we can't say for certain, and that interpretation is still hotly debated. I tried to include this by giving Sparta and Athens slightly different traditions in regard to the queen's role in prayer for divine intercession, and also in the story Pirithous tells Helen about Ariadne of Crete, and her association with the Labyrinth.

Concerning the other myths involved, I found it necessary to shrink the age gap between Helen and Theseus by maturing her character from a girl between the ages of seven and eleven (there is no consensus) to one of marriageable age with more adult sensibilities at thirteen, and fourteen when she meets our hero. Giving Theseus the benefit of the doubt, and assuming he accomplished his heroic feats upon the Isthmus road and at Crete as a true youth, his age of forty-eight in this story fits his mythology fairly well.

I also modified slightly the story of Helen's conception. Instead of the four children of Leda being hatched from two eggs (a result of Zeus's appearance as a swan), I separated their births into two sets of twins, Pollux and Castor first, and several years later, Helen and Clytemnestra. In part, this was to allow for the natural narrative of Helen's rescue and return to Sparta by her brothers—who could not possibly have accomplished half of what is attributed to them, even after I aged all four siblings up by several years—and in part because there is absolutely no agreement whatsoever as to the birth order or pairing of Helen and her siblings in or out of their eggs. Further, that Leda might have been duped once, and infuriated by it, then been punished by Zeus for not seeing his imposition as an honor seemed more reasonable to me than willing relations with a swan, no matter how beautiful that swan might have been. And contrasted against Aethra's experience with Poseidon, at Theseus's conception, it offers both women a role more complex than "passive victim." Leda and Aethra both deserved that much.

One last element I wanted to address is the false alliance between Egypt and Athens. Egypt rarely mixed its royal blood outside of its borders (or even married its heirs outside its own bloodline), preferring to keep ties strong and remove any potential rivals to the throne from external powers. However, there is *some* evidence for a marriage alliance between Egypt and Crete during the Bronze Age. Again, working under the assumption of the possibility of trade and travel, and mixing it with the reputation of Theseus as a powerful king during his time, as well as later mythology involving Helen and Egypt, it did not seem quite so far-fetched an idea that Egypt might be willing to accommodate the king of Athens if he desired to execute such a ruse. Egyptologists may feel free to disagree!

Writing *Helen of Sparta* felt to me like an archaeological dig through myth and history, and I sought to represent her story as faithfully as that reconciliation allowed. But it wouldn't be myth or history if there weren't multiple interpretations and constant debate surrounding the conclusions reached—mine provide just one very small thread in the tapestry of our shared cultural history. But I do hope you found it as satisfying to read as I did to weave.

Thomas G. Hale 2012

ABOUT THE AUTHOR

malia Carosella began as a biology major before taking Latin and falling in love with old heroes and older gods. After that, she couldn't stop writing about them, with the occasional break for more contemporary subjects. She graduated with a BA in classical studies as well as English from the University of North Dakota. A former bookseller and avid reader, she is fascinated by the Age of Heroes and Bronze Age Greece, though anything Viking Age or earlier is likely to capture her attention. She maintains a blog relating to classical mythology and the Bronze Age at www.amaliacarosella. com, and can also be found writing fantasy under the name Amalia Dillin, at www.amaliadillin.com. Today, she lives with her husband in Upstate New York, and dreams of the day she will own goats (and maybe even a horse, too).